Petra Hammesfahr, born in 1951, wrote her first novel at the age of seventeen. She has written over twenty crime and suspense novels and television series for radio and film. Her book *The Quiet Mr. Genardy* was her first bestseller and was made into a film. It was soon followed by the critical and commercial success of *The Sinner*. She has won numerous literary prizes, including the Crime Prize of Wiesbaden and the Rhineland Literary Prize, and lives near Cologne.

THE SINNER

Petra Hammesfahr

Translated from the German
by John Brownjohn

BITTER LEMON PRESS
LONDON

BITTER LEMON PRESS

First published in the United Kingdom in 2007 by
Bitter Lemon Press, 37 Arundel Gardens, London W11 2LW

www.bitterlemonpress.com

First published in German as *Die Sünderin* by
Wunderlich, Rowohlt Verlag GmbH,
Reinbek bei Hamburg, 1999

Bitter Lemon Press gratefully acknowledges the financial
assistance of the Arts Council of England

A CIP record for this book is available
from the British Library

ISBN 978–1–904738–25–1

Typeset by Alma Books Ltd
Printed and bound by Cox & Wyman Ltd,
Reading, Berkshire

The Sinner

1

It was a hot day at the beginning of July when Cora Bender decided to die. Gereon had made love to her the night before. He made love to her regularly every Friday and Saturday night. She couldn't bring herself to refuse him, being only too well aware how much he needed it. And she loved Gereon. It was more than love. It was gratitude and utter submission – something absolute and unconditional.

Gereon had enabled her to be a normal young woman like any other. That was why she wanted him to be happy and contented. She used to enjoy his lovemaking, but that had stopped six months ago.

It was Christmas Eve, of all times, when Gereon had taken it into his head to install a radio in their bedroom. He had wanted it to be a special night. They'd been husband and wife for exactly two and a half years and the parents of a son for eighteen months.

Gereon Bender was twenty-seven, Cora twenty-four. A slim five feet ten, Gereon looked fit and athletic, although he played no games, he never had time. His hair, ash blond at birth, had darkened little since then. His face was neither handsome nor ugly. It was an average sort of face, just as Gereon himself was an average sort of man.

Cora Bender was just as unexceptional in outward appearance, discounting the scar on her forehead and her scarred forearms. The dent in her skull had been caused by an accident, the gnarled skin on the inside of her elbows was the result of a nasty infection transmitted by hypodermic needles while she was being treated in the hospital – or so she'd told Gereon. She had also said she didn't remember any details. That much was true. The doctor had told her that lapses of memory were common in the case of severe head injuries.

There was a hole in her life. She knew it concealed some dark, squalid episode, but her memory of it was missing. Until a few years ago she'd fallen into that hole innumerable times, night after night. The last occasion had been four years ago, before she met Gereon, and she'd somehow managed to close it. She had never expected to fall into it again since her marriage to him. And then, on Christmas Eve of all nights, it had happened.

Everything was fine at first, what with the soft Christmas music and Gereon's caresses, which gradually became more urgent and passionate. Her mood didn't sour until he slid slowly down the bed, and when he buried his face between her thighs and she felt his tongue, the music swelled. She heard a rapid roll on the drums, the throb of a bass guitar and the shrill, high-pitched notes of an organ. Only for a fraction of a second, then it was over, but that brief moment was enough.

Something inside her disintegrated – or rather, burst open like a safe being attacked with an acetylene torch. It was an unreal sensation. As if she were no longer lying in her own bed, she felt a hard surface beneath her back and something in her mouth like an outsize thumb that depressed her tongue and caused her to gag unbearably.

Cora's response was purely instinctive: she wrapped her legs around Gereon's neck and squeezed it between her thighs. She was within an ace of breaking his neck or throttling him, but she didn't even notice, she was so far away at that moment. It wasn't until he pinched her in the side, gasping and panting and driving his fingernails deep into the soft flesh of her waist, that the pain summoned her back.

Gereon fought for breath. "Are you crazy? What's got into you?" He massaged his throat and coughed, staring at her and shaking his head.

He couldn't fathom her reaction. She herself was equally at a loss to know what it was she'd suddenly found so repulsive and

2

distasteful – so terrible that she'd momentarily felt his tongue was the touch of death.

"I don't like it, that's all," she said, wondering what it was that she'd heard. The music was still playing softly: a children's choir singing "Silent Night" – what else, on such a night?

Her unexpected onslaught had quenched Gereon's desire. He switched off the radio, turned out the light and pulled the covers over his shoulders. He didn't say goodnight, just growled: "That's that, then . . ."

He fell asleep quickly. Cora wasn't sure later whether she had also dozed off, but at some point she sat bolt upright in bed and lashed out with her fists, yelling: "Don't! Let go! Let go of me! Stop it, you filthy swine!" And her ears rang with the wild beat of the drums, the throb of the bass guitar and the shrill strains of the organ.

Gereon woke up, grabbed her wrists and shook her. "Cora! Stop that!" he shouted. "What is all this shit?" She couldn't stop, couldn't wake up. She sat there in the darkness, desperately fighting off something that was slowly bearing down on her – something of which she knew nothing, only that it was driving her insane.

She didn't recover her composure until Gereon had gently slapped her face several times. He asked her again what the matter was. Had he done something wrong? Still too bemused to answer right away, she merely stared at him. After a moment or two he lay back. She followed his example, turned on her side and strove to convince herself that it had just been an ordinary nightmare.

But it happened again the following night, when Gereon tried to make up for lost time, even though there was no radio in the bedroom and he made no attempt to do what he regarded as the supreme expression of love. First came the music, somewhat louder and longer lasting – long enough for her to realize that she had never heard the tune before. Then she fell into the dark hole and emerged from it yelling and lashing out. She didn't wake up. That she did only when Gereon shook her, slapped her face and shouted her name.

The same thing happened twice the first week in January and once the week thereafter. Gereon was too tired that Friday night

3

– so he claimed, at least – but on the Saturday he said: "I'm getting sick of this." That may also have been his reason the night before.

In March he insisted on her going to a doctor. "It isn't normal, you must admit. Something's got to be done. Or do you plan to go on like this indefinitely? If so, I'll sleep on the couch."

She didn't go to a doctor. A doctor would have been bound to ask if she had some explanation for this curious nightmare, or at least for why it happened only when Gereon had made love to her. A doctor would probably have begun to rake around in the dark hole – to persuade her to become aware of things. A doctor wouldn't have understood that there are things too terrible to become aware of. Instead she tried a chemist, who recommended a mild sedative. This cured the yelling and lashing out, so Gereon assumed that all was well again. It wasn't.

*

It got worse every weekend. By May her fear of Friday nights was like a wild beast gnawing away inside her. The first Friday afternoon in July was sheer hell.

She was sitting in her office, which was just a cubbyhole partitioned off from the rest of the storeroom. There was a light over the desk, and standing on the outskirts of the glow it shed was a fax machine displaying the time and date.

Four-fifty pm, 4 July . . . Ten more minutes to the end of office hours. Only another five hours or so, and Gereon would be reaching for her. She yearned to go on sitting there till Monday morning. As long as she was sitting at her desk, she was a smart, efficient young woman, the heart and soul and motive power of her father-in-law's firm.

It was a family firm: just Cora, her father-in-law, Gereon, and an employee named Manni Weber. They were plumbing and heating engineers, and nothing functioned without her. She was proud of her position, having had to fight hard for her place in the hierarchy.

Her father-in-law had asked her to take over the office-work the day after her marriage. He wouldn't take no for an answer. "What

4

do you mean, you can't? You've got a pair of eyes in your head; look at my books, you'll soon pick it up. You didn't think you were going to twiddle your thumbs in idleness, did you?"

Twiddling her thumbs had never been her style, and she told him so. The old man nodded. "That's settled, then."

Until then he'd had to handle the paperwork himself after hours. Her mother-in-law could just about answer the phone, which was little more than Cora herself could do to begin with.

The old man never offered her any tips or advice on how he'd done things hitherto. As for being guided by his books, they would have had to be better kept for that. There were times when he seemed to relish her helplessness, but she didn't remain helpless for long.

She quickly grasped the essentials and persevered. Nothing was handed to her on a plate – she'd even had to fight for the wooden partition that separated her miniature office from the rest of the premises.

For the first year she'd sat at a discarded kitchen table in the corner of the big, unheated, eternally grimy room. She dared not complain, although the old man didn't even pay her a wage. Gereon himself earned nothing but pocket money plus their board and lodging, and his car was registered in the firm's name. If they needed anything else, he had to ask.

Even Cora's pregnancy brought no concessions – not even a modicum of comfort. She continued to sit in the corner of the storeroom until the very last minute. When she went into labour she was working out an estimate for a gas central heating system – standing at the table because she couldn't continue to sit any longer, her back was aching so much. Her mother-in-law got hysterical because everything went so quickly. A few fierce pains, then her waters broke, and she felt intense pressure in her lower abdomen.

She hadn't wanted to go to hospital at first, but in the end she called out: "I need an ambulance! Call an ambulance!"

Her mother-in-law just stood there, pointing at the table. "You aren't through yet, finish it first. No one gives birth in ten minutes;

5

I was in labour with Gereon for a whole day. Father will be furious if that isn't finished by tonight, you know what he's like."

She knew it only too well, having lived under the same roof since her marriage. The old man was a tyrant, an exploiter, and her mother-in-law a submissive creature who bullied anyone in a weaker position than herself. Gereon was just a follower of orders, and Cora a slave. She'd sold herself cheap, almost for nothing, in return for the illusion of a well-ordered existence.

And suddenly, as she stood hunched over the old kitchen table, watching the puddle spreading around her feet with one hand clamped between her thighs and pressed against her bulging belly, she'd had enough. Finish it first? No!

In the hospital she found time to reflect on her life at leisure and grasp that a well-ordered existence also had its drawbacks. In such an environment, any hope that her dreams would come true by themselves was futile. The only question was, how much of a risk could she afford to take? Still, she told herself, it would be easier with a baby in her arms. Those seven or eight pounds of humanity would be enough to support any demand she made.

She proceeded to put her ideas into effect when she came home a few days later. This earned her the reputation of a brazen, ruthless creature – a hussy with hair on her teeth, as the old man often called her. She certainly wasn't that, but she could act like one if necessary. Besides, asking his permission would have achieved nothing.

She fixed up the office, complete with desk, filing cabinet and heating. She also took other liberties, like paying herself and Gereon a salary. The old man flew into a rage, accusing her of barefaced rapacity. "Where did you learn to pick other people's pockets?" he demanded.

Her heart was in her mouth, but she stood firm. "Either we get paid like other people or we go and work elsewhere, it's up to you. Ask around, find out what other firms are paying, then you'll see what a good deal you're getting. Me, pick your pockets? Never say that again! I *earn* my money!"

It was an arduous business, getting her way with the old man, but she managed it. She had even, well over a year ago, squeezed a house of their own out of him. More than once she'd been afraid he would chuck her out, child or no child. "Go back where you came from!" Gereon had merely stood there, looking hangdog. He'd never once backed her up or uttered a word in her defence.

To her chagrin, Cora had realized soon after their son's birth that her husband would be no help to her. That had ceased to matter now. Gereon was simply like that. He did his work. That apart, he liked a quiet life – and a bit of lovemaking on Friday and Saturday night. She couldn't baulk at this because lovemaking was something good, something wholly normal and natural.

Eight minutes to five on 4 July . . . Cora still had another invoice to make out. She'd kept putting it off so as to occupy her mind for those last few minutes. A new central heating boiler. Gereon and Manni Weber had installed it on Wednesday, and there were two more scheduled for next week. The new anti-pollution regulations were compelling people to scrap their old boilers. The regulations had come into force several years ago, but many householders had jibbed at the expense and waited until the district chimney sweep threatened to put their old boilers out of action.

It was funny in a way, that attitude. You knew exactly what you were in for and did nothing. You simply waited, as if an old boiler's emissions would conform to the stricter standards overnight, entirely by themselves and of their own accord – as if a hole inside you would close up from one minute to the next.

It had closed up four years ago, although not from one minute to the next. The process had taken a month or two. That was before she met Gereon, whose raids on her body kept dislodging the scabs that had formed in the previous few days.

Three minutes to five on 4 July . . . Nothing left to do but that invoice. Last Friday she'd been able to devote some time to the wage slips. Although only an illusion, it had kept her panic at bay. It wasn't just fear or a simple sense of unease; it was a reddish-grey mist that filled her brain, pervading every cranny and jangling every nerve.

Five pm! Stiff-fingered, she removed the sheet of paper from the typewriter and carefully checked the individual figures. There was nothing to correct, just a bit of desk tidying to do. Last of all she turned the calendar over to next week. Monday! Till then two eternities loomed like a double death, and she was half-dead already.

*

Her legs refused to obey her. Walking like someone on stilts, she emerged from her tiny office and made her way across the storeroom, then out into the yard. It was very hot outside. The baby-faced sun was smiling down out of a cloudless sky. It was so bright, her eyes started to water, but not, in all probability, because of the glare.

Her parents-in-law lived in the house overlooking the street; her own home occupied the former garden. It was a sizeable house equipped with all mod cons, the fitted kitchen a dream in bleached oak. As a rule she felt very proud of it all. At the moment she felt nothing in the way of pride or self-assurance, just this terrible fear of going mad. To her, going mad seemed worse than death.

She busied herself with housework until just before seven. Gereon wasn't home yet. On Fridays he regularly repaired to a bar with Manni Weber for a beer or two – never more than two, unless he switched to alcohol-free. They joined his parents for supper at seven on the dot.

At eight they returned to their own house, taking their son with them, and put him straight to bed. Cora's mother-in-law had already dressed him in his pyjamas and a nappy for the night.

Gereon sat down in front of the TV and watched the news, then a movie. At ten he developed his nervous expression. He smoked one more cigarette. Before lighting it he said: "I'll just smoke one more."

His manner was tense and uncertain – he hadn't known how to behave for weeks now. After a minute or two he stubbed out the cigarette and said: "I'll go up now." He might as well have brandished a whip or done something equally atrocious.

"Coming, Cora? I'm through." It was all she could do to get out of her armchair when she heard him call her from upstairs.

8

He'd showered and brushed his teeth, run the razor over his cheeks and neck and dabbed himself with aftershave. Clean, fragrant and good-looking, he was standing in the bathroom doorway in his underpants, his erection all too apparent beneath the thin material. He gave a sheepish grin and stroked the nape of his neck, where his hair was still damp from the shower. "Or don't you feel like it?" he asked hesitantly.

It would have been easy to say no – in fact she briefly considered doing so – but that would merely have postponed the problem, not disposed of it for good.

She wasn't long in the bathroom. Her sleeping pills were on the shelf above the basin – stronger ones than the first batch, and the packet was almost full. She washed two down with half a tooth-mug of water. Then, after a moment's hesitation, she swallowed the remaining sixteen in the hope that they would be enough to finish her off. Going into the bedroom, she lay down beside Gereon and forced a smile.

He took little trouble, being eager to get it over quickly. His hand located the objective and checked its condition with a finger. The outlook was unpromising, and had been ever since the night he'd tried to kiss her there. Having become inured to this, Gereon had acquired a tube of lubricant, which he gently applied before mounting her and thrusting his way inside.

That was when the madness began. Absolute silence reigned, except for Gereon's breathing. Restrained at first, it became ever louder and more hectic. Not a sound to be heard but his breathing, yet hear it she did, like the strains of an invisible radio. After six months the rhythm was as familiar to her as her own heartbeat: the rapid roll on the drums, the throb of the bass guitar and the high-pitched piping of the organ. The faster Gereon's movements, the more the tempo increased until she felt her heart must burst. Then it was over, cut off at the very instant Gereon rolled off her.

He turned over on his side and fell asleep in no time. She stared into the darkness, waiting for the sixteen pills to take effect.

Her stomach, which felt as if it were filled with molten lead, rumbled and burned like fire. Then its hot, scalding contents ascended into her throat. She reached the bathroom just in time to vomit. Afterwards she cried herself to sleep – cried her way through a dream that rent her night into a thousand fragments. She was still weeping when Gereon turned on the light and shook her by the shoulder. "What's the matter?" he asked, staring at her uncomprehendingly.

"I can't take it any more," she said. "I just can't take it any more." At breakfast she was still feeling nauseous and had a raging headache – she often did at weekends. Gereon made no reference to the incident in the night, just eyed her with a mixture of doubt and suspicion.

He'd made some coffee. It was too strong, and her tormented stomach rebelled once more. Gereon had also got the child up. He was holding his son on his lap and feeding him a slice of white bread thickly spread with butter and jam. An affectionate father, he looked after him whenever he could spare the time.

The little boy was cared for by his grandmother during the week. He also slept at the grandparents' house, in the room that had once been Gereon's. At the weekend Cora took him home with her. Looking at the boy as he sat perched on Gereon's lap, she felt he was her finest achievement in life.

Gereon wiped the jam off his son's chin and out of the corners of his mouth. "I'll get him dressed," he said. "You're bound to want to take him shopping."

"I won't be going out till later on," she replied, "and I'd sooner not take him with me in this heat."

Only nine o'clock, and the thermometer was already nudging eighty degrees. Her eyes were almost starting out of their sockets, the pain in her head was so intense. She could scarcely think, and everything needed careful planning and execution. A spontaneous decision like last night's wasn't good enough: it left too much to chance. While Gereon was cutting the grass she went across to her mother-in-law and begged one of her strong painkillers, the kind you could only get on prescription. After that she cleaned the kitchen, bathroom, stairs and hallway more thoroughly than ever before. Everything had to be spick and span.

At eleven she left the little boy with her mother-in-law and made her way to the car with an empty shopping bag in each hand. The car seemed the simplest solution, but she dismissed the idea as she drove off. Gereon was dependent on the car. How else would he get to their customers on Monday? Besides, it wasn't like her to destroy something that had cost as much as a new car.

Out of habit she drove to the supermarket. While filling the wire basket she debated other possibilities. Nothing occurred to her immediately. A dozen women were waiting at the sausage counter. She wondered how many of them were looking forward to tonight and how many felt as she did. None, she was sure.

She was the exception. She'd always been an exception, the outsider with the mark on her forehead. Cora Bender, twenty-five, slim and petite, three years married, mother of a two-year-old son to whom she'd given birth almost on her feet, just after getting into the ambulance.

A "precipitate delivery", the doctors had called it. Her mother-in-law took a different view. "You only have to whore around long enough to pup that easily, you get so big down there. Who knows what she got up to before? It can't have been anything good if her parents want nothing more to do with her. They didn't even come to the wedding. You can't help wondering why."

Cora Bender's shoulder-length auburn hair flopped across her forehead in a way that hid the dent in her skull and the jagged scar. Her pretty little face wore a questing, helpless expression, as if she'd merely forgotten to put some item of shopping in her basket. Her hands clutched the handle of the basket so tightly, the knuckles stood out white and sharp. Her brown eyes roamed restlessly over the contents of the basket, counted the pots of yoghurt, lingered on the papier mâché tray of apples. Six plump, juicy apples with yellow skins. Golden Delicious, the sort she liked. She liked life too, but hers had ceased to be a life. It had never been one, strictly speaking. And then it occurred to her how to end it.

*

11

That afternoon, when the worst of the heat was over, Gereon drove them down to the lake. Although he hadn't been delighted by her suggestion, he hadn't opposed it. He manifested his displeasure in another way, never guessing that he was only stiffening her resolve: he spent a quarter of an hour driving vainly around the dusty car park nearest the entrance.

There were vacant spaces further off, as Cora pointed out more than once. "I don't feel like toting the whole caboodle all that way," he retorted.

It was hot inside the car. They'd driven there with the windows up in case the child caught a cold. Cora had been calm when they set off, but all this driving around was making her nervous. "Come on," she said, "be quick, or it won't be worth it."

"What's the hurry? A few minutes here or there won't matter. Maybe someone'll leave."

"Nonsense, no one goes home at this hour. Either park somewhere or let me out and I'll go on ahead. Then you can drive around till nightfall, for all I care."

It was four o'clock. Gereon scowled but said nothing. He put the car into reverse and backed up for a spell, although he knew she disliked it. At long last he parked so close to another car that the door on her side wouldn't open fully.

She wormed her way out, relieved by the faint breeze that fanned her forehead. Then she reached into the stuffy car, retrieved her shoulder bag and hooked it over her shoulder, and released the little boy from his special seat in the back. She set him on his feet beside the car and went round the back to help Gereon unload.

They'd brought everything needed for an afternoon at the lido. Cora didn't want anyone to assume premeditation later on. She clamped the blanket and sun umbrella under her shoulder-bag arm and carried the two folding chairs in her other hand. All that remained for Gereon to carry were the towels, the cold bag and the child.

The sunlight made her blink. The big car park was completely devoid of shade. There were a few bushes around the edge, more dusty than green. Her sunglasses were at the bottom of the shoulder bag. She hadn't put them on in the car, just lowered the sun visor. The folding chairs bumped against her leg as she walked. A protruding piece of metal scraped the bare skin unpleasantly, leaving a red mark.

Gereon had already reached the barrier and was waiting for her. He was pointing to the wire-mesh fence and explaining something to the child. He was only wearing shorts and sandals. His chest was bare, the skin tanned and smooth. He had a good figure: broad shoulders, muscular arms and a narrow waist. Looking at him, she felt sure he would soon find someone else. He didn't move when she got there, nor did he make any attempt to take anything from her.

The charge for the car park covered the price of admission, but she'd stowed the tickets away. She put the folding chairs down and proceeded to rummage in the shoulder bag for her purse. She groped around in nappies and a change of pants for the child, passing two apples, a banana and a packet of biscuits on the way. Her fingers encountered a plastic yoghurt spoon and the blade of the little fruit knife, which almost cut her. At last she located the leather purse and opened it. Having extracted the tickets, she proffered them to the woman at the barrier and pushed through the turnstile in Gereon's wake.

They had to make a long trek across the grass, which was trampled flat, threading their way between countless blankets, seated family circles and frolicking children. The shoulder strap was cutting into her flesh, the arm with the blanket and umbrella clamped beneath it going numb, and her leg hurt where the skin was being lacerated by the chair's metal frame. But these were only superficial sensations; they had ceased to trouble her. She had finished with life. Her one remaining concern was to behave normally and do nothing that might arouse Gereon's suspicions, although it was unlikely that he would fathom the significance of a telltale gesture or remark.

He eventually halted at a spot that conveyed at least an illusion of shade, thanks to a measly little tree with sparse foliage. The leaves were drooping as though asleep; the trunk was even thinner than a man's arm.

She deposited the blanket, shoulder bag and chairs on the grass, put up the umbrella and stuck the end in the ground, spread out the blanket beneath it, erected the folding chairs and arranged them on it. Gereon stood their son on the blanket, then squatted down and removed the boy's shoes and socks. Finally, he peeled off his thin shirt and pulled his coloured rompers down.

The little boy sat there with a pair of white underpants over his nappy. His fringe made him look almost like a girl. Looking at him, Cora wondered if he would miss her when she wasn't there any more. She doubted it, considering that he spent most of the time with his grandmother.

It was a peculiar feeling, standing there in the midst of all those people. A large family lay stretched out on several blankets behind the little tree to their rear. Father, mother, grandfather, grandmother and two little girls of four or five in ruched bikinis. A baby sat kicking in a bouncy chair beneath a sun umbrella.

Just as she had in the supermarket, she wondered what was going on inside the other people's heads. The grandmother was playing with the baby. The two men were dozing in the sun. The grandfather had spread a newspaper over his face; the father was wearing a cap whose peak shaded his eyes. The mother looked harassed. She called to one of the little girls to blow her nose, rummaging in a basket for some tissues. An elderly couple were seated in deckchairs on their right. Some children were playing with a ball on an open stretch of grass to their left.

Cora pulled her T-shirt over her head – she was wearing a swimsuit underneath – and let her skirt fall around her ankles. Then she felt in the shoulder bag for her sunglasses, put them on and sat down on one of the chairs.

Gereon was already sitting down. "Like me to rub some sun cream on you?" he asked.

"I already did, at home."

"You can't reach the whole of your back."

"But I'm not sitting with my back to the sun."

He shrugged, sat back and closed his eyes. She looked out over the water, sensing its almost magnetic attraction. It wouldn't be

14

easy, not for a good swimmer like her, but if she went on swimming until she was utterly exhausted . . . She got up and removed her sunglasses. "I'm going in," she said. It was unnecessary to tell him that. He didn't even open his eyes.

She walked across the grass and the narrow strip of sand and waded out through the shallows. The water was cool and refreshing. An agreeable frisson ran through her when she submerged and it closed over her head.

She swam out to the boom that separated the supervised lido from the open lake, then along it for a little way. She felt a sudden temptation to do it at once – climb over the boom and swim out. It wasn't prohibited. There were a few groups of figures sprawled on blankets on the far shore, people who were reluctant to pay the admission charge and didn't mind lying among rocks and scrub. The lifeguard on his little wooden platform kept an eye on them too, but he couldn't see everything and wouldn't be able to reach the spot in time if something happened out there. Besides, a person would have to shout for help or at least wave their arms. If a lone head in the midst of all this turmoil simply sank beneath the surface . . .

Some man was said to have drowned in the lake and never been found; she didn't know if it was true. If it was, he must still be down there. Then she could live with him among the fish and waterweed. It must be nice in his watery world, where there were no tunes and no dark dreams, where nothing could be heard but faint gurgles and everything was a mysterious shade of green or brown. The last thing the man in the lake had heard wasn't a drum, that was certain, only his own heartbeat. No bass guitar or shrilling organ, just his own blood throbbing in his ears.

After nearly an hour she swam back. It came hard, but she had already left most of her strength in the water. Besides, she felt she needed to play with the child for a while and explain to him, perhaps, why she had to go away – not that he would understand. She also wanted to bid Gereon a covert farewell.

*

When she got back to their patch the elderly couple on the right had disappeared. Only the two deckchairs were still there, and the expanse on their left was no longer unoccupied. There wasn't a sign of the children playing ball. In their place, a pale green blanket had been spread out so close to her folding chair that it almost touched the tubular frame. Music was oozing into the afternoon air from a big radio cassette in the middle of the blanket.

Distributed round the radio were four people, all of them roughly her own and Gereon's age. Two men, two women. Two couples, one of them seated with their knees drawn up, just talking, their faces visible in profile. The other couple were faceless at first. They were lying stretched out: the woman on her back, the man on top of her.

Only the woman's hair could be seen. Platinum blond – almost white – and very long, it reached to her waist. The man had thick, dark hair that curled on the nape of the neck. His muscular legs were lying between the woman's splayed thighs, his hands cupping her head. He was kissing her.

The sight abruptly froze her heart. She found it hard to breathe and felt the blood drain into her legs, leaving her head empty. Purely to replenish it, she ducked beneath the umbrella and reached for a towel, and just to drown the hammering of her heart, which had started to beat again, she stroked the little boy's head, said a few words to him, dug his red plastic fish out of her shoulder bag and put it in his hand.

Then she turned her chair so that her back was towards the foursome with the radio. Although their image continued to float before her eyes, it gradually faded, and she grew calmer. It was no concern of hers what the couple behind her were doing – it was normal and innocuous, and even the music wasn't a nuisance. Someone was singing in English.

In addition to the music she could hear a woman's high-pitched voice and the low, unhurried voice of a man, presumably the one sitting up. He hadn't known the woman long, from the way he spoke. Alice, he called her. The name reminded Cora of a book she'd owned – for one short day – as a child: *Alice in Wonderland*.

16

She hadn't read it – she hadn't had a chance to, not in those few hours. Her father had told her what it was about, but what he'd told her was as worthless as his promise: "Things will be better some day."

The man behind her chair was saying that he planned to become a GP. He'd been invited to join a group practice – a good offer, he told Alice. Nothing could be heard from the couple lying down.

Gereon peered past her and grinned. Instinctively, Cora glanced over her shoulder. Still with his back to her, the dark-haired man was kneeling up beside the platinum blonde. He'd removed her bikini top and poured some suntan oil between her breasts. The little pool was clearly visible, and he was busy rubbing it in. The woman stretched voluptuously under his hands. She was enjoying it, from the look on her face. Then she sat up. "Your turn now," she said. "But first let's have some decent music. This stuff is enough to send you to sleep."

Lying beside the platinum blonde's legs was a brightly coloured cloth bag. She reached into it and took out a cassette. The dark-haired man protested. "No, Ute, not that one – that's not fair. Where did you get it from? Give it here!" He made a grab for her arm. She toppled over backwards and he fell on top of her. They wrestled around, almost rolling off the blanket.

Gereon was still grinning.

The man ended up underneath with the woman sitting astride him. She held the cassette in the air, laughing. "I win, I win!" she said breathlessly. "Don't be a spoilsport, sweetie. This is great stuff!" She leaned over, her long fair hair brushing the man's legs, and thrust the cassette into the slot, then pressed the start button and turned up the volume.

The words "don't be a spoilsport, sweetie" pierced Cora like a knife and set something inside her quivering. As the first bars of the music rang out, the blonde bent down and cupped the man's face between her hands. She kissed him, her hips moving rhythmically against his crotch.

Gereon was getting his edgy expression. "Like me to oil you now?" he asked.

"No!" She hadn't meant to be so vehement, but the woman's movements and Gereon's reaction to them were infuriating her. It was time to say goodbye to the child. She wanted to do so in peace, not in the immediate proximity of a bimbo who was all too vividly demonstrating where she herself had failed.

"They might at least turn the music down," she said. "Loud music is forbidden here."

Gereon looked scornful. "It'll be forbidden to breathe here soon. Don't get all worked up about nothing. I'm enjoying that music. I'm enjoying what goes with it too. At least she's got some fire down below."

She ignored this. Clasping the child in one arm, she picked up the red fish with her free hand. It soothed her and did her good, the feeling of his warm, firm body bundled up in its nappy and little white pants, the plump arm around her neck and the baby face so close to her own.

He flinched when she reached the lakeshore and put him down in the shallows. He'd been sitting in the heat for so long, the water felt cold. After a moment or two he squatted down and looked up at her. She handed him the red fish and he dunked it in the water.

He was a quiet, good-looking child. He didn't speak much, although he had a relatively large vocabulary and could express himself clearly in short sentences. "I'm hungry." – "Papa has to work." – "Grandma is making blancmange." – "That's Mama's bed."

One Sunday morning shortly after they moved into their own house, when he was just a year old, she had taken him into her bed. He went back to sleep in her arms, and holding him had imparted a sensation of warmth and intimacy.

Now, as she stood looking down at his slender white back, at the little hand wiggling the red fish in the water, the bowed head and almost white hair, the delicate little neck, that feeling returned. If there hadn't already been reasons enough, she would have done it for him alone, so that he could grow up free and unencumbered. She crouched down beside him and kissed him on the shoulder. He smelled clean and fresh from the suntan oil Gereon had rubbed into him while she was in the water.

She stood beside him in the shallows for half an hour, forgetful of the couple on the green blanket, forgetful of everything that might have disrupted their leave-taking. Then the lido gradually emptied. It was nearing six o'clock, and she realized that the time had come. If she hadn't had the child with her she would have swum out into the lake without wasting another thought on Gereon, but she couldn't bring herself to leave the helpless toddler alone on the lakeshore. He might have waded in after her.

She picked him up in her arms again, feeling the chill of his little legs and wet pants through her swimsuit and his firm, plump arm around her neck. He was holding the red fish by the tail.

She saw as she drew nearer that nothing on the green blanket had changed. The music was playing as loudly as before. One couple was sitting there, chatting away without any physical contact, the other lying down again.

Taking no notice of them, she changed the little boy into a clean nappy and dry underpants. Just as she was about to go, she was detained once more.

The child said: "I'm hungry."

A couple of minutes here or there wouldn't matter. She was totally focused on these last few moments with her son. "What would you like," she asked, "a yoghurt, a banana, a biscuit or an apple?"

He cocked his head as though seriously debating her question. "An apple," he said. So she resumed her seat and took an apple and the little fruit knife from her shoulder bag.

*

In her absence, Gereon had moved her chair so that she no longer had her back to the blanket but was sideways on. That way, he could see past her more easily. He was sitting there with his legs extended and his hands folded on his stomach, pretending to look at the lake. In reality, he was leering at the blonde bimbo's breasts.

19

He was bound to choose himself a bimbo like that when she'd gone, she reflected. The thought should have infuriated her, but it didn't even sadden her. The part of her that could feel was probably dead already, killed off – not that anyone had noticed – sometime in the last six months. Her sole concern was how to make things easier for herself.

She mustn't fight the water. Jutting into the lake at the far end of the lido was a small, scrub-covered headland. Once beyond it she would be hidden from view. Then out to the middle of the lake, duck-diving from the outset. That would sap her strength.

The radio cassette was belting out a drum solo. It flailed away at her brain, although she took no notice of it. Holding the apple firmly in her hand, she felt the nape of her neck prickle and her shoulder muscles tense, felt her back stiffen and go cold as if she were lying on some hard, cold surface instead of sitting in balmy air, felt something like an exceptionally thick thumb force its way into her mouth, just as it had at Christmas, when Gereon had meant to give her a special treat.

Swallowing hard, she took the knife and cut the apple into four quarters, three of which she deposited on her lap.

Behind her, a voice she recognized as Alice's said: "It's really hot stuff."

"Yes," said the man sitting beside her, "you wouldn't think it of him today. It was five years ago, of course. That was Frankie's wild and woolly phase – it only lasted a few weeks. He doesn't like being reminded of it, but I reckon Ute's right, it's great music – nothing to be ashamed of. Three friends, they were. A shame they never made the big time, just played in a cellar. That's Frankie on drums."

Frankie, friends, cellar, drums . . . The words rang briefly in her head, imprinting themselves on her memory.

"Were you there at the time?" Alice asked.

"No, I hadn't met him yet."

Gereon stretched. He glanced at the piece of apple in her hand. "He'll never eat all that. You can give me the rest."

"I'm eating the rest myself," she said. "Then I'm going for another swim. There's another apple in the bag; you can have it."

20

A last piece of apple! Golden Delicious, the kind she'd loved as a child. The very thought made her mouth water.

Out of the corner of her eye she saw the blonde on the blanket sit up. "Hang on," the woman said, pressing a button on the cassette player, "I'll wind it on a bit. This is nothing compared to 'Tiger's Song'! You won't hear anything better."

The dark-haired man rolled over and made another grab for her arm. Cora saw his face for the first time. It meant nothing to her. His voice too was just as unfamiliar when he protested again, more vehemently this time. "No, Ute, that's enough. Not that, give me a break!" He sounded very much in earnest, but Ute laughed and fended him off.

Cora thought of her house. Her mother-in-law was bound to go through it with a fine-tooth comb, but she wouldn't find any cause for complaint. Everything was spick and span. The firm's books were in order too. No one would be able to say she'd been slapdash.

She removed the core from the piece of apple and peeled it as thinly as possible, then handed it to the little boy and picked up the next piece, intending to peel and core it for herself. At that moment the music started again, even louder than before. Involuntarily, she glanced sideways. She saw the blonde subside onto her back, grasp the man's shoulders and pull him down on top of her, saw him bury his fingers in her hair and adjust her head to a convenient angle. Then he kissed her. And the drums . . .

The remains of the apple fell to the grass as she jumped up. Gereon gave a start when she began to shout.

"Stop it, you filthy swine! Stop it, let go of her! Let go of her!"

At the first words she hurled herself sideways and fell to her knees. As the last words left her lips she stabbed the man with the knife.

Her first thrust caught him in the neck. He gave a startled cry and swung round, grabbed her wrist and held it for a moment or two, staring at her. Then he let go and merely went on staring. He muttered something she didn't catch, the music was too loud.

That was it! That was the tune in her head, the prelude to madness. It rang out over the trampled grass, over the horrified faces and frozen figures of those around her.

The second thrust caught him in the side of the throat. He stared at her wide-eyed but made no sound, just clutched his neck with one hand and gazed into her eyes. The blood spurted between his fingers, red as the little plastic fish. The blonde screamed and tried to crawl away beneath his legs.

She stabbed him again and again. Once in the throat, once in the shoulder, once through the cheek. The knife was small but pointed and very sharp. And the music was so loud. It filled her head entirely.

The man who had merely been sitting there, talking with Alice, shouted something. It sounded like "Stop that!"

Of course! That was the whole point: Stop that! Stop it, you filthy swine! The seated man put out his hand as if to catch hold of her, but he didn't. No one did a thing. It was as if they were all frozen in time. Alice put both hands over her mouth. The blonde whimpered and screamed alternately. The little girls in frilly bikinis clung to their mother. The grandfather removed the newspaper from his face and sat up. The grandmother snatched up the baby and clasped it to her breast. The father started to rise.

Gereon got out of his chair at last. An instant later he was standing over her. He punched her in the back and tried to grab the hand with the knife just as she raised her arm once more. "Cora!" he yelled. "Stop that! Are you crazy?"

No, her head was clear as a bell. Everything was fine, everything was just as it should be. It had to be this way: she knew it beyond all doubt. And the man knew it too; she could read it in his eyes. "This is my blood, which was shed for you for the remission of your sins."

When Gereon hurled himself at her the seated man and the father of the little girls came to his aid. They each held an arm while Gereon wrested the knife from her grasp. Holding her by the hair with one hand, he forced her head back and punched her in the face several times.

Gereon was bleeding from two or three cuts on his arm. She had stabbed him too, although she hadn't meant to. The seated man yelled at him to stop, which he eventually did. But he gripped her by the back of the neck and clamped her face against the other man's bloodstained chest.

No sound was coming from inside that chest, nor was there much sound in general. A few more rhythmical beats, a final drum solo just before the tape ended. Then came a click. A button on the cassette player popped up, and it was over.

She was conscious of Gereon's grip, of the numb places on her face where his fist had struck her, of the blood on the chest beneath her cheek and its taste on her lips. The platinum blonde was whimpering.

She put out a hand and rested it on the woman's leg. "Don't be afraid," she said. "He won't hit you. Come on, come away. Let's go. We shouldn't have come here. Can you get up by yourself, or shall I help you?" The little boy on her blanket started to cry.

2

I didn't cry much as a child. Only once, in fact, and then I didn't cry but screamed with fear. I haven't given it a thought in recent years, but I remember the occasion distinctly. I'm in a dimly lit bedroom with heavy brown curtains over the window. The curtains are stirring, so the window must be open. It's cold in there. I'm shivering.

I'm standing in front of a double bed. One half is neatly made up, the other, nearest the window, is rumpled. The bed emits a stale, sourish smell as if the sheets haven't been changed for a long time.

I don't like it in the bedroom. The chill, the stench of months-old sweat, a threadbare runner on the bare floorboards. In the room I've just come from there's a thick carpet on the floor, and it's nice and warm. I tug at the hand holding mine, eager to go.

Seated on the tidy side of the bed is a woman wearing an overcoat and holding a baby in her arms. The baby is wrapped in a blanket. I'm supposed to look at her. She's my sister Magdalena. I have a new sister, I've been told, and we're going to look at her. But all I see is the woman in the overcoat.

The woman is a total stranger to me. She's my mother, whom I haven't seen for ages. Six months – a long time to a small child. My memory doesn't go back that far. And now I'm supposed to remain with this woman, who only has eyes for the bundle in the blanket.

Her face frightens me. It's hard, grey and forbidding. At last she looks at me. Her voice sounds the way she looks. She says: "The Lord has not forgiven our sins."

24

Then she folds back the blanket, and I see a tiny, blue face. "He has put us to the test," she goes on. "We must pass that test. We shall do what He expects of us."

I don't believe I could have registered those words at the time. They were often told me later on, that's why I still remember them so well.

I want to go. The woman's odd voice, the tiny, blue face in the blanket – I want no part of them. I tug again at the hand holding mine and start crying. Somebody picks me up and hushes me. My mother! I'm firmly convinced that the woman who takes me in her arms is my real mother. I cling to her and feel relieved when she takes me back into the warm.

I was still very young – only eighteen months. It's easy to work that out because I was one year old when Magdalena was born at the hospital in Buchholz, like me. We were both born in the same month: I on 9 May, and she on 16 May. My sister was a blue baby. Immediately after her birth she was transferred to the big hospital at Eppendorf and had an operation on her heart. The doctors discovered that Magdalena had other things wrong with her. They did their best for her, of course, but they couldn't put everything right.

It was thought at first that she had only a few days to live – a few weeks at most. The doctors didn't want Mother to take her home, but Mother refused to leave her on her own, so she stayed on at Eppendorf. But my sister was still alive after six months, and the doctors couldn't keep her there indefinitely, so they sent her home to die.

I spent those first six months living with the Adigars, our next-door neighbours. As a little child I firmly believed that they were my family – that Grit Adigar was my real mother and had handed me over to the woman in the overcoat because she wanted to get rid of me. Grit took me back with her at first but not, alas, for long.

Although I don't have any detailed recollections of this period, I've often wished I could remember at least a little about the weeks and months I spent with Grit and her daughters, Kerstin and Melanie.

Grit was still very young. She must then have been in her early twenties, having had her first child at seventeen and her second at nineteen. Her husband was seldom at home. Several years older than her, he earned a good living at sea. Grit always had plenty of money and plenty of time for her daughters. She was a cheerful, uncomplicated person, almost a child herself.

In later years I often saw her pounce on her daughters and roll around on the floor with them, tickling them until they squirmed and giggled so much they could hardly breathe. I believe that she must have done the same to me in the days when I was in her care; that I played with Kerstin and Melanie; that Grit took me on her lap in the evenings and cuddled me the way she cuddled her own children; that she fed me cake in the afternoons or told me funny stories. And that she said: "You're a good girl, Cora."

But those six months are a blank, like the few more weeks I spent with Grit after Mother returned from the hospital with Magdalena. All that has lodged in my mind is a sense of having been shunted aside – cast out and expelled from Paradise. For the only licensed inmates of Paradise are the angels of purity who obey God's word to the letter, question none of His commandments, never rebel against Him and can look at the apples on the Tree of Knowledge without coveting a bite.

I couldn't do that. Easily led astray, I was a weak, sinful little creature unable to control the desires aroused in me and covetous of all I set eyes on. And Grit Adigar, or so I thought, had no wish to live under the same roof as such a person.

That was why I had to say "Mother" to a woman I disliked and "Father" to the man who lived in our house. But him I was very fond of. He was a sinner like me. Mother often called him that.

I carried my sin around inside me. Father's was on the outside. I often saw it when he relieved himself while I was sitting in the bathtub. I don't know how I came to believe that that appendage was his sin. Perhaps because I didn't possess such a thing, nor did Kerstin and Melanie Adigar. Because I considered myself entirely normal, Father's bit extra meant that he wasn't. It made me feel sorry for him, and I often got the impression that he wanted to get rid of the thing.

We slept in the same room, and one night I woke up because he was so restless. I think I was three years old; I can't recall exactly. I was very fond of Father, as I said. He used to buy me new shoes when the old ones pinched, tuck me up at night, sit with me till I went to sleep and tell me stories of long ago, when Buchholz was still a wretched little moorland village. Just a few farmsteads, and the soil so poor and the cattle so emaciated they couldn't make their own way to pasture in springtime and had to be hauled there on wagons. And then the railway came, and everything got better.

I liked those stories. There was something hopeful, almost promising, about them. If a wretched little moorland village could develop into a nice little town, everything else could get better too.

On that particular night Father had told me about the Black Death, so when I woke up and heard him groaning I immediately thought of the plague and was afraid he'd caught it. But then I saw he was holding his sin in his hand. To me it looked as if he was trying to yank it off. He didn't succeed.

If both of us yanked together, I thought, I was sure we'd manage it. I told him so and asked if I could help. Father said there was no need. He got out of bed and went to the bathroom. There was a big pair of scissors in the bathroom, so I thought he meant to cut it off.

But a few days later I saw it was still there. Well, I would also have been scared to cut off something so firmly attached to me. I wished with all my heart that it would fall off by itself or go bad and be washed out by pus like the splinter in my palm.

Father smiled when I said this. Stowing it away in his pants, he came over to the bathtub and soaped me. "Yes," he said, "let's hope it falls off. We could pray that it does."

I can't recall if we did, but I expect so. We were forever praying for things we didn't have or didn't want to have, like a craving for lemonade. That often tormented me.

Which reminds me of an occasion when I was in the kitchen with Mother – I must have been four. I still didn't believe she was really my mother. Everyone said so, but I already knew how to lie and thought everyone did.

27

I was thirsty, so Mother gave me a glass of water. Just ordinary tap water, and I didn't want it. It tasted of nothing. Mother took the glass away. "In that case," she said, "you can't be thirsty."

I was too, and I said I'd sooner have some lemonade. Grit always had some lemonade. Mother didn't like me going over there, but she didn't have time to worry about what I got up to, so I seized every opportunity to escape from her and spend time with my real family.

I'd been playing next door that day too, but Grit wanted to pay someone a visit. She had a wide circle of friends and acquaintances. A lot of people invited her over because her husband was away at sea so often. She called to her girls to come inside and get washed and changed. I asked if I could come too, but the answer was no, "my mother" wouldn't allow it. So I had to go home.

I remember the occasion vividly. It was early one afternoon at the end of July or the beginning of August, and very hot outside. The kitchen window was open, and everything – all the shabbiness of my surroundings, for which there was no financial reason – was bathed in brilliant sunlight.

Father worked in an office in Hamburg. He sometimes told me about it, and I knew, even at the age of four, that he earned a good salary. We could have lived more comfortably than we did. My parents had done so in the old days. They often used to treat themselves to nights out in Hamburg, where they dined and danced and so on.

But Father had needed a lot of money himself since Magdalena's birth, and the hospital was expensive too. The doctors at Eppendorf were surprised by Magdalena's survival. She paid many visits to the hospital, sometimes for another operation, sometimes just for a few days' observation. Mother always went with her, and Father had to pay for her bed and board. It was the same old story every time they came back: another few weeks, a month or two at most.

We shared our home with death, and Mother fought for every extra day of life. She never let Magdalena out of her sight, not even at night, which was why Father slept in my room. There were only two bedrooms and a bathroom upstairs. My parents never expected to have children when they bought the house, so the second bedroom would have been a guest room.

Mother was standing at the stove when I asked her for some lemonade. It was an electric stove. We also had a refrigerator, but the rest of the kitchen amenities comprised the clumsy old second-hand furniture my parents had bought after their marriage. Everything in the house was old, Mother included.

She was forty-four at this time. A tall woman with a thin face, she looked much older than her age. She had no time to spare for herself. Her stringy grey hair hung down to her shoulders. When it grew too long she cut some off.

She was wearing a coloured apron and stirring a saucepan. Putting the tumbler in the sink, she turned to me and said: "Lemonade?"

Mother had a soft voice and always spoke quietly, so you were compelled to listen hard. She shook her head as though she found it utterly incomprehensible that I could have had such an absurd idea. Then she went on in her quiet, deliberate way. "Do you know what they gave our Saviour when He was dying and said He was thirsty? They took a sponge soaked in vinegar and put it to His lips. A mug of water would have rejoiced His heart and alleviated His sufferings, but He didn't complain – and He certainly didn't ask for lemonade. What does that tell you?"

This can't have been the first such conversation I had with Mother, because I already knew the answer by heart: "That our Saviour was always content with His lot."

Me, I was never content. I was a difficult child. Stubborn, quick-tempered and egotistical, I wanted everything all for myself; and if I wasn't stopped, I simply took it. That was the only reason why Magdalena was so sick, Mother explained. Magdalena had come from Mother's tummy, and I had been in Mother's tummy a short while before. I'd used up all her strength, which would have sufficed for at least three children, so there'd been none left for poor Magdalena.

I didn't care when she told me such things. Although I wasn't intent on being a bad person, being good wasn't so important where my sister was concerned. I didn't like Magdalena. To me, she was just an object like a piece of wood. She couldn't walk or speak – she couldn't even cry properly. If something hurt her, she squealed. Most of the time she lay in bed, or sometimes for an hour in an armchair in the kitchen. But that was on an especially good day.

I couldn't say what I thought, of course. I had to say the diametrical opposite, but at that I was an expert. I always said what people wanted to hear. Mother was satisfied with my answer. "Don't you also think you should follow our Saviour's example?" she asked. I nodded eagerly, and she went on: "Then go and beg Him for strength and grace."

I was still thirsty, but I knew she wouldn't even give me the glass of tap water until I'd prayed, so I went into the living room.

It was just as shabby and old-fashioned in appearance as the kitchen. A threadbare sofa, a coffee table on spindly, crooked legs and two armchairs. But no one entering the room had eyes for the worn-out furniture.

The first thing that met your gaze was the altar in the corner beside the window. It was really just a cupboard minus the top half, which Father had had to saw off. In front of it stood a hard wooden bench on which you were only allowed to kneel. The makeshift altar was draped in a white cloth embroidered with candles, and on it stood a vase of flowers, usually roses.

Roses were very expensive, but Mother bought them gladly even when the housekeeping money ran short. Making a sacrifice to our Saviour couldn't fail to fill one's heart with joy, she said. My heart was never filled with joy. It was filled with the supposition that I'd been given away. My real mother, Grit Adigar, must have realized a long time ago that I was a bad person. She didn't want Kerstin and Melanie to suffer in consequence and end up as sick as Magdalena; that was why she had taken me to live with this woman who knew exactly how to make a bad person good.

But if I showed everyone that I was a good girl, if I prayed diligently enough and didn't sin – or not so anyone noticed – I felt sure I would soon be restored to my real family for evermore.

I can't imagine that everyone genuinely believed my invalid sister's survival to be dependent on my good conduct. In any case, it would mean that I could never go home again – that I would have to remain with this peculiar woman and our Saviour for all eternity.

The Saviour stood on the altar between the vase of flowers and four candlesticks containing tall, white candles. But he didn't actually "stand" there: he was nailed to a twelve-inch wooden cross with tiny nails. His back was also glued to it. I took him down and examined him one day when Mother wasn't around.

I'd only wanted to see if he could open his eyes. Mother claimed he could gaze deep into people's hearts and see all their sinful desires. But his eyes didn't open even when I shook him, waggled the crown of thorns on his head, which was bowed in agony, and tapped his tummy with my knuckles. It sounded as if I'd tapped the tabletop.

I didn't believe he could catch me out. I had no respect for him, only for Mother, who compelled me to kneel before him three or more times a day and beg for grace and strength and mercy. He was supposed to purify my heart, but I didn't want a pure heart. I had a sound one – that was good enough for me. He was also supposed to give me the strength to go without things. I didn't want that either.

I always had to go without – without sweets, lemonade and other treats. Like the cake Grit Adigar regularly offered us. She baked them herself – one every Saturday, thickly sprinkled with icing sugar – and on Monday she would turn up bearing a plate with three or four slices on it. They were a bit dry already, but that didn't matter. Mother always declined them. The very sight of the plate made my mouth water.

If I stared at it for too long, Mother said: "You've got that greedy look again." And she would send me off to the living room, where I knelt before the cross on the cupboard in the corner, the one on which the Saviour had shed his blood for the remission of our sins.

31

*

She felt momentarily puzzled as she knelt beside the dead man, seeing his blood and the horror on the others' faces. The platinum blonde didn't want to be touched by her or helped to her feet and shepherded away. She lashed out at Cora with both fists. The seated man told Cora to leave her alone, which she did. Ute didn't concern her.

She apologized to Gereon for cutting his arm, but he punched her in the face again. The seated man had long since ceased to be seated. He was kneeling opposite her, examining his dead friend, but since this was a timeless moment, something for eternity, he had to remain the seated man. "Stop that, damn you!" he yelled at Gereon. "Give it a rest!" Gereon ignored him. "Are you mad?" he shouted at Cora. "Why did you do it?" She didn't know. It was embarrassing somehow.

She would have liked to be alone with the dead man, just for a minute or two, so as to be able to look at him in peace and savour the emotions the sight of him aroused in her: satisfaction, boundless relief and pride. It was as if some disagreeable, long-deferred task had been accomplished at last. She almost said: "It is finished." But she didn't; she merely sat there feeling good.

She continued to feel so even when the first policemen turned up: four uniformed officers. One of them asked if the knife was hers. When she confirmed this, he asked if she had killed the man with it.

"Yes, of course," she replied. "It was me."

The policeman said they would have to detain her. She need not make a statement, was entitled to a lawyer and so on.

She got to her feet. "Many thanks," she said. "I don't need a lawyer, everything's fine." And it was. Everything was absolutely fine. The joy, the inner peace – she had never experienced such wonderful sensations before.

A policeman told Gereon to take her clean underclothes and ID from the shoulder bag and hand them over. She wasn't allowed to touch the bag herself, she was only allowed to take her skirt and T-shirt. She forgot about a towel.

Gereon proceeded to rummage in the bag. "You must be out of your mind!" he snarled. "You stabbed me too!" She answered him in a calm, controlled manner. Then Gereon handed her underclothes to the policeman, who had no choice but to pass them on to her with a neutral expression.

They allowed her to freshen up. Two uniformed officers escorted her to the staff washroom in the low building beside the entrance. The washbasin was filthy, the mirror above it cloudy and spattered with countless splash marks, but she could see her face well enough. She felt her right temple. The skin there was broken, and her right eyelid badly swollen. She could only see through a narrow slit on that side, but it didn't worry her.

She ran the tip of her tongue over her upper lip, tasted blood and thought of the wooden figure in the corner of the living room, of the red paint on its hands and feet and the wound in its side, from which several thin threads trickled down. She knew it was only paint, even at the age of four. But the blood of the man, the blood on her face and body was genuine. And there lay redemption.

Everything was red. Her swimsuit, her arms, her hands – even her hair was smeared with it. She would have liked to leave it that way, but she didn't want to annoy the policemen so she turned on the tap, sluiced her hands and arms, held her head under the thin trickle and watched the blood run into the basin. It looked paler when mixed with water, almost like the raspberryade of her childhood. Not that it had been raspberryade, just syrup diluted with water.

Mother had eventually capitulated and made a concession to her sinful desires: one glass of diluted juice a day. Two, to be exact: one for her and one for Magdalena. She saw herself standing at the scratched and dented kitchen table; saw herself watching closely as Mother trickled syrup into two tumblers, taking care to pour the same amount into each; saw herself snatch the one that held maybe a millilitre more, then hurry to the tap before Mother noticed the minuscule difference and shooed her into the living room.

She hadn't thought of that for years, and now it seemed like only yesterday. Father and his attempts to wrench the sin from his body and his stories about Buchholz in the old days – always the old days, as if there were no today and no tomorrow. Mother with her coloured aprons, her stringy hair and the cross. And Magdalena, her bluish, translucent porcelain features imbued with flawless intensity by ever-present death.

It was over. The Saviour had shed his blood and, by his death, taken their sins upon himself and paved their way to heaven. She saw his face before her, the look of understanding and forgiveness in his eyes. "Father, forgive her, for she knoweth not what she doth." Well, no one could know everything!

She rinsed out her swimsuit and used it to swab her breasts and stomach like a sponge. The water she wiped off with her hands. There was a towel – it hung on a hook beside the basin – but it was so grimy, it might have been hanging there for weeks. Then she got dressed. The panties and T-shirt stuck to her skin, becoming damp and transparent. She hesitated for a moment and looked down at herself. Her breasts showed through the thin material. She couldn't go outside like this. There were policemen waiting outside the door. Men! It would look provocative if she confronted them in this state. Mother would have a fit – she would feel compelled to light the candles on the altar and force her to her knees . . .

She couldn't understand why this suddenly seemed so real. And so important! Try as she might, she couldn't shake it off. The candle flames continued to dance before her eyes. She blinked hard to banish the image. When that didn't help, she opened the door and spoke to one of the policemen. "Can you lend me a jacket?"

The two men, who were only wearing their uniform shirts, glanced at each other. The younger one lowered his gaze in embarrassment. The other, who could have been in his early forties, managed to look into her eyes: not at the breasts showing through the damp T-shirt. He seemed to grasp her problem. "You don't need a jacket," he said in a gentle, fatherly tone. "There are people over there with less on than you. Are you through? Shall we go?"

She merely nodded.

Still looking her in the eye, he asked: "Who did that to your face?"

"My husband," she said. "But he didn't mean to. He was very upset and lost his temper." The policeman frowned as though this information surprised him. He took hold of her elbow but swiftly withdrew his hand when she flinched at his touch. "Let's go," he said.

And the candle flames went out at last.

The lido had almost emptied while she was in the washroom. Everyone except the immediate witnesses of the incident had left. A group of figures could still be seen in the distance, where the green blanket with the dead man lying on it must be.

It was just after seven. Some twenty people were assembled on the terrace adjoining the low building. They all stared at her as she approached. She found their nervous, enquiring expressions unpleasant.

The three survivors of the green blanket party were sitting a little apart from the rest. The seated man was trying to comfort the two women. Ute thrust his hand away, sobbing incessantly. Standing beside them was a youngish man in a sports coat. He was asking questions and jotting down their answers in a notebook. Two medics appeared on the terrace. Ute was led away. Alice followed.

It was like a film set. Hustle and bustle everywhere, but she just stood and watched. The older policeman escorted her over to a chair and got one of the medics to examine her face, especially the swollen eye. He was very friendly and stood beside her while his younger colleague joined the man in the sports coat and exchanged a few words with him.

Gereon was still there too, holding the boy on his lap and looking at the dressings on his arm. The man in the sports coat went over to him and said something. Gereon shook his head fiercely. Then he got up and went over to the seated man. He didn't spare her a glance, either then or a little later, when she made for the wire-mesh fence flanked by the two policemen.

Parked in the shade of some trees near the entrance were two patrol cars and another vehicle. Gereon's car was parked a long way off in the full glare of the sun, she remembered. She stopped short and turned to the older policeman, who looked more mature and experienced than his colleague. "Would you mind telling me your name?"

"Berrenrath," he replied automatically.

She nodded her thanks. "Look, Herr Berrenrath, you must go back and have a word with my husband. Tell him to air the car well and close the windows before he drives off. I know my husband, it won't occur to him – he never thinks of such things. Our little boy has sensitive ears, he often gets ill. He so easily develops rigors when he has a high temperature."

Berrenrath merely nodded, opened the rear door of one of the patrol cars and gestured to her to get in. The younger policeman went around the car and got in behind the wheel, then turned, never taking his eyes off Cora. He looked almost afraid of her.

She would gladly have reassured him but she didn't know how. It was over! He wouldn't have understood that, though. She didn't understand it herself, she merely sensed it, as though she'd inscribed it on her forehead in the man's blood: OVER!

Berrenrath really did go back. He wasn't long. "Your husband will see to it," he said as he got in beside her.

She felt relieved of everything. Relieved and remote and somewhat isolated – numb with triumph, as if she'd swum out and submerged. A grand sensation, except that it was confined to her heart and stomach. In her brain she felt a gradual, sneaking inclination to view what had happened from another perspective: with the eyes of the people who had gone to the lido for an afternoon's recreation.

She thought suddenly of her son and the way he'd been sitting on the blanket, crying. The poor little fellow had witnessed the whole thing. She consoled herself with the thought that he was too young to have taken it in. He would forget what he had seen. He would forget her too. He would grow up with Gereon and her parents-in-law. His grandmother was very kind to him. Even the old man, that uncouth boor, watched over his grandson like a mother hen.

The trip didn't take long, and she was so preoccupied with her thoughts that she didn't register any of it. When the patrol car pulled up – when Berrenrath got out and asked her to do likewise

– she surfaced for a moment, only to subside at once into thoughts of the future so as not to have to dwell on the past.

Life imprisonment! She was quite clear about that. After all, she'd committed a murder. She was clear about that too. She had to be punished, but prison bars couldn't intimidate someone inured to the Cross. There was nothing ominous about the idea of a cell. Regular meals and a job in the kitchen or the laundry – even in an office, perhaps, if she behaved herself and showed everyone what she was capable of.

Prison couldn't be so different from her three years with Gereon. It made no difference whether she was being watched by her parents-in-law or a bunch of wardresses. The weekends would be a thing of the past, that's all. No more cigarettes whose dying embers in the ashtray signalled the madness to come.

The next time she surfaced she was sitting on a chair in a whitewashed room. More chairs were scattered around at random, and in the centre were two desks, each bearing a telephone and a typewriter surrounded by a clutter of papers. The sight of them worried her. She itched to tidy them up and wondered if she should ask the policemen for permission.

The younger one was standing near the door, Berrenrath beside a large window with two pot plants languishing on the sill. The sunlight was still strong enough to dazzle her, and she'd forgotten to bring her sunglasses. On the right, beside the pot plants, lay a folder. The Cora Bender file, she thought fleetingly. It could only be a slender file – the case was clear-cut, after all. They would have to ask her a few questions, of course, but . . .

Those plants needed attention badly. A pitiful sight, with brown blotches on the leaves, they must have been standing in the full glare of the afternoon sun. Ten to one the soil was bound to be bone dry.

"Listen, Herr Berrenrath," she said, "you should take those plants off the windowsill. They can't stand the sun – it's like putting them in a furnace. They probably need some water too. Mind if I take a look?"

Berrenrath seemed taken aback. After a few moments he nodded reluctantly.

There was a sink near the door with an old coffee percolator on the draining board. An ugly brown film had formed on the glass jug, which had probably never been rinsed properly. Beside the percolator was a dirty coffee mug. She rinsed it out carefully, then picked up the jug and started to rinse that too.

"No, leave that," Berrenrath said. "Please sit down again."

"Look," she protested, "you said I could water those plants, and the jug was dirty. Why shouldn't I clean up a bit?"

Berrenrath sighed and shrugged his shoulders. "Water the plants if you like, but cleaning up isn't your job."

"Then I won't," she said. "I meant no harm."

She filled the jug with water and went over to the window. The soil really was as dry as dust. Leaving the jug on the windowsill, she carried the two plants over to a desk, unobtrusively straightened a couple of chairs and shuffled some papers into a neat pile. This created a little more room and looked tidier. Then she fetched the jug and gave the plants a soaking.

The policemen watched in disbelief as she refilled the jug at the sink. "They needed it badly," she said when she'd emptied it and resumed her seat.

A good minute's silence ensued. She strove to marshal her thoughts and prepare herself for what would happen next. The interrogation! Being a moviegoer, she knew the form. A confession was all that really mattered – to the police; that was the most important thing, so an interrogation was superfluous in her case. She'd already confessed. All that remained was to type it out and get her to sign it. Odd that no one was troubling to do that. She turned to Berrenrath again. "What are we waiting for?"

"The officer in charge," he said.

"Aren't you in charge?"

"No."

She smiled at him. It was meant to be an endearing smile, but her battered features turned it into a crooked grimace. "Look, this is silly, one policeman's as good as another. I'd sooner we got this over. Write down what I say, and I'll sign it, then you can knock off."

"No, we'll wait for the officer in charge," Berrenrath said. "He should be here any minute."

He wasn't, of course. She had often seen movies in which suspects were left to stew in order to break down their resistance, but she couldn't understand why this technique was being used in her case. For one thing she wasn't just a suspect; she was definitely guilty. For another, she had no intention of causing difficulties.

The delay was making her nervous. She couldn't help thinking of Gereon and the way he'd acted on the terrace beside the lake – as if she were a total stranger. But she could understand that. It must have been a terrible shock to him. You had to put yourself in his place. He hadn't wanted to go to the lido at all. It was far too hot, he'd said when she broached the idea over lunch. He didn't like swimming in any case. And then, in a few brief seconds, she'd torn his world to shreds. No wonder he'd beaten her up like a madman. Was he home already? What would he have told his parents? They must have been surprised to see him come home without her.

She could picture it. The puzzled expressions. Her mother-in-law's voice. The old man never said much when family matters were under discussion. Gereon, pale and bandaged, clasping their son with his uninjured arm, would begin by asking someone to help him unload the boot. His mother would volunteer. Outside, where the old man couldn't hear, Gereon would say: "She stabbed a man to death."

Later they would sit together in the living room, while Gereon recounted what had happened, although there wasn't much to tell. His mother would moan about what the neighbours would say when they heard; the old man would merely wonder how it would affect his business and who would handle the paperwork in future.

*

It was almost nine o'clock when the door finally opened. Her vision of Gereon and his parents vanished abruptly. The man in the sports coat, the one she'd noticed on the terrace overlooking the lake, entered the room. He introduced himself, but she forgot

39

his name at once and tried to size him up. She hoped he wouldn't waste time asking her unnecessary questions.

But he did precisely that. As if there were any doubt about her identity, he sat down at the typewriter and asked her to state her name, her maiden name as well. He wanted to know how old she was, how long she'd been married and whether she was employed – totally irrelevant, all of it. Then he asked details of her parentage and siblings, if any.

She answered him reluctantly but truthfully up to her parents-in-law. Then she said: "My parents are dead, and I'm an only child."

He looked at the plants on his desk and asked if she was fond of flowers. Almost in the same breath, he enquired if she was in pain, if she needed a doctor or would like some coffee. She glanced at the old percolator and said no.

She was finding it hard to concentrate and remain calm. It seemed to be a longer business than she'd expected. As if she needed telling, the man in the sports coat informed her of the crime she was being charged with, quoted from the penal code, reminded her of her rights and repeated what Berrenrath had already told her down at the lake – that she need not make a statement and so on.

At that point she interrupted him. "Many thanks, but I already told Herr Berrenrath that's unnecessary. I don't need a lawyer. It would be best if you simply took down what I say. We can start right away."

But they couldn't. The man in the sports coat said they would have to wait for his chief, who had already gone home.

Another fifteen minutes went by. It made her feel quite sick, being unable to do anything but sit there, staring at the whitewashed walls. She wasn't used to being idle: you only started brooding. Like this morning in the supermarket, when she thought she'd found the answer.

It really was crazy, in a way. Having made up her mind to kill herself – having come to an irrevocable decision – she had then, quite suddenly, attacked a stranger. Just because the blonde – she couldn't recall her name for the moment – was playing that tape.

40

She would have done better to ask where the woman had got it and whether anyone could explain how the tune had got into her head.

Nobody spoke. The only sound came from the dripping tap, which she hadn't turned off tightly enough when she filled the jug the second time. The men took no notice of it. Berrenrath kept an eye on the door, and his younger colleague stood there with his hands clasped behind his back. The man in the sports coat was looking through the notes he'd made on the terrace.

What would the witnesses have told him? That she'd gone for the man like a lunatic. That's what it must have looked like to them. She suddenly realized why they were spending so much time on her: because they couldn't understand. Because they wanted, like Gereon, to know why.

That realization transformed her heart into a lump of lead and filled her brain with a reddish-grey mist. She felt her hands go moist and start to tremble. Every trace of her initial relief, jubilation and triumph had gone. She needed a rational explanation.

When the door finally opened again she started to count in her head – eighteen, nineteen, twenty – in the hope that it would help to calm her. The man who came in looked to be in his early fifties. He made an easy-going, good-natured impression, said hello all round and nodded to the two constables. Berrenrath returned the nod, combining it with a nod in her direction that struck her as somehow odd. The man in the sports coat got up, and the newcomer went out again, accompanied by him and Berrenrath.

Again she waited, wondering what the trio outside the door were talking about and what that strange nod had signified. If only the younger policeman would say something. She found the silence unbearable because it was only superficial. It was almost like a Saturday night. Her head wasn't silent inside; the tune was playing there. The dripping tap sounded almost like the drums. The tune was always followed by the dream, and she wasn't asleep now! If those men didn't come back soon . . .

They were gone for only ten minutes, but that was six hundred seconds, and every second spawned a new idea that gnawed away at her mind. What alarmed her most were the feelings aroused in her by the act of killing. Any normal person would have been in despair, horrified and tormented by guilt at having done such a thing. And she had felt good. That wasn't normal.

At last they returned. The man in the sports coat resumed his seat at the typewriter, and Berrenrath his place beside the window. The chief sat down facing her. He gave her an amiable smile and stated his name, which she registered as little as the rest of what he said. Everything inside her tensed. If she wasn't to be suspected of insanity, she must come up with some brief, precise answers and a demonstrable motive.

Berrenrath was holding something in his hand: her purse. She didn't know where he had produced it from so suddenly; she hadn't noticed it. The whole procedure was repeated: name, maiden name, date of birth, place of birth, marital status, occupation, parents, siblings.

"Is this a quiz?" she asked angrily. "If so, you're too late, I've already earned my points for the answers. Or are you simply trying to find out if I've lost my marbles? Don't worry, they're all there. This is the third time I've been asked the same questions – I noticed. Here's a suggestion for you: ask your colleague for a change, he's got all the answers written down. Besides, that man there has my papers."

She regretted having called Berrenrath "that man there"; he didn't deserve such a disparaging designation. He'd been really very nice to her so far, and besides, it would be more advisable to display a polite, cooperative manner. She *was* being cooperative, but they must hurry it up a bit. She couldn't endure it if they kept up this snail's pace.

Her insolence evoked no reaction. The younger constable gave a momentary frown, but that was all. Berrenrath brought her purse over to the desk, and the man in the sports coat took it from him. She became aware that she'd failed to register both his name and the chief's. She strove to remember them, but her every thought became entangled with the dead man's face. She couldn't say: "Sorry, I wasn't on the ball just now, I've forgotten your names." They would jump to the conclusion that she was deranged.

The two uniformed policemen left the room. She would have preferred Berrenrath to stay, he was such a sympathetic fellow, but she couldn't ask. It mustn't look as if she needed moral support. The man in the sports coat opened her purse, removed her ID and handed it to his boss. Then he examined her driving licence and glanced up quickly.

It was the face that had fazed him, she felt sure. The sick, grey face on her licence, which looked as if it belonged to an old woman. For a moment she was afraid he would remark on it, but he didn't speak. She swiftly tweaked her hair over her forehead to prevent him from noticing the scar. The chief, who had been studying the particulars on her identity card, also looked up at her. "Cora Bender," he said. "Cora sounds like an abbreviation. Or is it your full name?"

He had an agreeably warm, deep voice. Many people must have found it reassuring, but it didn't have that effect on her. She couldn't control her hands, which were trembling more and more. She put them on her lap and gripped her right hand with her left.

"Look," she said, "I don't want to seem rude, but it's getting late. Can't we dispense with the social chit-chat?"

The chief smiled. "There's plenty of time. Anyway, I find a bit of chit-chat relaxing. How are you feeling, Frau Bender?"

"Fine, thanks."

"You're hurt." He pointed to her face. "We really ought to send for a doctor."

"No doctors, thank you!" she snapped. "A medic examined me. It's not as bad as it looks. I've known worse."

"For example?"

"I don't see how that concerns you," she retorted.

"Very well, Frau Bender," he said quietly but very firmly, "if that's the way you want it. Please tell me if you're in pain or feel adversely affected in any way. You may also tell me if you'd like a coffee or something to eat. But say please, it sounds better."

She had riled him. She stirred uneasily on her chair and blinked her good eye. "Look, I'm sorry if I got a bit heated. I don't want to be difficult. It's just that I'm rather on edge, and I'd like to get this over. Why do I have to state my husband's name three times? It's completely irrelevant. Take down my confession and let me sign it, then we can have some coffee."

The chief nodded to the man in the sports coat, who deposited a small black box on the desk. She started when she saw it was a tape recorder. The man pressed a button. She put her hands over her ears before she could stop herself.

Her head seemed to be on fire at that moment. They knew! Someone had told them about the tune, and now they wanted her to listen to it again. God alone knew what the result would be. Perhaps she would jump up and hit one of them over the head with the nearest plant pot.

But no music emerged, no sound of any kind. The two men stared at her doubtfully. "Anything wrong, Frau Bender?" asked the chief.

She gave him a strained smile and lowered her hands. "No, everything's fine," she assured him hastily. "A sudden earache – very unpleasant. From swimming, I suppose. I dived, and . . . But it's gone already. I can hear you perfectly well, honestly."

The chief began at last. He devoted little time to the penal code and defined the situation as succinctly as possible. "Frau Bender, just after six pm today you killed a man at the Otto Maigler Lido. Several persons in the immediate vicinity witnessed the incident and were able to make a statement. Some of these depositions have already been taken down in writing and signed. To this extent the circumstances are clear-cut. We should nevertheless like to ask you a few questions. You are entitled to decline to make a statement. You are also entitled to an attorney, and —"

She raised a hand and cut him short. This time she strove to sound calm and reasonable. The black box was a recording machine, she realized. It would register her every word and play it back to all kinds of people. They would all hear what she'd said and draw their own conclusions.

"I know all that," she said, "and I've already said so twice. I don't need an attorney, I'm making a confession. I'll also sign an affidavit to the effect that you didn't subject me to pressure or do anything else to me, and that I've been advised of my rights several times, etcetera. All right?"

"All right, if that's the way you want it," the chief said again. He leaned forward and looked at her intently.

She drew a deep breath, wondering how best to convey, in her very first sentence, that she was a hundred percent in order, both physically and – of course – mentally. She now had the tremor in her hands well under control. If she gripped one hand with the other hard enough, it was barely noticeable. Besides, they were watching her face, not her hands. After a couple of seconds she said in a firm voice: "Shortly after six pm today I stabbed a man to death at the Otto Maigler Lido. I did it with the little fruit knife I was using to peel an apple for my son."

The chief produced a transparent plastic bag and put it on the desk. Inside was the bloodstained knife. "Is this it?"

She nodded, then realized that a nod was inaudible. "It is," she said simply.

"Is that why you took this knife to the lido, to peel an apple?" the chief asked.

"Yes, of course. We didn't have anything else with us that needed peeling, only the apples."

"But instead you used it to stab a man. Did you realize what would happen if you used this knife to stab someone?"

She stared at him uncomprehendingly. Then she grasped the point of his question and started to smile. "Look, I may be a bit nervous, but you don't have to speak to me as though I'm mentally deranged. Of course I knew what would happen if I stabbed someone. I would injure or kill them. I stabbed him in such a way that death would be inevitable, and I knew what I was doing. Does that answer your question fully enough?"

The chief betrayed no reaction to these words. All he said was: "If you stabbed him deliberately, Frau Bender, can you remember where you stabbed him first?"

She was still smiling. Did she remember? She would never forget it – everything else, perhaps, but not that! "In the back of the neck," she said. "Then he swung round and I stabbed him in the throat. It's a small knife. I thought I mightn't pierce his heart if I stabbed him in the chest, but the throat contains the jugular and the larynx. That's what I aimed for, and I succeeded. From the way he bled, I must have severed the artery. But I stabbed him in other places as well. The face, for instance. And once the knife got deflected and went into his shoulder."

The chief nodded. "What made you kill the man? I have got it right, haven't I? You did mean to kill him?"

"Yes, I did," she said firmly. And at that moment it dawned on her that she'd meant to do it for a long time: to kill that man. Not just any man, but that particular one.

3

It had ceased to matter what her motive had been for going to the lido. Things had turned out differently, and that was good. She hadn't meant them to, certainly not during the drive there, and if the woman at the turnstile had accused her of intending to kill a man, she would have thought her insane. It had happened because it had to. Realizing this, she felt a little calmer.

By contrast, the two policemen seemed taken aback by her bald statement. She could tell that from their expressions but had no time to reflect on whether she might have phrased it a little less bluntly. The questions now came thick and fast. The chief asked them; the man in the sports coat just sat there, never taking his eyes off her.

"Did you know the man?"

"No."

"You'd never seen him before?"

"No."

"You really didn't know who he was?"

"No."

That was the truth, and the truth was always right and good, but the chief seemed baffled by it. He shot a puzzled glance at the man in the sports coat, who shrugged his shoulders. Then, with a slight shake of the head, he turned to her again.

"What made you want to kill him?"

"The music was getting on my nerves." Although not entirely correct, that came closest to the truth.

"The music?" the chief repeated. The bewilderment in his voice wasn't lost on her.

She hastened to be more specific, without having to mention the tune. "Yes, they had a big radio cassette player with them. The woman had turned it up even louder. That infuriated me."

The chief cleared his throat. "Why didn't you ask her to turn the music down? Why did you attack her companion when she turned it up?" That was the crucial question and she had no answer to it. "I did ask her," she said. Then, because that didn't accord with the facts, she swiftly corrected herself: "I mean, I didn't ask her directly, I complained. She took no notice. Maybe I didn't speak loudly enough. I didn't want to shout, I . . . Well, I really wanted to go for a swim. I wanted . . . I . . ."

This really didn't concern him – it was completely irrelevant. She stopped stammering and said firmly: "Look, he was lying on top of the woman! I couldn't have got at her, but anyway, I didn't want to do anything to her, honestly not. I wanted to kill him, and I did. We don't have to argue the point. I admit it. That's good enough for your records."

"No," said the chief, shaking his head. "No, Frau Bender, it isn't."

"If you'd been there," she retorted, "you'd know it's more than good enough. You should have seen the man – he was all over her. I couldn't just watch. I had to do something about it."

The chief stared at her. "We aren't talking about a man assaulting a woman, Frau Bender," he said with a touch of asperity. "We're talking about a man you stabbed to death – a man named Georg Frankenberg – and I want to know why. So don't go telling me you . . ."

She didn't register what else he was saying; her ears seemed to be shrouded in gauze. She had a sudden vision of a prison cell. A wardress closed the door behind her. Strangely enough, the wardress had her mother's face. She was holding a lit candle in one hand and a wooden crucifix in the other. The figure on the cross was only glued to it.

The Saviour!

Georg Frankenberg, was that his name? His name wasn't important, but she let it drift like an echo past Mother's face, past

48

the candle and the crucifix, and waited for some connection to establish itself. She felt that the chief would be satisfied and leave her in peace if she said: "Ah yes, it's just occurred to me: I did know him after all."

But the echo died away, leaving no vestige behind. Her expression must have conveyed this, because the chief's tone was plain incredulous.

"Does the name really mean nothing to you?"

"No."

He sighed, scratched his neck and glanced uncertainly at the man in the sports coat, who was sitting quite still, contemplating the pot plants on his desk.

They already looked a little perkier. It might have been her imagination, but she thought she could see their limp foliage absorbing fresh strength from the moist soil. Water was the elixir of life, after all. Father had often told her about the hard layer of moorland soil that had to be pierced so the water wouldn't drain away when it rained.

But moorland soil was not under discussion here, and the chief's voice prevented her from dwelling on Father's stories. "So you're telling us he was a stranger to you, a man you'd never seen before. And just because he and his friends were playing loud music, you stabbed him like a madwoman."

"Don't say that," she snapped. "I'm not mad, I'm completely normal."

The man in the sports coat cleared his throat discreetly and pushed his notepad across the desk. He leaned forward and whispered something, tapping a passage in his notes.

The chief nodded and looked up again. "You weren't annoyed by the music, only by what the couple were doing, isn't that it? You just said he was 'all over her'. But it wasn't like that. Georg Frankenberg was merely necking with his wife, and the initiative was definitely hers. 'Stop it, you filthy swine!' That's what you shouted as you stabbed him. You meant the pair of them, didn't you?"

She registered only two out of all those words. They lodged in her throat like a foreign body. It was all she could do to spit them out.

"His wife?"

The chief nodded. "Georg Frankenberg had only been married three weeks. They got back from their honeymoon two days ago. They were still in the first flush, so to speak, and very much in love. It's only normal for newlyweds to kiss and cuddle, and nobody takes offence these days if they do it in public. You were the only person to get worked up about it. Why, Frau Bender? What gave you the idea that Georg Frankenberg might hit his wife?"

Georg Frankenberg? Something was wrong – something wasn't the way she'd instinctively expected. She had the same puzzling sensation as she'd had after the murder, when the blonde pushed her hand away. His wife! She felt utterly bewildered.

"Look," she said, "there's no point in telling me such things and asking stupid questions. That's all I'm saying. It'll save a lot of time if you take down my confession. I killed the man, I can't say more than that."

"You mean you won't," said the chief. "However, we already have several statements, and one of the witnesses says you tried to put your arms round Frau Frankenberg after the murder. You spoke to her too. Do you remember what you said?"

He was furious now, but she didn't care. Georg Frankenberg! And his wife! If the chief said so, it must be true. Why should a policeman lie – what would he gain? And Gereon hadn't even glanced at her afterwards.

He was probably lounging in front of the TV at this moment, watching a movie. That was his life, working and watching TV. But he was more likely to be still sitting with his parents in the living room, and they would all be furious with her. The old man: "She was a minx, I saw that the moment she walked into the room. We should have sent her back where she came from."

And Gereon's mother: "You should divorce her. You must, if only because of the neighbours. We can't have them thinking we want anything more to do with such a creature."

And Gereon would nod. He not only nodded whenever his parents made a suggestion but acted on it too, unless someone pointed out what nonsense it was.

50

There was no one there to tell him anything any more, but he would soon find someone else. He was a healthy, good-looking young man. He owned a house and earned a decent living: she'd seen to that. One day he would take over the business and become his own boss. He was a good catch, not only financially.

He didn't drink much, wasn't given to violence and avoided arguments. He was affectionate – yes, he was. She could have slept with him for years and decades to come, if only he hadn't tried to kiss her that way on Christmas Eve. Any other woman might have enjoyed it.

He was welcome to a woman who could love him the way he deserved. Who enjoyed being in bed with him. Who couldn't wait for him to go down on her and would do the same to him. Although it pained her to imagine it, she hoped with all her heart that he would soon find such a woman. He was a philistine, yes, but a thoroughly normal man. And she . . . She was normal too. Absolutely normal, and had been from an early age. Grit Adigar had said so.

*

That was the worst thing I had to come to terms with as a child: that none of my family was normal. I can't recall when I first realized I was a part of it and that nothing would ever change, nor do I remember if that realization dawned on a particular occasion or was a gradual process. I simply knew, at some stage, that that frightful creature was my biological mother. If I'd had to show my face in town with her, I would have denied her just as Peter denied our Saviour. But that made no difference to the facts or to anything else in my miserable existence.

Father tried to make things a little more bearable for me, but what could he do? There was the day I went to school for the first time. Father had bought me a satchel and a blue dress in Hamburg. It was a pretty dress with little white buttons down the bodice, a white collar and a belt.

Vanity being yet another sin, I had to burn it before the altar in the living room – in a tin bucket. Mother stood alongside with a watering can in case the house went up in flames.

Father shook his head that evening when I told him. Mother was a Catholic, he said, and Catholics are a bit stricter than most. And later on, when we were in bed, he told me about the first school in Buchholz.

It had been built in 1654, he said, and consisted of only two rooms. The schoolroom doubled as the teacher's living room. The local inhabitants didn't send their children to school because they needed them to work in the fields – because they themselves couldn't read or write and didn't think it mattered much. These days everyone knew how important it was to be able to read and write, Father said, and it was up to every schoolchild what became of it.

That was his way of saying: "Make the best of things, Cora. I'm afraid I can't help you."

He said it didn't matter what clothes you wore, only what was in your head. Children in the old days went to school barefoot and in rags. Well, I possessed shoes and didn't have to wear rags on my first day at school, but I still felt like a scarecrow compared to all those dolled-up little girls.

I set off with the new satchel on my back, like the rest, but in an old, sack-like frock that Mother had dug out of the cupboard as a penance, even though it was too small for me. I smelled of mothballs and went to school empty-handed. All the others turned up clutching bags of sweets in the traditional German manner.

Luckily, Mother had no time to accompany me to school that first day, but everyone knew. It's incredible how quickly such things get around.

I was an outsider from the first because I had an invalid sister. Yes, she was still alive. The doctors expressed surprise at her survival every few months, but that didn't worry Magdalena. It was her form of revenge, I often thought. I'd eaten up her strength in Mother's belly, so she stubbornly lived on.

I had no friends. Even Kerstin and Melanie Adigar wanted nothing to do with me in the playground; they were scared of

52

being jeered at too. During break I used to stand there alone every day, week after week. The others played and horsed around, whereas I had to commune with myself and pray to the Saviour for forgiveness and strength for myself and mercy and another day of life for Magdalena.

Her condition had worsened since I started school. I often came home with a cough or a cold or a sore throat. She regularly caught them, even though I didn't go near her. I had only to sneeze, and it would hit Magdalena like a hammer blow.

Mother attributed her more frequent illnesses to the fact that I had less time to pray than before. The morning was out, she said, so I must at least do my duty during break. And I did. The knowledge that Magdalena was my own flesh and blood had crippled me somehow. It meant that I would bear the same stigma for as long as she lived.

I didn't wish her dead, honestly not, but I wanted to have some girlfriends who would play with me in the schoolyard and come home with me in the afternoons. I wanted to go for walks on Sundays and sit in the ice-cream parlour with my parents – with a mother who'd taken the time to wash, do her hair and put on a pretty dress. I wouldn't even have expected her to paint her nails or use lipstick occasionally, like Grit Adigar.

I wanted a father who could laugh. Who didn't always tell me about the old days, about things that had long been dead and decayed. Who didn't have to slink into the bathroom at night to wrestle with his sin. Who sometimes referred to tomorrow or next weekend. Who would once, just once, say: "Let's pay a visit to Hamburg Cathedral! Let's have some candyfloss and a ride on the Big Wheel!"

I wanted to go shopping with Mother. I wanted her to ask me which I would prefer: a candy bar or a bag of crisps. I didn't want her to tell me, again and again, that I was a bad, greedy person.

The baby that had monopolized all the strength in her belly? I hadn't done so deliberately, damn it all! I couldn't have guessed that I would be followed by another child who also needed strength.

Sometimes I tried to get Mother to admit that she was exaggerating a little. I broached the subject very skilfully, but it was futile. If I told her I'd realized how bad I was and was trying to mend my ways, she merely looked at me as if to say: "High time too." When I told her that children at school were laughing at me, she said: "Our Saviour was also mocked, even when He hung, dying, from the Cross. He lifted up His eyes to Heaven and said: 'Father, forgive them, for they know not what they do.' What does that teach you?"

How I detested that question!

It was inadvisable to grant Mother even the smallest insight into what I was really learning: reading, writing, arithmetic – and lying. Ingratiating myself with the teacher so that she would intervene when the others laughed at me too loudly and pointed their fingers at me. Above all, I learned to hate my sister.

I really did hate Magdalena as fervently as only a child can. Whenever I saw her lying in the kitchen and heard her groaning and whimpering I hoped she was suffering the tortures of the damned.

I continued to do so until that day in May, when I had been going to school for a year. It was a normal day. No one had said anything special to me that morning except the teacher, who shook my hand during break. "Now you're seven years old too, Cora," she told me with a smile.

I came home at lunchtime as usual. Mother answered the door and sent me straight to the living room. There was no lunch, no saucepan on the stove, no loaf on the table. The bread was on the top shelf in the larder, but the door was locked, and Mother kept the key, her motto being "Lead us not into temptation".

She went upstairs to see to Magdalena. My sister had caught a cold from me at the beginning of April and couldn't shake it off. Her nose often bled without her blowing it or hitting it on anything; and she spat blood even when Mother brushed her teeth. She vomited frequently, yet she ate almost nothing. Her body was covered with blue and red contusions, her hair was falling out, and she had permanent diarrhoea. Mother dared not take her to Eppendorf for fear she would need another operation. "Let us pray for tomorrow," she would say as we sat down to supper every evening.

54

Father came home late that afternoon. Tummy rumbling, I was still seated in front of a bunch of fresh roses with such long stems that they overtopped the crucifix by several inches. Thanks to them, all we'd had for Sunday lunch was some bean soup without so much as a slice of sausage in it. Father walked into the kitchen and called me in a low voice. I saw when I joined him that he was holding something in his hand.

A bar of chocolate! My stomach leaped at the very sight of it. "For your birthday," Father whispered as he kissed me.

I knew what birthdays were from the other children in my class. When Grit's daughters had a birthday, she threw a big party, complete with cream cakes and potato crisps and ice cream. No one had ever broached the possibility of my having a birthday.

Everyone had birthdays, Father explained, and nearly everyone celebrated them. They invited friends, ate cake and were given presents. He never took his eyes off the door as he spoke. We could hear Mother moving around upstairs. She'd tried to get a couple of spoonfuls of chicken broth down Magdalena a short while before, but after the third spoonful Magdalena had brought it up. Mother had had to change the sheets and carry Magdalena into the bathroom to wash her.

We failed to hear her come downstairs. I'd just put the first piece of chocolate into my mouth when she walked in. After two steps she froze, her gaze commuting between my hand and my mouth. Then she turned to Father.

"How could you?" she demanded. "One of them can't keep a morsel down, and you stuff the other with chocolate."

Father hung his head. "It's her birthday, Elsbeth," he mumbled. "Other kids are showered with presents. All their friends turn up and bring something. Look at next door. Grit invites the whole street in, whereas we —"

He got no further. Mother didn't raise her voice – she never did. "In this house," she said quietly, "only one birthday counts: that of our Saviour. Let us now turn to Him and ask Him to grant us the strength to resist our manifold temptations. How can He show us compassion unless our hearts are pure?"

She put out her hand for the bar of chocolate. "Give me that," she said, "and light the candles."

The three of us knelt on the little bench for nearly an hour. Then Mother sent me to bed. She asked if I was willing to go without supper. I mustn't just say yes, she said. I must be genuinely prepared to make that sacrifice.

Although terribly hungry I nodded, went upstairs and got into bed without cleaning my teeth. I felt sick, had a tummy-ache and wished that I could be really ill for once. Or die, possibly of starvation.

I couldn't sleep, so I was still awake when Father came into the bedroom. It must have been around nine. He always went to bed at nine when he came home early from work, even in the summer, when it was still light outside. What else was he to do? Other people watched television in the evenings or listened to a radio programme or read a newspaper or a book.

We had nothing of the kind apart from Mother's Bibles. She had several: an Old Testament, a New Testament and a Children's Testament. The latter contained some nice pictures and stories about the miracles performed by our Saviour.

Mother would often read aloud to Magdalena from the book, then show her the pictures and tell her that she would one day sit before our Saviour's father on a little bench, rejoicing with the other angels. She hadn't read to her in recent weeks, though, because Magdalena was too weak. Whenever Mother started to talk or read aloud, she turned her head away.

Just as Father shut the bedroom door I heard him mutter: "It'll soon be over. If she doesn't stop all this nonsense then, I'll kick her arse for her." And he drove his fist into his palm. He hadn't noticed I wasn't asleep yet.

*

The chief's name was Rudolf Grovian. A lot of people mispronounced it deliberately, *Grobian* being the German for "roughneck", but he wasn't a violent man. On the contrary, he knew there were times when he should have been tougher in his private life. Now fifty-two, he had been married for twenty-seven years and a father for twenty-five.

His daughter had always been a rebellious creature who made impossible demands and rode her parents roughshod. It was his fault for leaving his wife to bring her up alone. Mechthild was too soft and too gullible. She couldn't bring herself to put her foot down and believed any old rubbish she was told. If he ever said anything, all he got was: "Oh, go easy on her, Rudi, she's still so young."

Later on, when she was older but still refused to listen to anyone, least of all to him, Mechthild changed her tune to: "Oh, don't get so het up, Rudi, think of your blood pressure. Girls are like that at her age."

Having now been married for three years, his daughter was riding roughshod over a nice, conscientious young husband. They'd had a son two years ago, and Rudolf Grovian had hoped she would come to her senses, acknowledge her responsibilities and moderate her demands.

Only that Saturday he'd been compelled to accept, to his chagrin, that many hopes aren't worth the time devoted to them. He'd spent the afternoon at a birthday party for his wife's sister. His daughter had turned up with their grandson, but not his son-in-law.

Rudolf Grovian overheard some scraps of conversation between his wife and daughter that aroused his direst fears. The word "attorney" cropped up a number of times, and he wasn't naïve enough to persuade himself that a traffic accident or rent dispute was involved.

He'd made up his mind to have a serious talk with his daughter during the evening, although he knew it was pointless and would only put his blood pressure up, but he was called away before he got the chance. In his job, it happened from time to time.

Rudolf Grovian was a detective chief superintendent and head of the homicide division. Age-wise and in other respects he could have been Cora Bender's father. As it was, he was the chief whose questions were taking her back, not forwards – thrusting her slowly but steadily back into the midst of the madness she feared more than death.

It was a baneful encounter for both parties: the policeman who was an often irritable and sometimes guilt-ridden father in his private life, and the woman who lived with the knowledge that fathers cannot help, and that they only make things worse if they try.

Rudolf Grovian might have been more irritable than usual this Saturday, but he set to work with his customary impartiality and detachment.

As soon as he was informed of the incident at the Otto Maigler Lido, he drove to police headquarters and sent for all available officers to conduct interviews, even those who did not usually deal with capital offences.

Although it was the weekend, things moved swiftly. The whole team was distributed around the adjoining interview rooms. Grovian conferred with everyone so as to form an initial impression of the case. His men were careful to mention every last little detail.

But it all came down to the actual crime. There was no indication of what had prompted the disaster. In such cases, as Grovian knew from experience, the trigger was to be found either in the past or in the nature of the perpetrator. He had never dealt with or heard of a case in which a woman launched a frenzied attack on a total stranger.

Women drowned their children, brained their husbands in their sleep or poisoned or smothered their invalid mothers in a mood of desperation. Women killed those with whom they were intimately connected, and all that Grovian heard between seven and nine o'clock on Saturday evening seemed to fit the usual pattern.

The most important statement he obtained came from Georg Frankenberg's friend and colleague Winfried Meilhofer, a fellow physician at the Uniklinik in Cologne. Meilhofer was a down-to-earth person who, despite his shock, indulged in only one remark of a non-factual nature. According to him, the woman had attacked Frankenberg "like an avenging angel".

58

Meilhofer himself had felt rooted to the spot and unable to react, he said. Besides, it had looked as if Frankie could cope with the woman by himself. After the first blow, which would definitely not have been fatal, he'd gripped her wrist.

This was confirmed by the father of the two little girls. "I still don't understand it. A big, strong fellow, he was. He grabbed her, then he let her go! I saw the whole thing quite clearly. She didn't break free – he could easily have hung onto her, but he let her butcher him without lifting a finger. And the way he looked at her! I felt he must know her and know exactly why she was doing it."

Winfried Meilhofer had merely shrugged when told of the man's supposition that Georg Frankenberg had known or recognized Cora Bender. "Possibly, I don't know. Only the husband and child were there when we arrived. The woman turned up later – she'd been swimming, I think. I noticed her because she was staring at Frankie and Ute so oddly. I got the feeling she was startled. But I don't think Frankie spotted her. I was going to point her out to him, but then she sat down and took no more notice of us, and I paid no more attention to her. When it happened, Frankie stared at her and said something, I didn't hear what. I'm sorry I can't tell you more, Chief Superintendent. I'd only known Frankie for two years, and he seemed a quiet, level-headed person. I can't imagine he would have given a woman grounds for such crazy behaviour. 'He won't hit you,' she told Ute. Frankie wasn't the type of man to strike a woman. On the contrary, he tended to put them on a pedestal."

Winfried Meilhofer went on to mention an allusion Frankie had once made to a girl he'd known and fallen head-over-heels in love with as a first-year student. Apparently, the girl had been killed in an accident.

"He didn't expressly say so," said Meilhofer, "but I gathered from the way he spoke that he was present when the girl died and took a long time to get over it. I don't think he had another affair until six months ago, when he met Ute. Till then he lived for his work."

Meilhofer went on to recall an incident that typified Georg Frankenberg's attitude to women and his profession. Just over six months ago they had lost a patient, a young woman who died of a pulmonary embolism after a routine operation. You had to accept that such things happened, but Frankie couldn't. He went berserk and broke two of the girl's ribs in his efforts to revive her. Afterwards he got drunk and wouldn't go home.

Unwilling to leave him on his own, Meilhofer had accompanied him to a bar. Music was playing in the background. Frankie had maundered on about their dead patient and his inability to understand how a young woman could die on them from one minute to the next. Then, quite suddenly, he'd started to talk about his music – about the wild, lost weeks he'd spent playing the drums in a combo. How a friend had talked him into it, what a great mistake it had been and how he would have done better to concentrate on his studies.

It was hours before he'd allowed Meilhofer to take him home. Once there he reverted to the subject of the girl he'd loved and lost. Then he showed Meilhofer the tape Ute had played beside the lake. He played it too, beating out the rhythm in the air with his fists. "I have to listen to it every night," he said. "When I do, she's here beside me. I can feel her, and when I feel her I can go to sleep."

A strange man, Georg Frankenberg. Very earnest, very conscientious, subject to occasional bouts of depression and overly fond of fast cars. One might have been forgiven for suspecting that his hold on life was tenuous. Meilhofer had more than once been afraid he wouldn't survive the weekend. Then Ute had jolted him out of his melancholia.

Having obtained this information about the victim, Rudolf Grovian was hoping to learn something about his killer's background from Gereon Bender. They had offered to drive Cora's husband home out of consideration for the little boy, intending to follow and interview him there.

Gereon Bender had vehemently opposed this. He didn't want to be the great exception among the witnesses. Go home with a police escort? Impossible! If everyone else had been summoned to headquarters, he insisted on going there too. The child would present no problem, he said, nor did he. The little boy was very good. He sat on his father's knee, nibbling a biscuit, and only once asked for his mother. "Where's Mummy?"

The child's piping voice lodged in Rudolf Grovian's memory for days, like a thorn in his flesh. "I've no idea why she snapped so suddenly," Gereon Bender told him. "I don't have a clue. All she ever said about her past was something about an accident. We didn't have any problems, though. She clashed with my father occasionally because she wouldn't knuckle under to him. She always got her way, and she always said she was very happy with me." The latter statement didn't entirely accord with the facts.

Berrenrath, the uniformed constable who had been one of the first to reach the scene of the crime, had overheard something of interest. When Cora Bender was being shepherded away from Georg Frankenberg's body, her husband had shouted and sworn at her. Quite unruffled, she'd turned to him and said: "I'm sorry, Gereon, I should never have married you. I knew what I was carrying around inside me. Now you're rid of me. You would have been in any case, after today. I was going for a swim."

An informative remark, Rudolf Grovian thought. He had drawn his own conclusions from it and collated some points that seemed to confirm them: two independent allusions to an "accident" in years gone by and two statements which, although dependent on personal impressions, reinforced his suspicion that the victim and his killer had met before that afternoon at the Otto Maigler Lido.

It didn't at first occur to Grovian that Georg Frankenberg's reaction to the attack on himself might simply have stemmed from shock and surprise. He proceeded on the obvious assumption.

When he confronted Cora Bender shortly after nine o'clock, he saw a tremulous picture of misery with a bruised and bloodstained face, one eye swollen shut and the other flickering with unadulterated panic. "She'll sing like a canary, chief," Berrenrath had told him. "She insists on confessing – wants to get it off her chest. She tidied up your office. If I'd let her, she'd have waxed and polished the floor for you." Berrenrath's knowledge of human nature was generally reliable.

Grovian had taken it for granted that she would promptly burst into tears and implore his sympathy – that she would supply a rational motive for her act by recounting the tragic story of a love affair that had turned out to be a big mistake – or something of the kind.

Within minutes, however, he was finding it hard to preserve the studiously calm and affable manner that had always served him so well. He had a momentary urge to thump the desk with his fist and call her to order. "Does that answer your question fully enough?" What cheek!

She sat facing him like a block of granite. He couldn't see her heart thumping or the reddish-grey mist in her brain. She still hadn't answered his last question. It seemed she was going to make good her threat: "That's all I'm saying." He waited for her expression to match the words and harden. But it didn't.

The tension on her battered face abruptly eased, her gaze turned inwards, the hands on her lap relaxed their iron grip and lay there as though forgotten. For a minute or two she was just a nice young woman in a white T-shirt, denim skirt and sandals, the next-door neighbour to whom one would happily entrust one's children for a few hours, the heart and soul of her father-in-law's family firm, worn out after a hard day's work.

He eyed her irresolutely and addressed her twice by name. She didn't respond. For a moment he felt an uneasy chill run down his spine. The contusions on her face disturbed him. There was something not quite right about her, despite her repeated denials – that was beyond question, although he ascribed this more to her physical than her mental state. He couldn't see that her mind was balancing on a knife-edge. But several hard punches to the head...

"I thought he was going to kill her," Winfried Meilhofer had said. Grovian couldn't exclude the possibility that she'd sustained some internal injury that was manifesting itself only now, several hours after the event. One occasionally heard of such things happening after a fight. If she collapsed in his office...

He shouldn't have relied on what she'd said. The woman did need a doctor. She probably needed one that would also sound her out on her putative intention to commit suicide.

Although it wasn't like him to pass the buck, he suddenly wished the district attorney had come and made the decision for him. Carry on questioning her, remand her in custody or take her to the nearest hospital, have her head X-rayed so as to preclude any subsequent charges of negligence.

The DA was engaged on another case. A man had been arrested in a Cologne bar on suspicion of having split open his girlfriend's skull with an axe. The DA's response to Grovian's phone call had been faintly indignant: "I'm in the middle of an interrogation. I'll come and pick up the papers tomorrow morning. When you're through with the woman, take her to the examining magistrate in Brühl. All clear so far?"

Nothing was clear so long as she disclaimed all knowledge of her victim. However, the witnesses' statements would be sufficient for the examining magistrate. Everything else could be left to an expert psychologist. One was bound to be called in. Let him break his teeth on her.

Something inside Rudolf Grovian urged him to offload her as soon as possible. There was something about her that not only infuriated but – although he would never have admitted it – disconcerted him. The longer he remained silent, the more clearly he felt it: a first smidgen of doubt. What if she were telling the truth?

Nonsense! A respectable wife and mother, stabbing a total stranger for some trivial reason? Out of the question.

She was toying with her wedding ring. A residue of dried blood was still visible under her fingernails. She began to dig it out. Her hands started trembling again. She raised her head and looked at him. A child's expression, helpless and forlorn.

"Did you ask me something?"

"Yes," he said, "I did, but you seem to be past concentrating. I think we'd better call it a night, Frau Bender. We'll talk again tomorrow."

That was the best solution. She might be more amenable after a night in the cells. Equally, she might use the time for another attempt to carry out her original intention. Going for a swim, indeed! But there were other methods. He would have to instruct his men to watch her incessantly. The smallest pointer in that direction would clinch the matter as far as he was concerned. Like when his daughter announced her intention of getting married. He'd breathed a sigh of relief and told himself: "Peace at last."

"No, no," she said quickly, "I'm fine. It's just that there are so many things going through my head at the same time." The tremor in her hands intensified, communicating itself to her arms and shoulders. "Forgive me for not being with it. I couldn't help thinking of my husband. It really upset him. I've never seen him so angry."

She sounded as if she'd put a dent in his bumper. Noticeably flagging now, she stared at her hands. She seemed wholly intent on preserving her composure. He wondered what would happen if she lost it. A fit of weeping? The truth at last? Or a repetition of the scene beside the lake?

His doubts recurred, somewhat more pronounced this time. What the devil was she? A young woman suddenly confronted by some distasteful reminder of her past, or one of those walking time bombs that convey a normal, innocuous impression for years on end, only to explode for no discernible reason? Would she attack him?

He was closer to her than his sidekick, Inspector Werner Hoss: the man in the sports coat, who was seated behind his desk like a graven image. Hoss was duty officer tonight, and he wasn't normally as reticent. But then, he normally agreed with everything Grovian said. Not this time, though.

When the three of them had been standing outside the door – when Berrenrath had predicted that the woman would sing like a canary, and Grovian briefly outlined his opinion of what had happened, based on his assessment of the witnesses' statements – Hoss had shaken his head. "I don't know. It would have to be one hell of a coincidence. A woman is unhappy in her marriage and plans to kill herself. Just then, she bumps into someone she once had an affair with. I can imagine something inside her snapping when she was confronted by what the Frankenbergs were up to."

64

Cora's voice jolted Grovian out of his deliberations. "Please might I have some coffee now?" she asked in a timid, humble voice.

He felt tempted to refuse. No, no coffee until we've wrapped this up. Come on, young woman, tell us what's going on in your head. You can't act as if you'd merely swatted a wasp that was trying to snack on your ice cream. You meant to drown yourself out there, didn't you? But a man had to die first. The man was young – he'd made it his vocation to save lives – and you attacked him like a rabid dog. Why?

Instead, he asked: "Would you like something to eat as well?"

"No thanks," she said quickly. "Just some coffee, please. I've got a headache, but it isn't too bad – I mean, I'm in full possession of my faculties. You needn't think I'll claim I was in such a state I didn't know what I was doing or saying."

*

Her assertion was inaccurate. She felt like someone on a roller coaster. Her thoughts roamed from Gereon to her father, from her father to her mother, from her mother to Magdalena, from Magdalena to the subject of guilt. She didn't want any coffee, just a breather in which to estimate the height of the mountain that had so suddenly loomed up in front of her.

Too much was happening all at once. She was overwhelmed with old memories and new impressions. Nothing remained of the peace and contentment, the boundless relief of those first few minutes. It wasn't over – she hadn't filled that yawning hole. Still in the midst of it, she seemed to feel its black walls steadily converging on her.

"How long have you had this headache?"

Rudolf Grovian rose to his feet with a mixture of resignation and reawakening professional ambition. It was a question of intuition and experience. He must carry on! Her voice, demeanour and sudden submissiveness were familiar to him – he'd encountered them a hundred times before. First they acted defiant, then they

65

recognized the hopelessness of their position and tried to gauge, by making some innocuous request, how much goodwill they'd already squandered.

He went over to the coffee machine, took the jug and held it under the tap. Behind him he could hear her tremulous breathing.

"Only a few minutes. But it really isn't too bad."

"So you didn't have it at the lido?"

"No."

"We ought to call a doctor and get him to look at your injuries," he suggested.

"No!" She spoke like a stubborn child refusing to put on a warm scarf. "I don't want a doctor, and if I don't want one, you can't call one. Doctors can't examine people against their will. That would be common assault."

Common assault, eh? Aloud he said: "Have you got something against doctors?"

Out of the corner of his eye he saw her shrug. After a few moments she said: "I wouldn't go that far. I just don't think much of them. They tell you some nonsense and you have to believe it because you can't prove the opposite."

"Do you know what Georg Frankenberg's profession was?"

It didn't escape him that her voice was swimming in a puddle of despair. "How would I, if I didn't know the man?"

That was the truth, the unadulterated truth. A stranger, but his wife had had that tape! "I'll wind it on a bit . . ." In her head something was winding back. The chief wasn't giving her time to reflect on how, when and under what circumstances the tune on the cassette could have found its way into her head. It would have been important to know that.

"Do you often get headaches?" he asked.

"No, only when I've slept badly."

"Would you like an aspirin? I think we've got some here." He oughtn't to give her anything even as harmless as aspirin – she could say he'd fed her something that had impaired her will. He'd only asked to make a change from saying yes or no.

"No thanks," she said. "Kind of you, but aspirin doesn't help.

66

My mother-in-law has some tablets. I take one occasionally, but you can only get them on prescription. They're very strong."

"Then your headaches must be bad," he said, spooning coffee into a paper filter. He inserted the filter, pressed a button and turned to face her.

"Yes, sometimes, but not now." She shook her head. "I'm all right, honestly. Hey, would you turn off the machine and clean the jug first? It's dirty. See that film on the bottom? You must wipe it off. It's no use just rinsing it out with water."

Her look of distaste was unmistakable. House-proud young woman, Grovian thought with a trace of sarcasm that didn't match his mood. "I bet you rinse out the jug every time," he said quietly.

"Of course."

"And everything else in your home is spick and span as well."

"I don't get much time for housework, but I do my best to keep everything clean."

"Your private life included?"

Although she was feeling so wretched she could hardly think, she grasped what he was getting at. Instinctively, her hands closed around the scars on her forearms. Her voice was hoarse and defensive. "What do you mean?"

"What I say. You don't like talking about the past, but your husband can't have been the first man in your life. Were you happy with him, Frau Bender?"

She merely nodded.

"So why did you tell him, only a few hours ago, that he should never have married you?"

She shrugged, put a hand to her mouth and started to chew her thumbnail.

"He beat you up," Grovian said, indicating her face. "Did he often hit you?"

"No!" The hoarseness in her voice had gone without her having to clear her throat. "Gereon never hit me," she said firmly. "Today was the first time, but put yourself in his place. What would *you* do if your wife suddenly jumped up and stabbed a stranger with

67

a knife? You'd also try to get it away from her, and if she resisted, you'd hit her. It was quite understandable."

Grovian rubbed the bottom of the jug clean with his fingertips, replaced the jug under the filter and pressed the button again. "I can't put myself in your husband's place, Frau Bender, because my wife would never do such a crazy thing."

Her reaction was fiercer than he'd expected. She stamped her foot and shouted: "I'm *not* crazy!"

Her earlier outbursts hadn't been lost on him. He took her renewed insistence on this point as a positive challenge to continue along the same lines. "Maybe not, Frau Bender, but that's what people will think if you provide no explanation for your actions. No normal person kills a stranger just because some music has got on her nerves. I spent a long time talking with your husband, and —"

She muttered something he didn't catch, but it stopped him in his tracks. "Leave my husband out of it!" she said fiercely. "He's got absolutely nothing to do with this." In a rather more moderate tone she went on: "Gereon is a decent man. He's hard-working and honest. He doesn't drink. He isn't violent."

She bowed her head, and her voice lost strength. "He'd never force a woman to do anything she didn't want to do. He never forced me to, either. Only yesterday he asked if I felt like it. I could have said no, but I . . ."

Grovian was feeling rather mean and couldn't understand why. Cora Bender had attacked a defenceless man like a maddened beast. She'd gone berserk with her little knife and was showing no hint of remorse or sympathy for her victim. Yet to see her sitting there with her lips trembling, enumerating her husband's good qualities, anyone would have thought *she* was the victim.

But then she smiled a self-assured, supercilious smile and exasperated him yet again with her habitual, introductory "Look . . ."

"Look," she said, "I've no wish to discuss my husband with you; it's enough if he's made a statement. He has, and he'll have to repeat it in court, but that'll have to do. We can settle the rest between us. I don't see why any outsiders should be dragged into this."

More harshly than he intended, Grovian said: "Plenty of outsiders will be dragged into this, Frau Bender. I'll tell you how matters stand: you suddenly lost control of yourself, and you either can't or won't explain why."

She opened her mouth to speak, but he went on quickly: "No, don't interrupt me again. I didn't say you were mad – no one has, to date – but you did something incomprehensible, and it's our job to find out why. We're obliged to do so by law, whether you like it or not. We shall have to interview a lot of people. Your parents, your parents-in-law – everyone who's close to you. We shall question them all, and —"

He got no further. She made to jump up, gripping the seat of her chair with both hands as if that were all that could keep her in her place. "Your parents . . ." The words reverberated in her head.

"I'm warning you!" she snarled. "Leave my father alone. You're welcome to interview my parents-in-law, they'll tell you what you want to hear: that I'm just a shameless, money-grubbing floozy. A floozy – my mother-in-law called me that from the outset. She can be an absolute bitch – she's always finding fault with me."

Grovian was unaware that she'd said her parents were dead. He saw Werner Hoss make a sign but construed it as a recommendation that the interview be discontinued, and that didn't suit him. Why stop just when he was getting somewhere? The glacier was melting, he could already hear its waters gurgling in his ears. Her parents, her father . . . He swiftly grasped that he'd touched a nerve. When she went on, he realized that more than one sore point was involved.

Hoss scribbled something on a piece of paper. *Parents dead*, Grovian read. Well, well, he thought, but he didn't have time to dwell on it. Her voice had lost its stability and was fluttering like a leaf in the wind.

"I didn't lose the child. It was a precipitate birth – the doctors said it can happen to anyone. It's nothing at all to do with whether you've slept with one man or a hundred. I haven't slept with a hundred men. As a child I used to imagine their things rotted off in due course."

She was gripping the fingers of her left hand in her right and kneading them as if she meant to break them. Grovian watched her with a mixture of fascination and triumph. Staring at the floor, she went on quietly: "But it was nice with Gereon. He never forced me. He was always kind to me. I shouldn't have married him because I . . . because I . . . I used to have this dream, but I hadn't had it for quite a long time, and I . . . I only wanted to . . ."

She broke off, raised her head and gazed into his face, her voice hoarse with panic. "I only wanted to lead a normal life with a nice young husband. I wanted what other women have, can you understand that?"

He nodded. Who wouldn't have understood, and what father wouldn't have wanted his own daughter to pursue the same aim: that of leading a happy, contented life with a nice, respectable husband?

That was the moment when a change occurred in Rudolf Grovian's attitude. He didn't notice it at the time; in fact, he still considered himself impartial days later, a conscientious policeman entitled to feel pity when confronted by the misery of an offender. Pity wasn't forbidden as long as you didn't lose sight of your objective, and that he never did for a moment. The aim of his work was detection and elucidation, rooting around in dark corners and searching for evidence. It made no difference whether those dark corners were located in a building, a patch of forest or a human soul.

Grovian did not aspire to usurp the role of an expert in the latter field, nor was it his intention to prove, by hook or by crook, that his initial assumption was correct. He was just a man who had been faced with a challenge, who failed to spot the preliminary alarm signals emitted by a mind on the brink of derangement, who was tempted and succumbed.

Cora Bender shut her eyes tight. "And that's the way it was at first," she said haltingly. "It was all quite normal. I enjoyed it when Gereon made love to me. I liked going to bed with him. But then . . . it started again. It wasn't his fault, he meant well. Other women like it – they're crazy about it. He wasn't to know what

70

he was starting when he did it to me. I didn't know myself till it happened. I ought to have discussed it with him, but what should I have told him – that I'm not a lesbian? But it wasn't that, I think. I don't know, but . . . I mean, I realize it isn't just women that do it with their tongues. Men do it too, and everyone enjoys it – everyone but me. And it never stopped. I thought it would be best if I went for a swim. It would have looked like an accident. Gereon needn't have felt guilty. That's the worst of it when someone dies – people blame themselves. They can't rid themselves of the feeling they could have prevented it. I wanted to spare him that. If the child hadn't stopped me, nothing would have happened. I'd have been long gone by the time she wound that tape on . . ."

Still with her eyes shut, she started to thump her chest with her fist. A note of hysteria came into her voice. "It was my tune! My tune, and I can't stand hearing it. The man didn't want to hear it either. Not that, he said, give me a break! He knew I fall into a hole when I hear it – he must have known. He looked at me, and he forgave me. I could read it in his eyes. Father, forgive her! She knoweth not what she doth.

"Oh, my God," she sobbed. "Father, forgive me! I loved you all. You and Mother and . . . Yes, her too. I didn't want to kill anyone. I wanted to live, to lead a normal life."

She opened her eyes again, glared at him and shook her finger in his face. "Remember this: it was all my fault. Gereon had nothing to do with it, nor did my father. Leave my father in peace. He's an old man, he's suffered enough. You'll kill him if you tell him."

4

In his own way, Father tried hard throughout those years. Even though I disappointed him a hundred times and gave him a thousand reasons to despise me, he never stopped loving me. And he did something for me that no other father would have done.

I don't mean what he did on my birthday that time, when I was lying in bed feeling hungry and he came in swearing to himself. Although even then he did something for me. When he saw I wasn't asleep yet, he perched on my bed and stroked my head. "I'm sorry," he said.

I was furious with him. If he hadn't given me that stupid bar of chocolate I'd have had a bowl of soup. "Leave me alone," I told him and turned on my side.

But he didn't leave me alone. He took me in his arms and rocked me to and fro. "My poor little girl," he whispered.

I didn't want to be a poor little girl. I didn't want a birthday either, just to be left in peace. "Leave me alone," I said again.

"I can't," he whispered. "One unhappy daughter is enough. I can't do anything for her, that's the doctors' responsibility, but you're mine. If you hold out for another half-hour, Mother is bound to go to sleep. Then I'll bring you something to eat. You must be as hungry as a wolf."

He sat on my bed for more than an hour, holding me in his arms, and this time he didn't tell me anything about the old days. Mother was still down below, praying for the last time that day. It seemed an eternity before we heard her climb the stairs at last. She went to the bathroom. Soon afterwards the bedroom door closed behind her. Father waited a few more minutes before he stole downstairs.

He returned with a bowl of soup. It was only lukewarm, but that didn't matter. When the bowl was empty he put it on the floor, then felt in his pocket for something: the rest of the chocolate.

I didn't want to take it, honestly not, but he broke some off and stuffed it into my mouth. "Go on," he said. "Don't worry, you can eat it. You can if I say so. It isn't a sin. I'd never encourage you to commit a sin. You needn't be afraid that Mother will notice. She thinks it's outside in the dustbin." So I couldn't help it.

The next day Magdalena was worse, and the day after that her condition deteriorated still more. Father insisted on taking her to the hospital. Mother didn't agree, but this time Father got his way. They set off very early in the morning.

I'll never forget that day. Mother returned at lunchtime – alone, in a taxi. Father had remained at Eppendorf with Magdalena to have a quiet word with the doctors. I was next door at Grit Adigar's. Father had told me to go there if no one was in when I came home from school. Grit had given me a good lunch and later some sweets for doing my homework properly.

I hadn't meant to eat them until Magdalena came home, but I told myself it wouldn't matter, not after the chocolate episode, so I was still sucking away when Mother came to collect me. She spotted I had something in my mouth, naturally, but she didn't tell me to spit it out.

Mother wasn't her usual self. She might have been made of stone, and her voice grated like the white sand in which nothing can grow. The doctors had told her that Magdalena was terminally ill. She had laughed at death often enough; now her time was finally up. No treatment, they'd told her. It would only be cruel.

Her various ailments had been joined by yet another. It had nothing to do with the cold I'd brought home. It was called leukaemia – cancer, said Mother, and I pictured Magdalena being devoured from within by a creature armed with crablike claws.

Mother fetched two suitcases from the basement: one for her and one for Magdalena. I had to accompany her upstairs and stand beside Magdalena's bed while she packed them. "Take a good look at this bed," she told me. "This is how it's going to stay, and you'll see your sister lying there for the rest of your life. To the end of your days you'll ask yourself: Was it worth it? How could I let my sister die such a terrible death for the sake of a moment's pleasure?"

I believed that. I genuinely believed it, and I was terribly frightened. Until then I'd never given any thought to how life would go on when Magdalena wasn't there any more. Now I did. I looked at the bed as Mother had bidden me, and I thought she was going to lock me up in there so that I could see Magdalena's empty bed for the rest of my days.

Mother took a taxi back to Eppendorf, leaving me alone in the house. She hadn't locked me up in the bedroom, so I was in the living room when Father came home that evening. I'd lit the candles and spent the whole afternoon kneeling on the bench, promising our Saviour that I'd never covet anything ever again. I begged him to make me drop dead and leave my sister in peace. When I didn't drop dead I thought I must show Mother what a great sacrifice I could make. I planned to burn my hands like the blue dress with the white collar, so I could never again touch anything sweet. But when I held my hands over the candle flames and the pain became unbearable, I took them away. The only result was a few blisters.

Father was horrified when he saw them and asked what Mother had said to me. I told him. He flew into a rage and swore terribly – "The stupid bitch! She's sick!" and things like that. Then he went to Grit Adigar's to call the hospital and tell the doctors that he'd changed his mind: they must treat Magdalena after all. If they weren't prepared to do so, he would report them and take Magdalena to another hospital.

He was very quiet when he came back. He made supper for us – string beans from a preserving jar, which was all there was in the house. Then he put a smaller saucepan on the stove and poured some milk into it. We always had some milk for Magdalena's benefit. I didn't want any. I found it easy to go without milk, but I always pretended it was a great sacrifice. That shows you what a deceitful, hypocritical child I was.

74

Father produced a little paper bag from his trouser pocket and smiled at me. "Let's see if I can do this," he said. It was custard powder – he'd begged it from Grit. "I must make her understand she can eat what she likes," he'd told her. "But what am I going to do about Magdalena? It would be best to let her die in peace. The treatment is sheer torture; the doctors explained that to me in detail. She won't survive it, and I'll have to live with the thought that she was tortured to death at my instigation. But I have to do it for Cora's sake."

Grit didn't tell me that until much later, but I always knew Father loved me. I loved him too – very much.

We were alone together for a long time after that. Those six months were the best time I'd ever had. Before Father went off to work in the mornings he'd make me a breakfast of cocoa, boiled eggs and bread and sausage, and he always gave me a nice big apple or banana to eat at break.

When I came back at lunchtime I went to Grit's and spent the afternoon playing with Kerstin and Melanie. They were always nice to me at home, in fact they sometimes said they were sorry for ignoring me during break.

The best thing was when Father came home at the end of the afternoon. He'd clean the windows and wash the curtains while I dusted and swept the kitchen, so everything looked neat and clean. When we'd done the housework he cooked for us. There was meat or sausage and a dessert every day. After supper we sat in the kitchen. Father assured me that Magdalena's condition would neither improve nor deteriorate if we had some blancmange. He also promised to urge Mother to allow me to grow up a normal child.

"It's enough," he said once, "if the person responsible for this evil practises self-denial. I'm firmly resolved to do so. God grant I manage it."

We always went into the living room before bed. Father never lit the candles. We simply kneeled before the altar in the darkness and prayed for Magdalena. Mother had asked us to, but I think we'd have done so of our own accord.

Father sometimes went to the hospital on a Sunday. He didn't take me with him. I wasn't allowed near Magdalena in case she caught some minor ailment from me. The treatment he'd insisted on for my sake was working, but Magdalena had grown so weak, a common cold might have carried her off.

While Father was visiting her I went next door, where Grit gave me cocoa and fresh-baked pastries sprinkled with sugar. I was happy – infinitely happy, especially when Father came home from the hospital and said: "It looks as if she's going to make it. There's nothing left of her but two great big eyes, but the doctors say she has an invincible determination to survive. You could almost believe she pumps the blood through her veins by willpower alone. She's such a frail little creature – too weak even to raise her head. The doctors can't understand it, but all human beings cling to life."

They came home in December. Magdalena had no hair left. She was so weak, she couldn't be allowed to wait until she did it of her own accord. Mother gave her an enema every morning, so she didn't have to strain. Magdalena hated those enemas. She had only to see Mother coming with the jug and the tube, and she burst into tears. But she wasn't allowed to do that either; it was too strenuous.

Mother completely lost it when Magdalena started to cry. She would shoo me into the living room, with the result that I couldn't come out and do my homework. I regularly got into trouble with the teacher the next day. She'd liked me to begin with, but now she thought me lazy and neglectful. I couldn't always blame my shortcomings on my invalid sister. A couple of times I even got a black mark in the class book.

Grit Adigar advised me to do my homework at night, after Mother had sent me to bed. I had to sprawl on the floor with my exercise books because there was no table in the bedroom. Then the teacher would complain about my untidy handwriting.

Although I was naturally grateful to our Saviour for having spared my sister's life, Magdalena's survival wasn't the way I'd imagined it. Sometimes I thought it would have been better if Mother had shut me up in the bedroom forever. Then I wouldn't have had as much hassle.

Every four weeks Magdalena had to go to the hospital for follow-up treatment. Mother went with her. They remained there for two or three days each time, and each time I wished they would never come back – that the doctors would say Magdalena had to stay at Eppendorf forever, that she could only survive there, and that Mother would stay with her. She never left her side, after all. Then I would stay home with Father, and he would be just like he'd been throughout those six months. I didn't want him to be so sad, but that was all.

*

It was like the nightmare she couldn't awake from, except that this time it was completely different. Nothing remained hidden. It all escaped her grasp, spilled out of her head and spread in all directions. She heard herself talking about her birthday, the bar of chocolate, her daydreams. Just Father and me! She saw herself gesticulating, seemed to see the chief's perplexed, attentive face through a mist.

From time to time he nodded.

And she couldn't stop talking, she couldn't afford to. She had to persuade him to leave her father in peace. Gereon too. Gereon didn't deserve to be troubled with something for which he bore no responsibility. As for Father, it would finish him to learn the truth.

She told the chief about him. Not too much, just what a kind, warm-hearted man he used to be. A man of wide interests, a walking treatise on local history. She also spoke of her mother, of the crucifix and the roses on the home-made altar, of the wooden Saviour and their prayers. All she omitted to mention was the reason for them: Magdalena.

Her body trembled spasmodically. Her brain did too, causing her head to jerk up and down like that of an automaton. But she still had some self-control left. No one must be allowed near Magdalena, certainly not a man. Any excitement, any exertion could spell her death.

She spoke of her conflicting emotions, of her need to be good and her desire for a life of sin. Sweets in her childhood, young men and their magical power of attraction in later years. There had been one in particular, the kind that had only to click his fingers. Everyone called him Johnny Guitar.

Grit Adigar had once told her: "When you're old enough, do as I did. Find yourself a nice husband and get him to father a child on you, then go away with him and forget all this nonsense." She would gladly have gone away with Johnny and had more than once wondered what it would be like to have a child by him.

The thought of Johnny brought her back to Gereon. She told of the day she'd met him for the first time. Gereon was her only route to normality, and normal was what she longed to be – had to be. A normal, grown-up woman who had long since left her childhood behind her. As for the unsavoury episode that had begun in May five years ago and ended six months later, in November, leaving such unmistakable traces on her forearms and forehead, that too must remain a closed book because it would stir up too much dust.

Her mother-in-law had often tried to pump her. "The hussy! Who knows what she got up to before!" And the old man with his stupid remarks: "You're a cunning little vixen, but you can't fool me."

You bet she could! She'd learned to fool people in her cradle. She could fool anyone she chose, the chief included. It helped her to recall her first meeting with Gereon. Four years ago, it was – five come December. It was shortly before Christmas.

Gereon was in town, shopping for some presents for his parents. Laden with parcels, he'd walked into the café on Herzogstrasse where she earned her living – an honest living, be it noted! A chance customer the first time, he'd sat down at a table and waited for service. He didn't know you had to order at the counter out front and was embarrassed when she told him.

"Do I have to go back out there?" He was clearly disconcerted. Feeling that he'd branded himself a country bumpkin, he blushed. "Couldn't you bring me something?"

"I don't know what you want."

"Anything," he said with a grin. "Something with whipped cream on it and a coffee."

"Pot or cup?" she asked.

"A cup'll do me," he replied. That was typical of him. He'd always been modest in his requirements.

She went out front and brought him a slice of Black Forest gateau and a coffee. "Nice of you," he said. "Would you like something too? My treat."

"Thanks," she said, "but I work here."

"Yes, of course." Embarrassed once more, he forked up a big piece of gateau, shoved it into his mouth and started chewing. His gaze followed her around the room. He smiled whenever she caught his eye.

Two days later he was back. This time he ordered out front and chuckled at her like an old acquaintance. Before leaving he asked: "What do you do when you're through here? When do you get off?"

"Six-thirty."

"Could we go somewhere after that? Have a beer, maybe?"

"I don't drink beer."

"Something else, then, it doesn't matter. It doesn't have to be for long either. Just half an hour. I'd like to get to know you properly."

Gereon was clumsy but very direct. Although he made no secret of the fact that he found her attractive, he wasn't pushy in the least. When she declined his invitation he merely shrugged his shoulders and said: "Another time, maybe."

He asked her three times for a date; and three times she refused. After the third time she talked to Margret about him, his good looks and his naivety. She said he was the kind of man you could convince that the earth was flat and that ships venturing too far would topple over the edge.

She spoke of her need to draw a line under the past and make a fresh start in some place where nobody knew her – to lead a life like thousands of others. And that would only work with a man who had no opinions of his own, a man who would believe that the scars on her arms resulted from a bad infection – which was essentially true – and that she'd acquired the scar on her forehead by walking in front of a car. Margret was thoroughly understanding.

But she couldn't tell the chief all that. He would promptly have asked who Margret was and added her to the list of people he had to interview at all costs. And dragging Margret into this business would definitely be a step too far.

Margret was Father's younger sister. Compared to Mother, Margret had always been a young woman. Young and pretty and modern, with revolutionary ideas about life and a sympathetic understanding of all the failings and mistakes to which a person can be prone.

When Gereon came into her life she'd been living for a year in Margret's cramped little apartment in Cologne. Two rooms plus a tiny kitchen and a shower room the size of a pocket handkerchief. When you sat on the loo you grazed your knees on the door. She slept on the sofa, which was all Margret had to offer. The bedroom was too small for a second bed.

Cora didn't want a bed. She couldn't have endured another bed so close to hers. Sometimes she wondered what would have become of her if Margret hadn't taken her in when she couldn't stand it at home any longer. To that there was only one answer: she'd be dead. And she wanted to enjoy life.

She finally learned to do so with Margret. It was Margret who got her the job at the café on Herzogstrasse, and Margret who said, when Gereon turned up and persisted in asking her for a date: "Why not go out with him, Cora? You're a young woman. It's normal to fall in love with a young man."

"I don't know if I'm in love with him. It's just that he reminds me of someone I was crazy about. Everyone called him Johnny – I never knew his real name. He looked like the archangel driving Adam and Eve out of Paradise in Mother's Bible. You know the passage? 'And the eyes of them both were opened, and they knew that they were naked!' That's what Johnny looked like. Gereon looks a bit like him, but only superficially, hair colour and so on.

Gereon is a nice fellow; he comes from a respectable family. He's told me about his parents, and one day he's bound to ask me —"

"Nonsense," said Margret. "Let him ask, we'll think of something. You say he isn't too smart. Anyway, you aren't obliged to tell him your life story. And besides, he won't necessarily ask about your family right away. Young men usually have something else in mind. If he does ask, tell him you couldn't stick it at home any longer. Tell him your mother isn't right in the head, but it isn't hereditary. That's true enough."

"But what if he wants to go to bed with me?" It was more of a murmur and not addressed to Margret at all.

But Margret heard it nonetheless. She looked at Cora intently, filled with sympathy and compassion. "Don't you think you could?" she asked.

Of course she could, it wasn't that. She often wondered what it would be like with some nice young man, but it would have been cheating. When she didn't reply, Margret said in her typically forthright tone: "That's no problem, Cora. If you don't feel like it, just say no."

It wasn't as simple as Margret imagined. You couldn't say no forever if you wanted to keep a man, and she did. She found Gereon attractive. For one thing, there was his superficial resemblance to Johnny. For another, he was very gentle and affectionate. Those first few evenings in his car were wonderful.

He picked her up at the café twice a week, drove her to some lonely spot and took her in his arms. It was usually too cold to remove her jacket, let alone anything else, but Gereon didn't hassle her. He contented himself with kisses and cuddles until well into the New Year. Only then did he want more.

She would have preferred to put it off a little longer, but her fear of losing him if she denied him outweighed her fear that he might be disappointed afterwards. He wasn't either. He didn't feel duped or deceived. All he said was: "You weren't a virgin, though."

Of course she wasn't! No girl was a virgin at twenty-one – she was bound to have gone to bed with some man or other, but there was no need to tell the chief that.

Cora had everything under control again. She managed to tell her story without mentioning Margret and without leaving a hiatus. Only the last sentence, Gereon's statement, slipped out before she could stop it.

The chief was looking at her. He wanted her to go on, his demeanour made that obvious. He wanted some explanation for the man's death and wouldn't rest until he got one. He would speak with Gereon, probably even with Father.

A long silence ensued. The man in the sports coat was eyeing the recording machine dubiously, the chief looking her insistently in the eye. She had to tell him something, anything. What if he wouldn't believe the truth? Now, when her head had cleared a bit and she was making some sort of sense again . . .

It occurred to her that Gereon's remark about her virginity and what Grit Adigar had said about her leaving home might well serve as the basis of a story. What about a name for the principal character? What had the chief said? "His name was Georg Frankenberg." Perhaps, but the name was unfamiliar, and she was afraid of stumbling over it if she used it. Johnny was more familiar, and if she combined what she'd wanted back then with what people had said about him . . . that would make an excellent basis for a good story.

"If I . . ." she began haltingly. "If I explain why I killed him, will you promise not to bother my family?"

He made no such promise, just asked: "*Can* you explain it, Frau Bender?"

She nodded. Her hands were trembling uncontrollably again. She placed one firmly on the other and pressed them both against her thighs. "Of course I can. It's just that I'd hoped I wouldn't have to. And I don't want my husband finding out. He mightn't understand, and his parents certainly wouldn't. They'd make his life a misery if they knew – I mean, for getting involved with a person like me."

Till then she'd spoken with her head down. Now she looked up, straight into his eyes, and drew several deep breaths.

"I was lying to you when I said I didn't know the man. I didn't know his real name, but the man himself . . .

82

"It was March five years ago when he turned up in Buchholz for the first time. Nobody knew his real name. He called himself Johnny Guitar. I'd had little experience of men. I was seldom allowed out and had to lie to get a few hours to myself. Usually I told my mother I found it easier to recognize my sinful desires and concentrate on curbing them in the open air, immediately beneath the eye of God. She was so impressed by such statements, she even allowed me to leave the house on Saturday nights. There wasn't much for young people to do in Buchholz. Lots of open countryside around with paths for walkers and cyclists and cafés and hotels for people in search of relaxation but no disco. Many youngsters went to Hamburg. I never did, although Father would certainly have lent me his car. He'd allowed me to take my test. We were allies, Father and I, but I didn't want to push my luck.

"I always went into town. There were a few ice-cream parlours and a place where you could dance on Saturdays. I had no friends of either sex. Most girls of my age had boyfriends and preferred to be alone with them. As for the boys, I got to know one or two but not in a serious way. I danced with them and let them buy me a Coke, but that was all. I was inhibited, and they lost interest when they saw they wouldn't make it with me right away.

"That never bothered me – not until Johnny turned up that night in March. I fell for him within minutes, I think. He wasn't on his own. There was someone else with him, a short, fat youth. Neither of them came from our part of the world; I could tell that as soon as I heard them speak. They looked around without noticing me and sat down at a table. After a minute or two Johnny got up and went over to a girl. He danced with her a couple of times. Later they left with the fat boy in tow.

"They were back again the following Saturday, the girl as well. She was sitting in a corner with two girlfriends. When they spotted Johnny and his friend they put their heads together and started whispering, but the girl didn't join them. I got the impression she wanted nothing more to do with them. Johnny took no notice of her either. It wasn't long before he was dancing with another girl.

He went off with her soon afterwards, the fat boy trailing after them. And next Saturday they might all have been strangers.

"It went on like that for several weeks. Perhaps my suspicions should have been aroused by their behaviour, and even more so by that of the girls, but I never thought twice about it. I was really very naïve in those days. And very much in love! I'd have given anything just to speak to him.

"I could hardly wait to leave the house on Saturdays. I'd never lied to my mother as brazenly as I did at that time. Everything revolved around Johnny. I knew I didn't stand a chance with him – all I wanted was to be near him. I asked around a bit, but no one knew anything definite. Some of the girls said he was a musician. The ones who'd been with him and his friend grinned when I questioned them. 'It was nice,' they told me, 'but not your cup of tea.'

"And then – it was on 16 May, a week after my birthday – Fatso spoke to me. There wasn't much action that night, and they'd been sitting at their table for quite a while before he came over. I danced with him because I thought he might take me back to their table afterwards. Big mistake! He got fresh, and I had trouble fending him off. He became abusive and swore at me.

"I left feeling pretty depressed. Then, outside in the car park, I heard Johnny calling after me. He apologized for his friend and urged me not to take offence. The fat boy was a hothead and didn't have much luck with girls. We stood outside for a while, talking. I could hardly believe my luck. He asked if I'd like to go back inside. It was too early to go home, he said, and he would make sure his friend didn't hassle me again.

"That's how it started with Johnny and me. It seemed like a miracle. I'd suspected that he only came to Buchholz to pick up a girl for the night, but he didn't act that way with me. His fat friend left as soon as we came in. We sat at the table on our own for nearly half an hour, chatting. Then Johnny asked if I'd care to dance with him.

"Nothing more happened that night. Fatso didn't reappear. When I had to leave Johnny accompanied me outside. He wanted to escort me home, but that was impossible. If my mother had seen us, I'd never have been allowed out again. We said goodbye in the car park. He shook hands with me and said: 'Any chance of seeing you again?'

"I said: 'I'll probably come again next Saturday.'

"He smiled. 'Me too, but I'd better come by myself, I guess. See you next week, then.'

"He really did come by himself, and he took things very slowly. It was three weeks before he kissed me for the first time. He was nice and gentle and seemed to understand whatever I told him; in fact, he didn't laugh even when I told him about my mother. All he said was: '*Chacun à son goût.*'

"I asked him his name, of course. He said it was Horsti. That sounded silly, so I stuck to Johnny. He said he couldn't stand girls you could bed right away – they were only good for a laugh. He said he'd never met a girl like me before and that he loved me. Everything was perfect. He was even a trifle jealous. A couple of times, when he couldn't make it to Buchholz the following weekend, he asked me to stay home in case someone else queered his pitch.

"I didn't know much about him. He was reluctant to talk about himself and seldom did so. He'd formed a group with two friends, he told me, and they practised in a cellar. Fatso was one of them – Johnny said he was terrific on the keyboard. He himself played the drums and the third member of the group played bass guitar.

"In August he asked if I'd like to hear them play. I wanted to, I said, but I didn't feel like being cooped up in a cellar with Fatso, where I couldn't get away if he got fresh again. Johnny laughed at me. 'I'll be there. He won't even give you the eye.'

"The following weekend he brought him along. Fatso behaved himself, so I agreed to go with them. It was a great night. They played a new number, 'Tiger's Song'. Johnny said it was my tune now – he'd composed it especially for me.

"They played for about an hour. Then the other two went off and didn't come back. Johnny gave me a drink and turned on the hi-fi. He played some tapes of their own composition. We danced, had another couple of drinks and sat down on the couch. And that was when it happened.

"I won't pretend he raped me. It was lovely, and I wanted it. I was a bit squiffy, my one fear being that he'd get me pregnant. I'd never been on the pill, you see.

"'Don't worry,' Johnny told me, 'I'll take care.' I relied on what he'd said, but my period failed to materialize. I was beside myself with fear. Johnny gave me some money and told me to buy a test kit from the chemist's. 'If it's positive,' he said, 'we'll simply get married.'

"It was positive. Johnny seemed overjoyed when I told him. 'So I'm going to be a daddy,' he said, hugging me delightedly. 'My parents will be amazed. I'll introduce you to them tomorrow. Think of some excuse so your mother lets you out and tell her you'll be gone a while. We'll meet in the car park at two. Don't give up if I'm half an hour late. Wait for me.'

"I waited till seven that evening. He didn't show up. I never saw him again. I did my best to find him, but that didn't amount to much. I didn't know his real name or where he lived.

"All I could remember was that we'd driven along the autobahn that night, in the direction of Hamburg. But we were sitting in the back, and I was too wrapped up in him to notice anything much. I didn't even know if we'd been at his parents' house or a friend's. I drove around for weeks, searching for the place. I thought some detail might occur to me while driving.

"Father parked his car in a side street when he came home from work every evening, so Mother didn't notice anything. I told him I needed to keep my hand in, and he accepted that.

"I couldn't tell him I was pregnant and had no one else to confide in. In the end I realized my quest was hopeless. I waited another few weeks for Johnny to get in touch – he knew my name and address, after all. I couldn't believe anyone could be such a louse, but the girls who'd been with him before me said: 'Did you really imagine he was serious about you?'

"By the end of October I could see my bump was getting bigger. My mother, who had noticed that I often felt nauseous, insisted on my seeing a doctor. So I left home, hitching a lift into the blue. Then I tried to kill myself. I threw myself in front of a car. I lost the baby – it was a girl, you could already tell. Nothing much happened to me, just a few scratches on the face. And the miscarriage, of course.

"I had to go home again, but my mother wouldn't have me in the house. Trying to die and killing my baby in the process was the gravest sin a person could commit, she said, and she threw me out.

"I went to Cologne and found work there. A year later I met my husband and got married. But I never got over what had happened. My mother's right: I'm a murderess. I killed an innocent child. Ever since my son's birth I've wondered what it would be like for him to have an elder sister to love him – to do everything for him and always be there for him.

"This afternoon, when I saw Johnny with that woman . . . At first I only saw him from behind. It can't be him, I thought, but then he sat up and I heard him speak. And then the woman played that tune. My tune, 'Tiger's Song' . . .

"I thought . . . I don't know what I thought. Everything happened so incredibly fast. Automatically, in a way."

At these last words she looked up, gazed into the chief's eyes, and felt relief surge through her like a warm liquid. His face had softened. He believed her story, but then, it was a good story. And, since it was based to a very small extent on the truth, no one could disprove it.

*

The little apartment in Cologne in which Margret Rosch had given her niece a temporary home overlooked a busy street. This didn't bother her in the winter. She aired it briefly night and morning, but in the summer it often became unbearable. If the windows were open, they let in the noise of the traffic and the all-pervading stench of exhaust fumes. If they were shut, the heat built up inside until you felt you were in an incubator.

Margret had come home shortly after nine that Saturday night five years ago, having spent the afternoon and evening with an old friend of hers. She never described him as anything other than a friend. Achim Miek, a physician with a practice of his own in the city centre, had been her lover for the past twenty years.

Margret had never been married, and now it wasn't worth it any more. After all those years as his mistress, the thought of giving up her personal freedom didn't appeal to her, even though Achim was urging her to do so. He'd now been a widower for over a year.

Margret had never pressed him or uttered the word "divorce", and she had only once asked him to do something for her – or rather, for her brother and her niece. That had been five years ago – and illegal. She later regarded it as a bad omen that Achim had felt obliged to remind her of it today of all days. "Blackmail" might have been a better word.

She'd said goodbye to him earlier than planned to avoid an altercation, so she wasn't in the best of moods when she entered her apartment. The place was stuffy, but it was late enough to open all the windows. The traffic had diminished, and it was several degrees cooler outside than in.

She took a lukewarm shower. Then, because the restaurant dinner they'd planned had come to nothing, she fixed herself a light supper. After that she read a few pages of a novel to take her mind off her disappointment and misgivings.

At eleven there was a movie on TV she wanted to see. When she turned on the set a good-looking evangelist was earnestly discoursing upon our Saviour, humanity's shining example.

Margret promptly forgot about her own problems, all except for her friend's "Don't forget what I did for you." Forget? How could she? She'd taken a far bigger risk than Achim Miek. She felt a sudden upsurge of cold fury, saw for a fraction of a second her younger niece's anguished, blue-tinged face, heard Elsbeth's soft voice murmuring a prayer. The scent of lighted candles seemed to sting her nose. The impression was so real, she couldn't help sneezing.

88

She blew her nose, picked up her book again and concentrated on the text while the good-looking evangelist continued to expatiate for a minute or two. No one who had experienced what Margret had experienced could endure listening to him, although she had experienced it only sporadically. Four times a year for a couple of days at most, and not at first even then. She hadn't started visiting her brother regularly until Wilhelm expressly asked her to. Cora had been nine at the time, and when Margret departed she uttered a prayer as fervent as the ones Elsbeth murmured in the living room: "Take care of Cora, Wilhelm. You must do something about her, or she'll go to the dogs."

Wilhelm had nodded each time. "I'll do my best," he promised.

Margret didn't know whether he really did his best and how much he *could* do. She didn't know much about him in general. There was eighteen years' difference in age between her big brother and herself, their mother's spoilt little afterthought.

Wilhelm had already volunteered for the Wehrmacht when Margret was born. He came home once in the ensuing years, but she didn't remember him. Her home at that time was in Buchholz, the little town near Lüneburg Heath to which Wilhelm moved later. In the spring of 1944 Margret and her mother left their old home and went to the Rhineland, where relatives of her mother still lived. Her big brother was often mentioned after the move, but Margret didn't get to know him until she was ten years old, and Wilhelm already a broken man.

It was never talked of openly. From the few allusions he made over the years, Margret inferred that he'd taken part in executions in Poland. Members of the civilian population, women and children included. Under orders. If he'd refused he would probably have got a bullet in the back of the neck or been strung up. Wilhelm, who couldn't see the matter in that light, had never come to terms with it.

He didn't stay long in the Rhineland with his mother and sister. His father had been killed in France, and he wanted to go back to Buchholz, perhaps because he hoped to rediscover some measure of his youthful innocence there.

Instead he found Elsbeth, a beautiful young woman from Hamburg. An almost ethereal-looking creature with pale golden hair and a china-doll complexion, Elsbeth had shared the post-war fate of many German girls: she became pregnant by a member of the Allied occupation forces. She hadn't carried the child to term. By the time Margret learned that she'd got rid of it with a knitting needle and almost died as a result Elsbeth was a lost cause. But it was one explanation, and explanations were the most important thing of all.

Margret had often spoken of this during Cora's eighteen months with her. They'd spent countless nights discussing guilt and innocence, faith and morality, Cora's parents and their long years of childlessness. Elsbeth's company had gradually dispelled Wilhelm's gloom and awakened his *joie de vivre*, his love of laughter and dancing. Margret described how he'd begun to enjoy life, how he and Elsbeth had gone travelling – a week in Paris, three days in Rome, the Oktoberfest in Munich, the Prater in Vienna.

Elsbeth refused to miss Cologne's annual carnival, so they used to visit the Rhineland once a year. She had the odd drink on those occasions, but one glass too many would put her into a melancholy mood and prompt her to talk about love, sorrow and the heavy burden of guilt she carried.

Elsbeth was nearly forty when she became pregnant for the second time. Wilhelm, then pushing fifty, was exultant. He invited his mother and sister to Buchholz after Cora's birth, insisting that they come and admire that gift from heaven, their little granddaughter and niece, a pretty baby with his dark hair and a healthy appetite. The birth had taken a lot out of Elsbeth. She lay there in hospital, pale, weak and almost drained of blood but as overjoyed as Wilhelm.

"Have you seen her yet, Margret? Go on, the nurse will show her to you. Everyone here says they've seldom seen such a pretty baby. And how strong she is! She can hold her little head up all by herself. I never thought I'd hold a child of my own in my arms. And such a beautiful one! If He's given me such a wonderful gift, God must have forgiven me. A child like that is well worth a little self-sacrifice. I'll soon get over it."

But before Elsbeth could recover she became pregnant again – with Magdalena, the candidate for death. Her *ductus Botalli*, which connects the aorta to the pulmonary artery and normally closes at birth, was open, and she also suffered from several septal defects. The vestibules of her tiny heart were affected, as were both chambers. There were other vascular abnormalities as well. The left-hand chamber of the heart was not fully developed, and the abdominal aorta displayed saclike formations or aneurysms. The affected section was too big to be removed completely, and the doctors suspected that other vessels were also affected.

Margret was a nurse. Nobody needed to tell her that the blue baby stood no chance, despite undergoing six operations in as many months. One of the surgeons told Wilhelm: "The thing that's beating in your daughter's chest isn't a heart, it's Swiss cheese. It looks as if someone has gone to work on it with a knitting needle."

Unfortunately, Elsbeth either overheard that remark or had it relayed to her by a thoughtless nurse.

But no matter how little time the doctors gave her, Magdalena proved them wrong. She even duelled with leukaemia and won. Elsbeth, who attributed this to the power of prayer, intensified her efforts to an extent that any normal person would have found intolerable.

Although aware of the situation in her brother's home, Margret had done nothing about it, pleading the physical distance between them and the impossibility of leaving their old mother on her own. Her visits to Buchholz had been rare for the first few years after Magdalena's birth. She would look in, put her head in the sand and go home again.

Then her mother died. Wilhelm attended the funeral in Cologne on his own, Elsbeth being unable to get away. They sat together that night, Margret and the brother who was old enough to be her father. He hummed and hawed for a while before coming out with it: would she pay them a visit in the next few weeks, and would she have a word with Elsbeth, woman to woman, about a normal man's needs? He found it hard to be explicit. The fact that he managed it, when they were such relative strangers, showed Margret how desperate he was.

"I've considered divorcing her, but that would be irresponsible. I don't want to shirk my responsibilities, but things can't go on like this. I can't take it any more."

After at least two minutes he added: "I've been sleeping in the other bedroom ever since Magdalena's birth. She won't let me go near her, no matter what I say. I used to go to a woman who took money – I didn't know what else to do. It was wrong, I know, and I stopped it a while back."

At that time, "since Magdalena's birth" meant eight years ago. Wilhelm was fifty-nine but looked considerably younger. He was a tall, powerfully built man. "It's not just me," he told Margret in a low voice. "It's Cora. She's nine now, and getting older all the time. I'm worried about her." Although Wilhelm certainly hadn't meant this the way Margret construed it at first, a shiver ran down her spine.

She set off for Buchholz two weeks later and tried her luck with Elsbeth. But all her efforts were in vain. Elsbeth listened placidly, her hands folded on her lap. "I'd let him if I had the strength for another child. My time isn't up yet – I could still conceive, but how am I supposed to cope? No! We all have to make sacrifices. Wilhelm is a man. He must bear it like a man."

Wilhelm must have coped somehow, probably by resuming his visits to the woman who took money, Margret didn't know exactly. He had never raised the subject again, just made a couple of references to his fears for Cora, who was beginning to display signs of puberty.

It hadn't been pleasant to wonder if Wilhelm was putting the lid on Elsbeth's insane treatment of Cora. Her own brother! Even if he were at the end of his sexual tether, he surely wouldn't lay hands on a child! Not his own daughter!

Margret found this hard to believe but had made a half-hearted attempt to discover the truth. She ran into a brick wall. If Cora didn't want to say something, wild horses wouldn't drag it out of her; Margret had discovered that even then.

It was predictable that disaster would strike sooner or later. From Margret's point of view, disaster had already struck five years ago – on 16 May, Magdalena's birthday, to be precise. Cora had seemed to vanish from the face of the earth for six whole months.

With a shudder, Margret remembered the phone call in December of that year. Her niece's voice: "May I come to you? I can't live here any longer. I don't think I can *live* any longer, period." She recalled Cora standing outside her door with the needle marks in her arms and the dent in her skull, recalled the nights, well into the following March, when she used to have to jump out of bed and hurry into the living room, her first step being to grab Cora's wrists to prevent the girl from harming herself. Frightful nightmares followed by raging headaches and resolute silence. Whatever had happened to Cora, she couldn't talk about it. She made one reference to an accident the previous October, but that was all.

She needed the assistance of a competent physician, but she wouldn't let anyone near her. Margret almost had to go down on her knees before she would agree to let Achim Miek examine her. Achim said that the headaches were probably caused by the injury to her head and expressed surprise that a wound sustained in October had healed so well. As for the nightmares, he surmised that they resulted from some traumatic experience. A good psychologist could probably help, he said.

Cora rejected this idea, and somehow she managed without any help. These days there was no need to worry about her. Cora was doing fine – she visited Margret every other Sunday accompanied by Gereon and her little boy, full of news about her own home and her exhausting work at the office.

It delighted Margret every time to hear how enthusiastically Cora had taken to such an unfamiliar job. Gereon Bender was no ideal husband in Margret's opinion. She thought him a fool, but since marrying him Cora had had something useful to do and no more time to brood. Her problems seemed to be over. She always made an equable impression when they came visiting, and they were due to come again this Sunday.

Margret had spoken with her niece on the phone just before lunch on Friday. Cora had sounded a little on edge. Lately she'd often sounded a bit edgy on Fridays, and no wonder, after a week's stressful office work.

Shortly before eleven, just after the movie started, Gereon phoned. He'd never called her before, so that was a bad omen in itself – the second tonight. He gave her a garbled account of what had happened, but all she caught at first was a single word: police!

She thought Cora had been hurt in some way. It would never have occurred to her that she could hurt someone else. Cora was rebellious by nature and tended to make an aggressive impression, but at heart she was gentle as a lamb. And lambs don't kill; they're born victims.

Margret continued to hold the receiver to her ear long after Gereon had hung up, feeling sure she'd misunderstood. She tried to call back but there was no reply, either from her niece's house or from that of her parents-in-law. It was a while before she could bring herself to call directory enquiries and ask the number of the district police headquarters. After that she needed a brandy.

It was like before. She wavered between not wanting to know and the need for certainty, between a desire for a quiet life and the knowledge that Cora had no one to vouch for her. No help could be expected from Gereon. His final words had made his position clear: "I'm finished with her."

Margret brewed herself some coffee and drank two cups to offset the brandy. Then, at long last, she dialled the number and stated her name and business. No information could be given over the phone, she was told, and there was no possibility of her speaking to the officer in charge of the case. That was information enough.

5

Rudolf Grovian turned off the recording machine when a deep sigh conveyed that she'd said enough for the time being. It was a few minutes after eleven. She was looking tired but highly relieved. He was familiar with this effect from other interrogations. The coffee had been ready for ages. He rose and went over to the sink, picked up the mug and rinsed it out thoroughly under the tap so she could see. Then he shook off the drops. There wasn't a clean cloth around for drying up, needless to say. Nothing was ever to hand when you needed it.

"Milk and sugar, Frau Bender?"

"No thanks. Black, please. Is it nice and strong?"

"Black as pitch," he said, and she smiled faintly and nodded.

He filled the mug and brought it over to the desk. His manner still accorded with normal interrogation tactics. No one, not even Grovian himself, noticed that there was something different about it.

"Would you like something to eat as well?"

He resumed his seat across the desk from her, wondering where on earth he could drum up something edible at this hour. He had a brief vision of his sister-in-law's groaning dinner table. In addition to the serious talk he'd planned to have with his daughter, the evening's agenda had included barbecued spare ribs. Still, the fat wouldn't have done his cholesterol count any good.

He watched her clasp the mug in both hands, then carefully take it by the handle and put it to her lips. She took a tiny sip. "Fine, just right," she murmured, and shook her head. "Many thanks, I'm not hungry. Rather tired, that's all."

That was unmistakable. He should have granted her a breather – she was entitled to one – but he only had a few questions left. She'd avoided giving the smallest pointer that would have enabled her story to be checked. No names apart from Johnny Guitar and Horsti. No dance-hall name and no make of car, let alone a licence number. It was typical of her refusal to involve anyone else.

But she must be made to understand that this wasn't good enough. He needed a lot more than she'd disclosed, or the DA would be bound to tap his forehead and draw attention to a few inconsistencies. For instance, to the fact that Georg Frankenberg came from Frankfurt. Born and raised there, he hadn't left his parental home until he was called up for national service in the West German army. After that he'd studied at Cologne University.

Buchholz? Why should Frankenberg have gone there? Grovian found it hard to believe he'd strayed so far north purely to pick up girls. He surmised that one of his friends came from Hamburg or its environs. He'd unfortunately neglected to question Meilhofer about the other two members of the group, but at that stage he couldn't have guessed that they might be important.

He didn't ask whether she felt up to answering a few more questions. All he said was: "The coffee will do you good."

It was pretty strong; he'd seen that when he poured it out. That was why he hadn't had any himself. Strong coffee gave him palpitations.

He restarted the recording machine and – unaware of the wound he was probing – reverted to the only specific detail she'd mentioned. "So you first met Georg Frankenberg five years ago. On May sixteenth, to be precise."

She eyed him impassively over the rim of the mug and nodded. He did a quick calculation. At that time Frankenberg had been twenty-two and in his first year at university. The summer term began in March and lasted until mid July. The summer vacation spanned August and September. That left the weekends. She'd only mentioned weekends, and not every weekend.

A young man with a penchant for fast cars could have covered the hundred miles or so in no time, and it was probable that

Frankenberg had had wheels during his time at university. His upper-class parents would have provided their offspring with all he needed for an existence in keeping with his social status. His father was a Herr Professor, a consultant neurologist and surgeon who had for seven years headed his own clinic, which specialized in plastic surgery. His son must have been expected to know whose footsteps to tread in.

But the son had a bee in his bonnet. He preferred the drums to the lecture hall, amused himself with a different girl every week and eventually fathered a child on a girl of obscure parentage who hadn't been an easy lay. Whether or not Frankie had really been pleased to become a father was neither here nor there. His parents certainly wouldn't have welcomed the news. It all fitted. Grovian possessed enough imagination to be able to put himself in Georg Frankenberg's place. Five years ago, whether to avoid trouble at home or on orders from above, a young man had left his pregnant girlfriend in the lurch. Sometime he may have heard that she'd thrown herself in front of a car. From his point of view, that transfigured the whole affair.

His conscience must have pricked him badly. When he spoke of that girlfriend later on – only once and obliquely – he pronounced her dead, killed in a road accident. Which was one way of putting it. But Frankie never forgot her. He'd often wondered what would have become of her and his child if he'd stood by her, and when she went for him beside the lake . . .

Grovian didn't notice that his tone had softened appreciably. "We at least need the names of the other two members of Frankenberg's group, Frau Bender."

"I don't know their names," she said with a weary shrug. "He called them his friends, that's all."

"Would you recognize them if you saw them again?"

She sighed. "The fat one, maybe, but not the other. I only saw him once. He was already in the cellar when we arrived. It was pretty dark down there and he was sitting in a corner. I paid no attention to him when he left with the fat one."

That was more or less what he'd expected, but it shouldn't be too difficult to discover who had shared Frankenberg's short-lived dream of a career in music. The next point: "What make of car was Georg Frankenberg driving when you knew him?"

She stared into her coffee mug. "I can't remember. I don't think it was his car we went in that night. The fat boy was driving." After a few moments she added hesitantly: "It was a Golf GTI, silver. The registration number began with a B. BN, perhaps, I'm not sure."

"And you headed in the Hamburg direction?"

She merely nodded.

"Can't you be a bit more precise, Frau Bender? How long did the drive take? Where did you turn off the autobahn?"

She gave another shrug. "I'm sorry, I didn't notice."

"So you've no idea what part of Hamburg the house was situated in?"

Her shake of the head exasperated him. "Can you at least describe the place? Was it a detached house? What were the surroundings like?"

All at once she flared up. "Who cares, after all this time? It's pointless! Listen, I've confessed to killing him and explained why I did it, so let's leave it at that. Why do you want to know all these things? You want to look for the house? Good luck to you. Hamburg's a big city."

She broke off, blinking nervously, and ran a hand over her eyes as if brushing away an unpleasant vision. "It was a big suburban house with a lot of trees around it," she went on with undiminished vehemence. "That's all I know, honestly. I was very much in love – I paid more attention to Johnny than I did to the surroundings or the architecture. If I describe the hallway for you, you can ring the doorbell of every big house in Hamburg and ask to see inside."

"I may do that," he said, "if you tell me what this hallway looked like."

"It wasn't a hallway as such," she muttered. She put the coffee mug down, working her shoulders to and fro as if to relieve the tension in her neck and bit her lower lip before continuing. "It was a huge lobby," she went on, "all done up in white except for

98

some little green squares between the white flagstones. And there was a painting on the wall beside the stairs leading to the cellar. I remember it because Johnny pinned me up against the opposite wall and kissed me while the others were going downstairs. That was when I caught sight of the picture. I was surprised anyone would want such a thing on their wall. It was nothing you could recognize – just splashes of paint."

*

It had been such a good story. Till now! Although she hadn't liked it when the chief asked some more questions, she'd had a few more answers up her sleeve. A silver Golf GTI and a licence plate beginning with B. Or possibly BN. She'd almost said BM, but at the last moment she remembered that Gereon's licence plate began with BM. The chief would have been bound to spot the lie.

She hadn't had to think for long where the car was concerned. It was a typical young man's car. Gereon had also owned a silver Golf when she first met him, but not for long – it was an old banger. She seemed to recall that Johnny's fat little friend had driven a Golf, but she wasn't sure. It didn't matter anyway. She'd never had anything to do with the other two.

And the house – some house or other in Hamburg. You only needed a bit of logic. A detached house, naturally. If there was a music room installed in the basement, there had to be a bit of space around the house, or the neighbours would complain of the noise. And a big detached house in Hamburg could only belong to wealthy people. And wealthy people hung paintings on their walls. She couldn't imagine, with the best will in the world, how she'd dreamed up a picture composed of splashes of paint. But that was just as unimportant as the car.

The chief broke in on her thoughts. "What did you mean by 'the others'?" he asked. "Just now you said that the third member of the group was already down below when you got there. Who else was on the stairs, apart from the fat boy?"

The others? She wasn't aware of having said that. She knuckled her forehead and tried to remember exactly what she'd said when she introduced the subject of the splashy painting. The chief was waiting for an answer – a logical one. A picture made up of splashes of paint wasn't logical. Wealthy people liked their art to be dignified.

"I don't know," she said in a strained voice. "It was a girl. The fat boy had brought a girl along." She nodded contentedly to herself. "That was it! I wouldn't have come otherwise – I didn't trust him. I'd forgotten – it's only just occurred to me. There was another girl with us."

She gave the chief an apologetic smile. "Now please don't ask me her name; I really couldn't tell you. I'd never seen her before; it was her first visit to the house. I don't think she came from Buchholz. The girls from Buchholz had become chary of Johnny and his friend; none of them would have come with us. It was a girl I didn't know, and she left with Fatso and the other one. I don't know where they went. Perhaps they drove off."

"How did you get home?"

"Johnny drove me home in the Golf. It was parked outside when we left the house."

"Then the others couldn't have driven off in it."

She sighed. "I said perhaps," she retorted irritably. "They may still have been inside. I didn't go on a tour of the house."

The chief gave a thoughtful nod. "And you didn't notice what the outside of the house looked like before you left? You didn't register your route on the return journey?"

"No, I was rather squiffy. I fell asleep in the car."

He nodded again, then: "How far gone were you when you lost the baby?"

She had to think. What had she said? That she'd had sex with Johnny in August? Had she mentioned August? She couldn't remember. All she could recall was mentioning that she'd noticed her bump in October . . .

That was a bit quick. No one developed a noticeable bump in two months. Was the chief aware of that? She mustn't make a mistake. "Not that again, please," she said, shaking her head. "I can't talk about it – I never could."

Grovian had no wish to press her unduly. He confined himself to pointing out, mildly, that he would be compelled to consult some other people if she didn't cooperate.

"How old are your parents, Frau Bender?"

"My mother is sixty-five, my father ten years older," she replied mechanically.

Werner Hoss cut in. "Why did you tell me your parents were dead?"

She looked puzzled for a moment, then glared at him and said harshly: "Because they are, as far as I'm concerned, and the dead should be left in peace. Or don't you agree?"

"No, I don't," said Hoss. "They're still alive, and when I notice that someone has lied to me about one thing, I become suspicious of any other statements they make."

Grovian's immediate inclination had been to cut Hoss short. Instead, he let him run on, curious to know where it would lead.

"You've told us a good deal," said Hoss, "and some of it strikes me as odd. For instance, that a drummer should call himself Johnny Guitar and a big, strong youngster should call himself Horsti."

She shrugged. "I didn't think it was odd, just silly. Who knows why anyone calls himself anything. He must have had his reasons."

"Maybe," Hoss conceded, "and we probably won't learn any more about them. So let's revert to your reasons. Why did you want us to think your parents were dead? Because they might tell us a different story?"

Her lips curled in the semblance of a smile. "My mother would quote you something from the Bible. She's crazy."

"But your father isn't," said Grovian, taking up the reins again. "He's a very nice man, you said. Or was that another lie?"

She shook her head mutely.

"Why does it upset you when I say I'd like a word with him?"

She heaved a tremulous sigh. "Because I don't want him upset. He knows nothing about Johnny. He asked me a couple of times, but I didn't tell him a thing. It wasn't easy for him when

I came home. He reproached himself. 'We should have gone away years ago, the two of us,' he said once. 'Then it wouldn't have happened.' But my father always was a conscientious man. He didn't want to leave my mother alone with the Saviour and Magdalena."

*

The name meant nothing to Rudolf Grovian. He saw her wince as if in pain. She picked up the coffee mug and put it quickly to her lips, but she didn't drink, just put it back on the desk.

"Could you add a little water, please? Coffee this strong makes me feel queasy."

"There's only cold water."

"That doesn't matter, it's too hot anyway."

The indiscretion had jolted her brain like an electric shock. Magdalena! But all was well. The chief didn't react, and the other man didn't follow it up by asking if her "only child" story had been another lie. She stroked her forehead and tweaked a lock of hair over the scar, gingerly fingered the scab over her right eye, massaged the back of her neck and worked her head to and fro.

"May I get up and walk around for a bit? I'm stiff from sitting for so long."

"Of course," said Grovian.

She went to the window and stared out into the darkness. "Are we going to be much longer?" she asked with her back to him.

"No. Just a few more questions."

Grovian saw her nod and heard her mutter: "I thought as much." In a louder, more resolute tone she said: "All right, let's go on. Have you turned that thing on again? I don't want to have to repeat everything tomorrow morning." She was regaining her old, brusque manner. To call it aggressive, as he had at first, now struck him as exaggerated. She was showing no signs of fatigue, still less of mental confusion, which was all that mattered. Next question: what was the name of the establishment where she had met Georg Frankenberg, alias Horsti or Johnny Guitar?

102

She hesitated before replying. "The Aladdin. We called it that because of all the coloured lamps. It didn't really have a name – I mean, not from Monday to Friday. During the week it functioned as an old folks' community centre, but on Saturdays it became the Aladdin. It was my usual haunt because you could dance there."

That could be checked if necessary. Precisely when had she tried to take her own life? This time her reply was preceded by a long sigh: "I already told you: in October. I don't recall the exact date."

And in what hospital had she received treatment? She answered with her back still turned. "It wasn't a hospital," she said hoarsely. "The man who ran me over was a doctor – he took me to his surgery. I wasn't badly hurt, as I told you. Besides, he'd had a drink or two. He was scared he'd lose his licence and was grateful to me for keeping the police out of it. He put me up at his place for a few weeks. Until the middle of November."

"What was this doctor's name and where did he live?"

She turned around, shaking her head emphatically. "No! Please drop it. I won't tell you about the doctor, I can't. He helped me. He said I must . . . He was very nice to me. He said I must . . ." She shook her head more vigorously still, clasped her hands together and kneaded them hard before making a third attempt. "He said I must . . ."

She managed to complete the sentence after a pause and several audible breaths. "He said I must go home. But my mother . . ."

She hunched her shoulders at the memory. Mother standing inside the front door. Her suspicious gaze. She saw herself wearing a new dress and an overcoat, likewise new. And the shoes, the underwear Grit Adigar had so admired, black lace underwear and silk stockings, all of them new. All paid for by a man who had felt obliged to help her. A doctor! That was no lie.

And in the middle of November he'd put her aboard a train and sent her home, although she still wasn't well. On the contrary, she was very ill. The journey home was just a blur. She had no recollection of where she'd changed trains or how she'd got there. Only of standing outside the door with legs like jelly and a head filled with lead – with lead and the desire to go to bed and sleep, just sleep. She heard her own voice and its note of entreaty: "It's me, Mother. Cora."

And Mother's voice, uncaring and indifferent: "Cora is dead."

That, more or less, was how she had felt in November five years ago. And how she felt again now. She oughtn't to have mentioned her mother, still less the doctor.

Her fingers were almost dislocated, she was kneading them so hard. Seeing this, Grovian ascribed her defensiveness to the reference to her mother. "All right, Frau Bender, no need to tell us again, we already have it on tape. But we definitely need the doctor's name. We mean him no harm. He won't be prosecuted for having driven a car under the influence of alcohol, not after five years. We merely need to interview him as a witness. He could corroborate the story of your pregnancy and attempted suicide."

"No!" she said tensely, clutching the windowsill behind her back with both hands. "You can forget it as far as I'm concerned. Yes, forget it. Let's simply say I had an affair with the man I stabbed to death. He abandoned me. I bore him a grudge, so I killed him when I saw him again today."

Grovian spoke with due emphasis. "Frau Bender, this just won't do. You can't make a statement, only to stonewall whenever we try to elicit something that would enable us to check its veracity. If you do, I'm bound to assume, like my colleague, that you aren't telling the truth."

She turned to face the window again. There was a finality about the movement, and her tone underlined this. "I said forget it! I wasn't gagging to tell you anything. You threatened me, don't forget, but now you must stop. I can't go on, I don't feel well. You said I should tell you if I wasn't feeling well, then we'd stop."

"But I didn't tell you to use it as a pretext."

"It isn't a pretext. I really can't go on." Firm and resolute only a moment ago, her voice had suddenly grown tired and tearful. Her lower lip started to tremble like that of a two-year-old on the verge of bursting into tears.

104

He could see this reflected in the windowpane, but he wasn't going to fall for such a cheap trick. His daughter had always adopted the same tone when she couldn't get her way.

"You'll be able to go on in a minute or two," he said. He couldn't help sounding sharper, nor did he want to. All his sympathy and consideration notwithstanding, she must be made to realize that she couldn't fob him off indefinitely with her refusals and evasions.

"So you came to Cologne in December five years ago. Was there any particular reason why you opted for Cologne?"

He assumed that she had discovered something about Frankenberg's true identity and had set off to look for him.

"No," she said quietly. "I got into a train which happened to be going there."

He'd believed her up to now, but that he certainly didn't believe. "Perhaps you'd care to think again, Frau Bender. There was a reason. We already know it, but we'd like to hear it from you."

"I've no need to think again. There was no reason. I didn't know anyone in Cologne, if that's what you're getting at."

She couldn't understand why he was so insistent. In her mind's eye she was still standing outside the door looking into Mother's face, hearing Mother's voice: Cora is dead . . . No! Cora was alive, the man was dead, and Cora was going out of her mind. She sensed that quite clearly, like a handful of water trickling through her fingers. No matter how tightly she squeezed them together, they couldn't stop it seeping away.

It wasn't a good idea to mingle lies with smidgens of truth. Lies took on a life of their own – they caught up with you. The truth hit you on the head like a club, and everything got mixed up. The splashy painting was a complete fabrication. She was well aware of that, yet she could clearly see it hanging on the wall in the whitewashed lobby with the little green squares between the flagstones. And his face . . . So close to her own, she had to shut her eyes because it went blurred. Impossible! Johnny was kissing her just the way she'd said. She could feel the pressure of his lips on hers.

It was only her fingers, which she was pressing against her mouth to prevent herself from crying out. She knew they were only her fingers, but that knowledge didn't help. Over his shoulder, she could see the two figures going downstairs.

A short, fat man and a girl. The girl had fair hair. She was wearing a dark blue satin blouse and a white skirt with a scalloped hem. The skirt was made of lace and almost transparent.

Where had those details come from? She must have seen them somewhere. In a film! That explained it. It must have been in a film, and every film had some dialogue. The girl on the stairs laughed and called over her shoulder: "Coming, you two? You can carry on downstairs, it's bound to be cosier down there." Every movie had music too. Sure enough, it came drifting up from below: a drum solo. And, while she was trying to recall the title of the film and how the scene went on, the chief asked her about Cologne.

She was past concocting a logical lie. Cologne meant Margret. Did he already know about her? Had Gereon mentioned her? Possibly.

A five-minute rest, that was all she needed. Just five minutes in which to dream up a plausible story, and if he ignored her request she would remind him of his invitation. "May I have something to eat before we go on? Please, I'm very hungry. I never got around to it down at the lake. I meant to eat the rest of that apple. A Golden Delicious, the kind I adored as a child."

*

We had an allotment, but it wasn't near our house. We had to walk a long way to get to it. It wasn't far in reality, but to me as a child everything looked immense. To me, the allotment seemed a terribly long way off. I often felt so tired, I thought I'd never get there. I didn't want to either, because the allotment was such a temptation.

We didn't spend much time there the year Magdalena was fighting off her leukaemia, and I was beginning to wonder what it would be like if she never came home. But there was a lot to do the following spring. We went there almost every day. I weeded the vegetable beds – that was my job – while Father wielded a spade or a rake, and Mother looked after Magdalena. It was a mild spring, and she thought the fresh air would do my sister good.

The allotment next to ours contained an apple tree and a strawberry bed. It wasn't fenced off – the boundary was just a shallow trench. The strawberry bed was so close to the trench, I'd only have had to bend down, not set foot in our neighbour's allotment. Sometimes the strawberries overhung the trench itself.

I could have picked one while weeding and popped it into my mouth unobserved, but I didn't dare. I'd seen what had happened to Magdalena after that bar of chocolate, and Father had given me that. Helping yourself to someone else's property was one of the major sins.

Being eight years old by now, I knew there were immense differences between one sin and another. I hadn't been told that by Mother, for whom all sins were equally grave. We talked about the subject in school as well. There were venial sins, the little ones that were forgiven if you repented of them at once; and medium-grade sins, from which you were cleansed in Purgatory when you died; and mortal sins, for which you atoned in hell for all eternity.

We were never told in school that someone else had to suffer or die for our sins. Only Mother said that, and I'd ceased to be sure that she knew any better than our teacher, who wasn't a Catholic.

It was a time of uncertainty from my point of view. I never knew whom or what to believe. Father said one thing one day and another the next. One night he would kneel before the crucifix and repent of his sinful urges; the next, he would roam the house in a restless mood or lock himself up in the bathroom. When he came downstairs again he would gaze at Magdalena and mutter: "What have I done to you, sweetheart?"

Magdalena was sicker than before. She had to be taken to Eppendorf every four weeks. According to Father, they injected her with poison and bombarded her with nasty rays. She used to cry a lot the day before Mother took her there, but very quietly because any form of exertion was bad for her. When she returned she was so poorly she couldn't be left alone for a minute.

Sometimes Mother sent me into her bedroom so I could see what I'd done and would never forget it. I used to stand beside her bed and look at her, and she would return my gaze. I would have liked to apologize to her, but I never knew what to say.

That spring was an especially bad time. It was like an obsession. I couldn't help imagining what would happen to Magdalena if I stole a strawberry. Terrible, the feeling that it was solely up to me whether she lived or died . . . I had to keep a constant check on what I said, thought and did. Sometimes, when it all became too much for me, I longed to go to sleep, to dream of something nice and live on inside that dream.

I was very relieved when the strawberry season ended, relieved and proud of myself for having resisted temptation. I was particularly proud because it seemed to have worked: Magdalena's health was gradually improving. Although you couldn't spot any difference from one day to the next, you certainly could from one month to another.

Mother always wheeled her to the allotment in an old pram. Magdalena lay in the pram like a bundle of clothes that spring, but by autumn she could sit up almost straight. Only for a few minutes, but it was a great improvement.

There wasn't much to do at the allotment during the summer, and Magdalena tended to find it too hot there, even late in the afternoon. In the autumn, however, we went there every day. When Father came home from work we would set off in a procession. Father in the lead with the tools on his left shoulder and a bucket in his right hand, Mother pushing the pram. Magdalena wore a cap. Although her hair had grown back a bit, it was still very sparse and almost white. She couldn't stand the sun on her head.

I brought up the rear, thinking of our neighbour's yellow apples – Golden Delicious; Father had told me their name and said they were sweet. The tree was so close to the trench that many windfalls landed in it or even on our allotment itself. I thought it wouldn't really be stealing if they were lying on our allotment and I picked them up, and that apples couldn't be as pernicious as chocolate and sweets. Grit had often told me that eating fruit was healthy. It

108

occurred to me that I could pick up a few windfalls for Magdalena and make her healthy. I didn't want them for myself, honestly not.

Our route to the allotment crossed a busy road, and beside it stood a big old wooden box that used to hold sand for gritting the roadway in winter. It was empty at present, so Father had told me. But then I had this dream.

We were on our way home. Magdalena was sitting in the pram, utterly exhausted and weeping with pain. Mother came to a halt, kneeled down in the roadway and started praying. I walked past them. Father had already drawn level with the sand box. I caught him up and we slowly walked on together.

Then I heard a sound behind me – a creaking sound, followed by a growl. I turned around and saw a black wolf leap out of the box. Taking no notice of Father and me, it made for Mother and Magdalena. It reached the pram with a single bound and gobbled up Magdalena in an instant. Mother it ignored.

Then it scampered back to the box and jumped in again. Before shutting the lid it looked at me and laughed like a human, the teeth in its gaping jaws still stained with Magdalena's blood. I should have been afraid but I wasn't – I knew from the way it laughed that it liked me. I wanted to take it home with me, like a dog.

Mother was kneeling beside the empty pram with her hands raised to heaven. Father put an arm round my shoulders, smiling contentedly. "That was the hellhound," he said. "A handsome beast, isn't he? Did you see what a magnificent tail he has? And those splendid teeth! He's done us a great favour. We're rid of her at last! Now we won't have to wish that our sins would rot away. Not any more. Now we can enjoy them again, Cora, and we will. Shall I show you something nice?"

*

It was a duel! After his brief intervention, the man in the sports coat was taking no further part in things – just sitting there, switched off so to speak. With the unerring instinct of a hunted beast, she realized that he was dissatisfied. She didn't know what was bothering him, her lies or the chief's mode of procedure: all this probing and digging and hassling.

He was demanding something of her she couldn't give. It was almost like it had been with Mother. That on its own she could have coped with – she'd learned the art of deception at an early age – but this time it was altogether different. She seemed to be bewitched. The image refused to be shaken off; it only conjured up others. That confounded painting, the splashy one, and the backs of those people going down the stairs, a man and a girl . . .

She now saw the backs of two people in the front of a car, but this time they were both men. One of them turned and smiled at her. His expression was like a promise. Johnny Guitar!

It was all in her imagination, all just a pipe dream. Wishes could easily generate images in the brain and make themselves at home there like memories. And the rest? The girl's voice, the satin blouse, the skirt with the scalloped hem, the drum solo? She must have seen and heard all those things at some stage. In a film! That was the only possible answer. Gereon watched masses of films – almost one a night. That meant over a thousand in their three years together. If only she could recall the title or the ending . . .

The chief gave her no time to think. He rustled up a snack from somewhere. Just a few biscuits and some fresh coffee. He told the other man to make it less strong this time. His voice seemed to reach her through a layer of cotton wool. He kept asking about Cologne. Why had she opted for that particular city? Bremen or Hamburg would have been nearer. Where had she obtained the money for such a long train journey?

"I stole it," she muttered, staring at the floor. "From my mother. Nearly eight hundred marks. That covered my ticket and a few weeks' living expenses. I found a job at once. Somewhere to live too."

"Where?"

She quoted Margret's address! She was so confused, nothing else occurred to her. It was a second or two before she realized what she'd said – and, almost simultaneously, realized how hopeless it was. If he checked her statement, as he undoubtedly would, he'd soon discover where the lies ended and the truth began.

110

Her heartbeat speeded up; her hands became moist at the thought of getting Margret into trouble. She'd made a big mistake. She should have said she'd run away with Johnny. Not immediately, not until August. August was important, she didn't know why. At the moment she didn't know much in general, there were too many things going through her head.

Give up! She had heard of people who cracked under interrogation, people whose resistance was broken by a constant reiteration of the same questions. Not her! She summoned up all her remaining energy. There was always something left in the tank. Her eighteen-year battle with Mother had made her strong and taught her how to tell stories that left no loose ends. She should probably be grateful to her for training her so indefatigably.

Outwardly, she seemed to have surrendered at last. She looked up for a moment, gazed sadly into the chief's eyes and bowed her head again, lowering her voice as well. Inside, she was grimly self-controlled and taut to breaking point. She clasped her left hand with her right and wiped off the sweat on her skirt. She had resumed her seat long ago. Her shoulders sagged. Georg Frankenberg was dead; they couldn't ask him for confirmation.

It was only a whisper: "You'll find out anyway, so . . . Yes. I did have a reason for going to Cologne – I didn't tell you the truth because I was so ashamed. The thing is, I went around with Johnny for a while. Do you understand? He didn't take me home at all that night we went to Hamburg. The others had gone, leaving us in the cellar on our own. He wanted me to stay with him, so I . . . He made love to me, and it was wonderful. Now we belong together, I thought. That was in August. Did I say it was in August?"

The chief nodded, and she spun him a yarn about the weeks they'd spent together, and about a trip to Cologne, where Johnny planned to visit a friend of his. He'd called him several times on the way to warn him of their arrival, but in vain. And once he'd written down the number on a piece of paper and sent her to call him. And later, when she was back home, she found the slip of paper and called the number when her mother threw her out. A young woman answered. She enquired after Johnny, but the name meant nothing to the woman, who advised her to call again that evening when her husband was at home.

A short break. She took a sip of coffee and waited, almost with bated breath, to see if this lie would also generate some images. Nothing happened. She bit off a tiny piece of biscuit but could hardly swallow it. The biscuits were coated with chocolate, every crumb of which had meant a death sentence for Magdalena.

The chief was watching her intently. She'd made another mistake. This "going around together for a while"! How had they travelled to Cologne to visit Johnny's friend? In what car, if the silver Golf belonged to the fat boy?

Hurriedly, before the chief could follow this up, she lied on. "That night I called the number again. The husband answered. This time I asked for Horsti. 'His name is Georg Frankenberg,' he said with a laugh. 'Not even he knows why he hit on that name, the idiot.' He asked what I wanted with Georg Frankenberg. I simply said I'd been a friend of his and would like to see him again. In that case, the man said, I must come to Cologne."

Werner Hoss gave his boss a meaningful look, but it was superfluous. At that moment Rudolf Grovian smelled a rat and felt compelled to question everything he'd heard so far. "His name is Georg Frankenberg . . ." Those had been the man's words. He didn't know what to make of them. Georg Frankenberg had been Frankie to everyone except his parents, even to his wife. That robbed the friend from Cologne of all substance. In spite of this, he asked: "This man – did he also have a name?"

She could detect the mistrust in his voice, but he didn't seem to have registered her blunder about the car, and she now doubted if Margret was involved or he'd have said so straight out. All that interested him was Georg Frankenberg and the names of any friends who could confirm her story.

"I'm trying to remember," she said. "It was an odd name, but I can't think of it just at present. I'm very tired."

"And his telephone number?"

"I'm sorry, I've forgotten it. I never could remember numbers."

"The address?"

She shrugged. "I don't remember," she said softly. "Maybe the name and address will come back to me tomorrow. A person can't remember things to order, you know."

"Yes, I know," Grovian said. "And if a person is lying through their teeth, their memories aren't worth much anyway. So you acted on the man's suggestion?"

She nodded mechanically. A dam seemed to have broken in her head. A chaotic jumble of images and words poured through the breach and swirled around in her brain. The four people on the blanket beside the lake. The tune. The apples from the supermarket and the ones from the allotment. The story she'd told and the film in which a young man and a girl descended a flight of stairs.

Dislodged by the flood, names went tumbling through her head like boulders. Mother, Father, Magdalena, Horsti, Johnny, Margret, Gereon. Masses of names – too many of them. Some she'd never heard before – ridiculous names like Billy-Goat and Tiger. Her face twitched as if she were on the verge of tears.

"I should have saved myself the trouble. Frankie wanted nothing more to do with me."

"Who's Frankie?" Grovian asked.

She gave a start. "What?"

"Who's Frankie?" he repeated, finding it difficult to give the question a neutral wrapping. He glanced at Hoss triumphantly. That was what he'd been waiting for. To him, it was confirmation. "You said Frankie wanted nothing more to do with you, Frau Bender. Who is Frankie?"

She wasn't aware of what she'd said, had forgotten she'd heard the name beside the lake. "What did I say? I'm sorry, I'm awfully tired."

She clasped her forehead. Her eyes roamed across the desk and came to rest on Werner Hoss as if he could put an end to the torture. Torture, that's all it was. Her head was full to bursting like a drawer with too much stuffed into it. Now the contents were spewing out.

But she couldn't find the little knife she needed so badly. She should have tidied everything first. If she had, she would have discovered that the knife wasn't in the drawer. It was lying on the table on which the lemons had been sliced, visible to everyone who walked in, but she hadn't seen it because she was too low down, and the table too high. And standing at the table was a short, fat man. He'd sprinkled some white powder on the back of his hand. He licked it off, drank something and bit into a slice of lemon.

"Tell him to stop," she mumbled, still looking at Hoss. "Tell him to leave me alone, or I'll go mad. I'm seeing things, stupid things. You'd laugh yourself sick if I described them to you."

She shook herself like a wet dog and looked down at her hands. "Something very silly happened to me once," she said. "I can't remember it, and I don't want to. I've walled it off. Lots of people do that with experiences they can't handle, Achim told me. They build a wall across their brain and hide their painful memories behind it. Achim said you must tear down the wall and digest those memories or you'll never know any peace. Personally, I found the wall solution a very good one."

She paused, lost in thought, then raised her head and looked at Hoss again. "The brain is incredibly capacious," she said, addressing him alone. "You don't need even half of it in order to think – less than forty per cent, I believe, but it may be the other way round. Maybe thinking takes up sixty per cent. Did you know that?"

Hoss nodded.

She gave a melancholy smile. "Wonderful, isn't it? It's like an attic where you store all your junk. It worked too – until Christmas. Then it all came back. When I hear that tune it leaps over the wall like the wolf jumping out of the sand box. It may have something to do with the birth of our Saviour, I don't know. I don't know what it's about at all. I wake up and there's nothing there. It's better that way too – it worried me. I still feel it today, when I have that dream."

The melancholy smile faded. She drew a deep breath. "It happened to me once as a child," she went on eagerly. "But that was another dream – I could always remember that one. I enjoyed it too. I enjoyed being an animal."

114

6

That dream about the wolf was awful. But it was wonderful as well. My dearest wish had been fulfilled. Magdalena wasn't with us any more, and it wasn't my fault. Mother didn't want to be with us either; she went on kneeling beside the empty pram. And Father had the bucket of apples. I thought he must have known in advance it would happen, or he would have filled the bucket with greens and potatoes.

I woke up feeling light as air, although it quickly dawned on me that it hadn't really happened. But that was what I found so wonderful. I knew it was one of the very gravest sins to wish a person dead. You would some day have to suffer endless torment.

Mother always said that hundreds of little demons armed with red-hot pincers would rip the flesh from my body in tiny little shreds, so my flesh would last for all eternity. She showed me pictures of this being done to other people. But I couldn't help it if I only dreamed it, so it definitely wasn't a sin.

I was still feeling light as air when I got up in the morning. It was going to be a very special day, I felt. At first I even thought a miracle had occurred, but it hadn't. Everything turned out quite differently.

In the afternoon Mother had to go shopping. She sent me upstairs to keep an eye on Magdalena. Standing beside the bed as usual, I thought she was asleep, but as soon as the front door shut she opened her eyes and said: "Will you read to me?"

It was the first time Magdalena had spoken to me. She didn't

115

speak much in general, and then only to Mother. I hadn't a clue what to say.

"Are you deaf, or don't you understand German?" she said.

"What do you want me to say?" I asked.

"Nothing. Just read me something."

I wasn't sure Mother would approve. "I think it'd be too tiring," I said.

"For you or for me?" she said. "Shall I tell you what I think? I think you can't read at all."

I was so surprised to find I could have a normal conversation with her, just as I could with the kids in the playground, that I spoke without thinking. "You bet I can read," I said. "I can read even better than Mother. I don't mumble, I read loud and clear, and I put the stresses in the right place, the teacher says. My classmates aren't half as good."

"I'll believe that when you've read me something," she said. "Or won't you because you don't like me? Go on, admit it. Nobody here likes me, I know that. But I don't care, I don't like anyone either. Why do you think I've kept my mouth shut till now? Because I don't talk to fools. I save my breath for people with something sensible to say."

So I took the Bible from the bedside table and read a passage Mother often read, the one about the miracle our Saviour performed when a woman touched the hem of his garment. I don't know if my conscience was pricking me because Magdalena had said we didn't like her, or whether I wanted to show her how well I could read. I may also have been feeling rather proud that she'd spoken to me at all.

I took a lot of trouble over my reading. She listened with her eyes shut. Then she said: "Now the bit about Mary Magdalene washing the Saviour's feet and drying them on her hair. I like that bit best of all."

When I'd finished reading that passage as well, she said: "But I'm out of luck."

I didn't know what she meant. "Well," she went on, "our Saviour isn't wearing any clothes, just a little cloth around his tummy. Think

116

we could dress him up? We could try, if you took him off the altar and brought him up here. We'll dress him in a handkerchief, and I'll touch the hem. After that I'll wash his feet and dry them on my hair. It's bound to do me some good."

"Your hair is far too short," I said.

She shrugged. "Not if I rub hard enough. I've always wanted to do that. Will you bring him upstairs, or are you scared Mother will catch you?"

I wasn't scared of Mother, just reluctant for Magdalena to do something she pinned such hopes on. "He can't help you," I told her. "He's only made of wood, and Mary Magdalene wasn't sick. She was a sinner."

"I can sin too," she said. "Shall I say a dirty word?" Before I could reply she said: "Arsehole! Now will you fetch him?"

I went downstairs. All at once I felt terribly sorry for her. That, I think, was when I realized for the first time that my sister was a normal child. A very sick child who might die at any moment. She would never be able to lead a life like mine, but she could speak like me, think like me and feel like me.

*

I brought the crucifix over to the bed, and we started with the handkerchief. I borrowed one of Father's, which was big enough. I tied it around the figure's neck and Magdalena rubbed it between her fingers. Then I fetched some water from the bathroom in a tooth-mug, and Magdalena washed the feet. The figure was so small, the legs got wet too. Magdalena didn't want me to dry them on the handkerchief. "It may not work," she said.

After I'd taken our Saviour downstairs again I asked her where she'd heard some dirty words.

"At the hospital," she said. "You wouldn't believe the dirty words they know. They say them too, when they think you're asleep. Not the doctors, the others. A lot of sick people get really mean. I'm in with the grown-ups as a rule, and they're always cursing. They don't want to die, that's why."

She fell silent for a moment. Then she went on slowly: "I don't want to have to go back to Eppendorf any more. Although it's nice sometimes – not as boring as here. They have board games there. The nurse brings me one when I'm well enough to sit up in bed. She also fetches some children, and we play together. Mother doesn't like that, but she doesn't dare say anything. The nurse told her off once, that's why. Mother said I couldn't play, I must rest, and the nurse said: 'There'll come a day when she can rest till she turns black. Till then you should let her play for as long as she feels like it.' The dead turn black, you see, and then they get eaten by worms and rot away."

She didn't look at me as she said that. Drawing circles on the bedclothes with a finger, she went on: "A girl of eighteen told me that. She had leukaemia too, but the treatment didn't work. They couldn't find a bone-marrow donor for her. She said she wasn't afraid of death. I am, though, a bit."

Still drawing circles on the sheet, she raised her head and looked me in the eye. "Not of death itself," she said. "Death doesn't worry me. It may be better when you're dead and nothing hurts any more. But if nothing works and you can't go to the bathroom on your own, it really is better, I think. Except that . . . I don't want to turn black – I don't want to get eaten by worms and rot away. Can you imagine how disgusting that must be? I told Mother to have me cremated. A lot of people are – it isn't all that expensive – but Mother said it wouldn't do. Earth to earth, she said. Our Saviour wasn't cremated either."

She fell silent again and shut her eyes for a while. I thought she must be tired after talking so much, and she was, but she insisted on telling me something else. She was simply wondering if she could trust me.

"For all I care," she began, "you can tell Mother what I'm going to tell you: I hate him! I hope he rots away now his feet got wet. Wood rots too when it gets wet. That's why I wanted to wash him – that was the only reason. Don't get the idea I believe he'll make my heart better. They only tell you that nonsense so you keep your mouth shut and do what they want. But I'm sick of it. Will you tell Mother?"

I shook my head.

"Then we're friends now?" she asked.

"We're sisters," I said. "That's more than friends."

"No, it isn't," she retorted. "Friends like each other. Sometimes sisters don't."

"But I like you," I said.

She pulled a face. It looked almost like a smile, but only almost. I think she was well aware that I'd lied. But at that moment I really did like her, and I'd told her so.

"Do you think we could play something sometime?" she asked.

"I don't know. What?"

"Do you know 'I Spy'? It isn't tiring. You can play it perfectly well in bed."

She explained the game and we played it for a while, but there wasn't much to see in the bedroom, and we soon got tired of it. After three goes Magdalena said: "We could also play the wishing game. I invented it myself. It's quite easy; you only have to say what you wish for, but it must be something you can buy, not like 'lots of friends' or that sort of thing. And then you have to say what you want to do with it. I'd better start, then you can see how it goes."

The first thing she wished for was a television set. She'd watched TV at the hospital, where some of the patients had sets in their rooms. She also wanted a radio and a record player and lots of records. "But it must be a hi-fi!" she said. "I'm so fond of music. Proper music, not the kind where one person sings."

"Shall I ask Father to buy you a radio?" I suggested. "There are really small ones. You could easily keep it hidden."

She shook her head. "That's no good. If he really did buy me one, where would I hide it? Mother would burn it in two minutes flat. Besides, I don't think he would buy me one. You, maybe, but not me. He wouldn't lift a finger for me. He wishes I was dead."

"That's not true!" I said.

"Yes, it is," she retorted. "When I'm dead he can sleep with Mother. All men sleep with their wives, they enjoy it. I know that from the hospital. A man asked the doctor when his wife was coming home – she'd had a heart attack – and whether he could sleep with her right away. He was very disappointed when the doctor told him it would be a while yet. Father's very disappointed too, that's why he's always such a pain."

She wasn't altogether wrong. Father really could be a pain at times. Not to me or to her, only to Mother. He'd shout at her when she put the supper on the table. Once he even hurled a bowl of soup at her. "You can take that pigswill into the living room. Our Lord isn't picky, but I expect something decent to eat for my money."

Then he ran upstairs and locked himself in the bathroom. Later on, when I knocked on the door because I needed a pee, he yelled: "Go and do it in the garden! I'm busy wrenching my dick off, and I could be some time. It's damned hard to shift."

But I liked him all the same. And I liked Magdalena too, certainly that afternoon. I didn't want her to turn black and get eaten by worms – I found the idea quite as revolting as she did. I remember thinking it would be best for her if my dream came true. To be gobbled up by a big black wolf would be quick, and it probably wouldn't hurt much either.

That night I had the dream again. It was a bit different from before. After devouring her the wolf came slowly towards me instead of going back to the sand box, as it had the first time. It stood in front of me, looking at me with Magdalena's blood still dripping from its muzzle. And it thrust its muzzle into my stomach. I thought it was going to eat me too, but it seemed more like smooching.

And then something funny happened. The beast's muzzle disappeared into my stomach, but it didn't hurt in the least, even when the rest of it disappeared too: its legs, its paws and its whole body, the bushy tail last of all. And my stomach was fine, not a hole to be seen. That was when I knew.

The thing is, in the playground a few weeks earlier I'd heard two girls talking about a man who turned into a wolf at night and ate people. By day he was an entirely normal person. He took a lot of trouble to be nice and helpful to everyone, and everyone liked him, so it distressed him terribly to turn into an evil beast every night. But he couldn't help it. It simply happened to him.

120

It must be the same with me, I thought, and Father had known it for ages. He was standing beside me – he'd seen the whole thing and was looking very grave. "Don't worry," he told me, "I won't tell anyone. Remember what I told you on your birthday? 'You must be as hungry as a wolf,' I said. I already knew you'd turn into an animal and kill her before she gobbled up your life."

I woke up on the spot, feeling as big and strong as the beast the girls in the playground had been talking about. After a few minutes it occurred to me that my bed felt cold. I'd wetted it, and I was so ashamed I couldn't help crying. Father woke up, came over to me and felt the sheet. "It's not a tragedy, Cora," he said. "It can happen to anyone."

My nightie and pants were wet too. Father helped me take them off. Then he let me get into his bed because the room was so cold.

*

For some minutes Rudolf Grovian felt he'd been duped. He didn't know what to make of Cora Bender's demeanour. Werner Hoss, who seemed equally baffled, was listening to her spellbound.

With clouded gaze and trembling lips she rambled on about the wall in her brain and the beasts inside Magdalena and herself, the one being a crab with sharp claws, the other a wolf that ate children and crawled into them. The wolf kept crawling into her belly, but it didn't hurt – it couldn't because she herself was the wolf. She was an awful child who wet her bed so as to get into her father's. She had stabbed the Saviour because he wouldn't rot. Six or seven times she'd thrust the fruit knife into him! And the Saviour had looked at her and said: "This is my blood, which is shed for thy sins." And the blood on the child's face had liberated her – freed her from the curse laid upon her by the archangel.

With the Saviour's blood on her breast and belly, the child realized that Johnny had never been an angel. His friend had called him Billy-Goat. He was Satan, who had led the woman into temptation by means of the serpent. And, when she was lying on the ground, the tiger came. There was no room left for him in the

121

woman's belly, so he stuffed his penis into her mouth, and, when she bit it, lashed out at her.

The tiger had paws of crystal transfixed by slivers of coloured light. Then came darkness, the great oblivion. And oblivion was death, and death was the dream, and the dream lay behind the wall in her brain. It was all quite simple as long as you knew.

Now she did know. Now she could see it all in context. Now she even knew why it had been so cruel of Gereon to smoke another cigarette beforehand. It lay in the ashtray as he turned out the light and conjured up the tune.

She was speaking too softly for the recording machine. Grovian, who was closer to her, could understand her nonetheless. He was feeling wretched – at a loss, uncertain and rather angry. He could well believe she was putting on a show of insanity so as to gain her objective and be left in peace, but he wasn't a hundred per cent sure.

"This is my blood", he thought, and "Father, forgive her!" He felt like swearing aloud. The Saviour and the fruit knife, Satan in the shape of a lover . . . Religious mania! If what she had told them about her childhood were true, allowances would have to be made for that and one or two other things. In that case, no one should be surprised if she went on to say that an angel of the Lord had bidden her to kill any man who kissed his wife in public.

He raised his hand, intending it as a sign to Hoss that he was terminating the interview. Just then she shook herself and sat up straight. "I'm sorry," she said calmly, in a normal tone of voice, "I wasn't really with it. We were talking about Frankie just now, weren't we? Frankie – that was the name! I couldn't recall where I'd heard it, but I've just remembered. The man in Cologne called him that."

She nodded as if in self-confirmation. Somewhat more briskly, she went on: "I also remember what his friends were called. Not the people from Cologne – I really can't recall their names at present – but the other two, the ones who were down in the cellar with us. I don't know their real names, of course, only what they called each other: Billy-Goat and Tiger."

She laughed softly and gave an embarrassed shrug. "It sounds silly, I know, but that's what I heard in Cologne, when Frankie and the man were talking about them."

Grovian didn't get this – didn't know what to make of it. She was back on track again, and this latest change in her manner banished his suspicion that it was all an act. What reason would she have for breaking off a successful performance? So it had just been a mental slip. The second that day, perhaps, except that the hand holding the knife had slipped as well.

He couldn't bring himself to interrupt her and didn't know what to believe any more. In a calm, controlled voice, she was describing those few days she'd spent in Cologne. How she'd desperately tried to regain the affections of Horsti, AKA Johnny or Georg or Frankie. How he had coldly, implacably brushed her off. How his friends, that young couple, had helped her. Genuinely nice people, very sympathetic and touchingly concerned on her behalf. She would definitely remember their names tomorrow. She was having trouble with names at present. Hardly surprising, perhaps, after such an awful day.

It was a few minutes after midnight when the phone went. All three of them gave a start at the first ring. She broke off in mid sentence. Werner Hoss picked up the receiver with evident relief. "Yes," he said. He listened for a few moments, then gave Grovian an odd look.

*

Equally relieved at the interruption, she saw Hoss hand the receiver to his boss. A short break would enable her to sort out the fragments. Her brain was in turmoil. The wall was collapsing. Big cracks had appeared in many places, and something was showing through them. The white lobby with the little green mosaics in the floor, the stairs, the splashy painting – they all belonged behind the wall. And that was only the start. At the bottom of the stairs lay a room filled with flickering light.

She hadn't fallen in, but she'd looked down and seen some

white powder on the back of a hand, teeth biting into a lemon. A crystalline paw, Billy-Goat and Tiger . . . It was terrible but ludicrous. Strange the chief hadn't laughed.

Hunched up with fear and apprehension, she studied his face. The look of surprise that flitted across it gave way to one of satisfaction.

"No, not necessarily," he said. "Tomorrow morning would be fine. Ten o'clock, say?" He listened some more – he even smiled. "All right, if it's so important to you. It won't be the first night's sleep I've lost."

Having hung up, he gave the man in the sports coat a meaningful, semi-apologetic nod, then nodded in her direction. His smile was tinged with compassion. He pointed to the telephone. "A young couple?" he said. "Friends of Georg Frankenberg's?" He sighed. "Really, Frau Bender!" His tone became indulgently paternal. "Why didn't you simply tell us your aunt lived here in Cologne? You took refuge with her in December five years ago. There wasn't any young couple. That was your aunt just now, Frau Bender."

She shook her head. The young couple had been a mistake. She sensed more fragments falling from the wall – she tripped over them and slithered a few steps down the stairs. There was no handhold anywhere, so she clung to Margret. "No," she exclaimed, "that's wrong! My aunt has nothing to do with this – she's never had anything to do with me. I've just remembered what the people were called. The wife's name was Alice, and the husband . . . Wait, it's on the tip of my tongue. His name was . . . He . . . Damn it, what's the matter with me? I thought of it a moment ago. He . . . He told me he planned to join a group practice."

Damn it, thought Grovian: Winfried Meilhofer and Alice Winger, the lake . . . That's all she remembers.

But she was still vociferating. "Why should I have gone to my aunt? You really think I'd have asked for help from a woman I hardly knew?"

"Yes," he said in a tone of disappointment and frustration. "I not only think so, I know so. Your aunt just told me. That poses the question of where you really heard the names Frankie, Billy-Goat and Tiger. Not from some man in Cologne. You picked them up at the lido this afternoon, am I right?"

She stared at him, her brow furrowed with concentration. She might almost have been debating his question, but she didn't reply. It was superfluous in any case. Everything was in doubt again. He'd been taken in by her, fool that he was. Why, for God's sake? Because she'd told him exactly what he'd believed at first to be the only rational explanation: an idyllic love story with a tragic outcome. He sighed and made a gesture of dismissal. "Let's stop."

"No!" It was all she could do to remain seated, he saw. She was once more gripping the seat of her chair with both hands. "I can't go through this again. Let's get it over."

"No," he said likewise, very firmly. "I've had enough for one day. I'm sending for the duty sergeant; he'll put you up in a cell for the night. A dose of sleep will do you good. You're very tired, you said so yourself."

"I said it, I know, but I'm not – not in the least." Almost in the same breath, she added: "What did Margret want? Why did she call?"

"She wants a word with us," he said, feeling that it was high time to speak with a member of her family. "And it's so important to her, she can't wait until tomorrow. She's on her way here right now."

"You must send her away again," she said imploringly. "You'll only be wasting your time – she can't tell you anything. No one can but me."

Grovian gave a mirthless laugh. "And you've said quite enough for today. It'll take us another three days to sort it out. Let's see if your aunt can help us."

She shook her head again, even more fiercely this time, and slithered a few steps further down the stairs. "She can't! I never told her anything – I never told a soul, I was far too ashamed. You've no right to question Margret. She knows nothing, I tell you."

She sprang to her feet, not that it helped much. Although her body rose from the chair, her brain slithered down the last few steps and landed in the midst of the flickering light. She blinked hard. "Please leave Margret alone," she entreated. "She hasn't done anything bad. No one has, only me. I'm a murderess, believe me.

I killed an innocent child. That's the truth. And Frankie! Him as well, of course, but I had to kill him because he . . ."

She started stammering, gesticulating frantically, helplessly with both hands as if to emphasize the truth of what she was saying and compel him to devote a few more minutes of his time to her. "He . . . He didn't know what to do. I told him to be careful, but he wouldn't listen. I told him to stop, but he didn't care. Do you know what he did?"

Grovian didn't know, naturally, but he could well imagine. Her halting words seemed to be an attempt to refocus his attention on her pregnancy and miscarriage. However, what followed was out of context.

"He threw himself on top of her," she said breathlessly, still blinking hard. "He kissed her. And he hit her. He kissed her and hit her in turn, over and over again. He was crazy, not me. He went on hitting her until she was dead – I heard her ribs snap. It was so terrible, so awful. I wanted to help her, but they caught hold of me. One of them lay on top of me, the other gripped my head and stuck his thing in my mouth. I bit it, and . . ."

The light flickered once more before it went out. She couldn't go on. The chief was staring at her. The man in the sports coat jumped up, hurried to the door and went out. The tape recorder was still running. Having recorded every one of her words till now, it recorded the rest as well.

"Call him back!" she shouted. "No one must leave. Please don't leave me on my own. Please! I can't stand it. Help me, for God's sake help me! Get me out of here. I can't stand it in this cellar. I can't see, turn on the light again. Help me, please!"

Everything was blotted out. The chief was simply standing there without moving. He ought to have done something – anything. Taken her arm, held her hand, led her over to the stairs. Or turned on the light, at least, so she could find the way there by herself. It was so dark. Only a few green, blue, red and yellow flashes pierced the gloom and wrested fragments from its depths. "Let go," she gasped. "Get off her, leave her alone. Stop it! Stop it, you swine! Let go of me!"

Grovian couldn't react, he was too shocked by a sudden realization: what she was saying sounded like rape, and what she'd blurted out before sounded like murder. And she'd mentioned a second girl who had been stupid enough to join them, so it may not have been as much of a fiction as he'd temporarily assumed.

He saw her gesticulate wildly, gagging as she did so, with one hand over her crotch and the other in front of her face as if trying to push something away. There was no doubt about it: she was reliving what she was trying to tell him.

He saw her throw up an arm defensively. Saw her clasp her head in both hands and cry "No!" Saw her sway, saw her puffy, contorted features abruptly go limp. But he wasn't quick enough. Almost within arm's reach, she was lying on the floor before he could reach her and break her fall.

It had happened too suddenly. He froze for a moment, incapable of reacting. Then he smote his thigh with a clenched fist. He felt more like punching himself on the jaw or kicking his own backside – if only he could have reached it. This was his nightmare. He hadn't summoned a doctor, in spite of her battered face and Meinhofer's statement: "I thought he was going to kill her."

Cerebral haemorrhage . . . The words flashed through his mind. At last he kneeled down beside her and raised her head. "Come on, girl, up you get," he said, unaware that he was whispering. "Don't do this to me. Come on, please! You were all right before."

A red patch the size of his palm was forming on her forehead. In search of further injuries he brushed her hair aside with trembling fingers, knowing only too well that he wouldn't be able to detect anything serious with the naked eye.

But he did see the dent in her skull and the jagged white scar on her hairline. Her breathing was shallow but regular. He lifted her left eyelid just as Werner Hoss re-entered the room closely followed by Berrenrath and his colleague, who had been detailed to hold her in custody overnight. Hoss picked up the phone at once.

"She fainted," Grovian said helplessly. "I was too late."

The doctor alerted by Hoss took ten minutes to get there – ten hellish minutes from Grovian's point of view. Although she recovered consciousness even before Hoss replaced the receiver, every spark of life seemed to have left her. She suffered herself to be picked up and deposited on a chair like a rag doll, but when Grovian laid a hand on her shoulder and started to say something, she struck out at him feebly. "Go away," she sobbed. "Why didn't you stop? Why wouldn't you help me? It's all your fault."

She turned to Berrenrath. "Can't you get rid of him?" she begged. "Please, he's driving me insane – he pulled down my wall. I can't take it any more."

Grovian felt obliged to leave the room and give her time to calm down. Hoss followed him out into the passage. He cleared his throat several times.

"How did it happen?"

"How do you think it happened?" Grovian snarled. "You heard her: I wouldn't stop – I pulled down her wall."

Hoss didn't speak for a moment or two. Then he said: "What do you make of her story?"

"I don't know yet. It isn't all make-believe, that's for sure. I've never known anyone to faint from telling a pack of lies."

"Me neither," Hoss said uneasily. "Still, I could have sworn she was taking us for a ride."

The doctor's arrival absolved Grovian from replying. The three of them entered the office together. She was still sitting on the chair as before. Berrenrath was standing beside her with one hand resting on her shoulder – either consolingly or supportively, it was hard to tell which.

But she seemed in no further need of support. As soon as she caught sight of the new arrival she shook off her apathy and started complaining bitterly. Despite her bemused, bewildered tone of voice, she claimed to be feeling fine. No headache, nothing. She certainly didn't need a jab.

The doctor checked her reflexes and, after a long look at her pupils, diagnosed a straightforward fainting fit. He blandly assured her that an injection would do her good. Just something for the circulation, a harmless restorative to get her back on her feet.

With a hysterical laugh, she began by hugging her stomach

protectively. "No need to soft-soap me. I know what you're after – you want to get at these."

Abruptly, she extended both arms in his direction. "Go on, help yourself. See if you can find a vein. Like to take a blood sample too? You'd better – you'll only regret it later. Who knows what was in that lake water I swallowed today."

After tapping her forearms for a while, the doctor opted for the back of her hand. He muttered something about skin like leather, scar tissue, and the fact that he'd never seen such craters.

Although Grovian overheard this, he was too relieved by her reaction to draw any immediate conclusions. Half an hour later he was facing her aunt across a desk.

*

Margret Rosch had found it hard to persevere in the face of something she would rather not have known about. Unwilling to take no for an answer, tempting though it was, she'd tried again and again until she was finally put through.

She insisted on seeing her niece, but Grovian put her off. Cora Bender was lying down in an adjacent room. The doctor was still with her, together with Berrenrath, whose presence she had requested. "One of you will have to guard me, I suppose. Would you be kind enough to take on the job? Compared to the rest of this bunch, you seem positively human."

Werner Hoss had brewed some more coffee. Grovian, taking two cups with him, ushered Margret Rosch into an interview room. She made a dismayed but resolute impression. A buxom, attractive woman in her mid fifties, she was of medium height and had luxuriant hair of the same auburn shade as her niece's. Her face also displayed a family resemblance.

Her response to Grovian's first and most important question – whether her niece had ever displayed any signs of mental derangement – was a vigorous shake of the head. Before giving him any further information, she demanded to be put in the picture herself.

There was no reason to make a secret of the facts, so he outlined the circumstances of the case. She heard him out, frozen-faced, before proceeding to answer his questions.

The name Georg Frankenberg meant nothing to her. Horsti and Frankie elicited a shrug, nothing more, but Johnny she'd heard of. Cora had mentioned him on one occasion, likening him to the archangel that drove Adam and Eve out of Paradise. "And the eyes of them both were opened, and they knew that they were naked."

His friend called him Billy-Goat, thought Grovian. He was Satan, who had led the woman into temptation by means of the serpent. And then came the tiger with its paws of crystal.

It sounded mad, naturally, but he'd seen the scar and the dent in her skull with his own eyes. And she'd also said something about an ashtray. It didn't take a lot of imagination to visualize what had happened in that cellar, and it was likely that anyone who had had to camouflage a Saturday night disco as the eye of God would also clothe a dire experience in biblical quotations.

Cora's aunt could not recall her mentioning a Johnny Guitar, nor did she know when Cora had made his acquaintance or what their relationship had been, but she indirectly confirmed her niece's statements, rambling and intelligible alike.

In May five years ago her brother Wilhelm had called her. He was worried about his daughter, he said, and suspected that she had got into bad company.

"I didn't take him too seriously," said Margret Rosch. "In a household where a television set is the work of the devil, any young man is bad company."

But her brother's fears were not as groundless as she thought. That August, Cora disappeared. For three months she seemed to have vanished from the face of the earth. Then, in November, Wilhelm received a call from a doctor.

According to this doctor, Cora had been found lying beside a road some weeks earlier. She had been badly knocked about and was unconscious. Later she claimed to have thrown herself in front of a car. However, the doctor surmised from the nature of her injuries that she had been thrown from a car on the move.

130

Grovian was feeling rather relieved. The rest of what Margret Rosch told him also fitted the picture. She spoke of a trauma. Whatever had been done to her niece, Cora couldn't bring herself to talk about it. So the suicide attempt could be consigned to the realm of fantasy – the pregnancy too, in all probability. He sought confirmation on this point. "Your niece has repeatedly claimed to have killed an innocent child."

Margret Rosch gave a nervous laugh. "She most certainly hasn't. She's never had a child."

"I was thinking more of a pregnancy," he said.

"An abortion, you mean?" Margret Rosch shook her head. "I can't imagine it, not in Cora's case."

"It may have been a miscarriage," he said. "That wouldn't be surprising if she was knocked about. Do you know the name of the doctor who treated your niece at the time?"

"No, nor do I know what hospital looked after her."

"She says she wasn't in a hospital."

"She says!" Margret Rosch broke in. "It's no use asking Cora about this business, she's in denial. Do you know what a trauma is?"

He nodded, thinking of the wall in the brain his questions had demolished.

"Good," she said, "then consult your common sense. I know a lot of doctors, caring doctors, but none that would pick up a badly injured girl lying unconscious by the roadside and take her home with him. That would be irresponsible. I've no idea why she told you that story. Maybe she wishes there *had* been such a person – someone who would really be there for her. She always was a bit of a loner."

That sounded logical. He hadn't forgotten the doctor's remark about the needle marks in her arms. Next question: "Did your niece ever do drugs?"

Several seconds went by before Margret Rosch gave a reluctant nod. "Yes, heroin, but not for long. It must have been around that time. I assume Johnny administered it to make her compliant. She certainly didn't shoot up herself – she didn't know how to handle the stuff."

131

She sighed. "She was in a wretched state when she came to me. She thought it was withdrawal symptoms, but that had nothing to do with it. Terrible nightmares, she had, and always just before two in the morning – you could have set your clock by them. I used to give her sleeping pills, but they might as well have been candies. At five to two, on the dot, she would be sitting on the couch, lashing out with her fists and yelling at the top of her voice: 'Stop it! Stop it, you swine!' She wasn't awake and I couldn't rouse her. If I spoke to her, she would mumble something about a cellar – about worms and tigers and goats."

Listening intently, Rudolf Grovian felt easier in his mind. He hadn't mentioned the names Billy-Goat and Tiger. It was one thing to torment a young woman with his questions but quite another to goad her into remembering things that could ultimately provide her with a motive.

"I urged her more than once to consult a doctor," Margret Rosch went on, "but she refused, and I didn't want to bully her into it. She was badly in need of help, though, so I ended by dosing her food with tranquillizers. Her condition improved after a couple of months. The nightmares petered out, and she recovered physically as well."

She lapsed into silence for a moment or two. Then: "You won't tell Cora what I've just said, will you? If you tell her I told you about the heroin, she'll slam the door in your face, believe me. To her, keeping it under wraps is the most important thing in the world. It would be best not to mention it at all. Anyway, there's no point in bringing it up again after all this time. Cora must already have told you a lot of things – how the whole thing began, no doubt. It seems Johnny didn't behave like an animal right away. Maybe I can get her to tell you something about the end of the affair. I don't know how much she remembers, if anything at all, but it's worth a try. Will you let me have a word with her?"

"Yes, in due course," said Grovian. He inched his way slowly towards the subject of Cora's childhood and parental home. All he wanted was confirmation of the mother's religious mania and the father's failure to resist it. And also, perhaps, of what was lurking at the back of his mind. Child abuse?

132

But he had scarcely begun asking about Cora's childhood when her aunt underwent a strange transformation. Her initial eagerness to be communicative vanished.

"I can't tell you much. I had very little contact with my brother's family, mainly because I couldn't stand my sister-in-law's insane goings-on. Cora made a normal impression on me whenever I came to visit. Her mother didn't allow her much freedom, but she managed to get her way despite this. Many a child would have snapped under such constant pressure, but Cora . . . How can I put it? She thrived on it. She was always very mature for her age, very sensible and responsible. She took over some of the household chores at an early age, not because she was asked to, but because she saw that her mother couldn't cope. You could say she assumed the role of an adult."

And what of her role in the marriage bed? All the typical signs were there. Bed-wetting at the age of nine, heroin at nineteen! Sexually abused children often ended that way, Margret knew, but Wilhelm had always been a decent fellow. That she also knew, and now he was an old man, worn out and tired of his miserable existence. He called her occasionally. "How's Cora?" he would ask, and was always delighted when she replied: "She's fine."

*

Margret Rosch had been sitting with Rudolf Grovian for nearly an hour. She was obviously disconcerted by what had happened. That apart, she revealed nothing of what was going through her head. She didn't even mention Magdalena's name.

"Now may I see my niece?" she asked at length.

He rose. "I'll go and see how my colleagues are getting on."

His colleagues were standing around in the passage. He only wanted to check on Cora Bender's condition. She was sitting up straight again when he entered the office. Berrenrath was standing beside the window in conversation with the doctor, and the latter's expression involuntarily reminded him of Winfried Meilhofer's reference to an avenging angel.

He must have got the relevant impression: the police and their brutal interrogation methods, an unconscious young woman with a battered face.

"Your aunt would like to see you, Frau Bender," Grovian said.

Her fixed stare seemed to bore into his brain.

"This woman needs rest," the doctor protested.

"Nonsense," she said. "You said that jab would perk me up, and it has. I've never felt wider awake in my life." She looked up at Grovian. "What has she been telling you?"

"I'll go and get her," was all he said.

He returned two minutes later with Margret Rosch at his heels. Gesturing to Berrenrath and the doctor to leave, he lingered in the background but watched and listened in silence. Margret Rosch remained standing in the middle of the room. He saw the fear on Cora Bender's face, heard the strain in her hoarse voice.

"What have you been telling him?"

"Nothing," her aunt lied. "Don't worry, I only came to see you. A shame you won't be paying me a visit tomorrow; I was looking forward to it. How's the little boy?"

She spoke as if she were visiting someone confined to bed with a broken leg, but Cora Bender's suspicions weren't to be allayed so easily.

"Fine. Have you really told him nothing?"

"Of course not. What's to tell?"

"How would I know? People talk a lot of nonsense in a situation like this. I did so myself – I blathered about the Saviour, Mary Magdalene and all that rubbish."

Margret Rosch shook her head. "No, I haven't said a word."

Cora Bender seemed relieved. She subsided a little and changed the subject. Grovian couldn't tell whether she was really appeased or pursuing some definite objective. She seemed genuinely concerned, just as she had at the lake that afternoon. Berrenrath had reported that she was worried about her son's ears.

"Did Gereon call you?" she asked. When her aunt nodded she went on: "How is he? Did he say anything about his arm? I stabbed him twice, I think. One of the medics at the lido bandaged him up. It was quite a dressing – it covered the whole of his forearm. Let's hope he'll be able to work with it, they're so busy at present. Manni Weber can't handle things on his own. As for the old man, forget it. You know what he's like. Talks big, but he doesn't know a screwdriver from a pipe wrench."

Her aunt nodded again, bit her lip and finally brought the conversation around to what had happened.

"Is there anything you need? Shall I get you a lawyer?"

Cora made a dismissive gesture. "Never mind that, but if you could bring me a few things. Some clothes and my sponge bag. The usual, you know what I mean."

"No, I *don't* know," Margret Rosch snapped suddenly. "What's 'the usual' when you're going to jail? This isn't a vacation, Cora. Do me a favour and tell these people the truth. Don't worry about anyone else, think of yourself for once. Tell them what happened five years ago. Tell them why you left home that August – they'll understand. Tell them everything."

"I already did."

"I don't believe you."

Cora calmly shrugged her shoulders. "Forget it, then. Leave me alone. Pretend Mother was right and I'm dead."

She was silent for some seconds. Then she said quietly: "Will you talk to Father? He'll have to be told, and I'd sooner you did it. But break it to him gently. Tell him I'm all right. I don't want him to get upset. I don't want him coming here either."

Margret Rosch merely nodded, then cast a yearning glance at the door. Grovian escorted her out and thanked her for her help. He meant it too. Johnny, heroin, brutally beaten, thrown out of a car on the move . . . He should be able to make something of that, not to mention the sound of the other girl's ribs snapping.

The dialogue between aunt and niece had also been informative. It illustrated the family's displacement mechanisms. When push came to shove, they preferred to talk about the weather.

Grovian was fairly sure that Margret Rosch could have told him a bit more – at least about "the Saviour, Mary Magdalene and all that rubbish". It puzzled him that Cora Bender seemed solely concerned to satisfy herself of her aunt's silence on these matters, even though she herself had talked at length about them.

He mentally corrected himself. No, she had only talked about the crucifix. He distinctly recalled how her face had twitched when she mentioned the Saviour in connection with the penitent Mary Magdalene and how she had promptly initiated a diversion by asking for some water in her coffee.

Not being very well versed in the Bible, he wondered what significance could be attached to a minor biblical figure if, five years after appearing as Satan with the serpent, Georg Frankenberg had now functioned as the Saviour. But it didn't pay to brood on the subject.

A trauma! Without realizing it, he'd touched her on the raw. It really wasn't his job to meddle with that trauma – that was a medical responsibility. Grovian never made the same mistake twice. She wouldn't collapse at his feet again. You had to know your own limits, and he had reached his. Or so he thought.

7

Margret's visits were a mixed blessing from my point of view. She came too seldom and never stayed long enough to really change anything. She came bearing hope for Father but took it away with her when she went home.

I scarcely remember her visits in my early years. There couldn't have been many of them, and she usually turned up accompanied by a very old woman, my grandmother. They always brought some cakes with them. Mother took them and put them in the larder with the bread. What happened to them after that, only Mother and the Saviour knew. Those early visits brought me no concessions, so I found them rather a nuisance. My grandmother kept on asking me if I was a good girl, if I obeyed my mother and father and always did as I was told. I nodded every time and felt relieved when she and my aunt went away again.

Then, for the first time, Margret came on her own, my grandmother having died in the interim. We talked together during that visit. She wanted to know if I enjoyed school, if my marks were good, what subject I liked best, whether I liked sleeping in the same room as my father, and whether I could draw her a picture of him because she didn't possess a photo of him.

I wasn't any good at drawing, so I painted her a matchstick man holding a rake and a bucket. She asked what the long thing sticking out of the matchstick man's side was, and I told her. That was the way I saw him.

The rest of the time Margret spent with Mother. During the day, at least, because Father had to work. Mother was strange for days after she left. I don't know how to describe it, but she seemed frightened. She was thoroughly upset and subjected me to endless lectures on "the true sins" – as if there weren't enough of the others.

The true sins, said Mother, were carnal desires. This meant nothing to me, being only nine years old. I thought it might have something to do with the joint she'd had to roast for Margret's benefit. Father had insisted on this, saying you couldn't feed a guest on bean soup two days running. He'd carved two slices of beef for himself and only one for me – the smallest, although Margret pressed me to have another. "Or don't you like meat, Cora?"

Of course I liked meat, but it occurred to me that, if I had another slice, Mother would give me an earful after she left. And she did.

And then, a week after Margret's departure, a parcel arrived. It was during the Christmas vacation, I remember distinctly. The postman delivered it one morning, but Mother didn't dare open it because it was addressed to Father. She put it away in the kitchen cupboard until that evening, when Father came home and cut the string with a grand gesture.

Margret's visit had changed him. A new wind was blowing in our home, he kept saying. Seven lean years must be followed by seven years of plenty, or if there'd been eight lean years, eight years of plenty. By then he'd be old enough to go without for good. I once heard him tell Mother: "If you don't give in soon, I'll get calluses on my hands." Those strange remarks of his made me feel uneasy. The people in our neighbourhood said Mother was crazy, and they said it so I could hear. I was afraid Father was also going mad.

He made a great song and dance about the parcel, almost as if it contained a new heart for Magdalena. The contents turned out to be sweets, some of which he handed around at once in spite of Mother's grim expression. Magdalena got a little tube of multicoloured chocolate candies – Smarties: I'd seen other girls with them in the playground. I got a tube too. I was about to hand it to Mother when Father gripped my wrist.

138

"They're yours," he said, "and you'll eat them. The rest we'll keep for Christmas, then Mother won't have to betray her principles by buying some herself."

As well as the sweets, Margret had included some other things done up in coloured paper tied with ribbon, and attached to the ribbon were little cards with our names on them. There was an envelope on top.

It was the first letter from Margret that Father read aloud to me, but not to me alone. Mother and Magdalena were also in the kitchen. Mother had fetched both armchairs from the living room and pushed them together so Magdalena could lie down. She wasn't too well that day.

Margret wished us all a happy Christmas and a happy and, above all, a healthy New Year. She was sorry her visit hadn't had the desired result, but she hoped Mother would reflect on her wifely duties and remember that the Saviour had never demanded abstinence of his followers. Other people had claimed that later on, but their only motive had been an unwillingness to distribute the riches they'd amassed among their heirs. Mother was urged to bear in mind that Father didn't have the other bedroom to himself, and it would do no one any good if something untoward occurred. She could well understand Mother's fear of becoming pregnant again, but that needn't happen these days – there were plenty of ways of avoiding it, and Margret felt sure the Saviour approved of them. No one knew human nature better than He, and sacrificing a second lamb would be a waste of which He could never approve.

Father read all this aloud to us. Then he came to the presents. Magdalena got a doll, a cloth doll with a funny face embroidered with sewing cotton. She had big blue eyes, red cheeks and a laughing mouthful of white teeth. Her hair consisted of yellow knitting wool braided into thick plaits. Margret wished Magdalena a face like the doll's, cheerful and healthy. Magdalena was allowed to unwrap the doll at once with my help.

Meantime, Father tossed a little packet to Mother. "Better take that into the living room," he said, "and ask Him if He objects to

139

it." Mother didn't budge. The little packet bounced off her apron and fell to the floor. Last of all, Father handed me my present. It was a book: *Alice in Wonderland.*

I never got to read more than the title. It was too late to dip into the book that evening, and the next day Mother asked me to put it in the bucket and burn it in front of the altar. She didn't exactly order me to; she preached me a sermon on Margret's letter and the depraved ideas it contained. I must tell her at once if Father exposed himself to me.

She's completely flipped, I thought. I'd known Father for so long, after all, and I also knew by then that he was my real father. I looked very like him and had long ceased to believe that the Adigars were my family. So I merely nodded to everything Mother said.

I also nodded when she asked me if I didn't believe, as she did, that all one needed in order to lead a full life was knowing the Book of Books. I knew it almost by heart. Mother had told me so much about the sins of mankind, they were coming out of my ears. And now that I could read myself . . . Oh, forget it!

She sent me to get the tin bucket and thrust the box of matches into my hand. Then we watched as *Alice in Wonderland* was reduced to a mound of ashes.

When Father came home late that afternoon and heard what had happened, I'd never seen him fly into such a fury. I only understood half of the things he said. He'd never expected a Tommy's whore to turn into a walking prayer book, he told Mother. She used to enjoy it once upon a time, he said. She'd not only welcomed the insertion of what Nature had provided for the purpose but followed it up with a knitting needle. Mother just stood there, frozen-faced. I felt sorry for her somehow.

Father and I sat together at the kitchen table for a long time afterwards while Mother did the washing up. He told me the story of *Alice in Wonderland*, although he didn't know it at all. He made up a completely new story about a girl whose mother went mad and wanted to drive the whole family insane. The girl didn't like living at home, but she couldn't run away because she was still too young and had no money, so she made up a world of her own.

She invented imaginary people and talked to them although they didn't exist.

"Then the girl was as mad as her mother," I said.

Father smiled. "Yes, probably, but how could she fail to be, with a mother like that? If you never see or hear anything else, it's hardly surprising."

Magdalena was in the kitchen too, stretched out in the two armchairs as before. She was recovering from a hard day: two enemas whose only result had been a stomach ache. She'd listened attentively, glancing at Father and Mother in turn. The thing was, she knew the story of *Alice in Wonderland*.

On one occasion, the hospital nurse who ensured that she was sometimes allowed to play with other children had pushed her wheelchair into a room where another mother was reading the book aloud to her sick child. Although she'd mentioned this to me later, she didn't tell me what *Alice in Wonderland* was really about. I didn't ask her, not wanting to know.

Father smiled at her and said: "How's our little sweetheart today?"

Magdalena didn't reply. By this time she spoke to me often but seldom to Mother and never to him. Mother answered for her. "She's not well. How could she be anything else, in a house where no one obeys the Lord's commandments?"

"*You* obey them, don't you?" said Father. He was still fuming. "But you must show me the commandment in question. I can't recall ever having read that the Lord commanded a child to burn a book. Book-burning was cultivated by the Inquisition and the Nazis. Strange company you keep!"

Mother just looked at him. He nodded to himself, bowed his head and stared at the tabletop. "But to revert to this Saviour of yours," he said after a while. "Didn't he say 'Unless you become like little children . . .'? I think he said something of the kind. If you obey his words to the letter, don't just cherry-pick the ones that suit you. Children like to do something occasionally apart from crossing themselves. If we're going to have to part with one of ours – and we'll have to sooner or later, you know that as well as I do – I want the other to be as hale and hearty as possible. I should have listened to those doctors, then it would have been over long ago. Then you could be performing your daft antics in the graveyard."

I thought my heart had stopped beating. I knew exactly what he meant, and Magdalena knew it too – she wasn't stupid. Her frequent visits to the hospital had taught her a lot about her illness and other things. She knew a great deal more than I did. She couldn't read or write or do sums, but she knew words like electrocardiogram, septal defect, insufficiency, aortic aneurysm, pathology and crematorium. What was more, she knew what they meant.

She stared at Father, hugging her doll and fingering its thick plaits. She seemed about to say something. Her lips moved a couple of times, but no sound emerged. At last it dawned on me. She was mouthing a single word: Arsehole!

I don't know if Father read her lips too. He drew a deep breath. Then he said, rather more softly: "Having made that decision, however, we should try to make her life as bearable as we can and give her a little pleasure, not spout pious platitudes the whole time. They're no use to her. I'm sure she would have enjoyed *Alice in Wonderland* too. Cora would surely have read some to her."

"She must sleep now," Mother said. "She's had a tiring day." She lifted Magdalena out of the armchairs and carried her to the door. Father watched them go, shaking his head. Then he stared at the tabletop again. "That was my sin," he said softly. "Not to have denied myself for once and bided my time. I'd have done better to stick it in a mouse hole."

He raised his head and looked at me. "We'd best go to bed, don't you think? It's your bedtime anyway, and I'm tired too."

We went upstairs. Mother was still in the bathroom with Magdalena, washing her and brushing her teeth. Father went to their bedroom and fetched the things he would wear to work in the morning. I retired to our room to put on my nightie. When Mother and Magdalena came out of the bathroom I went in there to wash.

Mother put Magdalena to bed and went downstairs to pray. Father came into the bathroom looking very depressed. He stood beside the basin, watching me wash my face and comb my hair.

My hair was all tangled – I used to twist it around my finger when I had to kneel in front of the altar for too long. Father helped me to comb out the knots, then pillowed my head against his chest and held me tight. "I'm so sorry," he murmured. "I'm so terribly sorry."

"Don't be sad about the book," I told him. "I'm not all that fond of reading. I like it better when you tell me about the old days. It's a long time since you told me about the railway and the old school and how they built the church."

"I've told you far too much about that," he said. "Anything, rather than talk about today or yesterday."

He clasped my head to his chest with one hand and stroked my back with the other. Then, quite suddenly, he pushed me away. Turning toward the washbasin, he said "Roll on the spring, when we're too busy working on the allotment to get any silly ideas."

*

It had been a silly idea to assume that Margret had betrayed her. But although Margret could be relied on – she herself had something to lose, after all – that realization did not detract from Cora's fear, bewilderment and uncertainty.

When Margret and the chief left the room, the man in the sports coat came in. On her own with him for a few minutes, she wished he would speak to her. Just a sentence or two, to dispel the dead feeling inside her head.

Ever since she had regained consciousness after that brief blackout, it had been as dark and cramped in there as a coffin. Or a cellar with the lights out. She knew she had seen and felt something frightful, but whatever it was that had broken through the wall in her brain had withdrawn behind it again. Only the sensation remained – that and her father's voice, which seemed to haunt the darkness.

She saw him sitting on the edge of her bed. He had done that night after night during the few weeks she spent at home after her return in November. She heard his imploring voice, suddenly so old and unsteady. "Speak to me, Cora. Don't be like her. You must talk to me – tell me what happened. Whatever you've done, I won't judge you. I'll never breathe a word about it, I promise. I don't have the right to judge you, nor does Mother. We each have something on our conscience. I'll tell you what I've done and Mother's done, then it'll be your turn. You must tell me, Cora. If you don't talk about it, it'll eat you up inside. What happened, Cora? What did you do?"

Just two or three sentences from the man in the sports coat might have drowned Father's voice, but he merely looked at her with a mixture of sympathy and uncertainty. Perhaps he was waiting for her to speak first. When she remained silent he transferred his attention to the tape recorder. He removed the cassette and added it to the others that had accumulated in the course of the night.

The cassette! "I'll wind it on a bit," the woman beside the lake had said and: "You'll never hear anything better."

The words flashed through her mind like an electric shock and found an echo somewhere.

"That's the best tune I've ever heard," said Magdalena.

She was lying in bed holding a tiny cassette player connected to her ear by a thin lead. She chuckled to herself. Her head rocked to and fro – only her head, which was all she could move – in time to the tune she was humming: "Bohemian Rhapsody". "I love that number," she said. "Freddie Mercury! Some voice he's got, really terrific. I wish I could hear it good and loud, like in a disco, but for that we'd need a really big stereo system, and if Mother saw it, she'd pull the plug on us as well as turn off the water. Did you find the stopcock?"

The chief had returned. "How are you feeling, Frau Bender?" he asked.

Still with Magdalena, she replied: "Afraid not. I'll go and get a bucket of water from Grit, that'll do to wash with." Then, realizing what Grovian had asked her, she said quickly: "Fine, thanks."

144

She felt sure he would start questioning her again. Then she remembered that his last question had remained unanswered: Where had she heard the names Frankie, Billy-Goat and Tiger? Where Frankie was concerned the answer was simple: down at the lake.

Only the truth would do. Lies made everything worse, Mother had told her so again and again, and she'd always been right, that had now been proved once and for all. The Lord punished those who incurred his wrath. He deranged them, either in speech or in spirit.

The truth, the whole truth and nothing but the truth! I didn't know the man. I really didn't know him, neither his name nor his face. I've no idea why I had to kill him. I only know I had to do it.

But the chief made no move to pursue the matter. Glancing at the man in the sports coat, he said something about them all being badly in need of sleep. He spoke in a tone of concern. As he said it she felt her limbs go leaden with fatigue. At the same time, she dreaded being left alone with the fragmentary memories that were imposing themselves on her – scouring her soul like dirty old cleaning rags. Everything inside her became stiff and hard. Bereft of the energy to protest, she could hardly rise from her chair.

The chief sent for Berrenrath and his younger colleague to escort her out. Moments later she was lying on a narrow bed, almost as lifeless as Georg Frankenberg but unable to go to sleep.

She wondered whether Margret had called Father yet. Probably not, at this hour of the night. There was no telephone in her parents' house. Anyone who wanted to give them an urgent message had to call the Adigars and ask them to go and get Father. And Margret would never get Grit Adigar out of bed in the middle of the night ...

She felt like an open wound. She had never experienced such a sensation before, and now it was spreading. A yearning for the old days, when she used to perch on Magdalena's bed and tell her about the outside world. About the disco, with its frenzied music, flashing lights and young men. Magdalena's questions: "What's coke like? They say it's an incredible sensation. You feel everything

145

much more intensely, especially sex. Have you tried it? What was it like? Go on, tell me."

A yearning to kneel before the altar again. To fold her hands again. To pray once more to the Saviour to grant Magdalena another day of life and herself the gift of self-denial. Then she would go next door to Grit, who regularly asked her: "Well, Cora, finished all your chores for today?"

Yes, not just for today but for all time.

She had killed a man: Georg Frankenberg! Heard a tune: "Tiger's Song"! Told a story: Father's version of *Alice in Wonderland*. Invented a world of her own and some non-existent people: Billy-Goat and Tiger.

Worst of all, she could feel her mind disintegrating, becoming friable and steadily losing substance until, in the end, it could be crumbled between finger and thumb. It was nearly five o'clock in the morning when she fell asleep at last.

*

Meantime, Rudolf Grovian was lying on the sofa in his living room. He had folded his arms behind his head and was staring up at the dark ceiling. He could hear her imploring voice: "Turn on the light again!"

He had got home at three, his thoughts in turmoil, exhausted and rather depressed by the awareness that he had started something whose completion he would have to leave to others. "Help me, please!" He couldn't help her. All he could do was prove that Johnny Guitar and Georg Frankenberg were one and the same person.

Werner Hoss doubted this, and his arguments could not be so easily dismissed. They had listened to the two most important tapes – the first and the last – before calling it a day. Hoss argued in favour of the first: "It was that tune." That, he said, was the answer, and it wasn't negated by her ramblings on the last tape. They were simply two different things. You couldn't tell what was going on in the head of someone who had been browbeaten with the Bible for nineteen years and smashed by a crystal paw five years ago.

146

Grovian had tossed and turned for so long that Mechthild had told him: "Rudi, do me a favour and bed down on the sofa. That way, at least *I'll* get some sleep."

He had long ago weaned himself from discussing his job with her. Mechthild had her own idea of justice and the law. She spent two afternoons a week working in a charity shop, handing out discarded overcoats and trousers to life's failures and other persons in need. As an unpaid volunteer, of course. In the old days, when he'd told her that one of life's failures had marched into a bank with a loaded gun in his hand, her usual response had been: "Oh, the poor fellow."

"Did Marita get home safely?" he asked, partly for something to say and partly in the hope that she would ask him why he was home so late and what the trouble was. Somehow, he had an itch to hear her say: "Oh, the poor girl."

"I suppose so," she said.

"What did she tell you? She must have told you something. I mean, I heard her say something about a lawyer."

"Rudi," she said in a plaintive drawl, "let's talk about it tomorrow. Look at the time."

"I won't get a chance tomorrow. I want to know now."

Mechthild sighed. "She wants a divorce."

"What?" He didn't even bother to sit up with a jerk. It was just as he'd feared. "She doesn't know when she's well off."

Mechthild heaved another sigh. "She isn't doing it for fun, Rudi, believe you me."

"If you believe it, that's good enough for me," he said. "But you believe any old guff she tells you."

"But she's right," said Mechthild, half-convinced. "Peter works too hard. She's always on her own. It's no kind of life for a young woman."

"Why not? I think she has a great life. He works too hard, and she spends the money he earns like it's going out of fashion. It's better than having to kneel for hours in front of a crucifix."

"Some comparison," said Mechthild. "What put that into your head?"

"Never mind. Tell me something, do we possess a Bible?"

"That's enough, Rudi! It's nearly half-past three." Mechthild turned over on her side.

"Do we or don't we?" he persisted.

"In the living room," she said. "In the cupboard beside the door."

So he went downstairs and, after turning out half the contents of the cupboard, came across a dog-eared edition with doodles in the margins. Evidently a relic of their daughter's schooldays, it was among her old schoolbooks. He lay down on the sofa and read the passage about the expulsion from Paradise. Then, remembering that an apple had been involved, he went so far as to surmise that Cora Bender's sole reason for taking some apples with her to the lake had been a wish to swim until Judgement Day.

Her expulsion from Paradise meant expulsion from her father-in-law's business and marriage to a man who had beaten her to a pulp and was quite unconcerned about how the police were treating her. When making his statement, Gereon Bender hadn't asked how his wife was or what would happen to her.

Then he remembered a reference to Mary Magdalene. He read a few lines on the subject and felt even more depressed. Mary Magdalene had been a whore. That fact, coupled with Cora Bender's heroin-taking and needle-scarred forearms, formed a combination he didn't like at all.

At half-past five he raided the refrigerator for the makings of a hearty breakfast and left a note for Mechthild on the kitchen table informing her that he would contrive to come home for lunch. It wouldn't take longer than that to deliver Cora Bender to the examining magistrate, he felt sure, and that was precisely what he intended to do – precisely what he should have done last night, when she displayed the first signs of mental confusion. It was unpardonable of him to have disobeyed his inner voice.

He was back in his office by six. Werner Hoss turned up shortly afterwards. They collated the documentation for the DA, listened again to the tapes, especially the last one, discussed them for a while and came to no firm conclusion.

"The tape from Frankenberg's cassette player," said Grovian, "has it been taken into safekeeping?"

Hoss grinned. "Want to listen to it?"

"No," he replied, grinning too. "On the other hand, if it really was his own composition . . ."

Hoss dug out the tape from Forensics, and they listened to it briefly. It was just music, rock music of a rather wild and woolly kind. To Grovian's ears it sounded chaotic and monotonous, but if it had some bearing on the murder, only the last number on the tape could be relevant. They knew from Winfried Meilhofer that the machine had switched itself off only a few seconds after the killing.

"We should try an experiment," suggested Hoss. "In other words, play her a sample and see if she can identify it straight off. I couldn't, not that kind of stuff."

Grovian firmly shook his head. "If it comes out that we've played it to her, we can kiss the case goodbye."

A copy of the autopsy report arrived shortly before nine. A total of seven stab wounds in positions that tallied with Cora Bender's account. One in the neck, one severing the carotid, and one through the larynx. The rest were comparatively superficial. Cause of death: aspiration. Georg Frankenberg had choked on his own blood before he could bleed to death.

The DA, who turned up not long afterwards, requested a thorough briefing.

"Do you have a confession?" he asked.

"We have a statement," said Grovian. He explained what he thought of it and mentioned the fainting fit. That couldn't be hushed up, nor did he try to gloss over it. He described Cora's alternate spells of clarity and confusion and ended with Margret Rosch's account of her nightmares. "I'd like you to listen to this."

At a sign from Grovian, Hoss started the tape recorder. The DA listened to Cora's voice with knitted brow. Although he didn't pursue the subject of her fainting fit, his expression clearly conveyed what he thought: such things simply shouldn't happen. Having listened to the halting voice on the tape for a while, he muttered "Good God!" and tapped his forehead in a meaningful way. "Is she . . .?"

149

Werner Hoss shrugged. Grovian gave an emphatic shake of the head. The DA asked if they thought she was putting on an act.

"No!" said Grovian. He couldn't resist a little sideswipe. "You wouldn't ask that question if you'd been there. These tapes should be listened to by people capable of interpreting them. I mean that. A transcript isn't good enough. She's carrying a lot of ballast around, that woman." He pointed to a few major features of her childhood, like her mother's religious fanaticism and her belief that her father's "thing" would rot off in due course.

"And there's something else," he said. "We'll look into it to-morrow. We don't have much to go on, just a few words, but we should at least make inquiries. A girl from Buchholz may have disappeared at the time in question. There may even be a corpse with broken ribs up there."

The DA shrugged his shoulders. He skimmed through the witnesses' depositions and the autopsy report. Then he looked up and said: "We've got one corpse already, don't forget. It may not have any broken ribs, but this stuff is more than enough for me. It's rare for a person to remember so precisely where they stabbed someone."

"What do you mean, precisely?" said Grovian. "She listed the points at which a stab wound can be fatal. Her aunt is a nurse. She lived with her for eighteen months, so she could have picked up a bit of medical knowledge."

The DA regarded him impassively for a moment or two. "Odd sort of conversations to have with an aunt," he said. "Anyway, Grovian, she not only listed the relevant points, she skewered them."

Grovian knew this, even though he hadn't seen it with his own eyes. He also knew that remembering such precise details was extremely rare, if not the great exception. No one committing a crime in the heat of the moment recalled the exact sequence of events, and this had been a crime of passion – it couldn't be anything else, and he wanted the DA to share his opinion. "Would you like a word with her?" he suggested. "I could send for her."

The DA shook his head. "Let her sleep. She must have had a tough night, but mine wasn't pleasant either. I don't care to prolong it at the moment."

Arsehole, thought Grovian.

*

It was late that morning when Berrenrath woke her. She didn't know he could have been tucked up in bed at home long ago, and it wouldn't have interested her particularly if she had. Last night his kindliness had possessed a certain value. Now he was just a link in the chain with which she had been fettered to the past.

She had a stale taste in her mouth, but her head was quite clear again. Cold, too, as if her brain had frozen in the night. Her fear – and with it every other sensation – was now encased in a block of ice.

She asked for a glass of water and was given one. Mineral water, which did her good. She sipped it slowly. Not long afterwards Berrenrath escorted her back into the chief's office.

There she was offered some breakfast. The chief was waiting for her, as was the other man, this time wearing pale grey slacks and a check shirt with an unobtrusive pattern. Both men looked weary, and both seemed concerned that she should really be feeling all right. On the tray set before her was a plate of open sandwiches topped with cheese and sausage. She wasn't hungry. The chief urged her to eat something, at least, so she obliged him by taking a mouthful of salami sandwich and washing it down with plenty of coffee.

Then she asked his name. "I'm sorry, I had so many things on my mind yesterday, I didn't take it in."

The chief stated his name, but in his case the name didn't matter. He'd driven her to the brink of insanity, thereby demonstrating the extent of his power over her and her mind. After him, no one else would be strong enough to do that to her.

He announced that they were going take her to the district court at Brühl and hand her over to the examining magistrate.

151

"You'll have to wait a while, then," she said, looking at Werner Hoss. Expressionlessly, she went on: "You had your doubts about my story last night – rightly so."

They listened closely, never taking their eyes off her, as she calmly proceeded to retract her whole edifice of lies about Johnny Guitar. She concluded with a tiny little new lie: in October five years ago she'd neglected to pay sufficient attention while crossing a road and been knocked down by a car.

She saw Werner Hoss give a satisfied nod. The chief shot him a furious glance and shook his head. Then, very cautiously, he raised the subject of his interview with her aunt. Margret had told him she'd been terribly mistreated, he said, and she herself had hinted as much.

It was a blow to learn that Margret had lied to her and talked after all – that she'd dished the little dirt she'd picked up from Father about the end of the affair. Terribly mistreated, yet! And she'd advised her to tell the truth about what happened from August onwards! From August onwards the truth couldn't hurt Margret. "Think of yourself for once!" Margret had been thinking of Margret, no one else.

"What is all this nonsense?" she burst out. "I hinted at nothing. Did I *say* I'd been mistreated?"

The chief smiled. "Not in so many words." He asked her to listen to a passage from one of the tapes, but only, of course, if she felt up to it.

"Yes, sure," she said. "I feel exactly the way someone in my position should."

He turned on the tape recorder, and she listened to her quavering voice: "He went on hitting her until she was dead – I heard her ribs snap . . ."

"My God," she said, "I sound awful – quite bemused. But you did badger me, you must admit. That quack you foisted on me said I'd been subjected to intense emotional pressure, that's why I fainted. Ask him if you don't believe me. Or ask Berrenrath, he heard it too. But don't worry, I won't lodge a formal complaint against you. You were doing your job, I realize that."

Grovian nodded. He glanced at Hoss with an indefinable expression. It was either a plea for understanding or a demand for silence, which amounted to the same thing. He drew a deep breath, trying to assess her state of mind. She seemed quite lucid, and she could save him a lot of work if she wanted to. All she had to do was name the girl the fat boy had gone off with.

He proceeded with extreme caution, intimating that he understood what had prompted her to retract her story: a fear of having to confront some terrible truth once more.

Her lips twisted in a mocking smile. "You haven't understood a thing. The fat boy didn't have a girl. It was Johnny who went off with her. The fat boy trailed around after them like a little doggie who's only allowed to sniff a bone."

"So Johnny existed," said Grovian.

"Of course, but not for me. He never even spared me a glance."

Grovian injected a touch of paternal reproof into his voice. "Frau Bender, your aunt said —"

He got no further. "Cut it out!" she snapped. "Margret doesn't have a clue, she wasn't there! Forget all that crap and listen to the first tape instead. That's where you'll find the right answers. I'd never seen Georg Frankenberg before yesterday. I overheard his friend talking about him, that's how I was able to tell you something about his music and the cellar."

"No," he retorted. "You spoke about a cellar years ago – you dreamed about one. You aunt was certainly there then. And you didn't faint last night because I'd subjected you to pressure. I did pressure you, I don't deny it, but that wasn't why you fainted. You remembered the cellar. You couldn't bear it, you shouted, and you begged me to help you. I want to help you, Frau Bender, but you must meet me halfway. Your aunt said . . ."

She pursed her lips and nodded. On her battered face, the grin that accompanied the nod looked strangely pathetic. "I could tell you something about my aunt that would make your ears flap. She did something – theft, I think it's called. But you'd never guess what she stole, not in your worst nightmare. Margret lied to you just as I did, take it from me. She can't afford to tell you the truth. Forget it, though, I don't want to get her into trouble. I had a few nightmares while I was staying with her, that's true, but they had nothing to do with Georg Frankenberg. They were about quite different things."

"I know," he said. "They were about goats and pigs and tigers. And worms and suchlike. It doesn't take much imagination to interpret them. To me they sound like rape."

Grovian couldn't have explained how he came to prompt her in this way. He caught a puzzled glance from Werner Hoss.

She laughed aloud. "Rape? Who put that idea into your head? Margret?" She emitted another little bark of derisive laughter. "Who else! It's too annoying she only said it to you. She'd have done better to discuss it with me; I'd have had a story ready for her – one that would make me as innocent as a lamb."

*

Margret often said I'd gone my own way in spite of everything. It may have looked like that to her, but it wasn't my "way", it was my test track. I sinned deliberately to see what would happen. I gambled with Magdalena's life as if death were merely a ball to be tossed from hand to hand. Thrill-seeking – that's what it was for a while. Later it became a habit.

It started with little things. With the dream about the wolf, which made me wet my bed. I never stopped hoping the wolf would reappear because he liberated me, at least for the space of a night. And he continued to reappear for almost a year, nearly every night. Or I'd sneak over to Grit's in the afternoon, beg a sweet or a slice of cake and hastily devour it. I inspected Magdalena every time I came home, and every time her condition was unchanged. So minor sins couldn't kill her.

Not that I wanted to kill her, honestly not. She was a great burden to me. She compelled me to lead a life I had no wish to lead. But after that episode with the handkerchief and the Saviour's wet feet I often wished I could do more for her than talk to her or read her Bible stories.

I think I'd begun to love my sister, yet I still cadged sweets from Grit . . . Perhaps I simply wanted to prove to myself that I could sin like mad without affecting Magdalena's state of health. If little demons eventually ripped the flesh from my body with red-hot pincers, that was my problem, not hers.

And then, in the street one day, I found a one-mark coin. I was eleven and already going to secondary school, but I'd never had any money of my own. The other girls in my class got something from their parents every Sunday, and on Mondays after school they went to a little shop and bought themselves wine gums or ice lollies. They used to tease me for never being able to go to the shop with them.

I caught sight of the coin lying there while I was on my way to school that morning. I knew I was allowed to pick it up but ought to hand it in. Instead, I pocketed it. During break I left the playground, which was forbidden, and went to the shop to buy myself an ice lolly. And when the teacher asked where I'd been I said I'd had to order some candles for my mother. Taken together, I thought, that must surely amount to a mortal sin.

I dawdled on the way home for lunch, feeling terribly apprehensive. Magdalena hadn't been at all well that morning, and I. . . Oh, I don't know. Although I was eleven by then, and although I didn't want to believe what several people had told me – that Mother wasn't right in the head – I did still believe it – somehow.

Beliefs like that are deep-rooted, impossible to prove or disprove. You can't do much about them; you can only try. Many people think they'll be dogged by misfortune if they walk under a ladder or come to grief if a black cat crosses their path. They contrive never to walk under a ladder and turn tail if they see a black cat. But I wanted to find out.

Instead of ringing the doorbell, as I used to when I was younger, I went around to the kitchen. I could hear Mother singing before I reached the door.

"Almighty God, we praise Thee. Lord, we extol Thy might. The earth boweth down before Thee and marveleth at Thy works. As Thou wert in the beginning, so shalt Thou remain for all eternity.

All that can extol Thee, cherubim and seraphim, sing Thy praises. All the angels that serve Thee cry: 'Holy, holy, holy . . .'"

If Mother was singing that song, all had to be well. And it was. I walked into the kitchen to find Magdalena sitting in an armchair with the little bed-table across her knees, spooning up chicken broth – unaided. She winked at me, meaning get a load of what happens next. She was much better than she had been that morning.

"I'm going to be bored stiff in heaven," she said. "I mean, singing 'Holy, holy, holy' all day long."

She was so well, she could afford to needle Mother a little. She enjoyed doing so because Mother often needled her. Magdalena wasn't a gentle child by nature. She couldn't do much when she was little. She could do equally little when she became older, but she could use her tongue. And Mother was staggered or shocked every time, perhaps because she couldn't shoo Magdalena into the living room whenever she poked fun at her opinions or at the Saviour himself, not in her condition. "Blasphemy" was Mother's verdict on such remarks, and that was another very grave sin.

"No more singing, please," Magdalena insisted. "It'll spoil my appetite. If that's all I'm allowed to sing up there, I'd at least prefer to hear something else while I'm still down here. Cora must tell me something about school."

As time went by, my telling her about school had developed from our wishing game into a substitute for television. Things often happened at school. Sometimes kids got into fights. Sometimes one of the bigger boys would be caught smoking. On one occasion a girl locked herself up in the toilet and swallowed some tablets. Later, an ambulance turned up. Magdalena found it exciting when I told her things like that.

That was her life. She seldom left the house except to visit the hospital with Mother every three months. One couldn't go for a walk with her in town, and at her age she was too ashamed to be taken out in the pram.

Father had offered to buy her a wheelchair, but she wouldn't have it. "I don't want him spending a pfennig on me," she told me, "not a man who tosses himself off three times a day because he made me."

Father wasn't as bad as she thought, and I often told her so. I'd also offered to push her in the wheelchair, but Mother was against it. Something might happen to Magdalena while we were out, she said, and I wouldn't know what to do.

I really wanted to do something nice for her. At eleven I felt the urge to do so almost daily, but I could only tell her what had happened at school. If it was nothing special, I made something up. She didn't know the difference.

That day I could have told her about the one-mark coin – she wouldn't have given me away – but we were still in the kitchen with Mother. So I told her a made-up story, while Mother cleared the table and did the washing up. Magdalena was exhausted by the time Mother had finished. Mother took her upstairs to rest, but she was downstairs again by late afternoon, when Father came home.

The next day I sinned again, only worse. Before going to school I took some money from Mother's purse: two one-mark coins. I left the playground again during break, but this time I asked the teacher's permission. Could I go and see if the candles had been delivered yet? "Of course, Cora," the teacher said. "Go by all means."

So I went to the shop and bought myself an ice cream and a bar of chocolate. The ice I ate at once, the chocolate I hid in my jacket pocket. At lunchtime I took it into our barn and concealed it under some old potato sacks in the far corner.

My heart was pounding as I neared the kitchen door, but before I opened it I heard Magdalena talking. She was seated in the armchair, as before, with a plateful of mashed potato and a soft-boiled egg in front of her. She was fine. After she'd rested for an hour and I'd prayed and done my homework, she insisted on playing with me. Not "I spy with my little eye" or the wishing game, but a proper game.

Mother sent me to borrow Snakes and Ladders from Grit Adigar. Before returning to the kitchen with the cardboard box under my arm I hurried into the barn and broke off a square of chocolate. I let it dissolve slowly on my tongue. Mother would have noticed if I'd chewed it.

Magdalena watched me as I unfolded the board and put the dice in the cup. She saw I had something in my mouth but said nothing. Later, when Mother had gone out, she said: "What were you eating just now?"

"Chocolate."

Magdalena thought I'd got it from Grit. "Will you bring me a piece when you take the game back? But make sure there's some silver paper around it. You must slip it under my pillow and I'll eat it when Mother has put me to bed. I'll make sure she doesn't catch me."

Mother didn't want her eating sweet things, although she didn't invoke the Saviour, as she did in my case, but the dentist. Magdalena's teeth were a major problem: they were too soft. Once, in the hospital, they'd had to extract a molar that had developed a hole. This entailed giving her an injection, and Magdalena had reacted badly to it. The doctors had told Mother it must never happen again; that's why she was such a stickler for brushing Magdalena's teeth.

I knew this, and I also knew you shouldn't eat anything sweet after brushing your teeth because they'd get holes in them. To put it bluntly, I knew I would harm Magdalena, genuinely harm her, if I put a piece of chocolate under her pillow. But I nodded just the same.

Magdalena picked up the dice cup. "Let's play, then. Don't go easy on me, Cora, I'm a good loser."

*

Don't go easy on me, Cora . . . I can still hear her saying that. It became my motto in life. I gave up going easy on anything or anyone. I lied to the teacher and the other children at school, even to my father. I stole anything I could. At least twice a week I took money from Mother's purse. I bought sweets, hid them in the barn and helped myself to them whenever I felt like it. Whenever I got a chance I would bring some into the house for Magdalena and put them under her pillow. When my supplies ran out I simply stole some more money.

158

At first I was afraid the people in the shop would say something to Mother, who also shopped there. My sudden prosperity must have surprised them. To guard against all eventualities I told them that my Aunt Margret had sent me some money in a letter, and she'd written that I mustn't tell Mother or she'd take it away and spend it on candles or roses. The woman behind the counter smiled and said: "I won't breathe a word."

That was when I grasped what it meant to have money. Everyone was suddenly nice to me – everyone who had previously teased or ignored me. By the time I was twelve I was robbing Mother of at least three marks a week, and at that stage I was already getting a regular sum of pocket money from Father.

I sometimes wondered why Mother didn't miss the money. I don't know if she'd grown neglectful as time went by, or if I'd convinced her that I was the most devout and docile child on earth. Perhaps I had. I never argued, no matter what rubbish she spouted. I helped with the housework, washed up the dishes unasked and dusted the rooms or brought in washing from the clothes line, leaving her free to look after my sister. I did those things whenever my conscience pricked me, which it often did because I had everything and could seldom pass any of it on to Magdalena.

I went without my supper whenever I couldn't get a mouthful down after gorging myself on too many sweets in the afternoon. "I discovered a sinful desire in my heart at lunchtime today," I told Mother. "Now I want to atone for it." She was naturally delighted by such discernment.

I was always eager to do the shopping. "Leave it to me, Mother," I used to say. "I'm young and strong. Carrying heavy shopping bags doesn't worry me, and you need all your strength for Magdalena."

I would also tell her I'd sooner shop at the supermarket because everything was cheaper there, and "shopkeepers mustn't be encouraged to line their pockets". Mother said I was a great help and had learned a great deal from our Saviour. Sometimes she even said she was proud of me.

When I told Magdalena how I'd put one over on Mother, she

would say: "That's right, fool her whenever you can. Stupidity deserves to be punished."

Magdalena thought I walked all the way to the supermarket just so I could tell her if anything of interest was happening in town. I never told her the real reason: for one thing, it was easier to pinch things there; for another, Woolworths was nearby.

A good half of what I brought home was unpaid-for. At the supermarket I stole sweets and some of the groceries I had to get for Mother. In Woolworths I took barrettes, lipsticks and other bits and pieces I could easily slip into my jacket pocket but didn't need myself. Those things I sold in the playground.

I was an unbelievably good shoplifter. I looked so nice and innocent, no one would have thought me capable of skulduggery. Plenty of people knew who I was. I was just "that poor child" to the checkout girl at the supermarket, who lived on our street, and at Woolworths one of the sales assistants was a good friend of Grit Adigar, so it was just as easy there.

Nobody ever caught on, not even the girls who bought things from me. All I had to tell them was: "My aunt has sent me another parcel, but the stuff's no use to me. My mother would crucify me if she saw me wearing lipstick." They were all delighted to buy the things from me at half price.

I was rolling in it. I had my pocket money from Father, the proceeds of my raids on Mother's purse and my income from the playground. And I spent very little. I hoarded it all, the cash as well as the confectionery. I often had so many sweets in the barn I couldn't eat them by myself. In summer the chocolate melted under the old potato sacks, so I often took some to school and gave it to the other girls. This made me their best friend, and they vied with each other for the privilege of playing with me during break.

And I went on gambling with Magdalena's life. It was like the ladder superstition. You screw up the courage to walk under it and nothing happens, so you do it again and again. In the end you become convinced you're immune to bad luck. But you can't cheat fate like a mother who isn't right in the head. Sooner or later, when you're least expecting it, disaster strikes.

For a long time it looked as if I had no influence on Magdalena's condition. No matter what I did or didn't do, she remained equally well or unwell. It depended on your point of view. She had survived leukaemia. After five years, the doctors said, you were safe to assume a complete cure.

Because even the doctors called it a miracle, Mother naturally attributed her recovery to our prayers. But I didn't pray any more; I kneeled before the crucifix and thought up stories for Magdalena.

Once I told her I had a regular girlfriend. I was nearly thirteen and could easily have bought myself one. With eight hundred marks stashed away in the barn, I knew that Magdalena had been wrong in one respect: money can get you anything.

She found the girlfriend story exciting and asked me to describe her. She wanted to know every detail. How tall was she? Was she fat or thin? Was she pretty? Did we talk about boys? Had she ever been in love with one? Did I think I could get her to walk past our house? Then she could see her.

One afternoon we were in the bedroom Magdalena shared with Mother, which overlooked the street. She was sitting on her bed, while I kept watch beside the window. When a really pretty girl came down the street I helped Magdalena over to the window. Holding her tight with one arm, I tapped on the glass to attract the girl's attention. She looked up but shook her head. She probably thought we were daft.

I told Magdalena my friend knew how careful we had to be because of Mother – that was why she'd shaken her head. Magdalena believed every word of it.

Once, when I'd frittered away half the afternoon shopping, I told her my friend had invited me to come to the ice-cream parlour and stood me a strawberry sundae with whipped cream. She'd raved about some boy she was very much in love with but the boy himself was unaware of this.

The next day I told her we'd written the boy a letter, and my friend had asked me to slip it into his pocket. Lies, lies, all lies! There were times when it seemed to me that my life was one big lie.

8

Rudolf Grovian was gradually losing his temper, but not with her, with himself. Her aunt's warning – "She'll slam the door in your face" – flashed through his mind. Damnation, he'd tackled things the wrong way, but it ought to be possible to get his foot in the door again. He cast around in vain for the right tone to adopt. Any references to Margret Rosch only bolted the door more firmly.

When he asked how Margret had lied to him and what she'd stolen – he would "never guess what it was, even in his worst nightmare" – she said: "Do your own work. You're paid for it, I'm not."

He reverted to the crucial question: if Johnny existed, was he identical with Georg Frankenberg? She didn't answer, so he felt obliged to threaten her although it was the last thing he'd wanted to do. "In that case, Frau Bender, I suppose I'll have to speak to your father after all."

She smiled. "Why not try my mother? She knows everything. But make sure your knees are well padded."

She drank the last of her coffee, put the cup down with an air of finality and looked up at him. "That wraps it up, doesn't it? May I change before you hand me over to the examining magistrate? My clothes are all sweaty. I slept in them, and I wore them all yesterday. I'd also like to clean my teeth."

He felt infinitely sorry for her at that moment. She had always been dependent on herself. Why should she believe him, of all people, if he offered to help her? That apart, what help *could* he offer her? Several years behind bars. With as much neutrality as he could muster, he said: "Your things aren't here yet, Frau Bender. We asked your husband to bring them here, but he still hasn't appeared."

She shrugged her shoulders indifferently. "He won't either. I said Margret should do it."

Margret turned up half an hour later. In the interim he made three attempts to elicit some information about the other girl. Who was she? The first time he put the question calmly. "Ask my mother," she suggested. "But you're welcome to try my father as well. He's bound to be pleased if you tell him I was raped while another girl was beaten to death."

He asked a little more forcefully the second time. She turned to Werner Hoss. "Does your boss need a hearing aid, or is he just pig-headed? He's got a major problem – sounds like an old gramophone record with a crack in it."

The third time he sounded almost imploring. She glanced at the coffee machine. "Is that a reject from home?" she asked. "Can't the police afford a new one? They aren't all that expensive. There are some that boil the water properly; it makes the coffee taste much better. I bought one like that. I'll miss it, unless they let me have one in my cell. If they do I'll send for it. Then, when you visit me, you can also have a cup. You will visit me, won't you? We can spend a cosy afternoon drinking coffee and telling tall stories. Let's see who's better at it."

Grovian's patience was tested to the limit. He felt almost relieved when there was a knock at the door, and her aunt came in. Margret Rosch had packed a small suitcase. Werner Hoss took it from her and examined the contents. They didn't amount to much, just two nighties, her toilet articles, two blouses, two skirts, some underclothes, two pairs of tights, a pair of flat-heeled shoes and a framed photograph of her son.

It was a peaceful picture taken on a terrace. The little boy was crouching down with one hand resting on a green tractor, blinking at the sunlight and the camera.

She waved the photo away when Hoss put it with the rest of her things. Her face had stiffened, her voice was harsh and impersonal, and the look she gave her aunt would have graced an ice maiden. "Take that away," she said.

Margret Rosch, who had made such a resolute impression on Grovian in the small hours, was now looking helpless and somehow apprehensive. "But why? I thought you'd like to have a picture of him. I'm sure it's allowed, isn't it?" She gave Grovian an almost despairing glance. He merely nodded.

"I don't want it," said Cora. "Take it away."

Like a cowed child, her aunt took the snap from the heap of clothes and put it in her handbag.

"Did you bring the tablets?" Cora asked.

Margret Rosch nodded. She reached in her handbag and took out a small packet. Grovian thought he knew why he'd failed to get his foot in the door. "That's not possible," he said.

"But she needs them," Margret Rosch protested. "She often suffers from violent headaches – they're the result of a serious head injury. Surely she told you yesterday about that accident?" The stress on the last word was unmistakable.

Grovian took the packet from her. "I'll give them to the people in charge. If she needs them, she'll be given them. In the prescribed dosage."

Margret stepped forward as though about to embrace her niece.

"No, don't bother," Cora said almost casually. "Pretend I'm dead, that's the best plan. You won't need my corpse for that, will you? If you do need one, try the hospital morgue. There are always a few lying around in there."

To Grovian, that remark sounded plain spiteful. Her aunt reacted accordingly. She swallowed hard, lowered her arms and made for the door without a word of farewell. A moment later the door closed behind her. With a jerk of the head, Grovian signed to Hoss to leave the room as well. As soon as they were alone together he embarked on a final attempt.

"Well," he said, "now we can talk in private, Frau Bender. Let's do so like sensible adults. The lake didn't work, and neither will these tablets. Don't even think of trying anything else; I'll make sure you don't get the chance."

She remained impassive.

"A serious head injury," he said deliberately. "That's a pretty deep scar on your forehead – not just skin-deep, the skull was obviously fractured. I noticed it last night. Before you fainted you said something about a crystal paw and how cruel it was of your husband to smoke a cigarette beforehand because the ashtray started it all. So don't tell me you walked in front of a car."

She smirked at him. "I'm telling you nothing more. There should be some of the weekend left once I've said my piece to the magistrate. What does your wife say when you work overtime? Or don't you have a wife?"

"Yes, I do."

"Good." The smirk became a grin. "Then tuck her up in the car and take her for a nice outing when you've handed me over. Drive to the Otto Maigler Lido and better take Herr Hoss with you. He can show you an interesting spot. A man was killed there yesterday. Just imagine, the poor fellow was butchered simply because he was necking with his wife and listening to some music – butchered by some stupid cow who flipped because she didn't like the tune."

"Frau Bender," said Grovian, trying to sound authoritative, "spare me the comedy act. How did you get that scar?"

She stared at him, her uninjured eye like a hole in her face. He longed to know what was smouldering inside it, rage or panic. For a moment he felt he'd struck the right note. Then she tapped the right side of her head. "I've got a scar here too, an even bigger one, like to see it? You'll have to brush the hair aside, not that there's much to see. It's a good repair job."

"Who inflicted these injuries on you?"

She shrugged, and the grin stole back over her battered features. "I already told you. If you don't believe me, that's your problem. My head hit the bonnet, more I can't say. I was high when it happened. The doctor explained to you about my arms, and I'm sure my aunt also told you what my problem was. I used to shoot up."

She held out her left arm and pointed to the inside of the elbow. "I wasn't careful enough – I didn't sterilize my needles. The skin got badly inflamed. See? It's all pitted."

165

She ran her finger over the scar tissue. "I tried everything on offer," she went on. "Grass, coke and finally heroin." She laughed softly. "But don't worry, you haven't missed anything, I've been clean for years. Now will you show me where I can change?"

Although offhand, her voice had a harsh, hostile edge. He had no idea how a traumatized person felt, but the wall analogy struck him as appropriate. In her case he was managing to do what he never succeeded in doing with his daughter: remain calm, sympathetic and patient. He simply imagined that she was standing in front of her wall, defending all that lay hidden behind it with tooth and claw.

"Why didn't you tell us last night you were an addict?"

She gave another shrug. "Because I didn't think it was any of your business. It's a few years ago now, and it's quite irrelevant. My husband knows nothing about it. I hoped he would never find out. It was long before his time."

"Whose time was it, Georg Frankenberg's? Did he give you the stuff?"

She cast up her eyes at the ceiling. "Who are you investigating: me or him? What are you trying to pin on the poor devil? You want to brand him a criminal, is that it? Doesn't it fit your idea of the world that a woman can kill someone simply because she's annoyed by some loud music? Shall I tell you something? I really wanted to stab the woman. It was his bad luck to be lying on top."

Grovian smiled. "And to look, from where you were sitting, as if he were attacking her. You were afraid he would hit her. Did it remind you of what happened in the cellar?"

She didn't reply at once, just heaved a deep, weary sigh. Several seconds went by. Then she said curtly: "If you insist on sticking to that story, find out for yourself. Question a few more people. You're fond of asking questions. Why should I spoil your fun?"

So saying, she took a blouse, a skirt, a set of underclothes and her toothbrush from the desk. She didn't ask again for permission, just walked to the door with Grovian at her heels. Werner Hoss joined them in the passage, where Grovian tried once more.

"Frau Bender, it really doesn't pay to be so stubborn. If Georg Frankenberg —"

166

"Who's being stubborn?" she broke in. "Not me, for sure. I just don't like this probing of yours. You've seen what comes out: a load of filth! And I spun you such a pretty yarn. Romantic to begin with and pathetic at the end. A dead baby – dead babies are always pathetic, not dirty. The truth is dirty. The truth is riddled with worms and maggots; it turns black and stinks to high heaven. I don't like filth or foul smells."

"Nor do I, Frau Bender, but I like the truth, and in a case like this it would only be to your advantage to be frank with us."

She laughed mirthlessly. "Don't worry about my advantage, I can look after it myself. I always did, even as a child. I went astray quite early on. Someone like me goes right off the rails sooner or later. There's the truth for you. No one had to give me anything, least of all 'stuff'. Anything I wanted I took."

He stood outside in the passage, chaperoned by Hoss, while she was having a quick wash and changing her clothes – with the door open. As he listened to the unmistakable sounds he ran through the nocturnal dialogue between her and Margret Rosch again and again.

It got to the point where he felt he must be paranoid to detect a covert message in their harmless words and suspect her shocked and worried aunt of being a bringer of death. But, paranoid or not, he would have to take another good look at the contents of her little suitcase. He could have sworn that she had preserved her imperturbability only because Margret Rosch had brought her something more lethal than painkillers. Perhaps they had merely been a ploy to distract attention from a razor blade or something similar.

*

Her brain still resembled a block of ice, impossible to melt or chip away, no matter how hard the chief tried. The only warmth inside her was a searing pain behind the ribs. Margret shouldn't have brought that photo with her.

It had jolted her badly to see the boy again, looking so innocent

167

and carefree, but that had been her last backward glance. Lot's wife had promptly congealed into a pillar of salt. She was stiff inside, as stiff and cold as Mother had been when she sat on the bed with Magdalena and spoke of the sins the Lord had not forgiven.

But the boy was in good hands with his grandparents – she no longer thought of them as her parents-in-law – and sooner or later they could tell him his mother was dead. When they told him it would be the truth. The chief could take as many precautions as he liked; she knew what she had to do. She also knew how to do it! Margret also seemed to have known that opportunities in a prison cell were limited and that she must restrict herself to something outwardly natural and innocuous-looking. The authorities were bound to close the case after the death of the accused. Why should they go on rooting around in filth?

They drove to Brühl in silence, Werner Hoss at the wheel, the chief sitting beside her in the back. He seemed at last to have grasped that she would remain adamant whether he threatened, implored or even entreated her on his knees.

Her confrontation with the examining magistrate passed off surprisingly quickly. In a businesslike tone, the chief stated what she was charged with. She listened to it all with an impassive expression. The magistrate asked if she wished to say anything. She said she had already made a detailed statement and had no wish to keep on repeating herself. The magistrate advised her of her rights and formally remanded her in custody. Then it was over.

A minor shock awaited her when the chief re-examined her suitcase with the greatest care. He even felt the lining as if he suspected the presence of a couple of grains of sand and ended by confiscating the tights.

"Hey, what are you doing?" she protested. "You've no right to pinch my things."

"I've every right," he said. "Besides, it's too hot for tights. You aren't wearing any at the moment."

Then he left her alone. She had lunch in her cell. It wasn't bad. Compared to what her mother used to dish up, in fact, it was excellent.

So there she was. It was as if the past had been her life's true objective – as if she were having to recollect once more, with extreme clarity, what a bad person she'd been. Yet the memories she had broached hitherto were still comparatively innocuous.

She could hear a noise outside the door at brief, regular intervals. So the chief really had given instructions for her to be watched, but he was much mistaken if he imagined he could compel her to delve into the past. Resentment of him stiffened her resolve; and her head, still frozen, generated ideas as clear as glass. She waited for someone else to ask her some questions, but she didn't have to wait for long.

Around ten on Monday morning she was taken to be interviewed by the district attorney. A thoroughly amiable young man with a big sheaf of papers in front of him, he pointed out that her statement was worthless in its present form. He couldn't accept it until she told him the names of the two men concerned. Not those absurd nicknames, Billy-Goat and Tiger. He needed their real names – and, of course, the name of the girl. It would, he said, be in her own best interests to cooperate.

She almost laughed. Did this youngster imagine he knew what was in her best interests? "Didn't Herr Grovian tell you I retracted all that nonsense yesterday?" she asked.

He shook his head. She stared at him uncertainly. "Then what shall I tell the judge?" she asked, managing to sound resigned. "What do you advise?"

"Tell him the truth," he said.

She bowed her head, looking disconsolate. "But the truth amounts to so little," she said quietly. "I was furious with the woman."

The DA raised his eyebrows. "What had she done to infuriate you?"

"Nothing, really," she said in a low voice. "My husband thought she was hot stuff – he said she'd got some fire down below. I'd always done my best to satisfy him. Then along comes a tart like that, and his eyes are out on stalks. It wasn't the first time either. He used to leer at the talent whenever we went to the lido, and afterwards he'd often want to do things I didn't like and call me

169

a prude. I could well imagine what I was in for that night, and I'd had it up to here, understand? I wanted to teach one of those brazen bitches a lesson, but I couldn't get at her, so I thought . . ."

She looked over his shoulder at some indeterminate point. "I thought it didn't matter who I stabbed, her or the man. He was enjoying it too. They're all pretty much alike, those bastards."

The DA had had enough. He enquired about the stab wounds, which he said she'd inflicted "with precision". When she merely shrugged he asked how she'd sustained the injuries to her head. She repeated what she'd told the chief the last time: she was high on H and had walked in front of a car. The good Samaritan – the tipsy doctor who had driven into her – was a pure invention on her part. Her injuries had been treated at the district hospital in Dülmen.

Cora couldn't help smiling as she said this. She didn't even know if there was a district hospital in Dülmen. Manni Weber had been born and raised in Dülmen, and his grandmother still lived there. A year ago he'd asked her for a few days' unpaid leave. His grandmother had had a fall and was in the hospital with a fractured thigh. Exactly where, he hadn't said.

The DA didn't smile. "We'll check that," he said.

She thought he would at last get her to sign a confession, but no. The whole thing must be taken down again from scratch, he told her, and it would be better to wait until her statements had been verified. Her confession could then be signed and submitted to the examining magistrate.

Shortly after noon she was taken back to her cell. She spent half the afternoon wondering how to end things. Eventually she hit on the tissue idea. Although she didn't have any tissues, she felt sure they would give her some if she asked. Tissues were as innocuous as going for a swim. When they brought her supper she asked for some.

"Have you got a cold?" the wardress asked.

She nodded and sniffed a bit. "I'll bring you some in a minute," the woman said and moved on.

She ate a little. She was still feeling good – not hungry, but all right in other respects. Having pushed the tray aside, she kneeled in front of the bed and folded her hands.

It was the first time in ages, and she found she could do it only because there wasn't a crucifix there. It wasn't too hard to ask an invisible Saviour to forgive her for committing the ultimate sin. She saw the man's bloodstained face as she did so. Georg Frankenberg! And his expression . . . *He* had forgiven her, that was certain.

Something inside her was still firmly convinced that it had been right to kill him. Frankie, she thought. A gentle soul! Married three weeks as opposed to her three years. Three was a magic number, it suddenly struck her, but she didn't immediately grasp what was so remarkable about it. When it dawned on her . . .

There had been three crosses on Golgotha, and the two men who were crucified with the Saviour had deserved to die. The man in the middle had been guiltless.

It smote her like a red-hot iron, transfixed her between the shoulder blades, crept up her neck into her brain and began to melt the frozen mass. How could she have lost sight of that, even for a moment? The Saviour was utterly unblemished, purer and more innocent than any mortal man could be. She trembled convulsively for minutes on end. Her father seemed to be standing over her. "What have you done, Cora? What have you done?" And hovering above her father's head was the cross with its guiltless occupant.

She struggled to her feet at last and shuffled over to the washbasin. When the tray was collected soon afterwards she was still washing her hands, forgetful of the tissues she'd asked for. The wardress had forgotten them too.

*

Rudolf Grovian had spent some hours at the Otto Maigler Lido on Sunday afternoon. Not on her recommendation, nor had he driven there with his wife. By the time he got into his car Mechthild was on her way to Cologne. She had waited lunch for him, naturally hoping that he would come with her, but he baulked at the idea of spending a fruitless afternoon at their daughter's flat when he hadn't even inspected the scene of the crime.

Except that there was nothing to see apart from water and crowds of people. No question, either, of sitting in the sun and letting the atmosphere or surroundings work on him. Grovian was feeling depressed – wavering between his own belief and Werner Hoss's opinion that Johnny, Tiger and Billy-Goat had nothing to do with Georg Frankenberg.

He sat on the trampled grass, watching the half-naked people, young and old, men, women and children. An elderly couple strolled down to the water's edge hand in hand. The man must have been on the verge of retirement age, if not older. Grovian couldn't remember the last time he'd walked hand in hand with Mechthild. In the old days they'd often talked of all the things they planned to do when their daughter left home – weekend trips into the blue, a few days in the Black Forest or beside the North Sea – but nothing had come of them to date.

Not far away a man and a little boy were playing football. The boy, who wasn't much older than his grandson, kicked the ball maladroitly in his direction. He picked it up and threw it back. The youngster smiled at him, and it occurred to him that his grandson would soon have little to smile at. Or maybe he would!

It was likely that Marita and her young son would move in with them if her marriage were really on the rocks. A sobering thought, and one that temporarily overshadowed all else. Goodbye to domestic peace and tranquillity! He had no objection to a few building bricks on the living-room floor, no objection to childish laughter or tears, but his restful evenings on the sofa would be a thing of the past once his daughter was back home.

He pictured the way it used to be: the living-room table strewn with nail varnish, lipsticks, mascara and all the other stuff she daubed on her face. He had asked her innumerable times to apply her war paint in the bathroom, but no! The light was too poor, she said, and Mechthild backed her up. "Leave her alone, Rudi. *Must* we have the same fuss *every* evening?"

Barely an hour later he was sitting in his daughter's apartment,

172

determined to save whatever could be saved. His son-in-law wasn't there, and his attempts to intervene were cut short. "Stay out of it, Rudi, you've no idea what this is all about."

Mechthild, who was holding their grandson on her lap, kept saying: "Yes, but what are you going to —" She never got any further; Marita had it all worked out. She wouldn't hear of coming home, of swapping a spacious apartment for a room in her parents' house or life in the big city for their claustrophobic suburban ambience. The financial aspect presented no problems: Peter would have to pay up, naturally. Three thousand marks a month, Marita envisaged.

"There are smaller sums," said Grovian.

"And larger," said his daughter. "And with an income like his, at least he'll know what he's slaving away for." Thereafter she forgot he was there and talked exclusively to her mother. She spoke of gross neglect, of irreconcilable differences, of a man with nothing on his mind but bits and bytes, RAMs and ROMs, the Internet and other such nonsense – a man with whom you couldn't hold a sensible conversation, still less enjoy a night out on the town.

"But that's how it is when a man works for a living and wants to get on in his profession," Mechthild said feebly. "A wife has to grin and bear it sometimes. Still, she gets something out of life too."

Yes, said Marita: nappies, saucepans and, just for a change, the two-year-olds' playgroup twice a week. Grovian couldn't listen to it any more. He kept trying to draw comparisons, but there weren't any. His daughter and Cora Bender were like day and night, fire and water. One of them didn't need his advice – didn't even want to know what he thought. Keep out of this, Rudi . . . What was a man to do when such limits were constantly imposed on him in private? His only option was to bury himself in his work.

On Monday morning Grovian did precisely that. He had a longish discussion with the DA that evening, and by Tuesday he had assembled sufficient material to confront her with her lies once more and chip away at her wall.

It was late afternoon when he entered the cell. He saw her start at the sight of him and was just as startled himself. The last two days had transformed her into an apathetic creature, seemingly incapable of any reaction.

He began with the district hospital at Dülmen. That had only cost him a telephone call and a few minutes' waiting around on the line.

He had spoken with Georg Frankenberg's father the afternoon before. He couldn't get through to Ute Frankenberg, who was still unfit to be interviewed, but it was doubtful if she could tell him much in any case, having met her husband for the first time only six months before their marriage.

"And I hardly think," he said with a faint smile, "that he would have discussed his previous affairs with her."

In his head he could hear the DA's voice: "I respect your commitment, Herr Grovian, but I must urge you not to investigate so one-sidedly. Let us assume that the woman really didn't know her victim."

But she *must* have known him! In the past two days, Grovian had compiled a few details that indicated as much. To call them evidence would be an overstatement. Facts would be a better description, and one of those facts was the body of a young woman.

There really was one – with two broken ribs! No missing persons report had been filed in Buchholz at the time in question, but then, Cora had stated that she'd never seen the girl there before. The missing persons report could be anywhere. Only the authorities at Lüneburg had documents relating to an unknown female aged fifteen to twenty at most.

Her skeletonized body had been found near a military training area on Lüneburg Heath, cause of death unascertainable. No head injury, larynx and hyoid bone intact. In the police pathologist's opinion, the ribs could have been broken after death, possibly by animals – a frequent occurrence.

The corpse must have been lying in the open for at least three months. Naked! No articles of clothing had been found at the scene, nor had anything else that might have facilitated identification. Appeals for information were published, but to no avail. The local police assumed that the girl had been a hitch-hiker.

174

Given that Cora Bender and her helpful aunt had lied through their teeth, however, it was quite conceivable that she was the girl from the cellar. It didn't take much imagination to see that, just some intuition, a little knowledge of human nature and an ability to memorize casual remarks and assign them due importance at the crucial moment.

Provided, of course, that Cora had been persuaded to go for a drive with Johnny and his fat friend back in May, not in August. That would fit. It was strange how she and her aunt had harped on about August.

Grovian intended to consult the CID's central records office and check all the missing persons reports for the time in question. A name would have made things considerably easier.

He had, in fact, elicited two names from Winfried Meilhofer on Monday morning: Ottmar Denner and Hans Böckel.

"Do they mean anything to you, Frau Bender?"

She shook her head. He continued to smile, just smile and be friendly and speculate on why she and her aunt should both have cited August as the source of her troubles. Why? Because they knew that the body had been discovered, he would have bet on it! Because they didn't want to be associated with it – because they dreaded what might happen if such a connection were established.

"They do to me," Grovian said. "I think Hans Böckel and Ottmar Denner are Billy-Goat and Tiger respectively. Denner was the group's composer, I'm told, and composers like to immortalize themselves. One of the numbers on that tape was called 'Tiger's Song'. Remember? You described it as your tune."

The DA had poured scorn on his theory. Billy-Goat and Tiger? As fictitious as the district hospital at Dülmen! She merely shook her head again, but he pressed on regardless: "I also find it interesting that Ottmar Denner came from Bonn. He studied at Cologne University with Georg Frankenberg and lived at home while there. At that time he drove a silver VW Golf GTI with – logically enough – a BN licence plate. We're currently trying to discover his whereabouts, but it isn't easy. It appears he may have gone abroad – a development aid job."

He had interviewed Ottmar Denner's parents only a few hours ago. And got nowhere. They claimed not to know where their son was at present. Ghana, Sudan, Chad – somewhere or other. His request for a photograph had also been rejected. Why did he need one? What was Ottmar charged with, if anything? The father had been a fat, forceful little man who knew his rights and those of his son.

Grovian had envisaged laying out five or six photographs on the desk and asking her to pick out Johnny's fat friend. No such luck! However, as things stood she would probably have shaken her head at a photo as well.

They still hadn't discovered anything about Hans Böckel. Grovian assumed that Böckel was the one from north Germany, but if he'd ever had any connection with a house in Hamburg, there were no reports of it. Nor could he have been a fellow student of Georg Frankenberg. There was no such name on the university roll.

Instead, there was a statement from Frankenberg's father. Grovian had been unable to interview his mother – she was still too traumatized – and Professor Johannes Frankenberg denied all knowledge of the names Denner and Böckel. His son's flirtation with music had been just a brief episode, a craze that had lasted only a few weeks. Georg had soon realized that his time was too precious to waste on playing around.

And in May five years ago Georg Frankenberg had been at home in his father's private clinic, recovering from a fractured arm. The clinic's records stated that he had broken it on 16 May. Precisely the day on which Cora Bender – according to her original version, which fitted the discovery of the body so neatly – had yearned to make his acquaintance at a disco in Buchholz.

According to his father, Georg Frankenberg had come home for the weekend on Friday night and suffered a bad fall on Saturday morning. Fortunately, it was a simple fracture, and his father's clinic was only a few yards away. It hadn't even been necessary to call in another doctor.

Professor Frankenberg's statement had sufficed to convince the DA that Cora Bender's retraction was simply a belated adherence to the truth. It didn't convince Grovian. The timing of the broken arm had galvanized him. Records could be doctored if you headed your own clinic and knew that your son was in trouble. May 16, of all days! Another date mightn't have aroused his suspicions, but . . .

"Professor Frankenberg is a respectable man," he told Cora. "He won't be too easy to discredit. We can only hope that Ottmar Denner and Hans Böckel will confirm your story if we locate them."

*

Till then she had merely listened, wishing he would go to blazes but secretly admiring his obstinacy. He shrank from nothing, not even from harassing the father of her victim.

She'd panicked when he mentioned the silver Golf GTI, but she soon recovered her poise. It had to be a coincidence that Johnny's friend had driven the same car as a friend of Georg Frankenberg. It was a typical young man's car, after all. Meantime, the chief was watching her intently.

"Nobody can confirm anything," she said. "I told you a pack of lies."

Grovian hadn't heard her voice for two days. In front of the magistrate it had sounded resolute and hostile, cold and indifferent. Now, her harsh, unemotional tone and hunched, introverted pose counselled caution.

He shook his head emphatically. "No, no, Frau Bender, lies don't deposit dead bodies on the edge of a military training area. I've found the girl who was in the cellar with you. A dead girl with two broken ribs, Frau Bender, and you heard them snap."

He'd saved that till last, intending it as a bolt from the blue in the event of her not admitting anything, but perhaps it was just a damp squib. If she really hadn't made that trip until August, the dead body was irrelevant. But her reaction conveyed that it was a skyrocket rather than a damp squib. She came to life from one moment to the next, and he saw her bosom heave before she spoke.

177

"Don't talk nonsense! Use your head, man! I can't have heard a thing in all that noise – *if* it had been the way I said. It wasn't, but let's assume it was. There'd have been five people down there and deafening music. I don't know what a snapping rib sounds like, but it can't be as loud as all that."

Her hands started to shake. She clasped the left with the right. He remembered that from three nights ago. It was the preliminary alarm signal. Or, as prior experience of her prompted him to regard it, the precursor of a truth she was unwilling to face. Reason bade him pay the closest attention, but, at the same time, raised an admonitory finger: "Stop it, Rudi. Leave it to the shrinks."

"You're a . . ." she said hoarsely. Either the appropriate term eluded her, or she considered it too coarse. Instead, she asked: "Do you think it's right, what you're doing? Some nerve, bullying his father like that! The poor man must be finding it hard enough as it is. Does he have any more children?"

He shook his head, watching her series of changing expressions, the rubbing and kneading of her hands. Her voice broke, and her shoulders sagged, her head too.

"Then you must leave him alone. What's done is done. It won't do anyone any good to discover that a girl died. All right, a girl did die, but it had nothing to do with me. I only have the man on my conscience."

A chill ran down his spine when she raised her head and gazed into his eyes. There was something about the look on her face. It took him a second or two to identify it, and he did so only because her words confirmed his impression. Insanity!

"An innocent man," she said, "and he won't rise again on the third day. He'll turn black, get eaten by worms and rot away. If you insist on harassing his father, tell him to cremate him. Will you do that? You must, and you must promise me something. I don't want to be cremated if I die, so make sure I'm not. I want an unmarked grave. You can bury me on the edge of a restricted area, like the girl. Just lay me down beside her."

Restricted area, thought Grovian. He hadn't described it as such, but he didn't pursue the matter. Her expression was still giving him the shivers. It couldn't be true, surely! She'd been in full command of her senses at lunchtime on Sunday. Agitated, temporarily bewildered by the gravity of her act and firmly resolved to take the consequences, yes, but not insane. That she should have lost her reason within two days . . . No, that was impossible. She was merely exhausted.

He changed the subject to her son, hoping that it would arouse her fighting spirit. Only two years old! Didn't she share his opinion that so young a child needed his mother?

"Who needs the plague?" she retorted.

"No one," he said, "just as no one needs worms or wolf's or tiger's penises in them. I'm sorry, Frau Bender, I'd hoped we could talk like normal people. If you either can't or won't, I understand. In any case, I'm probably not the right person to solve your problems. There are experts for that. I expect you'll be seeing one in the next few days."

"What do you mean?" she demanded. "I want nothing to do with experts," she went on fiercely before he could reply. "Don't dare let a psychiatrist loose on me! I'll tell you something: if anyone like that shows up here . . ."

She refrained from saying what would happen then. Breaking off in mid sentence, she wiped her brow on the back of her hand and smiled suddenly. "But why am I getting so worked up? I don't have to talk to anyone, least of all a shrink. Listen, you can send along a dozen shrinks if you like, but make sure they bring a pack of cards with them. They'll get bored otherwise."

Her outburst had a liberating effect on him. As amiably as ever, he enquired whether she would sooner talk to a woman than a man. If so, he might be able to arrange it. She didn't reply.

He rose and made for the door, meaning to take his leave. "I can't prevent a psychologist being called in. It's the DA's ruling, and I think he's right."

That broke the ice at last.

"You think!" she snarled, barring his path. "You think anything goes! First you try to pressure me with my family and now with your blasted expert. Do you imagine he'll get more out of me than you? I know what you want to hear. All right, you can have it. Let's save the government a few marks. Experts need paying, and they certainly earn more an hour than heating engineers. I don't want anyone accusing me of wasting taxpayers' money."

"You don't have to tell me anything, Frau Bender."

She stamped her foot. "But now I want to, damn it! Now I want to, and you'll listen. Want to take it down, or can you remember it? Frankie's father didn't lie to you. I didn't get to know Frankie in May; it was later. It may have been in August, I don't recall exactly. I was dopey – I'd been on the needle for quite a while – so I didn't know whether it was Christmas or Ramadan."

She sniffed and dabbed her eyes with her fingertips. "Would you have a packet of tissues for me? I asked for some, but they forgot. Perhaps they expected me to pay, and I don't have any money on me."

He felt in his pockets, found an opened packet and handed it to her. She removed a tissue, dabbed her eyes briefly and carefully replaced it with the others, smiling at him. "Thanks. And forgive me for flying off the handle just now, I didn't mean to. Oh, what the hell, of course I did. It's a rotten feeling when you don't even have the right to leave your own dirt under the carpet. There's a whole heap of it, I'd better tell you right away."

He smiled too. "I'm sure I've seen bigger ones."

She shrugged. "Maybe, but I haven't." Then she squared her shoulders. "Well," she said, "it was probably in August. I said May at first because I was ashamed. I got involved with him the very first night and clung to him like a limpet. He had stuff, and he had enough money to keep me regularly supplied with it – I didn't have to worry about that any more. In return he insisted I go to bed with him. That was okay – I did it of my own free will – but after a few weeks he wanted me to do it with his friends as well."

She laughed bitterly. "And I did. I did anything he asked. He wanted to watch with that girl. I don't know her name, honestly I don't, but it isn't important. She was some stupid cow he'd brought from home. He didn't do anything to her – he certainly didn't hit her. I wished he would, that's all. He was stuck on her and wanted

180

to show her what a hell of a fellow he was – that he could do anything he liked with me."

"Was that in August too?"

She shook her head. "No, in October."

"Where were you at that time? You weren't at home."

Another shake of the head. "It varied. Hamburg or Bremen. I slept rough mostly, but sometimes he'd give me money for a room. He used to come at weekends, and we'd drive around. And once we went to that fabulous house. That was the night it happened."

"What exactly did happen?" He didn't know whether to believe her. Her tone was calm and composed, with an undertone of resignation. It sounded like the truth.

"I was pregnant by him. He said if I did what he wanted, he would arrange for a good doctor to sort it out. I cried a bit, but I knew there wasn't much point. So I gave in."

She gave another laugh, though it was more of a sob. Her eyes roamed the cell like hunted beasts, and she drew a hand nervously across her brow. "Can you imagine how I felt? I lay on the floor with those two fellows mounting me in turn, and that bitch sat beside him on the sofa and told me to do it again with both of them at the same time . . ." She gagged, and it was several seconds before she could continue. "She said: 'Don't be a spoilsport, sweetie.' And then she told one of them: 'Give her a shot, it'll relax her.'"

She shuddered. Her eyes found their way to his face at last, and her voice sounded firm and controlled once more. "They held me down and pumped me full of stuff. I thought they were going to kill me, so I struggled and they punched and kicked me in the head and stomach. Then I suddenly started to bleed. They must have panicked, I suppose, because they all pushed off and left me lying there. I made it to the street somehow, and that was when I ran in front of the car. The man who drove into me was a doctor – that was my one stroke of luck. He saw I was having a miscarriage, and he also saw I was drugged to the eyeballs. But that's enough. Next you'll be asking me his name again, and that I'll never tell you."

"Why not, Frau Bender? The man hasn't committed a criminal offence. As things stand, he seems to be the only person able to confirm your story."

She stared past him at the wall. "He certainly wouldn't," she muttered. "He'd swear he'd never seen me before."

"Why should he do that?"

"Because he was a scumbag. He felt me up while I was still in a daze – I thought he only wanted to examine me. I woke up one night to find him masturbating beside my bed, and he'd pawed me before that. Anything else you'd like to know?"

He saw her hand tighten on the packet of tissues. Her eyes flashed. "He was a lecherous old goat," she blurted out. "The whole room reeked of sweat when he came in. I tell you, if I ever had to set eyes on that bastard again, and I would if I told you his name, I'd stab him the way I stabbed Frankie even if the courtroom were packed with policemen – no one could stop me. And now, leave me alone."

She turned away, propped her arm against the wall and buried her face in it, weeping. It was the first time Grovian had seen her cry. An instinctive desire to do or say something consoling prompted him to lay a hand on her shoulder. She shook it off.

"Just go away. You can't imagine what happens when I talk to you. It all comes back to me – it all comes alive again. I can't stand it. Go away, get lost. And leave my father alone. He's an old man, he's sick, he's . . . He never did anything to me. He still had natural urges at his age, he couldn't help it. It was all my fault."

9

It was the sweets. It had never occurred to me, when I was gorging myself on them, that they were bound to have an effect. When I was thirteen it became obvious: I'd put on weight. Puppy fat, said Margret, and teased me about it whenever she came to stay. I tried to give them up, not wanting to be fat, but it wasn't easy because I couldn't stop stealing.

The money I pinched steadily accumulated. I used to sit in the barn and count it sometimes. Then I imagined running away with it, far away. When I'd amassed 1,278 marks – I still remember the exact sum – I took eight marks in small change to the station and enquired about the price of a ticket to Hamburg. "I don't want to buy one now," I said. "I'd just like to know."

"Single or return?" asked the man behind the counter.

"Single," I said. "I'm never coming back. And can you tell me how much it costs to travel on a ship?"

He laughed. "Depends where you want to go. Flying is quicker, but you have to pay for every pound of excess weight."

Excess weight, I thought as I walked away from the counter. I took the eight marks to the ice-cream parlour and wolfed down a big strawberry sundae topped with whipped cream. Afterwards I went into the ladies' and stuck a finger down my throat. From then on I did that every time I ate something sweet.

Magdalena said I had to stop. "It's an illness," she told me. "Girls have died of it before now. Spend the money on other things." She thought it was only the pocket money I got from Father. "Like smart clothes," she said. "You can hide those in the barn too, then you can get changed before you go out and come in. You'll see. Once you've got something smart to wear, you'll like yourself again."

I couldn't imagine that clothes would change anything. I was far too fat, thought I was ugly, and I still wet the bed. Not every night but often, even though I'd stopped dreaming about the wolf long ago. I simply failed to wake up when I needed to go.

As a rule, I didn't notice that everything was wet again until Father came to check. He often got up two or three times a night, and the first thing he did was to slip his hand under the bedclothes.

It sometimes puzzled me that he was so patient, that he never got angry or uttered a word about it. My bed stank – our whole room stank – because my mattress got wet so often and never dried out properly. In summer I used to prop it up in front of the window. Then I bought myself a rubber sheet.

I was growing up. Only outwardly but unmistakably. I developed a bosom and hair in my armpits. Down below too. I felt embarrassed when Father came to bed at the same time, not that he noticed. When I went into the bathroom to get undressed he would follow me in because he wanted to tell me something. Like what had happened at work or in the car on the way there. He couldn't talk about such things to Mother, so he discussed them all with me. I thought that was great, but I didn't like him watching me get undressed.

Then I got my periods. I didn't know much about what was happening to me, although I'd naturally been acquainted with the facts of life in school. The purely biological aspect, how you got pregnant and so on. Margret had also spoken to me about it. In general, though, she'd only made sure my first period wouldn't catch me unprepared.

By the time Margret broached the subject, however, I'd long ago learned what I was in for. Mother had briefed me thoroughly. She told me that I must be careful not to open the gates of hell to any man, and that I'd soon be afflicted with the curse of Eve.

It was a curse too. I got terrible stomach cramps when the bleeding started. I was nervous for days in advance. I could sense it coming and felt like hiding in a corner, but I had to go to school.

And I was reluctant to ask to be excused games for fear of attracting attention.

I asked Grit Adigar what to do when we had swimming. Swimming and games in the gym were always on alternate weeks, and I couldn't go into the pool wearing a sanitary towel. Grit suggested I use tampons and explained what you did with them. I found it disgusting, but I took her advice. Afterwards I washed my hands in hot water until they were all red and swollen.

The other girls in my class were thrilled by the whole thing. They thought themselves grown-up and bragged about it, even when boys were around. "I've just got my period," they would say. The boys seemed to find it a turn-on.

Then came the magazine episode. I'd seen a girl reading it in the playground: *Bravo, the Magazine for Young People*. I had to have it at once, of course. I hid it in the barn and dipped into it that afternoon while Magdalena was having her rest. There were lots of articles that interested me – pieces on music, singers and rock groups, movie stars and how to apply make-up. There were also letters from teenagers asking for advice.

One of them was from a girl only a year older than myself, but she already had a boyfriend with a room of his own, where they could spend time alone together. Whenever he put his hand inside her panties, his penis went stiff and she became wet between the legs. The girl wanted to know if this was all right. She felt ashamed of this wetness, but her boyfriend thought it was great. He was a bit older than her. Seventeen, I think.

The reply to the letter stated that getting wet between the legs was quite normal – inevitable, in fact. To a man, the wetness signified that a woman was sexually aroused and ready for sexual intercourse.

My God, how ashamed I felt! I wondered what Father must think of me. Did he think I was trying to turn him on? I felt quite sick. All at once, everything had changed. My world had turned upside down.

I had to go outside the moment Father came home that evening. I couldn't bear to sit in the kitchen with him. As soon as he walked in I felt my cheeks burn. He noticed that something was the matter with me. So did Magdalena. Father drove off again after supper, and Mother retired to the living room. I did the washing up. Magdalena, who remained in the kitchen with me, asked what was wrong. "You went as red as a tomato," she said.

I told her about the letter. Only that, to begin with. She assumed I had a boyfriend and pressed me to tell her more – every detail of what we'd so far done together.

"No boy has ever touched me like that," I told her, "and no one will ever do it again."

"What do you mean, again?" she asked. "That means someone already has! Come on, Cora, don't be shy. Tell me!"

I didn't want to, but she went on pestering me until I gave in. She listened attentively. Then, when I'd finished, she said: "Show me exactly how he touched you."

When I showed her she laughed at me. "That doesn't count! You've no need to get worked up about *that*. He was only checking to see if you'd wet the bed. That's nothing – after all, he's your father. It's the same as if Mother or a doctor touched you. Think how often Mother messes around with me down there when she's giving me an enema or a bed bath. That would make her a lesbian! As for the doctors, you can't imagine. They don't wait till I need to pee to take a urine sample, they simply stick a catheter into me. No, believe me, Father hasn't done anything bad. Being abused is quite different."

She knew this from a young woman she'd shared a room with at the hospital one time. The woman had been a prostitute. She had also done drugs and drunk heavily, so her liver was shot. Her father was to blame, she told Magdalena. He had raped her even before she went to school. At first with his finger and then properly.

"Father hasn't done that, has he?" Magdalena asked.

I shook my head.

"You see?" she said. "You've really no need to worry. Ask Margret if you don't believe me."

I was loath to do that. If Father hadn't done anything bad, why should I ask Margret? The fact that I thought he had – that was my problem. Besides, I told myself, Father was an old man. Far too old to do anything like that. How wrong I was!

*

Those were the true sins, the desires of the flesh. It wasn't about coveting a slice of roast beef. It was about an old man who couldn't control his physical urges – who had exposed himself to me, as Mother would have put it, at a time when I still didn't know there were two kinds of human beings. And then, when I did know perfectly well, it happened again.

In April, three weeks before I turned fourteen, I woke up in the middle of the night needing to go to the bathroom. At first I was simply happy not to have done it in the bed. I made for the bathroom in the dark, not noticing that Father wasn't in his bed. Once there I turned on the light, and there he was, standing at the washbasin with his pyjama trousers around his ankles. He'd also pulled his underpants down and was gripping his penis. His hand was moving up and down. I knew what he was doing. The boys at school called it jerking off.

I thought it a vulgar expression for a repulsive activity, and it was appalling that my father should be doing it after I'd decided to write him off as a harmless old man. Still more appalling was the fact that I couldn't help watching him. Worst of all, he must have known I was there – I'd opened the door and turned on the light, after all – but he carried on regardless. It was disgusting, what with the look on his face and the noises he was making.

Suddenly he spun round. "Go back to bed!" he yelled. "What do you think you're doing, sneaking in here like a ghost?"

"I need to go!" I shouted back.

"Piss in the bed, then," he yelled. "It's what you usually do."

He shouted so loudly, he couldn't have failed to wake Mother and Magdalena, but he didn't care. I thought it was mean of him to broadcast my shame at the top of his voice. I couldn't help wetting the bed – he'd always said I couldn't. "They're the tears of the

187

soul," he used to say, and afterwards he would go to the bathroom. Perhaps for the same reason he'd gone that night.

I went back into the bedroom and threw myself down on the bed. I'd forgotten I needed to go. Father came in a few minutes later. He sat down beside me and stroked my hair. He'd washed his hands – I could smell the soap.

He stared at me as if he meant to hit me. Instead, he started crying. "I'm sorry," he blurted out, sobbing like a three-year-old with a grazed knee. I found that almost more revolting than the other thing. Once he'd calmed down, he said: "I hope you'll understand when you're older. Human nature is too strong. What am I supposed to do? There are women who do it for money, but that's just a business. When I do it by myself I can at least imagine there's someone there who loves me. Everyone needs to feel loved, even an oldster like me."

"I loved you once," I said, on the verge of crying too.

Mother and Magdalena had been woken by the din, as I'd feared. Mother gave me some funny looks at breakfast the next morning, but she didn't ask what the matter was. Magdalena wanted to know when I came home from school at lunchtime. She kept badgering me every time Mother left the kitchen. "Come on, tell! What did he do? Did he stick his finger up you after all, or did he go the whole hog?"

I shook my head. I didn't want to tell her what had really happened, nor did I need to. Magdalena could guess what I'd seen. She'd known for a long time why he sneaked into the bathroom at night. Why? Because he'd often knocked on their door and warned Mother he was going to do like the man in the Bible who spilled his seed on the ground. Could she reconcile it with her conscience that he had to keep on sinning this way?

Magdalena found it funny. "He's still pretty randy, our old man, but lots of them are at his age. The old ones tend to be the worst of all, take it from me, especially when they can't perform the way they'd like to. Did you really see exactly how he did it?"

I couldn't talk about it. I was in a complete turmoil for days. As for the nights! Father came home very late for the next week or so.

188

I was already in bed, as a rule, but I couldn't sleep. Sometimes I thought I ought to say something nice when he finally did appear. Like telling him I still loved him. I'd lied to him so often about other things, it wouldn't have mattered.

But when I heard him coming up the stairs and turning the handle I felt my stomach go as cold and stiff as the stone that seemed to be constricting my chest, and I couldn't breathe, couldn't utter a word. I pretended to be asleep and listened to his movements, trying to gauge whether he was getting up again, coming over to me or going to the bathroom.

I wished things could be the way they were in the old days, when I'd even slept in his bed – when he was simply my father, nothing more. He had suddenly ceased to be that. Now he was just a dirty old man who jerked off. The boys in school said you had to think of naked women while doing so. I grasped what Father had been thinking of three weeks later.

We were having lunch on Sunday when he suddenly said to Mother: "I'm switching bedrooms. This present set-up won't do."

Mother disagreed, of course. "Why get so worked up after all these years?" he yelled at her. "Surely you don't imagine I could still be tempted by your shrivelled flesh? Don't worry, I prefer juicier meat, and I'd like some within arm's reach of me every night. I don't want to be the one that sacrifices our second lamb, but if things go on like this, I can't guarantee I won't. And don't quote Magdalena at me. You'd be powerless to help her in a real emergency, however near to her you slept."

He had to sleep in my room once more that night. Mother took Magdalena up to bed a little earlier than usual and locked the bedroom door from the inside. The next day Father confiscated the key and carried his bedclothes across.

Magdalena moved in with me. This soured the atmosphere for weeks until Mother finally grasped that her chastity wasn't in danger and that Magdalena and I were getting on together. It's true I was anxious for the first few nights, not being used to Magdalena's funny breathing, but she laughed at me. "I always breathe like this," she said. "It's just that you don't notice it during the day."

After a few weeks I thought it was great, having her in my room. She did too. I usually took her upstairs after supper. She preferred me to help her rather than Mother. I couldn't carry her – it was a long time since even Mother had been able to do that – but she could walk very slowly if well supported. She could even manage the stairs as long as she took a breather after every step.

I used to hang onto her while she was brushing her teeth, a thing she preferred to do on her own. Then I had to wash her. She couldn't have a bath in the bathtub any longer. Mother used to sit her in it and lift her out. When she got too big, Father bought her a chair with a hole in the seat and a pail underneath. That worked all right. You only had to wipe the bath out afterwards.

I was pretty clumsy at first. I washed her the way I washed myself, but her skin was very sensitive from lying down so much, unlike mine. The rough flannel hurt her.

"Use your hands instead," she said. "Then take the sponge and rinse off the soap. And only dab me with the towel, don't rub. Mother never understood that. Maybe she thought if she scratched me when she washed me, I'd at least be making some contribution to the family's penance."

After washing her I applied some ointment to prevent bedsores, then pulled her nightie over her head and put her to bed. After that, if there was nothing more to be done in the kitchen, I used to stay with her. We always had a lot to tell each other before going to sleep.

I could talk in a different way once we were in bed with the door shut. Magdalena was the only person I could talk to really frankly about everything. Not about stealing, but about how disgusted I was with Father and myself and the fact that I never wanted a boyfriend.

Although Magdalena was a year younger than me, she took a different view of such matters. "Just you wait," she told me. "Once you've lost a few pounds your self-loathing will disappear of its own accord. As for the other thing, there's no comparison. Old men disgust me too. Why do you think I won't let Father touch me? Being messed around by him is the last thing I need. I'm sure

190

he'd sit me in the bathtub and lift me out if you asked him to, but no thanks. It's quite different with a young man. I've noticed that with the doctors. There's a big difference in the way they look and the touch of their hands. I like the students best of all. They often come crowding around me. To them I'm a sight to be seen, a medical miracle. I'm the half-heart with the inoperable aortic aneurysm, the survivor contrary to all expectations. Who knows, perhaps the thing in my stomach took over the heart's function long ago."

She laughed softly. "The youngsters stand there without a clue about how to use their stethoscopes. The poor fellows aren't allowed to do much more than that, just listen to what a balloon full of holes sounds like."

Magdalena wished she could have a boyfriend herself later on, when she was fifteen or sixteen. Or preferably right away, because she didn't believe she would live that long.

*

She took nearly an hour to calm down after the chief had gone. She didn't understand how she could have let herself be drawn into spinning him such a yarn, not when she already had the tissues in her hand. Having sex with two men at once! She supposed she must have done that during the darkest chapter of her life. Something of the sort had flashed through her mind.

And then she'd had a vision of her father with his trousers down and a look of diabolical fury on his face. She'd almost blurted that out too and only just stopped herself by making the doctor a scapegoat.

It was unpardonable of her. That man had saved her life and asked for nothing in return. A kindly, friendly person, he had never touched her in the way she'd described to the chief. He hadn't been a dirty old man, just a man in a white coat who had made the minor mistake of getting into his car while slightly over the limit.

He'd been in his early fifties at most, with a thin face and a dark, neatly trimmed beard and moustache. He usually appeared at her

191

bedside holding a syringe. His hands were slender and very well manicured, and his voice was warm and gentle. "How are you feeling? You'll be asleep in no time."

Her forearms were a mass of suppurating sores. There was a cannula inserted in the back of her hand. When he emptied the hypo into it, darkness promptly descended and oblivion claimed her. The pains in her head were unbearable. They hammered and drilled and stabbed away as if the bandage around her head were a vice.

Her skull had been fractured in several places, the doctor told her later, when she'd recovered sufficiently to question him. As for her other injuries, they could not have been caused by such a minor impact. He hadn't been driving fast, had braked at once and merely brushed her with the radiator grille when she staggered out in front of his car. Three weeks ago, when she appeared out of the darkness on the edge of a country road.

Unconscious for three whole weeks?

"Think yourself lucky," he said. "You've slept through the worst of it. Withdrawal symptoms are a terrible thing. Your whole body rebels, your nerves go haywire. But you were unaware of it."

He asked her name. She hadn't been carrying any papers, he said. He also asked if she knew what had happened to her. She didn't. It had all gone, and not only the three weeks he was talking about. Over five months had been obliterated.

The last thing she remembered was a Saturday in the second week of May. Magdalena's birthday! A bottle of champagne! Bought – not stolen – in honour of the occasion. Hidden for three days under the old sacks in the barn and brought out when Mother and Father had left the house to spend another evening in the company of those despairing souls who clung to heaven because they couldn't stand on earth unsupported.

The fizz was warm when she brought it into the house. She put the bottle in the fridge and left it there until just before eight. That was when Magdalena wanted to toast her new year of life. "I'm sure a sip won't do me any harm," she said. "Maybe it'll help me to make it through the year."

No one believed that except Magdalena and her. She firmly believed it too, of course, but not the doctors at Eppendorf – as usual. Magdalena had been to the hospital again in April. She'd had to spend considerably longer there than the scheduled two days, but she wouldn't say why.

"I pay no attention to the crap they dish out. If they were right, I'd have died long ago. They don't have a clue. As far as I'm concerned, they can shove my heart and my abdominal aorta up their backsides. And my kidneys too. All I need is willpower. That's it, Cora! You have to want to go on living, then you will. I've proved that for the last eighteen years. What's more, I'll show them that an operation is possible. How much money do we have?"

Magdalena knew she'd been born at eight on the dot.

"Will you stay with me till then?"

"I'll stay with you all evening. Surely you don't think I'd go out on your birthday?"

"But I'd like you to. One of us must celebrate at least. Next year we'll both have a proper celebration. We'll throw a party that'll make the neighbours' teeth rattle. Tonight you'll have to go out on your own again. I'll be happy if you're back by eleven. We'll save some fizz for then, and you can tell me how you got on. Will you be seeing Horst?"

"No, I told him last week I couldn't come. He said it didn't matter. His father had already asked him a couple of times to fix the car. He could do it then, he said."

"What a shame. Still, he may be there all the same – it can't take all night to fix a car. And if he doesn't make it, have a good time with someone else. A bit of a change can't hurt. Promise me you'll have fun with some gorgeous young man, and then come home. And then . . ."

That had been on 16 May, and suddenly it was October! The doctor didn't know what had happened in the interim. He smiled at her while she experimentally moved her fingers and toes, arms and legs. "You're bound to remember in due course. Give your head a little time to recover. And even if you don't remember, I don't think you'll have missed much."

"I must go home," she said.

"It'll be a little while before we can think of that." He lifted her left foot and pricked the heel with a pin. "Excellent," he said when she winced. "Now get some sleep. You still need a lot of rest."

He never said much during his visits. Her only other visitor was a nurse, a surly creature of her own age who never spoke or did anything unless it was absolutely necessary. She brought Cora's meals, plumped up her pillows, smoothed her sheets and washed her. The doctor made her do exercises to prevent her limbs from stiffening up after so long in bed. He also made her do sums and recite poems from school to discover whether her brain had been affected by her heroin intake and the physical punishment she'd sustained. He inserted needles into the cannula in the back of her hand, applied ointment to her inflamed forearms and changed the bottle under her bed, which was connected to a catheter.

She thought of Magdalena, who needed her. She had to go home as soon as possible. Magdalena was eager to show the doctors at Eppendorf what could be done. She wanted to have an operation in the United States if there were enough money for the flight and the hospital. There was far from enough. A vast sum was still needed, and she would have to get it somehow. That was her last thought before the injection took effect.

There was no day or night in her little room. There were no windows, just a dim wall light. It was on whenever she opened her eyes, and whenever the doctor came she tried to find out more. But he knew very little.

"I don't think it was an accident," he said on one occasion. "The circumstances rule that out: a naked young woman without any identification, pumped full of heroin." He spoke of serious lesions in the vaginal area and elsewhere. Typical of certain sexual practices, they allowed for only one conclusion.

He had formed a definite picture of Cora: she was a drug-addicted prostitute. Easy meat for a pervert, a sadist who enjoyed inflicting pain and had dumped his unconscious victim beside the road, possibly in the belief that he had killed her.

"I ought to have notified the police," he said, "but I was afraid of losing my licence. And then I thought that you yourself should decide as soon as you were able. The police would be bound to judge by outward appearances, and you might as well have worn a placard round your neck. Look, no matter what happened and what sort of life you were leading, you've escaped without any lasting damage. You're still young – not even twenty. You can make a fresh start. All you need is the willpower to keep off that poison. Your body doesn't need it any more; now you must convince your mind. Life is better without heroin, believe me. Above all, it's cheaper. Even a respectable job will earn you enough to live on."

"Where am I?" she asked.

"In good hands," he said with a smile. "Forgive me if I think of myself now."

Of course she forgave him. Nobody as nice and kind and understanding could be blamed for thinking of himself for once and not wanting to risk being rewarded for his kindness with a driving ban. He'd been little short of a saint. If she was now on the road back to a normal existence, she owed it to him alone.

And she had cast him in the role of a brute. Why? Because she couldn't admit what she'd been: a lump of filth that had drifted further and further down the gutter until she'd let anyone do anything to her.

But the chief wouldn't give up. He kept probing away at the old wounds until they broke open one by one. If he spoke to Father . . . That was the last thing he'd said before leaving: that he must pay a visit to Buchholz next morning. "I'm very sorry, Frau Bender. I can't leave your father in peace, but I assure you I won't upset him unnecessarily. I only want to ask him . . ."

Father knew about her perverted boyfriends. He also knew about other perversions.

The ultimate sin! It had ceased to matter whether the Saviour forgave her or sentenced her to burn in hell, as Mother had graphically described so often. "Hundreds of little demons will rip the flesh from your body with red-hot pincers." The little demons had begun their work long ago, and the chief was guiding them, showing them where best to apply their pincers.

After supper she waited another few hours until she felt satisfied that the wardresses would be less alert. They didn't come to check on her so often at night. Shortly after twelve she took out the packet of tissues, tore off two pieces, rolled them into balls and plugged her nostrils with them.

Breathing through her mouth, she crumpled the rest of the tissues into a big ball and took up her position facing the wall at the end of the bed. Then she emptied her lungs and rammed the tissues down her throat as far as they would go. Even before she had lowered her hand, she drew back her head and butted the wall.

*

Rudolf Grovian set off at six on the Wednesday morning. Mechthild was still asleep when he left the house. He had estimated that the drive would take him five hours – a miscalculation that failed to allow for extensive roadworks on the A1. The first tailback cost him half an hour, the second almost a full hour. He didn't reach his destination until half-past twelve.

Buchholz. Clean as a new pin, lots of greenery, scarcely a building in the centre of town more than ten or fifteen years old. These surroundings, where Cora Bender had spent her childhood, were grossly at odds with his mental picture of her battered features.

He drove around for a while, getting his bearings with the aid of a street map, before pulling up outside her parental home. A nice little house, probably built in the early sixties, as neat and trim as the rest of the neighbourhood. Small but well-tended front garden, gleaming windows with snow-white net curtains behind them. Grovian suppressed an urge to shake his head.

He had learned the address from Gereon Bender on Tuesday night. He'd intended to get it from Margret Rosch and ask her a few more questions at the same time, but Cora's aunt had unexpectedly disappeared, so he had to make do with the husband. He was informed that Gereon Bender had never set eyes on his parents-in-law.

"They washed their hands of her years ago. I ought to have

known better – they must have had their reasons, after all. She lied to me from the outset. For months she led me to believe that Margret was her mother, and that her father had died shortly before she turned fourteen. The truth didn't come out until we applied for a marriage licence. I'd have done better to send her packing. Which reminds me: what's the form? She used the knife on me too. I ought to be able to charge her with assault. Or doesn't it count if you're married to someone?"

That wasn't all Gereon Bender had said. He admitted that his marriage hadn't been too rosy in the last six months – another respect in which he felt duped and deceived. "Cora always was a bit of a prude. Still, I had the feeling that she enjoyed it but didn't like showing it. But since Christmas . . ."

Then came the radio in the bedroom and the highly disagreeable results of his unwonted lovemaking. Although faintly embarrassed, Gereon Bender went into detail, even using the specific term: oral sex. "Don't get the idea I demanded it of her, I'd never have done that. I simply wanted to make it special for her, and she almost broke my neck."

Since hearing this, Grovian had once more entertained the suspicion that had arisen during his interview with her: child abuse. It went better with the drugs and her disgust. Her latest outburst fitted too. "Leave my father in peace, he's an old man!" A dead man, or so she'd told her husband.

He still believed the crux of her story: that she had sometime witnessed the scene she described before she fainted. "I heard her ribs snap . . ." Nobody dreamed up a detail like that. But he was alone in believing that Georg Frankenberg could have been involved in this horrific episode.

Whenever Mechthild wasn't preoccupied with their daughter, she tended to side with offenders and find a host of excuses for them, culminating in the view that they ought really to be released. This time, however, she agreed with the DA, Werner Hoss and the press.

An innocent man, and a doctor into the bargain, had had to die because of some insane delusion. Mechthild considered doctors inviolable. Although not infallible, they were people to whom you entrusted yourself and looked up with confidence rather than be overcome with dread when they reached for a scalpel.

Cora Bender had snuffed out one of these estimable men – one who, according to the press, had lived for his profession alone. In Mechthild's opinion, his killer deserved short shrift. Having read about the case in Monday morning's paper, she gratefully seized on it as a means of avoiding any discussion of their daughter's forthcoming divorce.

He hadn't spotted this at first, genuinely delighted that Mechthild was once more, after many years, showing an interest in his work and giving him an opportunity to get something off his chest – not that it had eased his burdens.

True, she acknowledged that Cora Bender's childhood was a mitigating factor, but when he'd finished she said: "I wouldn't like to be in your shoes, Rudi. It can't be pleasant, having to give such a pathetic creature the *coup de grâce*."

"I'm not planning to give her the *coup de grâce*," he protested.

Mechthild smiled indulgently. "What do you have in mind, then? She stabbed a doctor to death in front of a host of witnesses. You can't just pat her on the back."

"If I can prove —"

"Rudi," she broke in, "don't kid yourself. You can prove what you like, it'll just be a question of prison or a psychiatric ward."

She was right, he knew, but he didn't know if he would ever find evidence of a link between Frankie and his killer. Five years ago Cora Bender's world might have collapsed between May and November, or some other happening might have prompted her to tell a pack of lies and her aunt to clear off in a hurry after conducting her voluntary reconnaissance operation. Until now, nothing but good had been heard of Georg Frankenberg. A quiet man, reserved and almost shy where women were concerned.

And Gereon Bender had said that Cora lied whenever it suited her book. Naturally she lied when lying was her sole recourse. If someone tried to kick her wall down, she tossed everything that came into her head into a melting pot, gave it a vigorous stir and slapped a ladleful of hotchpotch on the nearest plate. Then you

198

had to sift through her offerings and determine the source of each and every morsel.

It had now been established that she could have picked up most of what she had presented as facts about Frankenberg's past while down beside the lake. Most but not all. Winfried Meilhofer hadn't mentioned the nicknames Billy-Goat and Tiger because he'd never heard them before. Georg Frankenberg had always referred to Hans Böckel and Ottmar Denner, nor had Meilhofer mentioned the silver Golf GTI with the Bonn licence plates.

The car and the two names were still Grovian's only means of establishing a link between Cora Bender and her victim, although the names might merely have derived from her imagination. To someone with a penchant for mind games, however, another attractive possibility presented itself: Hans = Johannes = Johnny Guitar. Winfried Meilhofer thought he remembered Frankie mentioning that Hans Böckel was the trio's bass guitarist. If Georg Frankenberg had been in his father's care with a broken arm on 16 May, Hans Böckel could well have met her on that day and introduced her to heroin.

Grovian had little hope of gleaning anything of importance from her father. He didn't intend to pressure him either. "Did you sexually abuse your daughter, Herr Rosch? Are you responsible for this disastrous state of affairs?" An expert witness could deal with that later. He only wanted some information about the period from May to November. And the name of the hospital where her head injury had been treated.

*

When he pressed the bell, the door was opened by a woman whose appearance matched the town. He gave an involuntary gulp: she looked so trim and youthful. Then Cora Bender's words flashed through his mind: "Mother is sixty-five." In her mid forties at most, the woman in the doorway was smartly dressed and well made-up, with short, stylishly cut hair. The tea towel in her hand suggested that she'd been washing up.

He introduced himself without stating his rank or the reason for his visit. "Frau Rosch?" he said hesitantly.

She smiled. "Heavens, no! I'm Grit Adigar, a neighbour."

He felt relieved but only slightly. "I wanted a word with Herr Rosch. Wilhelm Rosch."

"He isn't here."

"When will he be back?"

Grit Adigar didn't answer. Instead, she asked: "What did you want to speak to him about?" Before he could explain, she seemed to catch on. She peered past him at his car, which he'd parked beside the road, and gave a thoughtful nod. "It's about Cora, isn't it? You're from the police. Margret said someone would probably show up. Come in, we don't have to deal with this on the doorstep."

She stepped back, and that changed everything.

Beyond her lay a dim, narrow passage lined with wallpaper as old as the house itself. On the left was a flight of stairs covered with threadbare carpet. A thin strip of daylight issued from the door straight ahead, which was standing ajar. On the right, another door. It was also open, but Grovian didn't see this until he was almost level with it.

The room beyond, whose window overlooked the street, was the living room. The snow-white net curtains were invisible from the inside, obscured by a pair of heavy brown curtains that plunged the room in gloom. Standing in the doorway was another woman.

He gave a start when she suddenly stepped forward. Her shrewish face was framed by long grey hair that reached to her waist and looked as if it hadn't been washed for weeks. It smelled like that too, enveloping her in a sourish, musty odour. Tall for a woman, she would have topped Grovian by a couple of inches if she'd held herself erect, but her shoulders seemed to sag under an invisible burden. Her scrawny frame was loosely encased in a faded floral apron.

Grit Adigar gripped the woman's shoulder as she passed her. "That wasn't part of our bargain, Elsbeth. Finish off your lunch first, then you can pray some more."

The woman didn't answer. She was eyeing Grovian with her head a little on one side. "Is he looking for the whore?" she asked.

"No, he wants a word with Wilhelm. I'll deal with it."

Something akin to a smile appeared on the woman's thin lips. She gave a slow, deliberate nod. "The Almighty's patience was at an end. He has punished Wilhelm. He has robbed him of his voice and strength and confined him to his bed. He'll never leave it again."

There was an immense difference between hearing Cora Bender talk about her mother and seeing and hearing the mother in person. Grovian felt his skin crawl, despite the summer heat. The thought of a child being exposed to that sanctimonious voice, day after day, gave him the shivers.

"All right, Elsbeth." Grit Adigar tightened her grip on the malodorous creature's shoulder and propelled her in the direction of the kitchen. "You're going to sit down at the table and do the Almighty's bidding. He likes empty plates. Dumping all that good food in the dustbin would be a waste, and you know what he thinks of that."

Grit Adigar turned to Grovian. "Pay no attention to her. She was bad enough already, but since Monday she's been completely round the bend. And if you're wondering who she was calling a whore, it wasn't Cora. She meant Margret. To our saintly Elsbeth, any woman who has an affair with a married man is a whore."

A superfluous explanation, he thought. And whenever anyone offered him an explanation unasked, he pricked up his ears and wondered why.

The three of them sat down at an old kitchen table. The dresser beside it held a large number of framed photographs, all of Cora Bender. On her own, with her little boy, with her husband, with both. A wedding photo, a snap of her in the maternity ward, a view of the new house. Grit Adigar, who had followed the direction of Grovian's gaze, produced another unsolicited explanation. "Margret sent photos regularly. That's Wilhelm's altar. He could sit here looking at them for hours. He dreamed of her paying a visit sometime – of being able to see his grandson in the flesh – but she never did. I think he realized he'd never see her again."

A good opening, he thought, for a frontal attack on the point that kept cropping up. A neighbour might be more communicative on the subject than her parents or an aunt who had seen fit to disappear after making a voluntary statement.

"Did Wilhelm Rosch sexually abuse his daughter?"

Grit Adigar glared at him indignantly. "Wilhelm? What on earth gives you that idea? Only a policeman would suggest such a thing – he'd sooner have castrated himself with his own hands. Cora was the apple of his eye. It broke his heart when she went away, and on Monday, when Margret . . ."

She recounted what had happened. Margret Rosch had turned up two days ahead of him. Her intentions had been of the best. Far from going to ground, she'd left for Buchholz late on Sunday night, intending to break the news to her brother gently and in person. But news of that kind could not be broken gently: Wilhelm Rosch had suffered a stroke. His condition was critical, and Margret had remained at the hospital with him.

Everything had happened so fast on Monday, there'd been no time for explanations. Margret had called Grit Adigar only once from the hospital. There was little hope that Wilhelm would survive, she said, and it was possible that someone from the police would turn up because Cora had done something immensely stupid.

"Did she try to kill herself?" Grit asked.

"No."

She buried her face in her hands and breathed a sigh of relief. "Thank God," she muttered. "I thought she might have tried it again, because Wilhelm was so . . ."

Again! To Grovian, it sounded as if this woman knew far more than an aunt who'd had little contact with the family. She could be just as helpful to him as Cora Bender's parents. Above all, she might be willing to tell him what she knew.

But Grit Adigar wasn't prepared to cooperate without more ado. First she wanted to know what Cora had been getting up to. It sounded innocuous, the way she put it, but the faint smile quickly froze on her lips.

Grovian decided to be frank with her. He outlined the situation in a few brief sentences. Grit swallowed hard, and it was several seconds before she recovered her composure. "Good God!" she said eventually.

Elsbeth Rosch, who had been bending over her plate with an apathetic expression, looked up. Her soft voice acquired a sharp edge. "Thou shalt not take His name in —"

"Shut up, Elsbeth!" Grit snapped, breathing heavily. "This man – what was his name?"

"Georg Frankenberg."

"Never heard of him."

He showed her a photograph. She shook her head. She hadn't seen a silver Golf with Bonn licence plates either.

"How about Hans Böckel and Ottmar Denner, or the nicknames Frankie, Billy-Goat and Tiger?"

She gave a regretful shrug. "They don't mean a thing to me."

"Johnny Guitar?"

A fleeting smile. "That does mean something to me, but you ought to ask my youngest girl about him. All I know is, Johnny turned half the female heads in Buchholz a few years ago. My Melanie was no exception. He was a musician. Girls rate musicians higher than motor mechanics."

A musician, he thought. That's something, at least. But Grit couldn't imagine that Cora had got together with him. "She had a regular boyfriend, Horsti." Grovian had almost forgotten about Horsti.

Grit gave another apologetic smile. "I'm afraid I only know his first name. We always referred to him as Horsti. He was the love of Cora's life. She was seventeen when she met him. After three months she announced she was going to marry him some day and leave here. She was absolutely besotted with the boy; nobody could understand why. A weedy little fellow, he was – looked almost like an albino, with pale skin and pale yellow hair. All he needed were the pink eyes. I caught a glimpse of him a couple of times when he was hanging around in the street, waiting for Cora. My Melanie could tell you more. She's in Denmark, unfortunately – won't be back till next week – but she often saw them together. Cora's infatuation tickled her. She christened him 'the Wimp'."

A wimp for a regular boyfriend? It looked as if he were fighting a losing battle. Next question: "What about her attempted suicide? Do you know what made her do it?"

Grit nodded slowly, but her response was qualified. "I only know what Cora told me. It didn't happen here. According to her, she threw herself in front of a car. She never told me the reason, but she didn't have to. It was obvious: she couldn't get over Magdalena's death."

10

The very sound of the name made Grovian's head throb with unbridled fury at the thought of Margret Rosch's duplicity. Grit Adigar talked for nearly half an hour without a break. She described the arrival of the blue baby, the burning of the pretty dress in the tin bucket, the candle-scorched, blistered hands, the knees sore from praying, the sodden bedclothes, the desiccated soul of a child.

It was painful simply listening to it all, and he felt the whole time as if he were on the point of grasping something, some factor of whose existence he had never even dreamed until now. Not that he wanted to grasp it, because it would point too unequivocally in the direction of insanity. He found it impossible to imagine, as he sat at the kitchen table with Elsbeth muttering to herself, that any child could have developed normally under such a mother's tutelage.

The one thing he did grasp was Cora Bender's reason for not mentioning her sister hitherto: that her death was associated with a burden of guilt of which nothing and no one could relieve her. She had been guilty, even before Magdalena's birth, of draining her mother's strength.

He could have strangled the pathetic creature with his bare hands. Looking at her bent over her plate, he felt satisfied that she was responsible for Georg Frankenberg's death – indirectly responsible, perhaps, but that did not detract from the onus that rested on her bony shoulders.

Grit described Cora as a quiet, self-willed, introverted child and a rebellious teenager who was touchingly solicitous of her invalid sister on the one hand, and, on the other, eager for a modicum of personal freedom with Horsti at the Aladdin on Saturday nights.

A disreputable dump, it was rumoured to have supplied more than music, dancing and drinks. Drugs too had been readily available. The Aladdin had closed down well over four years ago. The premises were now occupied by a nice, clean restaurant serving good and inexpensive food.

"Was Cora a drug addict?" he asked.

"Not while she was still living here," Grit said firmly. "She was far too responsible. As for later on, shall I be honest?"

"Of course."

"I don't think so. I always thought the state of her arms made that less likely than more so. They must have been covered with suppurating sores. I've never had any dealings with junkies, but I don't believe they'd inject into festering wounds. I spoke to her about it at the time, and she said: 'I don't believe so either, Grit, but I don't believe a lot of things and they're true just the same. It wouldn't be surprising if I'd done drugs after the drama here.'

According to Grit, the drama had occurred in August five years ago. She hadn't witnessed it in person. She was away visiting friends on the Saturday in question and hadn't got home until late that night. To that extent she could only voice conjectures, she emphasized, but they were conjectures that fell within the bounds of probability.

In April the doctors had ascertained that Magdalena really was on her last legs. In the middle of May her condition worsened. Cora no longer left the house, even to do the shopping. Wilhelm had to take it over. Meanwhile, Cora sat at her sister's bedside day and night.

This was the period at which Grit had sighted Horsti a few times when he was loitering outside so as to at least be near Cora or grant her a glimpse of the love of her life.

That conflicted with what Margret Rosch had said about her brother's two phone calls. Grit brushed this aside. "Margret must have misunderstood him. Bad company? Wilhelm would never have put it that way. Even if he did, he must have meant Magdalena, not Horsti. Wilhelm never got on with Magdalena, and the feeling was mutual. She wasn't an easy person. Just because someone's terminally ill, it doesn't mean they haven't got a mind of their own. Magdalena did, take it from me."

With a ghost of a smile, Grit proceeded with her account of Magdalena's last few months. She took her time dying. As often happens with the terminally ill, she seemed to recover shortly before the end. In August Cora decided to risk it. Wilhelm and Elsbeth had gone to Hamburg, so she treated herself to a Saturday night out with the faithful Horsti. She was gone only a few hours. By the time she returned her sister was dead.

Grit rose. "Come with me, I'd like to show you something." Leaving Elsbeth staring at her plate in the kitchen, she led the way out into the passage and up the narrow stairs. There were three doors on the landing, one of which she opened for him.

Beyond it lay a sparsely furnished bedroom. Two beds and a bedside table, nothing more. The little alarm clock on the bedside table had stopped at half-past four. Beside it lay a Walkman plus earphones and a stack of audio cassettes, and in front of them stood a photograph in a silver frame.

An amateur snapshot, it showed two girls seated side by side on one of the beds. Their long hair, silver-blond and auburn respectively, was cropped by the frame.

Grovian picked up the photograph and studied it. What most attracted his attention was Cora's face and auburn hair. He had never seen her smile like that. She made an earnest, solicitous, affectionate impression as she sat there with one arm around her sister's shoulders. As for Magdalena . . .

"Two extremely pretty girls," he said.

"Yes, they were both pretty," said Grit, "but in Magdalena's case that was an understatement. She had the kind of beauty that drives men insane. I sometimes thought her outward appearance was Nature's way of making up for all that was wrong with her inside, or that those defects ensured that no man would be lured to his doom by her lovely exterior."

She sighed and shrugged her shoulders, smiling sheepishly.

"You get peculiar ideas when you live on top of something like that. Elsbeth must have looked like her as a girl. No wonder she lost her mind, having a child like that. Cora takes after Wilhelm. Magdalena was the image of her mother at that age."

"You wouldn't know she was ill, to look at her," Grovian said.

Grit smiled again. "Diabolical, wasn't it? Her heart was so badly affected, her whole body was bloated. Her kidneys were failing too, yet she looked the picture of health. Her bluish complexion was the only sign that something was wrong with her. Cora wielded her make-up for half an hour before I was allowed to snap them. Magdalena didn't want to be photographed at all. She was very vain – she wouldn't agree until Cora had got her ready. It's the only photo of Magdalena in existence. I took it at the beginning of April, two days before she went to Eppendorf for the last time. We thought she was doing better than ever before. She'd put on weight – she was fuller in the face, and even her legs had stopped looking like twigs. It was only the fluid, in fact, but we didn't learn that till later."

He replaced the photograph and turned round. Above one of the beds was a shelf crowded with books.

"We found the books in the barn," said Grit. "Wilhelm fixed the shelf above Cora's bed after she left and brought them up here."

They were mainly medical textbooks, two of which bore titles suggestive of psychology. The topics were revealing: religious mania and self-healing by means of willpower.

Grit omitted to mention that Wilhelm had also found a slim little notebook in the barn containing nothing but figures. Over 30,000 marks! "How in the world did she amass so much money?" Wilhelm had asked.

"After the age of sixteen," Grit went on, "Cora spent most of her pocket money on these books. I often saw her sneak out of the house at nights and go into the barn. That was where she kept her trendy gear, make-up, and so on – things Elsbeth wouldn't tolerate but teenagers find so important. Her books were there too. She used to change and put on a bit of make-up when she went into town. You'd have thought she was setting off to have a good time, but she usually had one of these tomes beneath her arm, and you don't go dancing like that, or to the movies or the ice-cream parlour. Cora didn't gad around. She can hardly be blamed for meeting Horsti on Saturdays. She needed a bit of freedom, a few hours in the week to herself. The rest of the time she devoted to her sister."

Grit said that Cora had read a magazine article about heart transplants and how successful they'd been in the States, and that she'd often spoken of her intention to take Magdalena there some day. A heart transplant wouldn't have done the trick, but Cora was either unable or unwilling to grasp that.

"If that had been all," Grit said, "they'd gladly have operated on her at Eppendorf, just to show they could. I don't know the full details; you'd have to ask Margret. She fetched all the documentation from the hospital, the whole of Magdalena's medical history. While she was alive, nobody here knew exactly how things stood with her. Wilhelm took little interest, Elsbeth was too stupid to understand what the doctors told her, and Magdalena herself wouldn't accept the truth and kept mum. In April the doctors wanted to keep her at the hospital, but she insisted on dying at home. It seems she told them she got all the nursing she needed here, but she didn't breathe a word once she got back. Then Cora came home that night and found her . . . When Wilhelm went upstairs the next morning, because Cora hadn't come down for breakfast, she'd gone."

"When was that, exactly?" Grovian asked.

"Hang on, the date's on the death certificate. It's in their bedroom, I'll get it."

Grit darted out of the door and returned a few seconds later. She handed him the certificate. "Cardiac and renal failure," he read. The doctor's signature was illegible, but he didn't trouble to decipher it. His eyes had fastened on two dates. Date of birth: 16 May. Date of death: 16 August.

*

Two sixteens. You didn't have to be a psychologist to grasp their significance in Cora Bender's life and why her initial version had

209

dated from the beginning of her romance with Johnny in May. It was wishful thinking. So he could forget about the dead girl on Lüneburg Heath and her assertion that her aunt had lied to him.

Margret Rosch had probably told him the truth, or hinted at it anyway, but the things she'd withheld! His anger hadn't subsided in the least. How dare she volunteer to give him all the information he needed – indeed, ram it down his throat – only to suppress the most important point! It was obstruction at best, if not a deliberate attempt to mislead.

But that was something he would have to clear up with Margret Rosch herself. He now turned to what interested him most: Cora's fateful suicide attempt and ensuing medical treatment. Unfortunately, Grit Adigar could tell him little.

Some man had telephoned her in November, a few days before Cora returned. She hadn't caught his name. Too agitated to check, she had run next door and called Wilhelm to the phone. Wilhelm might remember the name, she said, having spoken with him at greater length. All she could say was, Cora had come home in a terrible state. From the look of her, the doctor who'd treated her must have been a bungler. No responsible physician sent a patient home in that condition.

Cora arrived in a taxi with Hamburg licence plates. The cabby had to help her out. She could hardly stand, but he drove off at once without giving her a second thought.

Grit shook her head. "She stood staring at the house as if she'd never seen it before. Then she came tottering up the path. I'd spotted her from my window, so I hurried outside and spoke to her. She stared straight through me. Elsbeth opened the door. She looked at her and said: 'Cora is dead. Both my daughters are dead.' Cora screamed. I'd never heard a person scream that way before – like an animal."

She went on to describe how Cora had buckled at the knees, then hit her head on the doorstep again and again. How Wilhelm had come hurrying along the passage. How they had carried Cora upstairs and undressed her. Her body was completely emaciated. The fresh scar and the dent in her skull had healed well, unlike her forearms. "Magdalena can't be dead!" she kept whimpering while they were undressing her. "She can't be, we're flying to America!"

Grit had got the feeling that Cora's mind was a blank – that she'd completely forgotten about that night, presumably because of some major trauma. She didn't seem to entertain the possibility that Cora might really not have learned of her sister's death until November because she hadn't come home at all that night in August.

Grovian did. Johnny Guitar, he thought. The boy who had turned half the female heads in Buchholz. Who had never looked at her twice – until that night. After a three-month vigil at her sister's bedside she ventured out, happy and relieved that Magdalena seemed to be improving. And what a thrill when Johnny noticed her at last! Horsti got the brush-off – maybe he wasn't even at the Aladdin that night. With a pounding heart she joined Johnny and his fat little friend in the silver Golf, possibly accompanied by another girl, possibly not.

For now, that wasn't the salient point. The trouble was: could one believe that the fulfilment of Cora's dream had prompted her to consign her ailing sister to her fate and drive off into the blue? Hard to imagine, in view of what Grit Adigar had said. But there was another question to which he'd hitherto attached insufficient importance. Could a serious head wound have healed within a few weeks? That was equally hard to imagine.

From Cora Bender's parental home he set off for the restaurant that served good but inexpensive food. No luck: it was shut between three and six, so he drove to the hospital in which Wilhelm Rosch was fighting for what remained of his life and his sister was keeping watch and ordering the nursing staff around. He was unable to speak to Cora Bender's father. As for her aunt, she fiercely defended her reticence.

What did a girl who had died of cardiac and renal failure five years ago have to do with the Frankenberg case? Absolutely nothing. The very mention of Magdalena's name was bound to cut the ground from under Cora's feet. As a concerned and caring aunt, Margret Rosch had preferred to leave this decision to her niece. If he would be kind enough to recall, she had told Cora: "Tell them why you left home in August." That Cora hadn't done so spoke for itself. It was a guilt complex of which a simple detective could have no conception.

He swallowed the simple detective bit without protest. But Margret Rosch gave him no time to rebuke her in any case. She proved adept at diverting the simple detective's attention from her sin of omission and steering him in another direction. On Monday, even before uttering a word about Cora's act of folly, she had asked her brother the name of the hospital in which her niece had been treated.

Wilhelm knew nothing of any hospital. The doctor had given him his name and an address in Hamburg on the phone. Later, however, when Wilhelm sent him a letter of thanks, it was returned "Unknown at this Address".

"Interesting, no?" Margret Rosch said in a milder tone of voice. "Why should the man have given him a false name? What had he done to her? I can guess!"

She blew out her cheeks and shook her head. "Know what annoys me most of all, Herr Grovian? That I didn't let Cora get on with it when she was sitting in my kitchen with that stuff."

"What stuff?"

Margret Rosch sighed and gave an embarrassed little shrug. "Heroin. I told you, didn't I, that she attributed her condition to withdrawal symptoms? She'd got hold of some at the railway station and asked me to fill the hypo. I took it away from her. At the time I simply assumed she didn't know how to handle one because the man had been injecting her. But now I think, if that had been so, she would at least have seen how he filled the thing. She didn't have the first idea. Try testing her if you don't believe me."

He didn't believe a word of it, neither the putative doctor with the false name, nor the rest. Margret Rosch had had plenty of time to liaise with Grit Adigar. The nice neighbour had prepared the ground; the enterprising aunt was sowing the seeds. Their intentions were obscure to him, however. As a nurse, Margret Rosch could hardly be naïve enough to believe he would entertain

212

the likelihood that Cora Bender's fractured skull had been treated by a first-year medical student.

He would have no choice but to question all the hospitals and medical practices in the Hamburg area. A job for some subordinate who enjoyed telephoning until his ear was sore.

Grovian lacked the information he needed to locate Horsti. Besides, he was hungry. After concluding his conversation with Margret Rosch he made another attempt to get a good and inexpensive meal. It was a few minutes past six. The steak was not only ample but excellent; the vegetables left nothing to be desired. He had told Mechthild he might be very late, so she wasn't to wait dinner for him.

He spent just over an hour in the agreeably unpretentious restaurant, trying to picture what it had looked like in its Aladdin days. The friendly waiter couldn't help. He'd only lived in Buchholz for the past two years and had never heard of Johnny, Billy-Goat or Tiger, let alone Frankie or Horsti.

Grovian set off on the long drive home just after eight, slightly wiser than before but not a step further – far from it. He encountered a total of four tailbacks on the return trip, despite the lateness of the hour. Thanks to those and the various roadworks, the drive took him seven hours. He got home at half-past three in the morning.

Mechthild was asleep. There was a note on his pillow asking him to call Werner Hoss urgently, but it was too late even for that. He slipped into bed as stealthily as possible. His eyes were smarting with fatigue, his head throbbed, his neck and shoulders were completely tensed up. He was asleep in less than two minutes.

Next morning he learned that Cora Bender had tried to terminate the investigation in her own way. The news hit him like a whiplash. He couldn't have felt worse had he handed her a loaded pistol.

Half a packet of paper handkerchiefs! How could he have imagined, even for a moment, that he had the least inkling of what went on in her head?

He sat at his desk for several minutes, just sat there staring at the coffee percolator. A fresh brown film had formed on the bottom of the jug. At half-past nine he left the office and bought a bottle of detergent and a scouring pad at a supermarket. Then he not only scrubbed the jug but also polished the old machine until it looked like new. And he didn't even see it.

All he saw was her hand gripping the innocuous little packet of tissues. He also heard her voice: "You can't imagine what happens when I talk to you – it all comes alive again."

Now he could imagine. At least he now knew what spirit he had conjured up: Magdalena.

*

She was lying on a bed. Her arms and legs had been pinioned with broad cloth restraints. Her head was aching and buzzing from the violent blow she had dealt it, and they'd given her a sedative injection. That she could remember. She had fought like a wildcat, lashing out with her fists and feet, biting and screaming almost uncontrollably.

Some of this had lodged in her memory, but her impressions of it were too vague to preoccupy her. Now that they'd brought her to this room, she lay quietly on her back, drowsing. Although she could feel the restraints on her ankles and wrists, the stiffness in her limbs and the big plaster on her forehead, none of it mattered.

There was no room for tears even when her head gradually cleared. Her heart was beating, and she was breathing. She could even think, yet she had ceased to exist. She had missed eternity by a few minutes and ended up in the worst place imaginable: a psychiatric ward.

Although her bed was not the only one in the room, the others were unoccupied. Not unused, though. The rumpled bedclothes testified to the fact that their users were permitted to move around freely elsewhere. But not her! Most shameful of all was the nappy. She could feel it distinctly.

At some stage the door opened. A pair of hands swiftly checked her restraints; an impassive face looked down at her. "How are you feeling?"

She turned her head away, not wanting to feel anything any more. Two or three tears appeared from nowhere and seeped into the pillowcase. Two or three more trickled down her nose and onto her compressed lips. She licked them off with the tip of her tongue.

She was thirsty, but she would have bitten off her tongue rather than ask for a sip of water. Her throat hurt, it was so dry and so sore from the rough treatment it had received. So was her nose. Everything had been scraped raw.

The early-afternoon light was very bright. One of the barred windows had been opened a crack, and sparrows could be heard twittering outside. The succulent sound of rubber-soled shoes receded in the direction of the door, leaving her alone again. Alone with her thoughts and memories, her fear and guilt.

Conscious of every heartbeat, she wished it would be her last. She concentrated hard. If one could survive by willpower alone, as Magdalena had done for eighteen years, why shouldn't one be able to die by willpower alone? No use, her heart went on beating.

Later the door opened again. It was still light outside. Someone came in with a tray. The Last Supper. Except that it wasn't the last for a woman free to make her own decisions: it was the first for a zombie. A feeding cup and an open cheese sandwich cut into bite-sized cubes. One hand gripped her chin, another held the spout of the cup to her lips. She turned her head away indignantly, spilling the contents on her pillow. A smell of peppermint filled the air. A man's expressionless voice said: "If you refuse to eat and drink, you'll be force-fed. Now, are you going to open your mouth or aren't you?"

She didn't open it. Her thirst had become almost unbearable; her throat was completely parched, her tongue swollen.

Whoever it was that had brought the tray went out again. The door closed, but not for long. It opened again, and this time HE came in.

She knew who he was as soon as he bent over her. He radiated professional expertise like an aura. It shone in his eyes, issued from him with every breath. "I possess the knowledge and the power! I am the one who can save you from eternal damnation. Trust me, and you'll feel better."

With a last vestige of defiance, she thought: "Wrong, you arse-hole. Got a pack of cards with you?"

His voice sounded friendly. "You don't feel like eating?"

She wasn't sure if she should answer him. Who could tell what he would deduce from her replies? He might never release her from this room, from this nappy, from his clutches.

She decided to try after all, just to show him what a tough nut she was. A drug-addicted whore case, hardened by life on the streets. Her raw throat didn't share her intention, so it was only a croak: "Thanks, I'm not hungry, but I'd be grateful for a cigarette if you've got one."

"I'm sorry," he said, "I don't have any with me. I don't smoke."

"What a coincidence," she croaked. "We've got something in common: I don't smoke either, I gave it up years ago. All I thought was, with a cigarette I'd at least get one hand free."

"Would you like that?"

"Not really. I'm quite comfortable like this. I'd like to scratch my nose occasionally, that's all."

She almost substituted arsehole for nose, but Magdalena's favour-ite vulgarity refused to pass her lips.

"If you're sensible, I'll get them to remove your restraints."

"Haven't I proved how sensible I am?" she demanded. "I tried to save the taxpayer a tidy sum. They ought to reintroduce the death penalty. An eye for an eye, the Bible says. A life for a life."

He didn't pursue this. "It's up to you," he said quietly. "If you eat and drink something and take your medication . . ."

It cost her an effort to speak, but having once started she wanted to go on. "Got something nice for me? Some Resedorm maybe?"

It was only a momentary image like a flashgun picture in her brain: a slender, well-manicured hand and a glass of orange juice. Then it vanished into the darkness, and in the darkness a woman's voice asked suspiciously: "What's that you're giving her?"

A man's voice answered, a familiar voice, not gentle but business-like: "Resedorm. It works quickest."

"But she isn't fully conscious," the woman protested. "Can she swallow?"

216

"That's what I'm trying to find out," the man replied, sounding faintly annoyed. "And I'd prefer you to keep quiet. I'm not sure if she can understand us."

The darkness persisted. She felt a hand slide beneath her neck, heard his voice say: "Blink if you can understand me."

She blinked, although there was nothing but mist before her eyes. "Good," he said. "Try to raise your head. I'll help you." The cool rim of the glass touched her lips. "Drink up," he said. "Nice and slowly. Go on, try, one sip at a time. Yes, wonderful, that's it. You can go back to sleep in a minute. You still need plenty of sleep."

Another flashgun picture in her brain, an image suffused with green and red, blue and yellow light. It meant nothing – it was suddenly there, that's all, perhaps because the chief had mentioned an ashtray. But it was accompanied by the metallic taste of blood in her mouth and a cry, more a scream, of pain: "She bit me, the bitch!"

A hand reached for the table and reappeared in front of her face holding a heavy glass ashtray. It came flashing down, then nothing more. Nothing but a thought, almost a grin, in her brain: don't torment yourself wondering who stove your skull in. You know who it was: your last punter, paying you in his own coin.

The expert was still standing over her, watching her closely. "Have you had experience of Resedorm?" he asked.

"I've had a lot of experiences," she said. "Which ones would interest you most?" Her throat was so parched, her vocal cords seemed to be juggling with a pincushion. "My experiences with my pious mother? With my weak-kneed father? With drugs?"

"Resedorm isn't that kind of drug," he said. "It's a soporific."

"I know," she muttered.

It came back to her as she spoke: Margret had given her Resedorm – on the advice of her boyfriend Achim Miek. The doctor and the nurse . . .

No! No, it hadn't been like that. Achim Miek had never held a glass to her lips, and Margret had never given her any orange juice. Two tablets and a glass of water – that was what Margret had given her, and that voice just now had not been hers.

It must have been the grumpy nurse and the doctor with the slender hands and the neatly trimmed beard. Strange, she had no recollection of him holding a glass, only of the injections. And of what he had said about her perverted clients!

She was tired now, just tired. "I know all that," she muttered. "And that's what you should let me do now, sleep."

He lingered beside her bed a while longer. She took no more notice of him.

When she closed her eyes she saw herself beside the lake. The little boy was squatting at her feet, waving the red fish. His thin white back, smooth round shoulders, delicate neck and white-blond hair made him look like a girl. Like Magdalena at the time when she was just a bundle to be carried from room to room, a creature she was at liberty to hate with all the innocent fervour of a child.

Why hadn't she swum out? He wouldn't have followed her. To him, she had merely been the woman who fed him yoghurt and apples on weekends instead of chocolate and jelly babies. That he called her Mama was unimportant. Some day his subconscious might associate the word "Mama" with the taste of Golden Delicious and the sight of a little bloodstained knife. Someday his grandmother would tell him: "Let's be thankful she's gone. She was a slut. To think of all we found out about her after she left . . ."

At some stage she heard footsteps making for the door. It didn't matter; the expert would return like a demon she herself had summoned from hell.

Now she would never be free from the ghosts she'd raised.

"The Sorcerer's Apprentice." She'd had to learn that poem for school. It was one of the ones the doctor had kept making her recite. She'd enjoyed doing so then, but not now. It had raised too many ghosts.

And the man who was shutting the door behind him could not let her rest until he'd dragged the last grain of dirt to the surface: a couple of perverts who beat up a drug-addicted whore once they'd had their fun with her. That was his job, the one he was paid for.

218

She could always rebel against him and spin the whole thing out, but there was no escape, no right to remain silent. She had forfeited her rights when she stabbed that man with the knife, and the people outside wanted to know why. So did she. That tune had been no rational motive. That she'd once been afraid of it had almost ceased to be true.

At some point she fell asleep. She was unaware of the women who came into the room and might have stood around her bed, possibly stroking her face, possibly her hair, before getting into their own beds. Next morning she had the impression that someone had stroked her face and hair during the night. It must have been her father, who had put his arms around her and wanted to bring her a bowl of lukewarm bean soup because he knew she was as hungry as a wolf.

The beds were empty again by the time she awoke. Feeling only half-alive, she recalled a crazy dream she'd had, just before waking, in which she'd plugged her nostrils with pieces of paper and thrust a gag down her throat. Then came a blow on the forehead, but she hadn't lost consciousness. Panic, asphyxia. A key rattling in the lock. The shrill voice of the wardress: "For God's sake! I told you she'd flip!" Fingers down her throat. Red rings before her eyes. The end of the line: a psychiatric ward. And that was no dream.

Breakfast came. She ate some once her left arm had been released. Shortly after breakfast they removed the restraints from her right arm and both legs. She was told to get up, get washed and dressed. Her limbs were stiff from lying down; her mind was numb with fear. She had a date with the chief at nine, she was told.

Something inside her refused to call him that. The chief was Rudolf Grovian, an awful man who failed to grasp what he'd done to her. But at least she could lie to him. Any attempt to lie to a psychiatrist struck her as hopeless.

Professor Burthe, they told her. He looked like a professor, too: short and puny. He was a dwarf, and he had to be. Only dwarfs could probe other people's brains, crawl into every convolution, peer around every bend. His manner was as amiable as it had been last night, serene and self-assured. The kindly god whose eyes could see deep into others' hearts. And his eyes were open.

219

No more recalcitrance, no rebellion. She had shrunk in the night. Father, perched on the edge of her bed and trying desperately to show how much he loved her, had reduced her to a tiny, transparent little creature who was permitted to sit in a comfortable armchair and bare its innermost self.

The professor began by asking how she was feeling.

"Like hell," she said, drawing a deep breath. Father shouldn't have come; she'd told Margret to stop him coming. She started to massage her left wrist with her right hand, staring at it and waiting for the next question.

She could hardly bear it, he was so gentle, because it was false and deceitful. He wanted to talk about the meaning of life and escaping punishment.

"I didn't try to escape punishment," she said. "I simply didn't want to listen to what the chief had heard from my father."

"What could he have heard?"

None of your damned business, you dwarf, she thought. That I . . . Father came into our room one time and poked around in our bedside table. It was a plain bedside table with a drawer at the top and a cupboard below. Magdalena kept her music in the cupboard and her medication in the drawer. And the candle! One of the ones Mother had bought for the altar. Mother never came into our room, but Father did. And he found the candle. He also saw I'd never used it for praying. The wick was still white and the end a bit smeary.

She saw Father standing in the doorway, torn between disgust and disappointment. He had the candle in his hand. "What's been going on here?" he demanded, holding it out. "What have you been up to?"

She heard herself reply: "Can't you guess? You aren't usually so slow on the uptake when it comes to human nature. Didn't you tell me it becomes too much for you when you're older? Well, I'm human too, but I prefer the dry variety. A candle doesn't come and it doesn't stink. Put it back where you found it and get out of here."

Father dropped the candle on the floor and slunk out with his shoulders sagging. He was weeping the way he'd wept the night he sat on her bed and tried to explain why he was so miserable. This time he merely muttered: "What's become of you? You're worse than a whore."

*

Everything changed as the years went by. It probably had to do with growing up, with perception and comprehension. There are things you don't want to understand but have to. That a father is a man. That he has his needs like any other man. That he becomes angry and unjust when denied gratification. I understood him in a way.

When I grew older I often wondered what it must be like to be loved. Loved with the body as well as the heart. Self-abandonment, passion, French kisses, orgasms – stuff like that. I became accustomed to my breasts and my periods. I no longer had any difficulty using tampons, and sometimes, when I was inserting one, I caught myself wondering. What if a man . . . It can't be all that different, I thought, and if a man needs it!

But I also understood Mother, who wanted nothing more to do with it. She deserved to be pitied, really. After all, a woman can't help being off her head. Mother genuinely believed all that rubbish. I mean, that you mustn't do it unless you're trying to make a child.

Even three times a day had been fine as long as she didn't get pregnant. She could tell herself she was straining every muscle to do the Almighty a favour. Mother had never grasped that two thousand years are a hell of a long time. Enough time in which to produce more than enough children.

It could well be the way Margret had put it in her letter that time: that the Saviour had nothing whatever to do with all these prohibitions. That all this horrendous nonsense had been concocted by his earthly representatives, and people were compelled to believe it. What else were they to do when they couldn't read or write?

When I think what Buchholz used to be like! Just a handful of farms on the poorest soil imaginable. There were many years when stripping the thatch from the roofs was their only means of over-wintering the few cattle they possessed. Father once told me that a fat pig weighed a hundred pounds in those days. A measly hundred pounds, imagine! It sounds absurd today. And then came the Black Death and the Thirty Years War.

They were poor, they were stupid, and they seldom knew how to fill their children's bellies. When a preacher told them it was a damnable sin to yield to their sexual urges, they looked at their children and said to themselves: "Hey, he's right. If we stop it, there won't be any more mouths to feed."

The womenfolk were particularly impressed. The curse of Eve. Nobody gave them anything when they were in labour. It was part of the process. In sorrow shalt thou bring forth . . .

When the responsibility became too much for her, and when she had no other recourse, Mother took refuge in this poverty and stupidity. And there she remained. She no longer had to cope with the birth of an unwanted baby. Although she doubtless realized that it was bad of her to abort it, there must have been a few people in her circle who thought it better for a respectable German girl not to bring an enemy soldier's brat into the world. And she believed them.

Mother always needed someone to tell her what was right and proper. As a girl she believed in Hitler. Later she believed in a victorious soldier. She never believed in herself. For a while she believed in me when I said what she wanted to hear. A few Biblical quotations, and you could twist her around your little finger.

Father never bothered. When he came home not only late but drunk, he would tell her his colleagues in the firm had been celebrating and he couldn't back out every time. Mother knew as well as I did that he'd been with another woman.

He often patronized whores after I caught him at it in the bathroom. Then, because he felt rotten, he would drink himself silly and take out the anger and self-contempt he felt on Mother. I felt so sorry for her when he shooed her away from the crucifix and made her warm up his supper, I couldn't help myself. "Leave that, Mother," I would tell her. "I'll do it."

I could have wept sometimes when I saw her slink back into the living room. I was only fourteen or fifteen, but I felt so old – almost as if I had two children. They were far bigger and older than me, but that didn't alter the fact that they were children for whom I bore a responsibility. I had to cherish and discipline them.

Mother didn't require much disciplining. She was a good girl – no dirty thoughts, just dirty underclothes – but Father was a bad boy deserving of the sternest reprimands. "How much did today's whore cost you?" I asked him, aged fifteen. "A hundred marks? Two hundred? I'll be needing three hundred this week. Everything's getting dearer, and you aren't the only one in this house with personal needs."

He would look at me when I put his meals in front of him. He never said anything, just took the notes from his wallet and shoved them across the table. He despised me for the language I used, I knew, and he knew the feeling was mutual.

We had become enemies just as a mother and her son become enemies in the course of time because the son does things of which the mother disapproves, and which the son knows that the mother herself did once – or, in my case, would do in years to come. But the mother is the stronger of the two. As long as they live under the same roof, she wields a great deal of power over her son. He loves her, after all. He wishes with all his heart that she loved and took pride in him too, however often he yells and curses and hurls his rage and disappointment in her face, motivated solely by despair, loneliness and fear of being abandoned by the last person on earth capable of giving him a little love.

I was the one who broke Father's backbone, not Mother. I was to blame that he eventually knuckled under to her; that in his declining years he shared not only her bed but the crucifix; that he forgot he was a man – forgot it entirely, as if the physical evidence of it had rotted off at last.

I often wondered afterwards how I could have brought myself to sleep with men for money. I know why I did it: because I needed the money. Later on I needed still more money for drugs to deaden my disgust. But I've never found that a sufficient explanation. And the silly thing is, I don't remember that phase of my life.

I do recall smoking pot in Horsti's car one time. He rolled a spliff and let me take a drag. Then he said I'd done it wrong because I blew out the smoke at once. That's all I remember. The rest has gone, whether as a result of my addiction or the head injury, I don't know.

The doctor said it might be one or the other. He said it could well be a case of suppression because I'd done things I knew no normal person does. And I wanted to be normal. I didn't want to think about the men I'd sold myself to, that's why I stowed them all away behind the wall in my head. I didn't want them to acquire faces and bodies and groping hands in my mind's eye. I didn't want to see or feel them when I cast my mind back. I simply didn't want to remember, period.

But I've often wondered whether they were old or young. To begin with, I think most of them must have been old. Men like Father, who got a raw deal at home and had to satisfy their needs in the bathroom or on the street at night. Whose only wish was a little affection and the feeling that they were still men. Sometimes I've even wondered why I never offered that to my father.

"You can come to me if you need it so badly. Be honest, it's crossed your mind. Don't worry, you won't be sacrificing a second lamb. I've never been a lamb. You've no idea of all the things I've stolen from shops the way I stole from Mother in her womb. I sucked all the strength out of her through the umbilical cord. I desiccated her brain and drove her mad. I'm a werewolf. I jump out of my box at night and devour innocent children. As for old, defenceless men, I strip the skin from their bodies and rip out their hearts. I'm evil personified, Satan's daughter. And, since you're my father, you must be Satan. Come into my arms, you poor thing! You said much the same to me when I was little; now I'm saying it to you."

I never did say it, but I suppose I tried to apologize to Father in my own way. Perhaps I saw him in every man with whom I at first had sex in a normal way. Perhaps I really did come to understand that men are slaves to their desires. Not everyone possesses the strength of a Saviour capable of self-denial – capable of understanding and pardoning even a whore like Mary Magdalene.

224

11

Her hour was up. The professor had asked her to recount her experiences with her pious mother and weak-kneed father, and she had. To get it over as quickly as possible, she had also unloaded the filth. It hadn't been easy, but she'd done it. She was feeling pleased with herself and satisfied that the professor would promptly pass on what she'd told him to the district attorney.

Perhaps someone would get the idea that Frankie had simply been a former client of hers. That wouldn't be a bad explanation! She'd had to kill him before he recognized her and gave her away to her husband.

Her eyes suddenly swam with scalding tears at the thought of Gereon, but only for a moment. Her years with him were like the barrettes and lipsticks she'd stolen from Woolworths and sold or given away to other girls in the playground: over and gone forever. Gereon would be bound to hear in court, if not before, what sort of woman he had exchanged vows with.

For lunch, there were mashed potatoes and some unidentifiable vegetable boiled to a pulp. The meat, which had been dissected into little cubes, consisted mostly of fat and gristle and was swimming in unappetizing brown gravy. A bowl of fruit yoghurt had been provided for afters.

Reposing on the tray was a white plastic spoon. It reminded her of the lake and stirred everything up again. Why couldn't her son have asked for a yoghurt? The most she could have done to Frankie with a plastic spoon was scratch his face.

She ate a little mashed potato. It tasted of cardboard. Taking the yoghurt with her, she went and stood at the barred window, looked up at the sky. She wondered where the occupants of the other beds had their midday meal. Was she considered too dangerous to eat with the others? Perhaps it was a test designed to discover how much of her wits she had left. Perhaps the professor would ask her at their next session how she was getting on with her room-mates.

For a while she debated what answer to give him. Then she devoted some thought to the Frankie scenario. If the idea that he'd been a client of hers didn't occur to the professor spontaneously, she would have to rub his nose in it.

Finally, she wondered whether Magdalena had been relieved to enter the pearly gates and find that Mother wasn't there yet. Whether she was getting bored singing "Holy, holy, holy!" all the time, or whether she was sitting face to face with the Saviour in some quiet corner. Magdalena had once pointed to a picture of the Saviour in the Bible and said: "Give the fellow a shave and a decent haircut, and he wouldn't be bad-looking."

Frankie hadn't been bad-looking either. A pretty face for a man – pretty but masculine. They probably wouldn't believe her if she said he'd been a client of hers. A man like him had no need to pay for sex, nor was he a pervert.

She could still see him clearly – without any blood – sitting up and complaining about that tune. Perhaps he'd found it as agonizing as she had. Perhaps he'd been grateful when she put him out of his misery. The way he'd looked at her . . .

She stood at the window until just after two – just stood there, feeling happy she hadn't been tied to the bed again. Someone came to collect the tray and scolded her for leaving her meat and vegetable mush untouched. She pointed to her throat with an apologetic smile. "It still hurts when I swallow, but I've finished the yoghurt. If there's some soup tomorrow, I'll definitely have two helpings." Then she was alone again.

Twice she heard a sound behind her and turned to look at the door. She knew what had caused it: a watchful eye at the spy-hole. A few minutes later a key turned in the lock. She thought of the

226

mugs of coffee and slices of stale cake at the hospital where she'd spent a few days after the birth of her son. They always brought afternoon coffee at midday and supper at teatime because they wanted to get off early.

The door opened. The instant she turned, fear sprang at her like a rabid dog. The chief! His neutral, almost businesslike demeanour concealed all that he must have learned from her father.

*

In fact, Rudolf Grovian's impassive face merely camouflaged his own emotions. *Mea culpa!* He had driven home at lunchtime, unable to endure the office any longer, with its gleaming coffee machine and the chair on which she'd sat. He never came home for lunch as a rule, so Mechthild hadn't been expecting him. He didn't have to say much; she asked what was wrong of her own accord.

After he'd explained and told her what he felt he must do next, she said: "You're mad, Rudi. Leave the poor thing in peace. You can't help her, you'll only make matters worse. She's fine where she is."

"Fine? Don't make me laugh! Have you any idea what it's like in a psychiatric ward?"

"No," she said, cracking a couple of eggs into the pan, "and I don't want to know. I already know what goes on in your outfit, that's good enough for me. Nobody says a word if you and Hoss come down hard on some fellow who deserves it, but a young woman like that? Think what she's been through!"

Grovian had been thinking of nothing else. The law obliged him not only to investigate Cora Bender but also to gather any evidence that might exonerate her. He explained this to Mechthild. "Then do it, Rudi," she had said. "Do it, for God's sake, and take anything you discover to the district attorney. But not to her, certainly not the news that her father is dying. How much more do you plan to burden her with?"

He looked at her standing beside the window, a picture of misery: her bruised face all the colours of the rainbow, her forehead adorned with a broad strip of sticking plaster. Thinking of the objects in his jacket pocket and the news he had to give her, he could still hear Mechthild's voice in his head: "You're mad, Rudi. Leave the poor thing in peace . . ."

The door was locked behind him. "I'm sorry," he began, fully expecting her to go for him with her fists and wondering how he could prevent her from being put in a straitjacket. But her body merely sagged a little. She stared at him moist-eyed, pursing her tremulous lower lip like a child on the verge of tears who knows that crying is forbidden.

"Wouldn't you prefer to sit down, Frau Bender?"

She shook her head. "A stroke?" she whispered. "How is he? Will he get over it?"

"The doctors are very optimistic," he lied. "And your aunt never leaves his bedside."

"That's good," she murmured. She went over to her bed and sat down after all. He gave her a minute or two to recover from the shock, saw her hopes revive and her shoulders straighten. She raised her head and looked at him. "So you weren't able to speak to him?"

"No."

A satisfied smile flitted across her face. "Good," she said. "And I don't want to speak to you either. Go away."

He didn't budge, although he suddenly felt it would be the best solution. Psychiatry might seem horrendous to someone who didn't need it, but Professor Burthe enjoyed an excellent reputation. Burthe would discover why Georg Frankenberg had had to die. He was also bound to discover whether, when and under what circumstances Cora Bender had met Frankenberg and whether heroin had played a part in it, or whether she had come into contact with the drug later on. His own intentions in regard to her were fundamentally nonsensical. They would yield no evidence that would stand up in court, nor were they likely to establish a connection with Frankenberg. As for his wish to satisfy himself that her aunt had merely been launching another diversionary manoeuvre . . .

228

He drew a deep breath. "I realize you're angry with me, Frau Bender. I also realize you've no wish to talk to me, but I didn't come here to talk, just to ask you to do something for me."

Her look of surprise and enquiry was still alloyed with satisfaction. He felt in his jacket pocket. The hell with it! He'd got hold of the stuff and now he wanted to know the truth. Taking a plastic bag from his pocket, he went over to the table in the middle of the ward and laid out the contents: a hypodermic syringe still in its wrapping, a metal spoon, a candle end, a tourniquet and a small sachet filled with white powder.

She surveyed them with a look of cold distaste. "What's this, taking a leaf out of the Americans' book? Lethal injections save the state a fortune, and we're pretty broke. What do you want me to do, OD?"

"There isn't enough in there for that."

She shrugged her shoulders indifferently. "A little something to cheer me up, then? Very nice of you, but no thanks. They give me enough dope in here already. I'll be interested to see if I can give it up as easily as I did that stuff there."

"*Did* you find it easy to give it up?" He almost grinned. It seemed a tiny indication that her aunt had been telling the truth in this respect. "If so, you're the great exception," he added. "Other people go through hell."

"I slept through it," she said tartly.

He nodded. "Thanks to that nice doctor of yours, I presume. Doctors have ways of easing withdrawal symptoms, of course. From all I've heard, though, most of them make an addict go through hell as part of the cure. Ah well, there are different kinds of hell. We'll talk about that later."

"I'm not talking at all," she said firmly. "Neither now nor later."

"Very well," he said. "You don't have to. You don't have to inject yourself either. Just show me you can do it."

She chuckled derisively. "Ah, so that's it: you've been talking to Margret. What did she tell you? That I didn't know how to fill a syringe? It's different when you're at your wits' end, you know. When you're scared of being thrown out because you've already

229

caused a lot of aggro and someone catches you shooting up. You have to think of something fast." She chuckled again. "What happens if I show you I can handle the stuff? Will you leave me in peace at last?"

When he nodded she got up off the bed and came over to the table. She raised her forefinger like someone bidding a child pay attention. "Good, then let's make a deal. I'll show you. In return, you must leave my father alone as well as me. I want you to shake hands on it."

He held out his hand, momentarily surprised by the firm grip of her slender fingers. Then he handed her a lighter.

She sighed, looking at the wrapped syringe and the tourniquet. "But I'm not putting that round my arm," she said. "I never liked the feel of it. It'll be good enough if I fill the syringe and apply it to the back of my hand, won't it? I couldn't get it into my arm anyway. Will that be all right?"

He nodded again.

"Let me think, then. It's been quite a while." She put a finger to her head, then said: "First we stick the candle to the table. If it leaves any wax behind, you can explain it to them. It was your idea."

"You don't have to stick the candle to the table, Frau Bender," he said, but she'd already lit the wick and was dripping wax onto the tabletop by rotating the candle end.

"But it's safer if your hands shake," she said, "and they usually do. That way the candle won't fall over, at least. You can concentrate on the spoon and make sure you don't spill any of the precious stuff. So, what next?"

She picked up the sachet, rubbed it between her fingers and peered at the white powder through the transparent plastic. "What is this? It isn't H! You can't give me H!"

She eyed him thoughtfully with her head on one side. "But you wouldn't do that, you aren't that stupid. You know perfectly well I'd grass on you as soon as your back was turned. What did you put in there? It isn't flour – flour isn't as white as that."

When he didn't reply she said: "I'm only asking because of the solution. There mustn't be any lumps or it wouldn't go through the needle."

He still didn't speak. With a shrug, she carefully tore open the sachet and sniffed the contents. Then she moistened a finger and inserted it. Never taking her eyes off him, she slowly put the finger to her lips and dabbed it with the tip of her tongue.

"Icing sugar," she said. "That's not fair, when I've always had such a sweet tooth. You wouldn't have a knob of butter in your pocket, would you? I could make us a few nice caramels. They'd be more enjoyable than this nonsense of yours."

When he didn't respond, feeling suddenly stupid and privately cursing Margret Rosch and her opinions, which were just a tactical smokescreen, she shrugged again. "All right," she said, "let's get it over."

She tipped the contents of the sachet into the spoon, went over to the washbasin and turned on the tap. Having adjusted it until it was only dripping, she held the spoon underneath and gave a nod every time a drop landed in it, almost as if she was counting. Twice she carefully stirred the solution with a fingertip. Then, apparently satisfied with the consistency, she turned off the tap and came back to the table. She smiled at him as she held the spoon over the candle flame. Grovian did his best to look non-committal.

"At least the water here is clean," she said. "We used to scoop it out of the loo. Heaven knows what sort of shit I pumped into my arms. No wonder they look as if they've been gnawed by rats."

She was uncertain, that was unmistakable. Her eyes flitted back and forth between his face and the spoon. Eventually she removed the spoon from the flame, smiled at him and said casually: "I think that's hot enough. I mustn't let it boil."

Grovian found it hard to suppress a grin. When she picked up the hypo with her free hand, he caught hold of her arm. "Thank you, Frau Bender, that'll do. You don't have to fill it."

He didn't know whether to laugh or swear, nor did he know what bearing this had on the Frankenberg case. He only knew that her aunt had been right: Cora Bender genuinely had no idea how to prepare a fix. She had never shot up by herself; she could at most have seen someone else fill a hypo on television.

He blew out the candle, took the spoon from her and rinsed off the sugar solution under the tap. Then he stowed everything in the plastic bag and replaced it in his pocket.

"So," he said. "Remember our bargain? If you showed me you could handle the stuff, I'd leave you in peace. Well, now you've shown me you *can't* handle it, I'm at liberty to ask you a few more questions."

She was so startled, she simply stared at him for a few seconds before shaking her head and glaring at him angrily. "Did I do something wrong? Yes, I know, I ought to have unwrapped the syringe first. But I'd have done that – I could have managed it with my teeth and one hand. It was mean of you to grab my arm before I could show you, and now you say I couldn't have done it."

"It wasn't that, Frau Bender."

"What was it, then?"

"Why do you want to know? If you've washed your hands of heroin, you've no need to know."

To hell with fear and feelings of guilt, his own and hers. He was feeling good at this moment – damned good, in fact. The first step had been taken, now for the second. He was undeterred by the fact that she'd sat down on the bed again and was ostentatiously staring out of the window with a face like stone. He felt sure he could induce her to talk. He'd always managed to loosen her tongue and chip away at her wall in the past. Another few well-aimed hammer blows were all it needed.

"I couldn't speak to your father," he began, "and I never even tried to speak to your mother, but your neighbour proved helpful." He inserted a minute pause before adding the name. "Grit Adigar. I'm sure you remember her."

She didn't reply, just sucked in her lower lip and went on staring out of the window.

"She told me about Horsti and Johnny Guitar," he went on, mingling Grit Adigar's statements with his own conjectures. "Johnny was a friend of Georg Frankenberg's, and Horsti was

232

a little weed with pale skin and colourless hair. You'd been his girlfriend since you were seventeen. Your neighbour also told me about Magdalena. She told me you were very fond of her. You did everything for her, and her death sent you right off the rails."

Grovian never took his eyes off her, but all she did was stare out of the window and bite her lower lip. She'd gone pale under the rainbow-hued bruises and the big strip of plaster on her forehead. He felt almost sorry for her, but not quite. Pity wouldn't help her.

"So," he said again. The word was like an audible punctuation mark. "I'd like you to get something straight, Frau Bender. I'm not your father. I'm not your mother. I'm not your aunt or your neighbour. I imagine you must have been subjected to a lot of questions and recriminations when you came home that time, but I'm not interested in Magdalena. I don't want to know why you left your sister by herself on that particular night. It's completely irrelevant to me, understand?"

She didn't respond, so he went on: "All I want to know is, what happened that night at the Aladdin and afterwards? I want to know what became of Horsti, whether you stayed with Johnny, when and where you met Georg Frankenberg, whether and when you came into contact with heroin and who gave it to you. Above all, I want to know the name of the doctor who treated your injuries."

Still no reaction. Her hands were lying in her lap as though she'd forgotten them. Her lower lip should have been bleeding by now, she was biting it so hard.

"And don't lie to me again, Frau Bender," he said sternly, as though speaking to a child – which was, in a way, how he looked upon her. "I'll find out one way or another. It may take time, but I'll get there in the end. Two of my men have been on the phone since lunchtime, each with a long list beside him. They're calling every doctor, every hospital in the Hamburg area. You could save us a lot of time and money if you volunteered the information."

He gave a start, it happened so suddenly. As she repeated the words, her voice rose from a whisper to a shout: "I don't know. I don't know! I don't *know*! I've no wish to know, either; when are you going to grasp that? I didn't go out at all that night – I wouldn't have left my sister alone on her birthday!"

He raised his hands in a soothing gesture. "Easy, Frau Bender, easy. I'm not talking about your sister's birthday. I know you didn't go out that night. I'm talking about the night in August when she died."

She shook her head like a wet dog, breathing heavily. Almost a minute went by. Then she slowly raised her arm and pointed to the door. "I'm not talking, I've told you a dozen times. Once and for all: get out! Go away, get lost, you're the bane of my existence. Do you seriously believe I'd confide in you again? You'd have to beat it out of me. If I tell you shit, I'll never be rid of the stink."

Still shaking her head, she underlined her refusal by stamping her foot several times. "No! That's it! Enough! Stop it, or you'll send me to join my sister. Go away, or I'll shout the house down. I'll tell them you tried to give me some heroin and I tipped it into the washbasin. They'll believe me – you've still got the stuff in your pocket. I'll say you wanted to have sex with me. Try proving the opposite! If you don't go this minute, I'll give you a dose of your own medicine. The boss of this place – he's the only one I'll talk to. I told him everything this morning."

"Everything?" he said, ignoring her threat altogether. "Did you really tell him the whole story, Frau Bender?"

Seconds went by. She stared past him at the door with an inscrutable expression. "I told him all he needed to know," she said, rather more calmly.

"And what did you withhold from him?"

Another few seconds went by. She swallowed a couple of times, girding herself to reply. "Nothing that matters." She faltered, clearly finding it hard even to get a word out. "Nothing that isn't irrelevant from your point of view. That I had a sister who died of heart failure at the age of eighteen."

Grovian cursed his conflicting emotions. Reason pointed to the door; compassion urged him to take her in his arms. There, there, it's all right, it wasn't your fault. You weren't responsible for any of it. No one is born guilty.

Instead, he said: "Your sister was terminally ill, Frau Bender. She came home to die when she left the hospital that April, only she didn't tell anyone."

"That's not true." She sounded as if she could scarcely breathe.

"Yes, it is," he said firmly. "The doctors will confirm that. Ask your aunt if you don't believe it; she has the hospital records. It's all down there, Frau Bender. Your sister would have died in any case, even if you'd remained at home that night. You couldn't have prevented it."

The corners of her mouth twisted in a kind of smile. She began to laugh or sob, he couldn't tell which. "Shut up! You don't know what you're talking about."

"Then tell me, Frau Bender. Tell me."

She shook her head to and fro, to and fro, so slowly and deliberately that her nose and chin were almost aligned with each shoulder in turn. That was her sole response.

*

I can't talk to anyone about Magdalena. If I were to be entirely open and honest about her, everyone would think I hated her – hated her enough to kill her. Father thought so, Margret thought so, and Grit didn't know what to think.

I didn't kill Magdalena, I can't have. She was my sister, after all, and I loved her. Not always, I admit – not at the start, but that was only natural. Any child would have felt the same in my place.

Magdalena stole my childhood from me. She robbed me of my mother, and my father of the wife he so badly needed, the cheerful, lively person she used to be, according to Margret. A woman who could laugh and dance and enjoy the occasional drink. Who regularly had sex with her husband because it was what she herself wanted. Who wanted a child. Who became a mother and was overjoyed by the birth of her elder daughter.

I never saw my mother laugh, only pray; never saw her happy, only demented. It was Magdalena who drove her mad. But for Magdalena, I would never have had to hear that I'd sapped all her strength. I would never have had to pray till my lips were numb and my knees sore. I wouldn't have had to share a bedroom with my father or see him masturbating. I wouldn't have felt such disgust or wet my bed for years on end. I wouldn't have had such trouble with my periods. I'd have had a mother to explain things and help me cope with my problems – in fact, I mightn't have had any problems at all.

But Magdalena missed having a mother as much as I did. I remember her talking about it once when she'd just turned fifteen and spent another two days at Eppendorf, being checked over again from top to toe. ECG, blood tests – all kinds of tests, the doctors gave her, and all they'd ever come up with in the end was a number – a very low number. This time it had been a five. Another five months, that was all they'd given her.

Her heart had become overdeveloped and completely worn out. The doctors were quite frank with her. They'd tried to be frank with Mother at one time, but it wasn't much use. As for Father . . . Well, he'd stopped taking an interest in what went on at home.

We were lying in bed the night after she returned from the hospital for the last time. It was still light in the bedroom. "I don't care how long they give me," Magdalena said, staring up at the ceiling. "They've always been wrong so far, and it'll be the same again, you mark my words. My ticker and I will grow old together, and you'll probably be the only one to see it. I strongly suspect that our beloved mother and our drunk of a father will have kicked the bucket long before that."

She folded her arms behind her head, only to remove them again in a hurry. "Damn it!" she said. "It's hell, not being able to lie the way you want. All the same, it'll be a while before I breathe my last. You must promise me something, Cora. Don't let me rot – don't stick me in the ground with the worms. Make sure I have a nice, clean cremation. If there's no other way, haul me off into the woods and tip a can of petrol over me. I'd sooner go to hell than have to sing duets with Mother in heaven. I dread the thought of finding her waiting for me at the gate."

236

She chuckled. "Can you imagine what'll happen when Mother moves in? St Peter will be able to retire, I guarantee you. She'll become the head receptionist – she'll sort out who's allowed in and who isn't. By the time she's through, no one will qualify. Still, if she gets bored she can always chat about the old days with Peter. I bet you Mother knows more about them than he does. All she doesn't know is what's needed down here."

She fell silent for a minute or two, gazing up at the ceiling as if she could see through it into Mother's fantasies. "I'm really glad she doesn't know," she went on slowly. "I'm thankful she doesn't come near me when she's been too busy praying to wash for three days, but there were times when I wished she would take me in her arms. Especially when I was so ill in the hospital. You've no idea how nauseous I felt. I retched so violently, I thought my aneurysm would burst at any moment. And who held the bowl under my chin? Who wiped my sweaty forehead? A young student nurse! Mother, who'd come to give me strength, courage and God knows what else, was down on her knees and getting in the nurse's way. I sometimes wished the girl would kick her backside. I needed her so badly, Cora, and she wasn't there. She was always nearby but never there. But who am I telling? She's never been there for you either."

She turned her head and looked at me. "Did you ever wish she would put her arms around you?"

"Not really," I said.

She sighed. "Well, you had Father. And now you've got a boyfriend outside. Tell me a bit about him."

So I told her about a wonderful, non-existent boy who was two years older than me. He had finished school and rode a motor scooter, and we used to meet down at the lake in the evenings. His parents were rich and very modern-minded. They owned a fantastic house, one of the ones in the woods beside the road to Dibbersen – you could only see their roofs as you drove past. Theirs was the height of chic – no expense spared – and his parents naturally had no objection to his bringing me home. On the contrary, they liked me a lot and always made me welcome. But they never kept us talking for long because they knew we wanted to be alone together. We went upstairs to his room and lay on the bed, listening to music and necking.

I told Magdalena about this boy every night. Every night I helped her up the stairs, got her undressed, held her while she brushed her teeth, washed her, creamed her and put her to bed. "I can't wait to see him," I would tell her.

I'd christened him Thomas. There was a boy at school named Thomas who I thought was very nice. He wasn't as rough and vulgar as the others. I didn't know much about him. He was in a higher class, so I only saw him in break. He usually spent it sitting in a corner on the ground, reading a book. He took as little interest in girls as they did in him. He wore glasses.

My Thomas didn't wear glasses, of course – Magdalena would have considered that a flaw. For her, boys had to be tall, strong and handsome, high-spirited but gentle. Thomas was my second such invention.

When Magdalena was in bed I would go downstairs and tell Mother: "I feel the need to commune with God in the open air." I couldn't remain in the house or Magdalena would soon have smelled a rat.

Then I would walk into town. There was always something happening in the centre of Buchholz. A lot of new buildings were going up, and I'd look at the construction sites and imagine that they would some day wall us in, surrounding our house and isolating us like the plague victims Father used to tell me about. Sometimes I also imagined meeting Thomas – the real, bespectacled one – and pictured us sitting down somewhere and reading a book together.

I owned some books myself – books I'd ordered specially and bought, not stolen. They were quite expensive, but I had plenty of cash. I spent barely a third of the housekeeping money I extorted from Father every week, yet we lived better than before. I'd given up selling hair slides in the playground. Lipsticks and other items of make-up, yes, but mainly perfume and other stuff that fetched good prices and was easily concealed – even, on one occasion, a Walkman.

I'd got hold of a Walkman for Magdalena as well. She always had it in bed with her. There was no danger that Mother would catch her with it. Mother never entered our room any more. She divided her time between her home-made altar and her bed, having devolved all her earthly responsibilities onto me.

I made breakfast for us all and attended to Magdalena before going to school. I cooked lunch when I came home, did the shopping and the laundry and kept the house clean. And I spent every spare minute with Magdalena until she was tucked up in bed and I could go out on the town.

A girl in my class used to tape the latest hits for me in return for a small fee. Magdalena wouldn't have benefited from her Walkman otherwise. She loved music, and used to listen to one cassette after another during the three hours I was away at school.

Before going into the house I would pay a short visit to the barn. The potato sacks no longer concealed a hoard of candy bars, but lots of other things, including cigarettes and a little lighter. I would light a cigarette and take a few puffs, then stub it out and replace it carefully in the packet. That way, one cigarette lasted me a couple of days.

I thoroughly disliked smoking – it made me cough and feel dizzy – but Magdalena thought it was cool and could tell from my breath if I'd had a cigarette. A few months later, after the Thomas episode, I gave it up. I told her my new boyfriend hated cigarettes and couldn't stand girls who smoked. He said you might as well kiss an ashtray, and I didn't want to risk losing him because he looked fantastic and I got wet between the legs if he so much as touched my knee. Magdalena appreciated this.

I made this new boyfriend three years older. I can't remember what I called him; there were so many names in the course of time. He was the first boy I went to bed with, and Magdalena asked me to show her what it was like.

I genuinely did all I could for her. Sometimes she said: "I'm going to have another operation when I'm old enough to decide for myself. I'll find a surgeon who'll do it."

We planned to fly to the States together, to one of the great cardiac hospitals. We kept working out how much money we'd have by her eighteenth birthday if we put aside a hundred marks a week. I'd told her I could spare that much from the housekeeping. I didn't tell her it was twice that amount in case she became suspicious and thought I was helping myself to our hoard.

She said a hundred marks a week wouldn't do the trick. I told her that I'd found a wallet at the station containing a thousand marks, and that I always kept my eyes peeled because a lot of people were pretty careless and didn't notice when they lost things.

Magdalena laughed. "You're a dear," she said, "but you're a dope. You'd have to rob a bank to get that much money together. Fancy relying on people losing things!"

I was on the point of telling her that I hadn't found the money, and that there was far more in the barn than a thousand marks, but I'd read in a newspaper what operations cost and that you had to pay for them out of your own pocket. I didn't have anything like enough, and I didn't know how to get it.

It wouldn't have been such a problem if I'd been able to work after leaving school, but someone had to look after the house and Magdalena. Mother couldn't do that any more, even if she'd wanted to. Father had bought her a modern washing machine, but she couldn't cope with the thing and wanted nothing to do with it. I think she was afraid of it. She said it was the work of the Devil and turned off the water, saying we must fast for forty days in the wilderness. Although I managed to talk her out of that, we had to be constantly on our guard in case she did something silly.

Magdalena thought it would be better if I stayed at home. "Work?" she said. "What work would you do? A trainee's job is the most you'd get at your age. That means three years of earning next to nothing. If you're really serious about raising the money for my operation, we must think of something else. I've had an idea. There's a job that pays better the younger you are, but I don't know how you'd feel about it."

12

Cora Bender's transfer from the remand centre to the district hospital compelled the judicial authorities to appoint an attorney for her. Her family had so far made no move in that direction.

Her husband and her parents-in-law seemed to have forgotten her existence. Her aunt, the qualified nurse, was in north Germany, keeping watch over an elderly, dying man who was past helping. As for her mother, nothing could be expected from that quarter.

The district court at Cologne kept a list of attorneys available for *pro bono* work. One of them, Eberhard Brauning, was highly regarded for his courtroom technique. His friends, who included several judges, called him Hardy. Thirty-eight years old and unmarried, he shared a house with his mother Helene, the only woman in his life who really mattered to him.

Helene Brauning had for many years worked in the same field as Professor Burthe. Frequently called as an expert witness, she had only twice failed to prevent the imposition of a term of imprisonment. She had specialized – and not only in court – in cases of severe mental disturbance. Her retirement two years ago had been prompted in part by the fact that she'd found it more and more depressing not to be able to help people, only to keep them under lock and key.

To Eberhard Brauning, psychiatry and psychology were double-edged swords. Mentally deranged offenders had fascinated him since his earliest youth, but only in theory. In real life he abhorred them. Fortunately, however, they tended to be the exception in his daily routine.

If a husband killed his wife while drunk or consumed with jealousy, Brauning could handle it. If a hitherto inoffensive office clerk raped a female colleague after a firm's party, he could act for such a man, despite his personal distaste.

Eberhard Brauning liked calculable reflexes and comprehensible motives. He required candour but not necessarily remorse. If remorse was also on offer, he welcomed it; but he could cope just as well with denial.

None of these things could be expected from the creatures to whom Helene Brauning had devoted half her life. They inhabited a world to which he had no access. Their behaviour could provide the makings of a lively conversation with his mother in the evening. Where his work was concerned, however, he preferred cases in which a client's circumstances and mental state were clear-cut.

To the examining magistrate, the Frankenberg case appeared to be one such. A young woman had killed her erstwhile lover in the presence of a dozen or more eyewitnesses. Having at first denied knowing the man, she had later, when pressed by the interrogating officer, come clean about their relationship and her motives. Since then she had attempted suicide.

The district attorney's file was almost complete. All that was missing was the psychologist's report, but that could take a little while longer. Professor Burthe was snowed under with work.

Also missing was a signed confession, because the young woman had retracted her original statement and was once more stubbornly disclaiming all knowledge of her victim. It was obvious what she hoped to achieve, and Eberhard Brauning was just the man to convince her that prison was preferable to a lunatic asylum.

To Brauning, Cora Bender's current detention in a psychiatric ward was adequately explained by her attempted suicide. Paper handkerchiefs! That idea entailed some ingenuity. He considered it an extremely clever ploy and relied on the personal impression of the examining magistrate, who had described her as cold and unfeeling. He also realized, however, that the magistrate was loath to take a risk.

Having requested a sight of the file, Brauning was issued with copies of all the available documents five days after Georg Frankenberg's death. That was on Thursday. Early that evening he began his perusal of the file by studying the witnesses' statements made shortly after the killing and later amplified with details not directly related to the incident itself.

The victim's behaviour seemed as clear to him as it had to the gullible paterfamilias who had put it on record. A note had been subsequently added to the file containing Cora Bender's personal particulars. A sister, Magdalena Rosch, had died five years ago of cardiac and renal failure. Brauning attached no importance to this addendum.

He felt fleetingly uneasy while reading the transcripts of the tapes. Either Cora Bender had been in a state for which mental confusion was a very mild description, or she'd staged a first-class performance for the benefit of the officer interviewing her. Although he inclined to the latter view, he would have liked to hear his mother's opinion. Unfortunately, Helene had already gone to bed by the time he laid the file aside. It was long past midnight, and he didn't have time for an exhaustive discussion when they breakfasted together the next morning. He merely mentioned that he'd landed a new and extremely interesting case: yet another woman who imagined that the district hospital was a sanatorium.

Brauning arranged a meeting with his client as soon as he got to his chambers. He was firmly resolved to make it clear to her that a full confession would be likely to render the court more lenient. Early on Friday afternoon, at three o'clock precisely, a door was unlocked, and he saw her for the first time.

She was standing by the window in a plain skirt and a simply cut blouse, both of them creased and grubby. She wore no stockings, so the feet in her flat-heeled shoes were bare. Her hair looked as if it hadn't been in contact with water or shampoo for several days, and her face, when she slowly turned towards the door . . .

Brauning involuntarily caught his breath, assailed for the first time by doubts about his assessment of the situation. Such apathy! Her eyes reminded him of the glass eyes in the head of an old teddy bear he'd dearly loved as a little boy. They'd been quite big, those button eyes, and when he held them to the light he could see himself reflected in them – just himself and his bedroom, nothing more. They never revealed any stirrings of emotion inside old Teddy's straw-filled frame.

The briefcase in his hand seemed to have doubled in weight. He slowly expelled the breath he'd been holding, swallowed once and said in a studiously calm, deliberate tone: "Good afternoon, Frau Bender. I'm your attorney, Eberhard Brauning."

She looked him up and down, betraying no emotion of any kind.

"My attorney?" she said in a low, expressionless voice.

"The court has appointed me to safeguard your interests. Or, to put it more simply, to conduct your defence. You know what you stand accused of?"

He could have sworn, from the way she was standing there, that she didn't know. Nor did she answer his question. "It's rather warm in here," she said, turning back to the barred window. "The sky looks cloudy, though. Not the weather for a swim. I should have stayed in the water the first time. I'd have forgotten everything by now – I could be leading a peaceful life with the man down below."

She drew a long, tremulous breath.

"We talked about it this morning, the professor and I. The fact that I wanted to live with the man in the lake. And on Friday I said to him, 'You're wrong, my friend, it's Monday already.' But today is Friday, isn't it? I asked the professor this morning, and he said today is Friday."

She was silent for some seconds. Then she turned her head and eyed him appraisingly over her shoulder. "Or was he lying? If you want to do me a great favour, tell me he was lying. These quacks are a curse. When you think they're telling the truth they're wrong, and when you think they're wrong they're telling the truth. For instance, one of them told me I was a drug-addicted whore who only had sex with perverts."

She gave a little shrug. "He wasn't wrong, unfortunately. Perverts simply pay better, and I had to raise a lot of money in a hurry. It

244

all depended on me – she asked me to do it. She wanted me to pay for her heart with my body."

A rueful smile brought her face to life for an instant, but it vanished as quickly as it had come. "I would have done anything for her," she went on. "I'd have ripped out my own heart and given it to her if I could, and she knew it. She knew a lot about messed-up types like me. She knew I was so messed up, I wouldn't have cared."

Eberhard Brauning could only stare at her and try to make some sense of her effusions. Heart, sister . . .

She nodded to herself, lost in thought. "But I couldn't do that for her. I was only sixteen, and I'd never gone to bed with a man before. I wept. I prayed all night long that she'd think of another idea. And do you know what she told me? 'You've no need to fuck anyone, you idiot. Normal sex doesn't pay well. SM, that's the only thing that makes real money. You wouldn't have to offer your pussy to scum like that. All you need to do is give the dirty old men a regular walloping. Thrash them with a whip. Kick them in the crotch, stick pins in their peckers – that's what they enjoy.' But I couldn't torture old men either. The very idea!"

She put a hand over her mouth. Her deliberate nodding was succeeded by an equally deliberate shaking of the head. "She said I should simply think of Father and the way he'd got off on me. She said she'd only wanted to stop me getting hysterical when I showed her how he'd felt between my legs. That was the only reason why she'd told me it meant nothing. 'Feeling between your legs to see if you'd wet the bed? A glance at the sheets would have been enough.' I knew she was a beast when she said that. Still, everyone tries to survive in their own way, don't they? She only wanted to live."

Brauning managed a nod. "So do we all," he said.

She nodded too. "I ought to have done it. A lot of people genuinely enjoy being hurt and humiliated – you're only doing them a favour. I could have got her off my back in a legal way. I had to get rid of her somehow or other. She would never have died of her own accord, but after an operation she could have lived on her own, she wouldn't have needed me as much. Why didn't I do it while there was still time? Why did I only do it when she was dead? Was I trying to kill two birds with one stone? Apologize to my father and, at the same time, be able to say: 'Hey, you up there, look at me. I'm doing it, you see? I'm doing it for you.'"

She looked at him, and a spark began to glimmer in the depths of those glassy eyes. Not a spark of life, though, only of torment.

"I did it," she said with a long sigh. "But not in the way she'd suggested. I could never have brought myself to stick a pin in someone's penis. I swapped roles and offered my own flesh instead, but even that I couldn't handle. In order to endure the filth I was exposed to, I shot up. Sounds logical, doesn't it? I think it does, thoroughly logical, but the chief doesn't believe me. Do you?"

Brauning had an urge to hammer on the door and ask to be let out. To be spared the sight of those eyes, in which the spark was now glowing more brightly. To be released from this room – even, if possible, from this assignment. Cardiac and renal failure! That, he supposed, had been an error – not the only error in this case, and he had let himself in for it.

Instead of hammering on the door, he started to whistle a tune in his head. A cheerful tune. It had steadied his nerves even as a boy, this soundless whistling.

The beds in the ward were neatly made up. You could only tell they'd been used from the pillowcases, which were stained and creased like Cora Bender's clothing.

She had been silent for at least a minute. He didn't notice this until she followed the direction of his gaze and grinned. "Looks as if I've got company here, doesn't it?" she said sarcastically. "Don't be deceived by those beds, they're just a ploy. The only people I've seen here so far are the nursing staff, the professor and the chief. I imagine they're testing me to see if I'm still in my right mind, or if I'll start talking to non-existent people."

The change caught him wholly unprepared. Her voice and even her expression were suddenly those of someone amusing herself at other people's expense. They'd played a trick on her and failed to discern that she'd seen through it long ago, so she was fully entitled to laugh at their stupidity.

246

"On the other hand," she said with a shrug, "maybe it's because I sleep too much. I only have to lie down and I doze off in two seconds flat. You could fire a gun in my ear, and I wouldn't wake up – they always have to shake me in the mornings. The professor thinks it's a bad sign, my sleeping so much and enjoying it into the bargain. He must have read that sleep is death's little brother."

She laughed derisively. "But that's nonsense, the little brother idea never occurred to me. I shared a bedroom with the big brother for years. What's more, I welcomed it when Father moved next door and the big brother moved in with me. People are so stupid sometimes, it ought to be prohibited."

Brauning had already breathed a sigh of relief and was looking for a way of introducing the speech he'd prepared when she suddenly blinked. Her next words were uttered in a voice as bemused and apathetic as it had been at first.

"I'm sorry, you probably don't know what I'm talking about. I don't know myself, sometimes. My head isn't always as clear as it might be. They keep pumping me full of some shit or other. The professor claims it's just something to counter my depressive symptoms, but they're a bunch of liars in here, believe me."

She squared her shoulders. "But I'll make it," she said, sounding thoroughly wide awake. "I always have. I used to say, if someone gives you a kick in the backside, it's an incentive to move on. Or don't you agree?"

Her tone became harsh and mocking. "Now don't look so scared. I'm not mad; I only act that way. It's practical, being mad in here. I didn't take long to discover that. You can talk utter crap. If they ask unpleasant questions, you can fob them off with any old rubbish. They like that. They need it to justify their existence – that's what they're paid for, after all. But the two of us are talking sensibly together. You mustn't tell anyone I'm still capable of it. As my attorney you're pledged to secrecy, I presume. Except that I don't need you. I'm sorry you've had a wasted journey."

Eberhard Brauning felt like someone exposed to an alternation of hot and cold baths. He didn't know what to make of her outpourings or how to respond to them. "The court has entrusted me with your defence," he repeated lamely.

She shrugged, and an arrogant smile appeared on her bruised and battered face. "What makes the court think I want to be defended? Tell them I chucked you out. Or say you changed your mind after speaking with me."

"That's impossible, Frau Bender," he said. "You need an attorney, and —"

"Nonsense," she broke in coolly. "I don't need anyone. I get on best when I'm all alone, not that I ever am. Do you know 'The Sorcerer's Apprentice'?"

He nodded, looking baffled, and she went on: "I didn't summon the spirits. It was the chief. That bastard summoned them from hell, one after the other. Now he's ramming Magdalena down my throat. I knew that would happen if I brought her into it, that's why I kept quiet about her. But then he talked to Grit, and now I don't know how to get rid of her. I can't get rid of the others, either. Johnny, Billy-Goat, Tiger – I've no idea where I got them from, and I don't know where to put them or how to stop them trampling around on my mind."

She drove her fist into her palm and drew a deep breath. Then she smiled again. Pathetically this time, not arrogantly. "I'm in good company here, believe me. It wasn't my ambition to wind up in a loony bin, but beggars can't be choosers. It's not much different from prison; in fact, it may even be preferable. At least I don't get into arguments with other women. I swallow my pills like a good girl, finish most of my meals and tell the professor what he wants to hear. But let's leave it at that. I don't want anyone turning up and bugging me with questions so he can defend me in court. I've no wish to be defended. I can defend myself."

Eberhard Brauning was feeling just as Rudolf Grovian had felt during his first few hours with her. He failed to see the knife-edge on which her mental state reposed. Although he felt like losing his temper, he strove to remain calm and businesslike.

"No, Frau Bender, you can't. In this country, accused persons can't defend themselves in a jury trial. Not even I could, if I stood

248

accused of a capital crime. The verdict would have no legal validity and could be challenged at any time if the accused person had no defence counsel."

He waited for a moment to see if she would answer. When she remained silent he went over to the table and deposited his briefcase on it. He didn't open it at once, just pulled up a chair. "That's the fact of the matter. Whether or not we like it is irrelevant. When I was appointed your counsel I couldn't refuse. Now I could. I could tell the judge that Frau Bender refuses to cooperate and I cannot represent her under the circumstances. The judge would appreciate that. He would release me from my undertaking and appoint another attorney. You could naturally reject him as well, and a third, and a fourth. I don't know how long the judge would stand for this little game before his patience ran out. But you've only two alternatives: me or someone else. Perhaps you understand that now."

He didn't know why he'd explained this to her. It would have been far simpler to apply to the judge, except that he couldn't for the moment see anything that would have prompted him to regret his words. He felt she was leading him a dance and could have sworn she was playing the same tricks on him as she'd played on the police officer who had questioned her.

Johnny, Billy-Goat, Tiger! Not again, not with him! She was good at her role. She was almost brilliant, but he'd lived with Helene for as long as he could remember, and if there was one thing he'd learned from her, it was this: those who could laugh at the idiots who blithely swallowed their stories knew exactly what they were doing.

It was fascinating to watch her face and see the derision that twisted those lips and breathed life into those glassy eyes. No doubt about it: she was having fun at his expense. He felt sure Helene would have confirmed his impression had she been there. Cora Bender thought she could lead everyone by the nose.

"So we're both in the same boat, aren't we?" she said, coming over to the table and sitting down. "Where do we go from here? I'm really sorry you've been landed with me, but if that's the way things are I'd sooner hang onto you. I mean, they might send me some old fogey. At least you're easy on the eye. I don't want this case to overtax you, so I'll make things as simple as I can. I'm guilty, that's beyond dispute. I don't deny it. I've made a full confession, but I don't intend to make any further statements. Will that do?"

Brauning sat down at last. He opened his briefcase, took out the sheaf of papers and put it down in front of him. "It'll suffice for a conviction," he said. He laid his hand on the file. "This doesn't look good for you."

"I'm used to that," she said, grinning again. "Nothing has ever looked good for me. Put that away, I know what's in it. 'Deliberately inflicted wounds . . .' And that's not all. Heaven alone knows what else the chief is digging up, and when the professor's through with me he's bound to write a nice report for the district attorney. Perhaps he'll do you a favour and mention a few mitigating factors."

She heaved a big sigh. "We'll see," she went on. "When you've got everything together, work out your strategy. Then pay me another visit, and we'll talk it over quietly. I may be a bit wiser by then. At the moment we're only wasting our time."

She cast a yearning glance at the window, and her voice took on a melancholy note. For a while, it seemed to Brauning that she was merely trying to demonstrate her mental faculties.

"The thing is," she said, "I have to be rather careful what I say. Have you ever felt you had to cling to your sanity with both hands? It's quite a job, believe me. There are times when I have to look at those bars again and again to convince myself that I'm not back home. Everything seems so real, as if I'm right in the middle of it all. I help her up to bed and hold her while she cleans her teeth or see her sitting in the kitchen. Why must I go through it all again? I'd left it far behind me and shut the door tight. The chief kicked it open. He shouldn't have threatened me. That's what started it."

She shook her head in surprise and corrected herself. "No, it started down by the lake, but there I only tasted the raspberryade and saw the little cross. And now I taste his blood and see the three big crosses. It doesn't matter where I look, I see them everywhere. And the one in the middle bears an innocent man."

He felt reluctant to interrupt her monologue, but it really wasn't appropriate for her to put on such a show for his benefit. High time she understood that. "Who threatened you and what with?" he asked.

She continued to stare at the window, looking as detached as she had to begin with. "The chief," she muttered. Then, somewhat louder: "Rudolf Grovian, that's his name. A persistent swine, believe you me. He told me he'd found the girl with the broken ribs."

Her eyes returned to Brauning's face, glassy once more. "Terrible, isn't it?" She nodded slowly to herself. "But there's nothing to be done. He's only doing his job. I know I've no right to complain, and I've no wish to. But now he's collected so much information, surely he could give it a rest. He won't, though. He won't stop till he's done for me. I'm going crazy in here."

Her voice sent shivers down his spine. The last words were just a hoarse whisper. She smote her chest with a clenched fist, clamping her eyes shut as though in pain. Then she regained her composure.

"I could wring his neck, but I like him in a way. Love your enemies, the Saviour always said. The chief was my first enemy. I felt so strong to begin with. That man was lying there, bleeding to death, and I felt great. I felt like Goliath – I *was* Goliath. I was so tall, I could see the knife on the high table and pick it up. And then along came this little David, and said he had to have a talk with my father. I lost my nerve and lied. And the funny thing was, the more I told him, the more I could see. The splashy picture and the green mosaics in the floor and the girl on the stairs. And now I can see the three crosses. I know I killed an innocent man, and I'm frightened. I'm terribly frightened of his father's anger."

Brauning couldn't bring himself to do as he'd intended and bring her back to the point. He wished his mother were there. He would have liked her advice on what to do.

Cora Bender's lips tightened. She covered her face with both hands for seconds on end. "Sometimes," she whispered, "when I think I'm asleep at night, he appears at my bedside. I don't see him, I just feel him. He bends over me and says: 'My son wasn't to blame for this disaster. He did his best.' Every time he says that I want to shout: 'That's a lie!' But I can't. I can't open my mouth because I'm asleep."

After an eternity she lowered her hands. Her face was just as he'd imagined a madwoman's face as a child.

"Don't worry," she murmured wearily. "I know how all this sounds, but I also know who I can say it to and who not. I never breathe a word to the professor about the Saviour and Mary Magdalene. At first I wanted nothing to do with her, but then she washed his feet and everything changed. Do you know the Bible well?"

The look that accompanied the question was appraising and matter-of-fact, like that of an expert trying to explain something to a layman. He gave another involuntary shrug. "A bit," he said.

"If you've any questions about it," she went on, "just ask me. I know every word. I even know the bits that were never written. She was only trying to ingratiate herself with me when she washed his feet. She wanted to destroy him, and she did. I did it, I don't know why. I honestly don't know. That tune can't have been the only reason."

Her fingertips started drumming rhythmically on the tabletop. "It was his tune, and I had it in my head. How did it get there? I must have known him after all, don't you think? So why can't I remember him? Do you think he could really have been one of my clients? I can't remember them either. All that happened after she died is gone. I've buried it so deep, I can't get at it any more. I've turned over the whole of my brain and found nothing. Perhaps it's behind here."

She tapped the hair covering her forehead. "I won't find anything, even if I dig away till I die. That's the spot where he hit me first, I remember that now. And again on the side of the head. Then everything went black. I suppose they thought I was dead. They dumped me beside the road. Do you think I should tell it to the professor the way I told it to the chief? That might be an advantage, then there wouldn't be any inconsistency. It's best to be consistent or they catch you out right away."

"So what did you tell the chief?" Brauning asked hesitantly.

"Well, about the two men and Frankie sitting on the sofa. Don't you have that in your file?"

He shook his head. "That's odd," she said, "I didn't think he was slipshod. I told him they were friends of Frankie's," she went on eagerly, "and that the girl wanted me to do it with both of them at the same time. I'd like to stick to that story, and I'd also like to explain that Frankie was my pimp."

"And was he?" Brauning asked.

"Of course not," she said, sounding almost indignant, "but no one can prove the opposite. I'd already thought that over, but now . . ." She broke off and smiled apologetically. "Things sometimes get mixed up when I'm thinking, but don't worry, I'll work it out."

She sat back in her chair. "Well," she said, nodding thoughtfully, "we've discussed everything now. It's been worthwhile, at least from your point of view, and you won't need to come again. I'm going to try to think some more. Perhaps you'd better go."

Brauning thought so too. He had now gained some understanding, if not of her and her motives, of the police officers who had questioned her. It was time to discuss the case with Helene.

*

She kept tripping over fragments, picking herself up and roaming on across the rubble-strewn wasteland that had once been a brain neatly divided into two halves by a wall. The chief's visit had left her in such a bad way, she'd lost herself. Although she occasionally came across bits of herself, they usually dated from another time.

When her lawyer appeared, this chaotic jumble spewed out bits of the Cora who had defied her father-in-law and extracted an office, a salary and, finally, a house from him. Except that these fragments disappeared while Brauning was seated across the table from her.

She found herself seated once more at Magdalena's bedside and down at the lake with Frankie. She dipped her face in his blood. The next moment, Johnny was smiling at her from the front seat

253

of a car, even though she knew full well it couldn't have happened that way. It was as unreal as God the Father bending over her at night, when she thought she was asleep, and speaking of his guiltless son.

She badly needed someone to help her clear away the biggest fragments, but it would have to be a very special person. Someone who understood and, if need be, believed in miracles and desires that turned into mental images. You had to believe in them when there was no alternative. But no such special person appeared, so she made a lone attempt to create a little order, a somewhat tidier impression.

She realized that the other beds weren't a ploy soon after the day of her attorney's visit. How long after, she couldn't have said – one day resembled another – but that was unimportant. She had no contact with the other women. Unlike her, they lived in relative freedom. She left the ward only when another session with the professor was due. Her fear of him was soon a thing of the past. She got on well with him and quickly discovered what he wanted to hear. She even ended by telling him about Magdalena because she assumed that he would hear about her from the chief in any case.

And Frankie was to blame for Magdalena's death. She had eventually discussed this with her attorney. The professor didn't believe her at first because Frankie's father was a colleague of his and a professor like himself. He said a handsome young man of good family had no need to go pimping.

She'd thought the same at one time, but what she'd thought had ceased to matter. All that mattered now was to marshal her thoughts like a flock of frightened lambs and prevent them from stampeding. They usually did that when wolves were chasing them but not during her conversations about Frankie the pimp. Then the flock stood firm, and the wolves kept their distance.

Why shouldn't Frankie have been a pimp? He thought it chic to have a girl who danced to his tune. He'd never spoken about it to his father, of course. Nobody knew, but it was true! He'd accosted her that night in August and insisted on her having sex with two men at the same time.

Frankie had expected a lot of her – too much, in fact. And when Magdalena was dead – when she needed him badly – he'd grown tired of her and found himself a new girlfriend. And, because she wouldn't go away of her own accord, he'd told his friends to teach her a lesson. They'd beaten her up while he and his new girlfriend watched.

Her attorney would have been proud of her if he could have heard her. Although the professor was the expert, it was as easy to lie to him as it had been to Mother. She spent a total of three sessions drumming the pimp scenario into his head. She went into detail, adding the occasional embellishment and coming out with every enormity the human brain could devise. The little demons with red-hot pincers provided excellent models for the perverted clients she described.

The professor had her taken back to the ward when he'd heard enough. There she was a madwoman who could let herself go, and she did. When no one else was around it didn't matter where she was or whether she herself was present. Plenty of other people were there. Mother and Father, Magdalena and Johnny, Billy-Goat and Tiger, Frankie and a doctor. Not to mention her fear and shame and guilt.

Members of the nursing staff came in periodically, but since they entered by the door she knew exactly how to behave. She spoke normally to them, confining herself to trivialities for fear of making a mistake. "What's for lunch today?" she would ask. "It smells nice." Or she would look at the mush on her plate and say: "I wish I had a better appetite, but I've never been a great eater."

Sometimes she would also ask: "Do you think I could have a really decent cup of coffee? I'm always so tired. Some coffee would do me good, I'm sure."

She wasn't anything like as tired as she made out. That was because she only took her prescribed medication at night. Then she went straight to sleep and didn't have to cope with the other women, one of whom might have asked why she was there. But the pills on her tray in the morning she got rid of. The nursing staff were careless, and she herself was very convincing.

She had the situation under better control without medication.

255

She could ask Father's forgiveness, enthuse to Mother about communing with God in the open air and tell Magdalena about her randy boyfriends and their forthcoming flight to America. Frankie and the other young men were the only ones she didn't say a word to. Her throat seized up when Frankie gave her his forgiving look. He must have known he'd been born a sacrificial lamb destined to wash away her sins with his blood. What else could have accounted for the look on his face?

Perhaps Mother's preachifying hadn't been so crazy after all. If the Saviour had ascended into heaven two thousand years ago, who or what was there to prevent him from returning to help and redeem people once more? To enable her to experience a few minutes' absolute freedom? Perhaps he had brought that platinum blonde to the lake for one reason alone: to demonstrate to her that Magdalena had been a dirty beast. Perhaps he wanted her to fight, not for her outward freedom but only for the inward sense of being redeemed by him.

She would have liked to discuss this with her lawyer, but she didn't see him again for the time being. The chief paid her another visit and wanted to talk about irrelevancies with her, but she shook her head, and he left it at that. He hadn't come as a policeman, just as an ordinary visitor.

And, like anyone visiting the sick, he came bearing gifts. A newspaper, a bottle of shampoo and some fruit. Three apples. Golden Delicious. No knife. He looked rather sheepish as he deposited the paper bag on the table.

"I hope you'll enjoy them, even if you can't cut them up first," he said.

His embarrassment rendered him harmless and human. So did his first few questions. Had she had any visitors?

"My attorney came one day."

"No one else?"

Who, for instance? She knew what he was getting at: Gereon. But that chapter was closed. It was almost as if she'd invented her years with him. Family, job, a child, a house, a nice life. It was over. Her stories only had a dramatic ending, never a sequel.

The chief had had another word with Margret. He'd gone to the trouble of driving all the way to Buchholz again to ask after her father, because he thought she might be interested. Of course she was interested, and it almost moved her to tears that an enemy should display such a generous human emotion.

Margret was still with her father. She sent her love and said how dismayed she was to hear that Cora had been transferred to a psychiatric ward. He repeated what Margret had said, word for word: "For God's sake get her out of there before she really loses her mind. Have you any idea what you're doing to her?"

The chief spoke of this quite openly. He was straight with her too. Unfortunately, he said, he had no influence in this respect. It all depended on her, on how well she cooperated with Professor Burthe. Had she now told him about Magdalena?

"Yes, of course," she assured him.

Rudolf Grovian wagged his head at her. Her smile spoke volumes. She might just as well have said: "I told him a pack of lies." He injected a hint of fatherly reproof into his voice.

"You must tell him the truth, Frau Bender, so that he can form an accurate impression. You'll only harm yourself if you lie to him. Your future depends on his report."

She gave a low laugh. "I don't want a future. I've enough of a past to last me for a century. Please give Margret my love and tell her she's wrong; it's like being on vacation. You don't get a tan, but everything else is fine. The service here is no worse than in a cheap hotel, and the staff are nice. No one complains, no one expects a tip. During the day I even have a room to myself, as you see. I'll tell you something: if the word gets around, they'll be run off their feet. Some day you'll be happy to be able to keep me company in here. It's restful, I can guarantee you that. Now and then you have a civilized conversation with an educated man, but the rest of the time you can devote yourself to your own thoughts."

"What thoughts do you devote yourself to, Frau Bender?"

She shrugged. "Oh, it varies. My favourite thought is that I killed Frankie's wife instead of Frankie himself, and that I only tried to take the knife away from her. To be honest, I'd have preferred it if the little demons had concerned themselves with my sins at a later stage. I'm not Pontius Pilate."

Grovian nodded. He'd had a row at home, the first real row for twelve or fifteen years. He couldn't even have said how long ago it was since Mechthild had lost her temper. She'd made a hell of a scene when he casually asked her at breakfast if he could take the spare bottle of shampoo from the bathroom and maybe a newspaper or something else to read.

She'd stared at him with a mixture of surprise and suspicion. "Why, planning to give Hoss a shampoo and read to him, or have you something else in mind? Rudi, don't tell me you're . . ."

Of course he was, he had to. He'd learned a lot on his second visit to Buchholz – far more than he'd dared to hope – but it still wasn't enough to complete the puzzle. For that he needed another few pieces, and they were buried in her head. He'd tried to explain this to Mechthild.

That had started it. It ended with: "All right, go! Go and see her if you can't leave well alone. She can keep you, for all I care!"

Then Mechthild had rushed into the living room, snatched the apples from the fruit bowl and slammed them down on the table in front of him. "Here, you'd better take these too. You can use them to reconstruct the course of events."

She was barking up the wrong tree. What he wanted to reconstruct had nothing to do with apples.

He proceeded to chat in a casual, innocuous way. Her father was genuinely a little better. The doctors said he was over the worst. Margret wanted to find him a good nursing home. She was also thinking of returning to Cologne in the course of next week. Then he asked Cora whether she was allowed to talk to him at all. Private visit or not, her lawyer might have advised her to keep her mouth shut.

This made her smile again. "No, he looked as if he could use some good advice himself. He reminded me of Horsti in a way. Not that he's a weedy little runt, but he's just as shy and just as easily impressed."

Grovian had really wanted to spend a little longer talking about

258

her attorney. Eberhard Brauning . . . The DA had mentioned the name, but it didn't mean anything to him. He would have liked to know if Brauning was a tough customer. The court-appointed attorneys included one or two tough customers who did their best for their clients.

Mechthild was of the opinion that Cora Bender needed a really tough attorney whose first concern would be to keep a certain policeman away from his client because the said policeman was on the verge of insanity himself. That was, perhaps, the favourable aspect of the aggro at home: that Mechthild was concerned about him. "You're wearing yourself out, Rudi. Just look at yourself! My God, you aren't twenty-five any more – you need your sleep."

And he hadn't had much sleep in the last few nights. Too many thoughts racing around in his head. He would gladly have given a few away – to her lawyer, for instance. It was understandable that she should deny him, a policeman, access to her last line of defence. He had been her assailant from the outset, whereas an efficient defence counsel would be quick to convince Cora Bender that he was on her side.

What she had just said did not smack of efficiency or powers of persuasion, and Horsti was the second item on Grovian's agenda. He seized upon the subject, grateful not to have to rack his brains for a way of bringing her round to it.

He hadn't undertaken yet another long drive to Buchholz to talk to Margret or enquire about her brother's condition. There was nothing more to enquire about. Wilhelm Rosch was dead, and Margret was looking for a nursing home for her sister-in-law, who couldn't be left in the neighbour's care indefinitely. But Grovian couldn't have brought himself to break this news, even if Professor Burthe hadn't specifically advised against it: "Frau Bender couldn't cope with it." Of course not! So Horsti had been approved as a harmless topic of conversation.

It hadn't taken him much of an effort, just a few questions, to locate Cora's first boyfriend. Grit Adigar's daughter Melanie, now back from Denmark, had recalled that Horsti's surname was

Cremer and knew where to find him: at Asendorf, a small village not far from Buchholz. But that wasn't all Melanie knew.

*

The three of them had sat in Grit Adigar's modern, airy living room while Melanie dredged her memory.

She had once seen Cora at the Aladdin with Johnny Guitar. On Magdalena's birthday. Grit sought to contradict her daughter on that point. "You must be wrong," she said. "Cora would never have gone out that night."

"I know what I saw, Mother," Melanie said reproachfully. "I was surprised myself – I even spoke to her about it. She was on her own, and . . ." A touch of jealousy manifested itself. Johnny Guitar was a blond Adonis, a fascinating youngster. Melanie obviously wouldn't have kicked him out of bed herself, although he was to be treated with care. He always went around with a fat little acolyte.

Melanie had once seen a girl come back into the Aladdin after going for a drive with the pair – in tears! She retired to the ladies' with a couple of girlfriends. Melanie was curious, so she eavesdropped on them. "The swine!" she heard the girl say between sobs. "Johnny didn't lift a finger – he simply let him do it. I'm going to report them!" Someone else said: "You'd better keep your mouth shut. We did warn you, but you went with them of your own free will."

They all kept their mouths shut. However, Johnny had found it harder to pick up girls after that, and it could only be a matter of time before he changed his stamping ground. Melanie doubted whether Cora had learned of his dangerous reputation because she was always with Horsti.

But not that night. Johnny promptly seized his opportunity, and Cora became absolutely infatuated with him. They danced and necked. Watching them, Melanie made up her mind to warn Cora before Johnny talked her into going for a drive. But then a miracle occurred: his fat little friend also got lucky that night. She saw him dancing, almost without a break and always with the same girl. She was new to the Aladdin, blonde and rather plump but quite cute. Just right for a boy like him.

"We left around half-past ten," Melanie said. "He was still dancing with her, and Cora was with Johnny. I didn't want to spoil her fun. Besides, I thought nothing much could happen if she was in a foursome. That was the last time I saw Cora. Johnny and his friend never reappeared after that either."

Horst Cremer confirmed and amplified those particulars. He had last seen Cora the first weekend in May. She told him she couldn't meet him for another two weeks. She gave no special reason. She certainly didn't say anything about her sister being worse, but then she very seldom mentioned her sister at all.

Horst had stayed at home on the night of 16 May. On 23 May he waited in vain for Cora to show up at the Aladdin. He hung around outside her parents' house for the next two evenings, hoping to get some explanation from her. Also without success. He didn't dare ring the bell; he was too intimidated by the horror stories she'd told him about her martinet of a father.

He tried his luck once more on the last Saturday in May, but Cora still didn't show. When he asked around, he was told that she'd done the dirty on him on the sixteenth. Melanie Adigar wasn't the only one who'd witnessed the start of her liaison with Johnny Guitar. Several other people claimed to have seen her get into a car with Johnny and his fat friend later that night, accompanied by another girl whom nobody knew.

This information had instantly reminded Rudolf Grovian of the skeleton on Lüneburg Heath. Nothing much could happen if she was in a foursome? Like hell it couldn't!

He failed to discover the make of the car in question. Melanie Adigar had no precise recollection of it. "They didn't always turn up in the same car. It may have been a silver Golf on one occasion, but that would have belonged to the little fatty. Johnny went in for classy motors like Porsches or Jaguars. Once I saw him getting out of an American job, no idea what make. Lime green it was, I remember, with huge fins and lots of chrome – an oldie, a regular show-off's car. I remember thinking his daddy must be rich or in the second-hand car business."

Horst Cremer couldn't provide any information about the car either. No one had mentioned a make. She'd got into it with Johnny, that was all. Horsti had begun by drowning his sorrows in drink. Until the middle of June he wavered between despair and the hope that Cora would make it up with him. Johnny was notorious for coming to Buchholz for one reason only: to pick up girls.

Horsti spent every weekend at the Aladdin and kept watch on her parents' house night after night. One Sunday at the end of June he took the plunge. Instead of hanging around on the street corner he rang the doorbell.

"It was answered by an unkempt old scarecrow of a woman," he told Grovian. "I asked for Cora, and she said: 'There isn't any Cora in this house, not any more. My daughter has disappeared.' I couldn't believe my ears."

Grovian couldn't either. Disappeared? At the end of June, when her aunt and the neighbour were convinced that Cora had remained at her dying sister's bedside until 16 August?

However, Grit Adigar and Margret Rosch suddenly weren't so sure any more. After what her daughter had said, Grit Adigar started backtracking. She hadn't actually set eyes on Cora between May and August. It was odd, now she came to think of it. Wilhelm seemed to have taken a sudden dislike to her popping in, but she hadn't thought twice about it when he shooed her into the kitchen. She'd believed him when he gestured at the ceiling with a mournful expression and murmured: "Cora never stirs from her side." Why should Wilhelm have been lying?

Margret asked herself the same question. If Cora had already disappeared on 16 May, as Grovian surmised, why had Wilhelm merely spoken of her getting into bad company when he called his sister the following day?

Wilhelm was past being consulted, so Grovian had tried his luck with Elsbeth Rosch. Margret, who had moved into the house after her brother's death, reluctantly left them to it in the kitchen. Elsbeth informed him that Magdalena was sitting at the Almighty's feet, her beauty blossoming afresh now that every stain and every sinful thought had been eradicated from her earthly body.

It didn't make much sense. He thought at first that Elsbeth had forgotten her elder daughter, but then she told him about the satanic creature who had duped them all. Who had frequented the temples of sin instead of communing with God. Who had left her ailing sister to her fate because she was dazzled by fleshly desires. Exactly when the satanic creature had turned her back on her parental home, Elsbeth didn't know.

He could forget her blathering. The other two statements were more productive, though not, unfortunately, from an evidential point of view. All that Horst Cremer had to offer was indirect hearsay. He couldn't even recall who had informed him of Cora's breach of faith. As for Melanie Adigar, she hadn't seen whether Cora had left the Aladdin alone or accompanied by Johnny, his fat little friend and the unknown girl.

*

She seemed glad that Grovian had spoken to her former boyfriend. "How is he?" she asked in a voice fraught with melancholy. "What's he doing these days? Is he married?"

She listened to what he had to say, wondered if Horsti had asked after her and then, in her turn, started to talk about those nights at the Aladdin. How she used sometimes to dance and sometimes to stand on the sidelines. She laughed softly. "Horsti was a nice boy. My conscience often pricked me because I only used him to keep the others at bay. I was waiting for the right one to come along. Mean of me, wasn't it?"

Grovian merely shrugged and let her run on. He cudgelled his brains for a way of skirting the reef named Magdalena and steering for 16 May all the same. Her time at the Aladdin and the brief scene in the car park – that was all he wanted to talk to her about. The last thing he wanted was to drive her back behind her wall as he had the last time they spoke, when he'd watched her shaking her head for a full fifteen minutes before he grasped that she'd switched off.

He had to know the sequel to her meeting with Johnny. There must have been one. Johnny was Johannes = Hans Böckel, that was the only possibility. Böckel landed the girls, had his fun with them and made sure his friends got their share. And if Cora had been treated like the girl whose sobs Melanie Adigar had heard outside the ladies', it all made sense.

Her infatuation had put her at the mercy of two other men. Even if the fat boy had also had a girl with him that night, there was still Georg Frankenberg. And however studious and serious Frankie may have been, many another young man had lost control of himself before him. It only remained to prove that his arm had not been broken on 16 May, but somewhat later.

It hadn't taken much imagination to work out how the injury was sustained, just a few sleepless nights in which Grovian had pictured a young man coming home, beside himself with fear, and telling his father about a dead girl, possibly two. His father calms him down and asks a few questions. He learns that no one saw his son with the girls, and that it happened a long way from home. "Don't worry, my boy, we'll sort it out. You won't feel a thing, I'll give you a local anaesthetic beforehand."

Grovian and his thoughts were far away in Frankfurt, in the Aladdin and various other places, but not really with her. However, he didn't appear to have missed anything of importance. She was still talking about Horsti, who had really ceased to matter.

She sighed. "I hope he's happily married, I really do. He deserves it. He always tried to do the right thing by me. He gave me a cassette for my birthday, one he'd recorded himself. By Queen. We already had it, but his recording was much better, no background hiss at all. 'We Are the Champions' and 'Bohemian Rhapsody'. Magdalena was so mad about them, she listened to nothing else for a week. She adored Freddie Mercury's voice, and now he's dead too, long dead. My God, why are they all dead?"

She clapped a hand over her mouth, abruptly wide-eyed with horror. "I didn't kill him too, did I? I couldn't have, he was ill – very ill. I think I read that somewhere."

Grovian had missed the connection; he thought she was still

talking about Horst Cremer. Seeing her horrified expression, he hastened to reassure her. "No, don't worry, Frau Bender, he's in the best of health. His wife is expecting a baby soon, and he's so looking forward to it. He couldn't be better, honestly. He's opened a small service station."

"You're lying," she said. She bit her lip and shook her head. As she did so, a picture took shape in her mind.

*

She forgot about the chief. All her attention was focused on the little alarm clock on the bedside table. She could see it clearly. The hands were registering a few minutes past eleven.

Magdalena hadn't heard her coming up the stairs because she had the Walkman plugged into both ears and the volume turned up as high as it would go. She sat up with a look of mingled surprise and satisfaction. "You're very punctual. Nothing doing at the disco?"

She went over to the bed, brushed a long strand of hair out of Magdalena's eyes and kissed her on the cheek. "No, it was a dead loss. I didn't feel like hanging around any longer. I'd sooner be here with you."

Freddie Mercury's distorted voice was issuing from the tiny earpieces in Magdalena's hand. "Bohemian Rhapsody". "Is this the real life?" No, that wasn't it, that was a lie. "I've been tarting for you for years; we'll soon have enough money." No, we won't, because stealing takes too long. "I've given my boyfriend the push – he kept bugging me with his stupid questions – but I've already got another. His name is Horst, a really cool type." Crap! A little runt everyone laughs at. "I'd sooner be here with you." The hell I would!

I'd like to have stayed. Johnny was there. I've never told you about him, and I'm not going to now. Johnny belongs to me alone. He's young and strong and so handsome, you've never seen anyone like him outside a movie magazine. He looks like the archangel in Mother's Bible. And I touched him, his shoulders, his face. I had my arms around his waist and his hands on the back of my neck.

Her hand was still resting on Magdalena's head. She stroked her sister's smooth cheek, traced the outlines of her lips. "Do you need to go before I get into bed?"

Magdalena shook her head. She got up off the edge of the bed.

"Then I'll go and get the rest of the bubbly."

The bottle was nearly full. They'd only had a sip or two at eight. Magdalena had said she didn't like it, and she herself had been careful because Magdalena had badgered her into driving to the Aladdin. She was grateful now for Magdalena's persistence.

Magdalena, who was sitting up against her pillows when she returned with the bottle and two glasses, greeted her with an appraising smile. "You're in an odd mood. Anything wrong?"

"No. Why should it be?" I'm eating my heart out, that's what's wrong. I'd been wanting him to speak to me for so long – just that, nothing more – and tonight he actually touched me. We danced together, and I wanted him to go outside with me, to make love to me. He was excited, I could feel it while we were dancing. It almost broke me up when I had to go. Next week he won't even recognize me. I should have stayed with him. Some opportunities only come once, and I only got lucky this time because he was on his own and feeling bored, I realize that. And now I've squandered my only chance. But I promised I wouldn't stay too long.

I hate you sometimes! And now I hate you even more than I did to begin with. It isn't a child's hatred any more: it's the hatred of a woman who's been cheated out of her life. If it weren't for you I'd be free. I wouldn't have had to hang around in the Aladdin with that nerd Horsti for the past two years. Everyone laughs at me. I'm a figure of fun. Cora doesn't stand there praying in the playground any more, she hangs around in the Aladdin with her nerdy boyfriend. She doesn't have time for a real man; she's too busy with a sister who's eating her life away.

But tonight I showed them all – all the ones that matter. Melanie and her gang were there. You've never met Melanie. We chatted together for a little. Melanie asked where Horsti was. "Where did you leave that Tarzan of yours?"

"At home pumping iron," I told her. Just as I was about to finish my drink and drive home, they came in. Johnny and his friend.

Perhaps I ought to tell you about him. Everything, every detail, just so you see I'm not letting you destroy me and that I can still have normal feelings. Want to hear? They came in, sat down at a table, looked around and said something to each other. I could guess what: no action tonight – we'd better go somewhere else.

But then the fat boy saw a girl. He sees one every time, but he never gets lucky. I don't know how many times I've seen him sent off with a flea in his ear. I thought it would be the same this time. He got up from the table and went over to her. Surprise, surprise! She actually went onto the dance floor with him.

Johnny was sitting at the table on his own. He was bored, I could tell. You're out of luck tonight, I thought. Then he looked over at me and smiled. I don't know if I smiled back. At that moment I felt as if my face had gone to sleep and my heart had turned to water.

Then he got up and came over to me. Do you know what he said? "Left your steady at home to give another poor guy a chance?"

I couldn't believe it: he asked if I'd like to dance. Would I! While we were dancing he told me the only reason he'd never dared to speak to me was that Horsti was always with me. He held me so tight, I couldn't help thinking of the candle. It isn't as thick as what I could feel.

I felt Johnny's lips on my forehead and waited for him to kiss me, but he only asked if I'd care to go somewhere else with him and his friend. With him alone I'd have gone like a shot – you'd have had to wait a bit longer for me. But with his friend? They're a double act, those two, someone told me once, and I could guess what she meant. I don't think the girl the fat boy was dancing with wanted to go with them either, not when she'd only just met him. I reckoned she was dancing with him only as a way of getting to know Johnny.

So I said: "I'd like to, but it's no good, I can't stay out too long. My sister's alone in the house."

He looked surprised. "How old is she?"

"Eighteen," I said. "Today is her birthday."

He laughed. "Why is she at home, then? Why didn't she come too?"

"She wasn't feeling too good."

He was all for my staying and coming with them – with him alone, if necessary. He glanced across at the fat boy. "Tiger's busy. I'm sure he won't mind us leaving him alone for a while."

I thought it was funny, him calling his friend Tiger. He looked more like a pink piglet.

"Can't you call your parents?" Johnny said. "Can't you tell them about the party and ask them to babysit for once?"

"Our parents are dead," I told him.

They are too. We never had any parents, just ourselves, and since I'm the older and stronger of us I have to look after you. So I left, although it nearly killed me. It was like ripping out my heart. Johnny was going to tell me his real name if I stayed. He begged and pleaded: just another half-hour, just one more dance. He went out to the car park with me, and before I got into the car he kissed me at last. It was different from kissing Horsti. He'd been drinking whisky and Coke. Maybe that was it. Sweet as honey, it was. I could have stood with him like that for hours, and it only lasted a second or two.

He let go of me and said: "Sing your sister a lullaby and then come back, won't you? I'll be waiting for you." He stood there and waved me goodbye as I drove off. And I thought I might really go back when you'd gone to sleep. Sing your sister a lullaby . . .

13

Just a momentary slip, and that was that. Rudolf Grovian had scarcely uttered the name Magdalena when she switched off. He watched her go over to the bed and sit down sideways on, facing the pillow. She stroked the crumpled pillowslip with one hand, her change of expression clearly conveying that she wasn't with him any more.

He hoped for some remark, even a few muttered words, that would enable him to tell what was going through her mind at that moment, but she didn't do him that favour. As for reading the look on her face . . . It was eloquent of disgust and repugnance. She gulped again and again, almost as if she were fighting back an urge to vomit.

Minutes went by. He didn't dare break the silence – heaven alone knew where in her memories he would have caught her. Then, all at once, she surfaced again. She drew a hand across her forehead. "I drove home," she said, loud and clear.

He breathed a sigh of relief. "Of course you did, Frau Bender," he said hastily.

"I didn't abandon Magdalena."

Not a word about Magdalena! After what had happened at their last interview, he was only too glad to leave the subject of her sister to Professor Burthe. "Of course not, Frau Bender. But we aren't talking about Magdalena, only about Horsti. He asked after you several times when you stopped going to the Aladdin."

She merely stared at him with a puzzled, hesitant expression. Uncertain if she was still capable of following him, he went on slowly: "That was in June, so you must still have been living at home. Or had you left already?"

Of course she had, he would have staked his life on it. She had vanished in May, not in August, and for some undiscoverable reason her father had said . . . Or the others had thought it was better to locate her at Magdalena's bedside until they knew for certain what had happened to her.

By now he could play the lying game as well as her, her aunt and Grit Adigar, but she didn't notice. "Horst spoke to your father on one occasion. Your father told him you wanted nothing more to do with him. And that was in June."

He didn't know how he'd expected her to react. Somehow, anyway, and she did: she bowed her head and murmured: "No, I drove home."

Something in her tone puzzled him. He trod even more cautiously.

"Of course you did. But you were with Johnny one time?"

"Yes."

"Do you remember when that was?"

"Yes, I remember now. It was on Magdalena's birthday. But I drove home."

No, you didn't, he thought. "Of course, Frau Bender," he said. "I don't doubt that for a moment. Do you remember the night?"

"Yes, perfectly, it's just come back to me. I drove home shortly before eleven."

He was getting nowhere like this. He tried another tack. "Why did you go home?"

"Because I'd promised Magdalena. Besides, I was afraid Tiger would come too. The girl certainly wouldn't have, she'd only just met him."

The girl! He could have whooped with delight. All right, carry on, tell me, take it slowly and carefully. "Who was she, Frau Bender?"

"I don't know."

Okay, nor did anyone else. No wonder there hadn't been a missing persons report in Buchholz at the time in question. Heaven alone knew where the poor creature had come from. Back to the crucial point:

"Was Frankie there too?"

She looked at her hands, spread her fingers, rubbed her nails. Her manner reminded him involuntarily of a difficult child. "Don't you remember, Frau Bender?"

"Yes, I remember. He wasn't there. I never saw him."

He drew a deep breath and decided on a frontal attack. "Yes, Frau Bender, you did see him. Once, in the cellar, that night. But it was after eleven, I know that for a fact. If you drove home at eleven you must have driven back again. I can well understand your doing so. I would have returned to the Aladdin in your place. You were very taken with Johnny and wanted to be with him. That was quite natural. Any normal girl would have done the same, Frau Bender. And you were a normal girl, weren't you? You weren't crazy. Ditching Johnny and going home – *that* would have been crazy."

He'd almost said "going home to sit with your invalid sister", but he stopped himself just in time. With a trace of relief, he went on: "That night you got into a car with Johnny, the fat boy and another girl; I've got witnesses. Frankie must already have been in the cellar when you got there with the others."

"I don't know." She plucked at her fingernails, sounding close to tears. "I only know I drove home at eleven. And then it was October. I don't know how it happened."

Her fingers entwined themselves, rubbing, twisting and kneading themselves together as if her hands were her only means of support. A hint of panic came into her voice. Her eyes implored belief and understanding.

"I didn't abandon my sister. I did everything for her – everything except prostituting myself. I wanted to do it with a man I loved, and Johnny . . . I thought of that while we were dancing – that I wanted to do it with him, even if it had only been the once. I wouldn't have minded. I'd have had that one time, and no one could have taken it away from me. Sing your sister a lullaby, he said, I'll wait for you. And I thought, if she gets really tired, if she goes to sleep, maybe I will . . ."

Her eyes widened. "But I was careful. I was always careful, you've got to believe me. I loved her. I'd never have done anything to harm her. I knew what to look out for. When she held her breath I stopped at once, and when she started panting I went slower. I always kept one hand on her chest, so I could feel her heartbeat. I never lay on top of her. I did it with my fingers as a rule. Very seldom with the candle, honestly. And once with my tongue . . . But that was too . . . She'd raved about it. I tried it that once, but it revolted me. And besides, it was too risky. I couldn't check on her breathing."

She sucked in her lower lip and shrugged helplessly. Her voice was heavy with unshed tears. "I know it wasn't right. I oughtn't to have done it. It was contrary to nature. That's why Sodom and Gomorrah were destroyed. I didn't want to either, but she said only fathers and brothers were forbidden to do it to you, not sisters. She got so little out of life. She longed to have sex with a man, but all she had was me. She had feelings too."

Her voice broke. "You won't tell the professor, will you?" she entreated between her sobs. "Promise?"

"Of course, Frau Bender. I promise." He said it before he'd really absorbed what she'd just told him.

"She always said an orgasm was a wonderful sensation, and I didn't know what it was like. That night I wanted to find out, but I had to go home. She saw it in my face and kept on at me. You're in a funny mood, she said. There's something the matter with you. And then she told me to finish up the bubbly by myself. She said she didn't like it – it made her feel dizzy."

Her sobs died away. She wept dry-eyed, staring at her hands, at her twisting, writhing fingers. He had an urge to take her in his arms or at least say something comforting, but he didn't want to disrupt her train of thought. He let her stumble on.

"I stayed with her. I did all she asked. I painted her nails and we listened to music. I don't know what happened, but I can still hear her saying 'dance for me!'"

Her fingers had knotted themselves together on her lap. He heard the knuckles crack and tried to make sense of what she'd

272

just said. A mental blackout! Her stubborn denial amounted to confirmation. His assumption was correct: she hadn't been at home when her sister died. She hadn't heard of her death until November . . .

Her voice jolted him out of his cogitations. The words came out in a breathless rush. "Dance for me! Live for me! Smoke a cigarette for me! Prostitute yourself for me – pick the ones that pay best. And, so you have something for yourself, go to the disco. Choose yourself a boyfriend and go to bed with him, then tell me what it was like. I told her about the lights in the Aladdin and the way they flickered when the music got louder. Red and green and yellow and blue."

She paused, then blurted out: "The lights in the cellar were like that too! I can't go down there, please don't make me! I can't bear it. Do something – *do* something! I don't want to go down there!" She flailed the air with her arms as if trying to keep her balance.

He ought to have sent for Professor Burthe, but he dismissed the idea as soon as it occurred to him. The professor was a busy man. It was doubtful he could spare the time to explore the cellar with her. He would probably consider a sedative injection more appropriate.

Grovian felt quite capable of keeping the situation under control. He sat down on the bed beside her. Taking her hands, he squeezed them hard and tried to adopt a soothing tone of voice, although his heart was in his mouth. She was completely beside herself. Her eyes darted around the room; her bosom and shoulders rose and fell convulsively in time with her rapid breathing.

"Steady, Frau Bender, steady. I'm here, I've got you. Can you feel my hands? Nothing can happen. We'll go down there together and look around. Afterwards I'll take you back upstairs again, I promise."

It sounded crazy, but what else could he have said? Her hands clung to his, trembling so violently that his own arms shook in concert with them.

"Tell me what you can see, Frau Bender. What's in the cellar? Who's down there?"

273

She described a room bathed in flickering, multicoloured lights. A bar against the left-hand wall, a mass of bottles on a shelf with a mirror behind it. In the opposite corner, the instruments and amplifiers on a platform. "Tiger's Song". She danced to it, danced all alone in the middle of the room. Against the right-hand wall, a sofa with an ashtray on the low table in front of it.

"Tiger's Song". It was a wild tune, a wild dance. Frankie tossed his sticks aside, went over to the sofa and sat down beside the girl. Johnny inserted a tape, and the tune rang out once more. Tiger went to the bar. Although he'd drawn the short straw again, he didn't seem to mind.

She was still dancing, but not by herself any more. Johnny was holding her in his arms and kissing her. It was like a dream, even when he slid his hands up her skirt. She relished his touch. Not for Magdalena this time, only for herself. She couldn't always live for them both.

Then they were lying on the floor. Johnny undressed her. Everything was fine. Frankie, still sitting on the sofa, took no notice of them. He was talking to the girl. Tiger quartered a lemon at the bar and sprinkled some white powder on the back of his hands, then licked it off, washed it down with a jigger of colourless spirit and bit into the lemon. Having done that three times, he felt in his trouser pocket and said: "I've brought something for us. A little coke. Let's get comfy."

Listening to her, Grovian held her hands tight and squeezed them in the hope that she could feel the pressure. She was still lying on the floor. Frankie and the girl were watching Johnny make love to her. Tiger came sauntering over. He wanted his share. "My turn," he said.

Johnny made no attempt to fend him off. The girl said: "Give her a shot, it'll relax her."

The next few words were very clear: "Hey, what are you doing? I don't want any! No coke! Take it away!" She started muttering indistinctly, then jerked her head aside. "What are you doing?" she gasped. "Stop that! Stop it at once! Are you crazy? Leave her alone, damn you! Leave her alone!"

An electric shock seemed to run through her. "No!" she yelled. "Stop it! Stop that!" Her cries were succeeded by whimpering. She turned her head abruptly and gazed at him wide-eyed, but he could have sworn she didn't see him.

"Don't hit her! Stop it, you'll kill her! Stop it, you swine! Let go of me! Let go!"

He was thoroughly familiar with those words, or another version of them, but he wasn't prepared for what came next. She wrenched her hands away with astonishing strength, breaking his grip, and sprang to her feet. It all happened so fast, he couldn't react in time. She clenched her right fist and drove it into his neck. "I'll break your neck, you swine!" she gasped. "I'll slit your throat!"

She was precisely duplicating the blows listed in the pathologist's report. Once, twice, three times she struck him before he managed to catch hold of her wrist. No sooner had he grabbed it than she lashed out with her left. It was a few moments before he succeeded in grabbing that too and getting to his feet.

He held her at arm's length and shook her. "Frau Bender!" he shouted. "Stop it, Frau Bender!"

She stood there for a full five seconds, staring at him with blank incomprehension. Then she muttered something unintelligible and passed out.

*

Professor Burthe didn't trouble to hide his anger at the fact that a CID officer had, for the second time and in spite of warnings to the contrary, bullied a severely disturbed person into a state of collapse. "What on earth were you thinking of?" he demanded, shaking his head. "Didn't I expressly warn you not to treat Frau Bender like an ordinary criminal? That's the last time you'll interview her! Frau Bender's attempted suicide was a direct result of your interrogation technique, don't you realize that?"

Grovian couldn't summon up the energy to justify himself. They'd already established that he hadn't said a word to her about her father's death. Still unconscious, Cora Bender had been

275

hurriedly carted off to undergo tests of some kind. He would have given a great deal to undo that last half-hour with her. He failed to understand how he could have indulged in such an asinine experiment. "I'll take you back upstairs again, I promise . . ."

Wrong! It wasn't as simple as that. He'd done his best, patting her cheeks, calling her name and splashing her face with cold water for several minutes before he could bring himself to leave her to the doctors. And all the time he'd been thinking, despite himself, of what would have happened had she been holding a knife.

He was feeling rather sick. Sick but satisfied as well. Had the killing been premeditated? No, certainly not. If she hadn't happened to be peeling an apple for her son, she would only have attacked Georg Frankenberg with her fists and done what she'd been prevented from doing years before – in a situation in which every blow would have been delivered in defence of herself or someone else.

He would have liked to discuss this with Professor Burthe, but he couldn't get a word in. He was bombarded with technicalities: schizothymia, psychical detachment, a deliberate distinction between oneself and the outside world, a vulnerable, partly apathetic withdrawal from one's fellow creatures, pre-eminence accorded to the world of dreams, ideas and principles.

Impressive though this sounded, Grovian found it thoroughly uninteresting. His own interpretation was only that of a layman but far more cogent. After five years, self-defence was out. After five years, Cora Bender's act was homicide – unless someone could demonstrate that she had been in that confounded cellar at the time of the killing, not at the Otto Maigler Lido. And he couldn't prove that. That was the professor's job.

He submitted to Burthe's dressing-down without batting an eyelid. The professor eventually calmed down and asked what Cora Bender had been saying just before she passed out. Grovian outlined the scene in the cellar and their preceding conversation. He forbore to mention that she had attacked him, but he did touch upon the subject of self-defence and her wish to defend the other girl as well as herself.

When he had finished the professor gave a curt nod. It didn't signify approval, far from it. Burthe was naturally familiar with the cellar scene; in fact, he had heard two versions of it, one on tape mentioning the broken ribs, and the other with the pimp on the sofa.

There had to be a third version – one to which Cora Bender was denying all access. This third version, said Burthe, must embody what had really happened in the cellar. Her own desire had probably rebounded on her. Consequently, the cellar episode was unimportant. It was just a small part of a dark chapter in her life, and she defended that entire chapter from intruders with all her might, if necessary at the expense of her mental health. As if I didn't know that already, Grovian thought to himself.

Professor Burthe talked at length about the difference between truth and falsehood and Cora Bender's attitude to both. When under pressure she began by telling the truth. When the pressure subsided and she had come to terms with the situation, she sought to turn it to her advantage. This she could only do by lying. However, her lies created further pressure. The agitation she then displayed might convince a layman that she was disclosing the truth at last.

That was what had happened when Grovian questioned her, said Burthe. She had tried the same game with him, but he was an expert – she couldn't pull the wool over his eyes. No one disputed that Cora Bender had undergone some traumatic experiences at the hands of a man – several men, probably – a few years ago. It was also beyond doubt that she had been badly mistreated on one occasion. Her self-destructive tendencies must have acted as a spur to men of the appropriate disposition.

Grovian raised his first objection at that point. "If you're implying that she went on the game, she didn't. Her sister expected or even demanded it of her, if I understood her correctly, but she couldn't do it."

The professor smiled an omniscient smile. "Most certainly she could, Herr Grovian. After her sister's death she chose the worst form of punishment she could think of: having sex with perverts. She described a few of their practices to me. I've heard a thing or two in my time, but even I found them a bit much. No woman confesses to such activities unless she's actually engaged in them, you must admit. She was prompted by a yearning for atonement, coupled with a subconscious desire for an incestuous relationship with her father."

"That's nonsense," Grovian protested. It sounded feeble, he could hear that himself, almost as if he were half-convinced of Burthe's point of view. He wasn't. It was only helplessness that robbed him of speech – that and the self-assurance with which the professor had spoken. He sounded as if he'd been standing there watching.

Which he had – although only, of course, in the metaphorical sense. Burthe stressed that what he was presenting to Grovian was Cora Bender's inner belief. Being a trained and observant interviewer, he was capable of extracting grains of truth from a pack of lies.

"I'm afraid," Grovian said dryly, "that you've extracted a few lies as well. I don't know why she told you such a load of nonsense, but her chronology is all wrong. She was . . ."

He wanted to explain what he'd just discovered – that Cora's memories leapfrogged from Magdalena's birthday to the cellar and from there to October – but Burthe silenced him with a gesture. Timing wasn't the issue here, he said, nor was prostitution. There was no reason to get worked up about it.

The only issues were Georg Frankenberg's death, Cora Bender's motive and her ability to distinguish right from wrong. The latter was missing. Cora Bender was incapable of guilt. She couldn't be held responsible for her act. It had nothing whatever to do with the man and his behaviour. The woman had been the trigger.

"It was his bad luck to be lying on top . . ." Although Grovian could hear her saying it, he shook his head. "I don't know what put that idea into your head, Professor, but you're making a big mistake if you dismiss the cellar episode so readily. I've now been through it twice, and I myself am a trained and observant interviewer. Frau Bender was raped and nearly killed by two men in a cellar. Another girl was killed on the same occasion, very probably by Georg Frankenberg. That's why he had to die."

278

Professor Burthe had simmered down by now. He leaned back in his chair and eyed Grovian thoughtfully. "What makes you so certain?" he asked. "Frau Bender's statements, or do you have proof?"

Grovian swore under his breath. All he had was words. A few here, a few there. Horst Cremer, Melanie Adigar, Johnny Guitar . . . It wasn't even certain that Hans Böckel and Johnny Guitar were one and the same person, and Böckel was his only link with Frankenberg. No attorney could cite "Tiger's Song" as an argument in court.

"You feel sorry for the woman," the professor said when he didn't answer. The words hung in the air like an incontrovertible statement of fact. "You want to help her and are trying to find a rational explanation. You have a daughter, don't you? How old is she, Herr Grovian?"

When Grovian still didn't reply, Burthe nodded to himself. In the same infuriatingly sympathetic tone of voice, he went on: "I've listened to all the tapes, not just the last one, so I can understand your emotional involvement. A young woman whose only wish was to lead a normal life. So helpless, so desperate. Destroyed by circumstances beyond her control, she pleads for sympathy. Completely beside herself, she utters a cry for help and collapses. You were alone with her when it happened, weren't you? Cora Bender's cry for help was addressed to you alone. You not only personified her father at that moment, you felt like him too. The same scene recurred earlier today. Every father wants to believe his daughter, Herr Grovian. Bear that in mind and ask yourself how you would assess your behaviour had a colleague engaged in it."

Grovian involuntarily gritted his teeth. "I'm not here to be psychoanalysed," he said. "I've merely been trying to clarify some new information."

Burthe nodded thoughtfully. "And Frau Bender was able to confirm it?"

"Yes, in a way."

The professor gave another thoughtful nod. He didn't enquire into the nature of this new information. "She'll confirm anything,

Herr Grovian – anything and everything that establishes a connection between herself and Georg Frankenberg. She herself is seeking a rational explanation. His death had a liberating effect on her, and she's searching for the reason, trying desperately to incorporate him in her life and supply a demonstrable motive. To achieve that, she even sits him on a sofa in the role of her pimp."

Grovian's attempt to say something was silenced by another gesture. "I'll try to explain something to you, and I very much hope you'll finally grasp where your work and commitment end and mine begin. Let's forget about Georg Frankenberg and the cellar. Frau Bender's trauma has a name: Magdalena."

To Professor Burthe it was simple: Georg Frankenberg was only a chance victim. His fate could have been that of any man accompanied by a woman with something about her that reminded the killer of her sister. Cora Bender couldn't have brought herself to kill the woman who had ruined her life a second time. In her distress, which was very great, she had attacked the man. His death killed two birds with one stone. She had sent Magdalena her heart's desire, a good-looking man. What was more, Frankenberg's wife, deputizing for Magdalena, had pushed her hand away and thereby signalled that she no longer needed any help. Cora Bender was free at last – so free that even the certainty of life imprisonment had failed to shake her resolve. As she saw it, she deserved to be punished.

Grovian listened to this itemized account without expression. A life like a criminal record: mendacity, deceit, theft, drugs and, to crown it all, a murder. No, not Georg Frankenberg; he was supposed to forget all about him. The victim's name was Magdalena!

Professor Burthe didn't know whether Cora Bender had killed her sister with malice aforethought because she regarded her as the destroyer of herself – and not only of herself because her father, whom she worshipped, had also been destroyed – or whether she had done it in a drug-induced rage. The fact remained, the ribs that had snapped were Magdalena's.

Cora's words came back to Grovian: "I always kept one hand on her chest . . ." That was enough for him. You quacks, he thought, unaware that he had adopted her own way of thinking. Listen to you for half an hour, and you'll end up believing in Santa Claus.

But not him! He had assembled some facts. "I'll make you a suggestion," he said, getting to his feet. "You do your work, and I'll do mine. Put all that in your report, and I'll demolish it in three sentences." Professor Burthe expressed a wish to hear the three sentences right away. Grovian listed his facts. First, Cora had been absent from home for three months when her sister died. She was lying in some private clinic with a fractured skull and hadn't been discharged until November. Secondly, prostitution after her sister's death as a form of atonement, coupled with a subconscious desire for an incestuous relationship with her father. Prettily phrased, that. He could never have put it so well. Unfortunately, however, there hadn't been time. No one prostituted themselves with a fractured skull. That apart, there hadn't been any subconscious desire or idolized father.

"You should consult the Bible, Professor Burthe. It's all down there. The Bible keeps trying to tell us the truth in its own way. Magdalena was the whore."

He shook his head and laughed. "Magdalena did the spadework, and they finished her off in the cellar. If you don't believe me, try experimenting with a lighting console or play her 'Tiger's Song'. That was the trigger, not Frankenberg's wife, I'll bet you anything you like. She herself said it was the tune. If you try it, though, make sure there's someone else with you for safety's sake. You've got some tough male nurses here."

He made slowly for the door and played his last trump card. "And sometime ask Frau Bender how many drops of water a junkie scoops out of the toilet to lend his fix the requisite consistency."

Professor Burthe wrinkled his brow. "I'm not sure I . . ."

Grovian's hand was already on the door handle. "You heard me. Give Frau Bender a junkie's works and inspect every square centimetre of her body. If you find even one scar indicative of sadomasochistic practices, I'll turn in my badge. But I won't have to."

He opened the door and stepped out into the corridor. "Bear that tune in mind, Professor. I didn't dare play it to her, I'm afraid, but I'll make up for lost time the next chance I get. My investigative methods may have landed Frau Bender in this place, but they'll get her out again. That's a promise, Professor."

*

Grovian had seldom felt so angry as when he left the district hospital. Or so helpless. He'd worked his way up the police service without a university degree. How, if it came to the pinch, could he hope to rebut the findings of an eminent professor? He couldn't commission a second opinion.

He drove to Hürth and consulted a phone book. There were two numbers listed under the name Eberhard Brauning, one professional and one private. Grovian dialled the former. Herr Brauning wasn't available, unfortunately, and his courteous receptionist couldn't arrange an appointment until tomorrow at the earliest. However, a little pressure persuaded her to put Grovian through after all.

Eberhard Brauning was startled when Grovian stated his name and urgent business. "Ah yes," he said, "the chief." He chuckled, then turned businesslike. "I was going to call you anyway in the next few days. There are a few points that need clarifying."

"Only a few?" Grovian gave a mirthless laugh. "I'd much appreciate it if you could spare me a little of your time. I realize you're a busy man, but my own time is in short supply. I won't have any at all for the next few days, and the matter's urgent."

That was putting it mildly. From the way Burthe had spoken, it sounded as if his work was drawing to a close. Once his confounded report was with the DA . . . Burthe's assertions were buzzing through his head like a swarm of bees. It could have happened to any man accompanied by a woman . . .

That wasn't altogether true. At all events, he himself hadn't been accompanied by a woman when she struck him. Grovian could still hear her counting out the blows. Unaware that Brauning was hesitating, he didn't return to the present until a long, drawn-out

"Well . . ." came down the line. "Looking at my desk diary, I see . . ." Brauning didn't disclose what he saw. Instead, he asked: "Would this evening suit you? Do you have my home address?"

"Yes."

"Good. Shall we say eight o'clock?"

"Can't you make it a bit sooner?" It wasn't even four, and he didn't know how he would while away the afternoon. Until he'd got this off his chest, he couldn't concentrate on anything else. "How about six?" They compromised on seven.

That settled, he brewed himself some coffee. While drinking his first cup he dipped into the tapes again. "I only wanted to lead a normal life, can you understand that?" And: "Gereon shouldn't have done that to me." Oral sex, he thought, Magdalena's dream. That was why she'd freaked out when her husband tried it. In a way, that explained everything.

Over his second cup he noted down her description of the cellar as far as he recalled it. The reconstruction was excellent. He could see it in front of him. The bottles on the shelf with the mirror behind them. In front of them, a pudgy little man sprinkling white powder on the back of his hand, licking it off and biting into a lemon. Tequila, he thought. Tequila, coke and "my turn". Her own desire rebounded on her? What nonsense! All the same, he had Margret Rosch's statement about the nightmares Cora had suffered from at a time when everything was still fresh in her mind.

He wondered whether she had regained consciousness and had found the way back on her own, or whether she was cursing him again for having left her in the cellar despite his promise.

His gloomy deliberations were interrupted by Werner Hoss, who came in with a few items of news. There was still no clue to Ottmar Denner's whereabouts, and Hans Böckel was still just a name. They'd had no luck with the Hamburg hospitals, but Ute Frankenberg had been discharged.

Wonderful! He must definitely have a word with her. Perhaps Frankie had told her where he and his friends had made music together. He pocketed one of the interrogation tapes and set off for Cologne.

He got there almost on the stroke of seven. Eberhard Brauning's home address was an oldish but very well maintained apartment house with an ornate, freshly painted façade. He rang the bell, and the electrically operated door clicked open.

The lobby was dim and agreeably cool, the floor tiled in black and white. Her words came back to him: "White flagstones with little green squares between them . . ." They simply had to find the house in question.

There was a lift, but he decided to use the stairs. Brauning's apartment was on the second floor. Big old rooms with high ceilings and tall windows, choice antique furniture interspersed with a few luxuriant pot plants. All the doors to the hallway stood open, bathing the apartment in the subdued light of early evening.

Cora Bender's attorney greeted him at the door. The impression he made was tense rather than diffident. He ushered Grovian across the spacious hallway and into the living room. "I hope you don't mind," he said, "but I'd like my mother to sit in on our conversation."

Hell, thought Grovian. Aloud, he said: "Not at all." He saw her as soon as he entered the room, a distinguished-looking old lady with an alert expression and a neatly cut helmet of silver-grey hair. She probably goes to the hairdresser twice a week, he thought, and wondered if Cora Bender had used the shampoo he'd brought her.

Grovian said a polite good evening and returned her firm handshake. The heavy gold ring on her right hand was set with a ruby the size of a thumbnail, but all he could see in his mind's eye was Cora Bender's stringy hair. Why hadn't she washed it yet? Had she written herself off so completely? Perverted clients! She must realize that a statement like that would bar her way back for good and all. Her husband wasn't the type to come to terms with it.

Then he was sitting in an armchair with candy-striped upholstery. Beside him, on a little knee-high table with barley-sugar legs and an inlaid top, was a dainty china cup. The decaffeinated coffee was just the right colour. He didn't know where to begin.

Robin Hood, he thought wryly. Avenger of the disinherited and protector of widows and orphans. And of the legally incapacitated!

284

Go on, Robin, make it clear to this youngster what his client needs: a sensible expert who won't brand her on the forehead. She needs a woman to talk to. She can't trust an older man – she might see her father in him – but a woman . . . Then he visualized Elsbeth Rosch sitting at the kitchen table and shook his head. It was all nonsense.

He gave the distinguished-looking old lady a faint smile and transferred his attention to her son. "I paid Frau Bender a visit today. She said she'd spoken to you. Did you visit her in person?"

When Brauning nodded hesitantly he asked: "You consider one interview sufficient?"

"Of course not, but I don't yet have all the documentation. I'm still awaiting the psychologist's report."

"I can tell you what it'll say: not responsible for her actions. Georg Frankenberg was a chance victim. It could have happened to anyone."

Brauning stared at him, frowning slightly. Having waited in vain for some comment, Grovian asked: "What impression did Frau Bender make on you?"

He was well aware that the distinguished-looking old lady had been watching him closely. He also noticed the smile with which she awaited her son's reply, not that he could interpret it. She seemed almost amused. Brauning still said nothing.

Grovian grinned. "Come now, Herr Brauning, this can't be the first such interview you've had. What did you make of Frau Bender? She told you a load of nonsense, am I right? Did she also quote from the Bible – stuff about the Saviour and Mary Magdalene?"

Eberhard Brauning was by nature an exceedingly cautious and suspicious man. This certainly wasn't the first such talk he'd had. Policemen like Grovian were normally in favour of long custodial sentences and strove to impress that on you.

He still had a vivid recollection of the "nonsense" his client had talked, and he'd discussed it with his mother often enough in the last few days. Not just the nonsense, but also the clearly intelligible statements about her sister. "I had to get her off my back somehow or other . . ."

Helene shared his opinion. Having read the interrogation transcripts, she'd said: "I can't assess this woman's mental condition from my armchair, nor can I tell you if she knew her victim. One shouldn't altogether exclude the possibility that he was merely a former client – prostitutes often appeal to young men from respectable families – but the police will find it hard to establish such a connection, and it'll be to your disadvantage even if they do. I don't want to meddle in your work, and I'm aware that you regard psychiatry as an unsatisfactory solution, but perhaps you'll reconsider your attitude. In this case it would be the best solution. You can't do much for this woman in any case. Persuade her to tell Burthe how God the Father appeared at her bedside. That sounds more intriguing than the irrational act of a former prostitute." Helene was right!

"Herr Grovian," he said with a knowing smile, speaking slowly and deliberately, "I'm not of the opinion that Frau Bender told me a lot of nonsense. I can well imagine that you'd sooner see her in the toils of the penal system, but —"

Grovian cut him short with a single, emphatic "Wrong!" After a momentary pause he went on: "I'd sooner see her sitting in her garden, putting her little boy to bed or busying herself at the kitchen stove – even working in the cubbyhole she called her office. She felt good there – she felt mature, efficient and contented. Have you seen the place? You should; it doesn't even have a window. In the Bender household she was no more than a welcome beast of burden, but she was free, despite that. It was her heaven on earth. One wonders what her hell must have looked like!"

He could hardly believe he was saying all this, but it flowed from his lips with ease. It was the truth too. For the first time, he admitted to himself that Burthe hadn't been altogether wrong about him. The hell with it! Nineteen years with Elsbeth Rosch were punishment enough. A person sentenced to life imprisonment could hope to be released after fifteen years. From that angle, Cora Bender had already served four years too many.

"How much do you know about her childhood and adolescence, Herr Brauning? Only what's on file, or has she told you about it?"

She hadn't, so he did it for her. He summarized those miserable years in fifteen minutes and took the cassette from his pocket as he brought his account to a close. "And then it happened," he said. "I'm absolutely sure it happened just as she describes it, but I can't prove it, Herr Brauning. I can't prove it!"

A pinch of sarcasm was the only antidote to the depression those words aroused in him. "You've got a nice hi-fi there, a tape deck and all the trimmings. I'm now going to grant you the opportunity Frau Bender denied you: to be present at her interrogation. You've missed a great deal. One has to have heard it – reading a transcript isn't the same. Start the tape, it's at the right place."

Her voice issued from the big loudspeakers as if she were sitting beside the distinguished-looking old lady on the sofa. He heard once more her tear-choked, imploring, faltering words, her agonized cry of "Help me!"

He saw Brauning swallow hard a couple of times and took a sip of coffee to suppress his own urge to do likewise. After a few minutes, Cora Bender's voice died away. "I brought her back to that pitch today," he said quietly. "She went for me just as she went for Frankenberg. If she'd had a knife, I wouldn't be sitting here now."

Brauning didn't reply, staring at the tape deck as if he felt there must be more to come. His mother remained equally silent and uncommunicative.

"I don't quite understand what you expect me to do, Herr Grovian," Brauning said at length.

Grovian felt annoyed. It was on the tip of his tongue to say: "What do you usually do as a court-appointed counsel, just go through the motions?" But he controlled himself. "Get her another psychologist," he demanded and was rather surprised when the distinguished-looking old lady suddenly intervened. "Professor Burthe has a first-class reputation," she said.

"Maybe," he retorted, "but even the finest reputation isn't proof against Cora Bender's stories. She tossed him a tasty morsel, and he swallowed it whole. Prostitution and perverts!" It struck him, as he went on, that Eberhard Brauning's expression was changing. He wouldn't have won many hands of poker. "Did she spin you that yarn too?" He got no answer, just that meaningful expression.

"Listen," he said, "I have to know what she told you – every word, even if you think it's rubbish. She drops a lot of hints. You only have to interpret them correctly."

Brauning removed the cassette from the tape deck and handed it to him. "I'll need copies of all the tapes," he said for form's sake. "Including the one that was played beside the lake."

"Did she talk to you about that?"

Brauning didn't answer at once. Very deliberately, he resumed his seat with a disapproving frown. "Really, Herr Grovian, you can't expect me to divulge my conversations with a client to the other side."

"But I'm not the other side, damn it all! Do I have to go down on my knees to persuade you to talk? I may be here in my capacity as an investigator, but I'm not the woman's enemy."

"She thinks otherwise." Privately – Helene wasn't helping, just sitting there smiling – Brauning came to the conclusion that it couldn't hurt to disclose a few of Cora Bender's effusions.

He began with David and Goliath, went on to the three crosses with the guiltless figure in the middle and ended with God the Father, who sometimes appeared beside her bed at night, bent over her and assured her of his son's innocence.

Grovian listened attentively, but he soon realized that any input on his part would be a waste of time. "Well," he said, rising from his armchair and giving the distinguished-looking old lady another brief smile, "we're all tempted to take the line of least resistance sometimes, and in a case like this it suits us all perfectly. Don't condemn the poor creature, just lock her up – no need to wonder why she did what she did. I'd reached that stage at one time, but then I developed this itch to get to the bottom of the affair. And now I'm up to my neck in it. However, I'm afraid they won't let me delve any deeper. Burthe blames my investigative methods for Frau Bender's presence in a psychiatric ward. That should be grist to the mill of any good defence counsel."

That was the moment when Eberhard Brauning remembered his role, or rather, had his nose rubbed in it. Defence counsel . . . He felt a trifle uneasy. He would have to discuss the matter with Helene, of course, and work out what was to be done, if anything. Perhaps he shouldn't leave the initiative to the DA. If a policeman was rooting for this woman, her chances couldn't be that bad.

He cleared his throat. "Just between the two of us, Herr Grovian: if I produce a contrary expert opinion, do I stand a chance of an acquittal?"

"No," Grovian replied calmly, "you don't. But a few years' imprisonment are better than a death sentence, and that, I'm afraid, is the way she's headed. Cora Bender needs no judge or jury. She has already passed sentence on herself and is currently engaged in providing us with the grounds for it. She may be luckier carrying it out the next time. Once in prison with normal offenders, I think she'll refrain from committing suicide. To get there, all she needs to do is admit she recognized Georg Frankenberg and wanted to take revenge on him."

"Revenge for what?" asked Brauning, and Grovian told him. What he suggested was far from legal. He was sticking his neck out, but at that moment he didn't care.

*

It was nearly nine o'clock when he took his leave. During that last hour with the Braunings he'd kept asking himself why the mother should seem so interested until the son explained what her profession had been. Not a bad combination, he thought, and wondered if Cora Bender would be prepared to cooperate with Helene Brauning.

Although it was pretty late to go calling on someone else, Ute Frankenberg had so far been treated with great consideration. No one had asked her any distressing questions. Two or three answers were all he needed.

He pulled up outside Frankenberg's home, a modern apartment house, at ten past nine. Winfried Meilhofer opened the door to him. A young woman was sitting in the living room. She'd been too distressed to be interviewed the previous Saturday, like Frankenberg's wife, but Werner Hoss had since taken her statement.

Although Grovian had never set eyes on her before, he knew her name. She was Alice Winger, whose flirtation with Meilhofer had been so rudely interrupted by Cora Bender. The couple seemed to have drawn closer in the interim, because their manner to each other was suggestive of something more than friendship.

"I must apologize for disturbing you at this hour," he began, "but I was in the neighbourhood and I didn't want to drag Frau Frankenberg over to Hürth specially. She can just as well answer my questions here."

"Ute has gone to bed," Alice Winger informed him. "What questions?"

Nothing of great importance. He merely wanted confirmation of when and where she had met her husband. Alice Winger was able to answer that one herself. "Last December, at the Ludwig Museum. I was there myself."

Next: had Frankenberg ever mentioned the name Cora to his wife? Her lips tightened. "I strongly doubt it."

Well, one or two other names had cropped up in the course of his inquiries. "I'd really prefer to speak to Frau Frankenberg in person. It's just a formality."

"I'll get her." Alice Winger rose and left the room. Meilhofer used the time to ask: "Are you making progress with your inquiries?"

Grovian nodded. It was a good thing, in a way, that the man who had witnessed the murder at close quarters should assume that inquiries were still under way.

"I can't get it out of my head," Meilhofer said quietly. "The way she sat there, looking at Frankie. She seemed happy. I shouldn't say this, perhaps, but I felt sorry for her. Strange how one reacts. I should have been horrified. I was too, but more by Frankie's reaction, by her husband and myself. I'd never have thought a situation could arise in which I was rooted to the spot. I could have prevented it. Not the first blow, but the second and . . ."

He was interrupted by Alice Winger's reappearance. "She's coming," she said. "Please go easy on her, the whole thing is still so fresh. They were so happy."

"Yes, of course." Grovian felt almost ashamed. These people were the "other side", the one he was paid to uphold. Respectable citizens whose lives had been turned upside down, in the twinkling of an eye, by an incomprehensible act.

It was several minutes before Ute Frankenberg appeared in the doorway. All he noticed at first was the pink velvet ankle-length housecoat in which she had swathed herself as if she were cold. Surmounting the collar was a plump grey face, tearful and tired, the nose and eyes reddened from weeping, and a close-fitting cap of platinum blond hair gathered at the neck with a barrette.

He repeated his first question, which Alice Winger had already answered. Ute Frankenberg confirmed her reply in a low, almost inaudible voice. He turned to the subject of her husband's former friends. She knew only what Frankie had told her, not that he liked talking about them. Once, when she questioned him about the tune he listened to every night, claiming that he couldn't go to sleep without doing so, he showed her a few old photos and told her the music was associated with the silliest thing he'd ever done.

She had never heard him mention the name Cora, but he'd never been a skirt-chaser, unlike the other two. He said he'd often felt disgusted by what they got up to. Girls and coke, coke and girls. And once he'd told her he'd been waiting for her forever, his dream woman – just the person he needed to cure him.

From the way she spoke, Ute Frankenberg seemed to be heavily sedated. Grovian could only nod from time to time, although her reference to photographs had electrified him. Careful, he told himself, careful.

"These old photos, Frau Frankenberg – do they still exist?"

"Frankie wanted to throw them away, but I wouldn't let him. I think I put them . . ." She got up off the sofa with an effort and went over to a chest of drawers. Bending down, she opened a drawer and removed a photograph album. "They may be in here."

They weren't. There was another album in the bedroom, she said, but she didn't feel up to fetching it. Alice Winger went instead. Ute Frankenberg sat down again with the album on her lap. Her gaze fastened on a postcard-sized snapshot: Frankie! She stroked the print with her fingertips and burst into tears, unable to go on turning the pages.

Grovian strove to suppress his impatience. Alice Winger took the album from her. She looked through it and removed a photograph. "Is this what you mean?"

Yes, it was! Relief dispelled the constricted feeling in his chest. He wouldn't have to lie or manipulate, wouldn't have to do what he'd suggested to her lawyer less than an hour ago: "If it comes to the pinch, we'll make Frankie a nice but ill-brought-up youngster of good family who – possibly under the influence of alcohol and cocaine – allowed his friends to rape a girl in August five years ago. This can't be proved, but neither can it be disproved. His arm would have healed by the sixteenth of August, if we stick to that date. Let's make use of her stories. I can produce a witness who'll testify under oath that she saw Cora Bender getting into Georg Frankenberg's car on the night of August the sixteenth. I'm sure her neighbour will do that for her if we guarantee there won't be any untoward consequences. You must impress on your client that she mustn't say a word in court about the Saviour and Mary Magdalene or pimps and prostitution. What we need is a nice love story with a dramatic outcome."

Yes, there it was! The photograph was underexposed, but with a little goodwill and her description at the back of one's mind it was possible to make out quite a lot. The musical instruments on the platform in the corner. Even the figures of two men. The one behind the drums had to be Frankie. His arms were raised; his face was just a blur. The figure at the keyboard was clearer, plump and fair-haired, with a dreamy expression. Not very tall but thickset.

"Who's that?"

Ute Frankenberg bent over his outstretched hand. "That must be Ottmar Denner."

Tiger, he thought. "Did your husband ever mention Denner's nickname? Tiger?"

"No, never."

"No other nicknames? Billy-Goat or Johnny Guitar?"

"No."

What a pity! "There are only two people in this photograph, Frau Frankenberg. Where's the third, Hans Böckel?"

Where indeed? Behind the camera!

"Bueckler," she said mechanically. "Not Böckel, his name was Bueckler."

Winfried Meilhofer mumbled an apology. "I must have misheard the name, then."

"But there must also be a photo of Hans Bueckler," Ute Frankenberg muttered to herself. She took the album back and turned a page, shook her head, turned another. "Here," she said, extracting a print from its transparent sleeve and handing it to him.

Grovian registered two things at the same time: the man in the photo, who matched Melanie Adigar's description perfectly – a fair-haired Adonis who might have been a Greek sculptor's model for the god Apollo; and Ute Frankenberg's hair. Still held by a barrette on the nape of her neck, it reached to her waist.

He felt his heart give a jump, because at the same instant he saw himself standing in front of the old bedside table holding the silver-framed photo in his hand. Magdalena, he thought. This woman was the trigger.

Damnation, that gnome of a psychologist was right! But it couldn't be! The snapshot he was holding was evidence. He concentrated on it once more. Hans Bueckler was standing at the cellar bar, glass in hand.

"Do you know where these photos were taken, Frau Frankenberg?"

She nodded. "The cellar where they used to practise."

"Where is this cellar?"

"I don't know. Is it important to you?"

"Very much so."

"I really don't know. Maybe in Denner's parents' house, maybe at Hans Bueckler's. Yes, that would be it. I don't know where he lived, though. Somewhere up north. His father had something to do with music. I think he was an agent, but I'm not sure."

"I'll have to take these photographs with me, Frau Frankenberg. These and any others that show the cellar. There may even be one of the house itself."

There wasn't, but there were another two good prints of the cellar, one of them showing Georg Frankenberg seated on the sofa with the low table in front of it. There was also a snapshot of him and Denner standing beside a red sports car.

"Do you know who the car belonged to?"

Ute Frankenberg merely nodded, gazing at the photo in his hand. She couldn't trust herself to speak. Winfried Meilhofer answered for her. "That was Frankie's car. He still had it when I first met him."

Grovian left feeling relieved, but only a little. He didn't have much to go on, just a photograph that might or might not be of the famous Johnny. Besides, an inner voice told him he would have done better to take one of Ute Frankenberg and show it to her. "Who is this, Frau Bender?" he ought to ask her.

In his mind's eye he saw her smile as fondly as she had at the photo in her bedroom, and in his head he heard her say, in a low, melancholy voice: "That's Magdalena."

14

Her hair was still damp. She'd washed it after breakfast, and she had no hairdryer. It was afternoon now, she knew. She knew little more than that, only that her hair was still damp. She could feel it lying cool against the nape of her neck. When a puff of wind came in from outside, she also felt the coolness on her scalp. That apart, she felt nothing.

Some time ago her right calf had started itching just below the hollow of the knee, as if some insect had landed there, possibly a mosquito. She'd debated whether to scratch the spot or shoo it away. Concentrating hard, she'd tried to discover whether she could identify the creature or induce it to fly off by an effort of the will alone. She hadn't looked at the spot or touched it. The itching had eventually stopped half an hour ago. She was sure of that, having counted off the seconds.

Counting had been her exclusive occupation ever since she returned from seeing the professor. She had got to well over ten thousand when her itching leg interrupted her, and she had to start afresh. Eighteen . . . Magdalena's age when she died. Nineteen . . . Her own age at that time. Twenty . . . She'd gradually begun to live. Twenty-one . . . The age at which she'd imagined she could lead a life like a thousand others with a husband too stupid to be dangerous. But that had been a mistake. Twenty-two, twenty-three, twenty-four . . .

"I see you've washed your hair, Frau Bender," the professor had said.

It was still wet at that stage, not just damp. The professor was pleased. He asked how often she used to wash it before. Every day, surely! Were those curls natural or a permanent wave, and what shampoo did she use? It had such an agreeably fresh smell.

"It's a very good shampoo," she replied. "The chief brought it for me. Where is he? Did I kill him?"

She knew she'd stabbed him – with the little knife lying on the bar. She'd managed to get hold of it somehow, and the moment she stabbed him he wasn't the chief any more, just someone doing something he shouldn't. Then she'd seen his face again, just for a fraction of a second. She'd recognized him too but without being able to tell if he was bleeding – even if he was still alive. The next moment, darkness fell.

Then she was lying in a white bed with a thin, worried face bending over her. The neatly trimmed beard was missing. He's shaved it off, was her first thought – he must have shaved while I was asleep. She waited for him to make her drink some orange juice or move her arms and legs, ask her to recite a poem from her schooldays or inject something into the cannula in the back of her hand. Or check the bandage around her head or prick her heels.

And the fear, this terrible fear that everything had begun again from the beginning – that she must go through it all once more: her homecoming. Mother's uncaring voice in the doorway: "Cora is dead. Both my daughters are dead."

And Father at her bedside: "What have you done, Cora?"

And Grit with her anxious, worried expression, not knowing whether to speak or remain silent, groping her way along, every sentence a hammer blow: "You've no need to worry, Margret has taken care of everything. Her death certificate says it was cardiac and renal failure. Margret fetched the papers from Eppendorf and got hold of a body, a junkie, I believe. Her boyfriend helped her. He made out the death certificate too."

Grit had shaken her head and shrugged. "It was a young woman. Margret brought her here by car. A suicide mission, but we needed something for the funeral. We had her cremated. Magdalena wanted it that way, and Margret said that wrapped it up. If anyone asked any stupid questions later on, there wouldn't be any answers."

296

It almost stifled her, the dreadful fear of having to hear it all again. She cried out, reached for the hand that was taking her pulse and clung to it tightly. "I don't want to go home. Please don't send me away, let me stay here. I can assist the staff – I'll do anything you ask, but don't send me home. My sister is dead. I killed her."

She didn't know how long she begged and pleaded and clung to that hand. It seemed an age before she realized her mistake. He hadn't shaved – he'd never had a beard in the first place. It was the professor, and now she'd told him. He knew, however many times he pretended not to have heard and however many times he asked her what shampoo she'd used to wash her hair. He had attained his objective – squeezed the truth out of her at last.

Four thousand three hundred and twenty-seven . . .

Four thousand three hundred and twenty-eight . . .

Magdalena's bones lying in the dust, parched grass all around . . .

Four thousand three hundred and twenty-nine . . .

Four thousand three hundred and thirty . . .

An unidentified girl! A skeletonized body near a military training area on Lüneburg Heath.

Four thousand three hundred and thirty-one . . . Don't think! She mustn't think and had no wish to.

Grit had said: "I couldn't believe it at first when your father knocked on my door that Sunday morning in May and said: 'The girls have gone.' I thought you must have taken Magdalena to Eppendorf. We called the hospital, but no dice. That afternoon we found your car parked outside the Aladdin. We couldn't understand it and didn't know what to do. I told your father he should go to the police, but he was dead against it. I almost got the feeling he thought you'd done away with Magdalena."

Grit had heaved a big sigh. "I'll never understand how he could have got such an idea into his head – him, of all people, who knew you'd have cut off your right hand for her. Well, we let it be known in the neighbourhood that Magdalena was going downhill fast and that you wouldn't leave her side. It was lucky Melanie was sleeping over at a friend's place that weekend. She mightn't have been able to keep her mouth shut."

Then Grit had spoken of August. "I still think it's wrong, what Margret did, and I reproach myself for saying anything at all when I read in the newspaper about a body being found. I didn't want to mention it to your father at first – I thought it would upset him unnecessarily. And it did. He called Margret right away, and do you know what he told her? 'Magdalena has been found.' I said: 'Wilhelm, that's just not true! They've simply found a body, the remains of some unidentified girl. It can't be Magdalena. They'd have been bound to find some clothing. A nightie at the very least – she always wore a nightie.' But he gave me a funny look and shook his head. And Margret said: 'It doesn't matter who the dead girl was. We must do something – we've waited far too long as it is.' And she was right, really. We couldn't go on saying you were sitting beside her bed, not indefinitely. Besides, we didn't believe she was still alive."

Four thousand three hundred and thirty-two . . . And so on for evermore, with that image before her eyes – bones mouldering in the dirt – and Magdalena's voice in her ears: "I'd sooner go to hell." But the body out there had not been cremated. It had rotted away and turned black, infested by worms.

*

At eight thousand seven hundred and forty-three she heard the key turn in the lock. She kept on counting, firmly convinced that they'd come to take her to the professor a second time.

The morning's session had been very unproductive from his point of view. He'd wanted to know what she and the chief had talked about at their last meeting. He already knew, the cunning dog! She wasn't so dumb that she couldn't infer from his questions how much he knew.

He asked if she would care to talk to him again about the cellar and said he knew what a burden Magdalena had been to her. And then he wanted to talk about music with her. In particular, about the songs Magdalena had enjoyed listening to. Did she recall any particular titles?

But he wouldn't tell her where the chief was, or whether he was still alive, so she refused to answer him any more. And then he played her some music. Drums, guitar and the high-pitched strains of an organ: "Tiger's Song"!

The hypocritical swine had asked how she was feeling and what the music made her think of. Eighteen . . . Nineteen . . . Twenty . . . Twenty-one . . . She'd had to clench her teeth until her jaw muscles creaked, but it worked. Twenty-two . . . Twenty-three . . . Twenty-four . . .

He became edgy. It didn't show, not outwardly, but she sensed it and went on counting, counting.

Eight thousand seven hundred and forty-four . . . The door opened, and a male nurse came in – the one who had looked in on her twice during the night. On one occasion he'd brushed the hair out of her eyes and asked: "How are you feeling, little lady? Better?"

His name was Mario. A nice fellow, always friendly, always good-natured, and as dark-haired as Father used to be. And strong, immensely strong. He could clamp a grown man under his arm and carry him off with ease, even though the man kicked and struggled and thumped him on the back with both fists.

Having seen him do this once on the way back to her ward from the professor's office, she'd reflected that Father might have been the same at one time. As tall as Mario and as strong. As handsome as Mario too, as a young man. And she had imagined how Mother had fallen in love with Father and let him kiss her for the first time. And how she had gone to bed with him for the first time. And how she had enjoyed it. And how she had conceived her first child with him and how happy her husband and her belated pregnancy had made her. And she had pictured herself in Mother's place and Mario in Father's.

Last night, when she was still so bemused by her medication that she could scarcely think, only form a wish, she had also imagined Mario lifting her out of her bed and bearing her off, far, far away.

Back into the cellar. She pictured him putting her down on the floor and standing in the middle of the room like Hercules, then tucking its occupants under his arm, one by one, and carrying them upstairs. And killing them there – all of them! And, when he had killed them all, he would come back, pick her up off the floor and say: "It's all over, little lady." And then he would let her sleep for evermore.

It was a sin to wish for something like that. The whole of life itself was sinful. Death too. She had killed her sister. And then, when she saw Magdalena lying dead in front of her, she had run out of the house in a panic. She had driven back to the Aladdin, where Johnny was waiting for her. He had helped her to take the body to the heath. They had left Magdalena where she wouldn't be found in a hurry, at a spot near the prohibited area where no one went, not even soldiers. There Magdalena could turn into a stinking, disgusting lump of dirt.

That was how it must have been. She didn't know for sure, but Grit saw it that way. Grit assumed that Magdalena was already dead when she came home. That was her mistake, and now the professor knew. If she stopped counting she would have to ask herself some questions. Why didn't I cremate her? I'd promised to. Didn't we have any petrol? Father always kept a full can in his car, but his car was parked outside the Aladdin. It couldn't be used for that trip, so someone must have helped me. I can't have been alone with her. If I'd been alone, she'd have got her cremation. Whoever was with me didn't want to drive Father's car. Someone who didn't have a full can of petrol in his own car. Who was afraid the flames would be spotted. Johnny? It was the only answer.

Mario gave her a conspiratorial wink. He was carrying a tray, she saw. On it were a small, white china coffee pot and two cups and saucers. He deposited the tray on the table and put a finger to his lips. "Just between the two of us," he said, "I made this coffee myself. It's really good."

She bit her lip and blinked away a tear.

"Now, now," said Mario, "you don't want to water it down. One cup for you and one for your visitor."

"Has the chief come? Is he still alive?"

"Of course he's still alive." Mario smiled broadly. "But he won't show his face here again in a hurry; the professor read him the riot act. No, it's your lawyer. Now come and have your coffee with him." He turned to the door and called: "Come in, she's fine." He gave her another wink and a thumbs-up. "I'll stay here, okay? I'll make sure nothing happens." And he stationed himself beside the door like a sentry, hands behind his back in the at-ease position.

When Brauning came in she slid off the bed like a child whose legs are too short to reach the ground. She remembered speaking to him for a considerable time on some occasion, but . . . "I'm sorry, I've forgotten your name."

"Don't worry," he said. "I have to make notes of everything myself, otherwise I forget half of it. Brauning's the name."

He smiled at her as he spoke. Unlike Mario's smile, his made a tense impression. He felt uneasy in her presence, she could tell.

"Are you scared of me?"

"No, Frau Bender," he said. "Why should I be scared of you?"

She didn't know, but it was a fact. "I won't hurt you," she assured him. "I'll never hurt anyone again. If Frankie had told me he was a human being I wouldn't have hurt him either. But he didn't – he wanted me to do it. I forgot to tell you that the other day."

"It's all right, Frau Bender," he said. "We can talk about that later."

"No," she said, "I'm not going to talk any more. All I do now is count, then nothing bad can happen."

Brauning had brought his briefcase with him, as he had on his first visit. He deposited it beside the table and sat down where he could keep one eye on the door and the nurse, a tough-looking character with biceps like a wrestler's. There was something reassuring about the sight.

"There are one or two matters I need your help with, Frau Bender," he said.

Helene had rehearsed him thoroughly. She had been impressed by Rudolf Grovian's statements and, above all, by his readiness to stand up for Cora Bender, at the risk of his job if necessary.

"He knows how to make a thing sound palatable," she'd said. "Not, of course, that I approve of his suggestions, in fact I strongly advise you not to act on them. Besides, it may not be necessary to do so. Burthe really does enjoy an excellent reputation, Hardy. It's just that he's overly fixated on Freudian theory, and in such a complex case that isn't enough. Grovian may be absolutely correct in his assessment. A layman's opinion shouldn't be underestimated, and he's assembled a certain amount of evidence to support it. The fact is, he knows how to handle her – he gets her to talk. You managed to do that too, Hardy. It's a question of authority, that's all. But the decision is yours, I don't want to interfere. You must simply bear something in mind when you talk to her: treat her naturally. Invite her help, appeal to her sense of responsibility." It was easy for Helene to talk.

"May I pour you some coffee?" She didn't even ask what he wanted her help with.

"That would be nice," he said.

"Do you mind if I remain standing? I've spent the whole day sitting down. An hour with Professor Burthe and the rest of the time on my bed."

Helene had said: "Don't let her sidetrack you, Hardy. If she tries to, and she certainly will, bring her back to the point at once. And don't let her provoke you – she will, if she's reasonably clear-headed. Imagine a child dependent on itself alone. If someone suddenly turns up and says 'I like you and want to help you', that child is bound to put him to the test. Don't lose patience, draw a line and stick to it. Be calm but firm, Hardy. You'll cope with the child in her."

"I'd sooner you sat down," he told her. He was prepared for anything, thanks to Helene's instructions and predictions: a grin, a contradiction, an air of boredom or indifference.

Nothing of the kind. Obediently, she pulled a chair from under the table and sat down with her feet close together, tweaked the hem of her skirt over her knees and smiled at him. "I still don't know if it was a mosquito on my leg or a nerve twitching," she said. "I ought to have looked, it was silly not to. If it were a mosquito, it

302

must still be around. That means it'll come back during the night. I should have swatted it, beaten it to death."

Brauning couldn't tell how lucid she was. Was she bearing out Grovian's theory and expressing a cryptic death wish or simply talking nonsense? He decided to act on his mother's advice. "I'm not here to talk about mosquitoes, Frau Bender. I've brought some photos with me. I'd like you to look at them and —"

He got no further. "I don't want to look at any photos," she said flatly.

Just a child, he told himself like someone repeating an incantation, just an unloved child. "It's very important, Frau Bender. I want you to look at these photos and tell me if you know any of the men in them."

"No!" She underlined her refusal with a vigorous shake of the head. "There's bound to be a photo of Frankie there, and I don't want to look at it. I've no need to refresh my memory. I could draw a picture of him, I can see him so vividly."

Her voice abruptly broke. She emitted a sound like a dry sob. "I see him with and without blood. I see him behind the drums and on the cross, and he's always in the middle. He was the Saviour. No! No, please don't look at me like that. I'm not mad, I could see it in his eyes. But I'm not Pilate either. No bowl of water for me!"

There's no point, Brauning thought. If we really make it through to a main hearing, one such outburst and that's that.

"He didn't want to die," she went on in a choking voice, putting her hands over her face. "He begged his father to let the cup pass from him. He had such a lovely wife. Why don't you let me die? I don't want to think any more! I can't take it any more! Now I can start again from the beginning. Eighteen, nineteen, twenty, twenty-one . . ."

Brauning drew several deep, regular breaths. Privately, he consigned Helene and her newly reawakened love of her profession to the devil – closely followed by Rudolf Grovian, who had put the idea into her head.

The male nurse continued to stand motionless near the door,

seemingly blind and deaf to what was going on. He wasn't there as a bodyguard for Brauning or a watchdog for her. He was there on the instructions of the district attorney, who would gladly have eavesdropped on them himself. Professor Burthe had managed to talk him out of it. He had also firmly declined to let a detective anywhere near her, so the lot had fallen to her attorney. But they needed an impartial witness, if possible one to whom she reacted favourably. If not, said the professor, any attempt would be futile. At present, no one could get a word out of Frau Bender.

There were twenty prints in his briefcase. He didn't know who they depicted. Rudolf Grovian had brought them to his chambers shortly after lunch. The police laboratory had worked overtime. Twenty men, all of around the same age. Only their heads, and the backgrounds were so indistinct, they offered no clue to the men's whereabouts.

He took a sip of coffee and put the cup down. She had got to forty-five when he finally brought himself to interrupt her. "Stop that, Frau Bender. You're now going to look at these photos. I don't know if they include one of Frankie. If you see one, tell me and I'll take it away. You don't have to look at it, just at the others. Tell me if you recognize anyone. And tell me his name, if you know it."

She actually stopped counting. Not having expected this, he construed it as a personal triumph. When he bent down to open his briefcase the nurse came over to the table and took up his position beside it.

Brauning found it slightly reassuring to have him closer at hand. Not that he was scared, but just in case. After all, she'd even gone for Grovian. He took out a big brown envelope, put it on the table and gave her an encouraging nod as he removed the prints.

She stared at them as if they were a nest of vipers. "Where did you get them?" she asked.

"From Herr Grovian."

Her eyes betrayed a flicker of interest. "How is he?"

"Fine. He sends his regards."

"Is he angry with me?"

"No, why should he be?"

She leaned across the table. "I stabbed him," she whispered.

"No, Frau Bender." He shook his head vigorously. "No, you didn't. You hit him, but he understands that. You were very upset because he'd provoked you. He really isn't angry. He'd simply like you to look at these photos. He went to a lot of trouble to collect them all. There's even one of his son-in-law, so he told me."

She sat back, pursed her lips and folded her arms. "All right, I'll take a look at them."

He slid the packet across to her. She bent over and looked at the first print, then shook her head and laid it aside. The second, the third, the fourth – all were rejected with a shake of he head. "Which is his son-in-law?" she asked when she got to the fifth.

"No idea, Frau Bender. I'm not allowed to know."

"A pity," she said. She stopped short at the sixth print, frowning and chewing a fingernail. "Could that be him? I've seen him before, but I don't know where. I don't know his name, either. What shall we do with him?"

"Put him to one side," he said.

She examined the seventh and eighth prints. At the ninth she clamped her eyes shut. "Quick, take it away," she said hoarsely. "That's Frankie."

He took the photo and added it to the pile she'd already discarded. It was a couple of minutes before she could continue. The nurse rested his hand soothingly on her shoulder. She looked up at him and nodded. Then, with lips tightly compressed, she turned her attention to the tenth, eleventh and twelfth prints.

At the thirteenth she said: "I don't want to know this swine, and I don't want to know his name either." Abruptly, she pushed the photo across to him.

"But I have to know his name, Frau Bender."

"Tiger," she said curtly. She gave the fourteenth print a long look. The fifteenth brought a smile to her face.

"My God, what a big nose he's got!"

"Do you know him?"

"No, but look at that nose!"

305

It was going better than expected. He felt proud of himself and had ceased to expect any dramatic incident, but the eighteenth print proved critical.

*

Brauning didn't notice at first. It was the nurse who spotted that something was wrong. He put his hand on her shoulder again. Then Brauning saw the way she was staring at the latest photo.

"Do you recognize that man?" he asked.

She didn't react. He couldn't identify her expression. Sorrow or hatred?

All at once she thumped the table with her fist. The cups gave a jump, slopping some coffee on the table. Her voice rose above the clatter. "What have you done to me? I only did it for you! I didn't want her to die, just sleep. You said I should leave her to sleep and come back to you. Did I? You should know!"

Brauning couldn't summon up the courage to repeat his question. He took a handkerchief from his pocket and mopped up the coffee to prevent it from smudging the prints.

The nurse stepped in. Bending over her, he said soothingly: "Hey, little lady, don't get upset, it's only a photo. He can't hurt you, I'll make sure he doesn't. Tell me who he is, and I'll inform them downstairs. Then they won't let him in if he shows up."

"He can get in anywhere," she sobbed. "He's Satan. Have you ever seen a picture of Lucifer, Mario? They always show him with a long tail, cloven feet and horns, like a billy-goat with a pitchfork. But he can't look like that really. After all, he was one of the angels. He drives the girls insane – they all want him. They won't listen when they're warned against him. I didn't listen either. His friend called him Billy-Goat. I should have known what that meant. You always have a choice between good and evil. I chose evil."

Brauning didn't dare take the photograph away from her. Mario did it for him. "Billy-Goat, eh?" he said. "Well, let's put him with Tiger. I reckon that's where he belongs."

She nodded.

Mario continued the interrogation. "What about this guy here? Does he belong with them too?"

She took another look at the first print she'd picked out and shrugged. "I had the feeling I'd seen him with the chief, that's why I thought it might be his son-in-law. But it can't be. Or is his son-in-law a policeman too?"

"We'll ask the chief the next time he comes," said Mario. He turned to Brauning. "Is that it, or do you need me still?"

Brauning replaced the prints in their envelope. He couldn't afford to mark the ones of Billy-Goat and Tiger. She would have to identify Hans Bueckler and Ottmar Denner to the examining magistrate as soon as she could be brought before him. He shook his head. "No, I think you can leave us now." He didn't sound too convinced.

Mario went out. Brauning drank the remains of his coffee, which was cold. She hadn't touched hers.

"Are we through?" she asked, gazing wistfully in the direction of the window.

"Not quite." He didn't know how to put it.

Rudolf Grovian had said: "If she can identify the men, it'll be a big step forward. Then we'll need the name of the hospital. We had no luck in Hamburg. We didn't interview every last doctor, of course, but we can forget about the doctor in any case, even if her aunt thinks otherwise . . ."

She had been thoroughly examined in the interim. Her skull had been X-rayed too, and the neurologist's report was with the DA. It was highly improbable that such injuries had been treated in a general practitioner's surgery. The X-ray had revealed a regular spider's web of cracks. Among other things, there was a probability that epidural bleeding had occurred.

It was naturally impossible to form a precise diagnosis after five years. However, the very fact that Cora Bender had survived her injuries without physical impairment was evidence of expert treatment, and that entailed the requisite equipment. There was no escaping it: she must have been treated in a hospital or, at the very least, a private clinic.

Brauning pretended to be busy. He hoisted the briefcase onto his lap and proceeded to rummage in it without removing anything. Helene had given him a long lecture on Cora Bender's motives for lying to the police on this point and others.

"She has nothing to lose," his mother had told him. "Make that clear to her. We know about the drug-addicted whore. Coax her out of her shell by telling her what Grovian thinks of her alleged addiction. If you can also convince her she was never a whore, Hardy, you've won. Then offer her what she so desperately craves: a normal, decent life."

He tried, albeit half-heartedly. At least she listened, and there were times when her expression seemed to justify Helene's approach. When he'd finished, however, she shrugged and gave an apologetic smile.

"Nice of you to say all that," she said. "I only wish it were true." She sighed and looked past him. "What happens to a person who thinks a crime has been committed and makes every attempt to hush it up?"

"Nothing, if it doesn't come out. But now, Frau Bender, we must talk about the hospital."

"No," she said and proceeded to polish a left-hand fingernail on her right thumb. "We'll do that later. I must ask you something. You're my attorney, so you mustn't tell anyone. Let's assume a woman's body was found somewhere and buried. Nobody knew her name – her bones were simply buried. Let's assume I knew she'd wanted to be cremated. Could I go to the authorities and say 'I'd like to grant this poor woman's last request and have her remains cremated.' Could I do that?"

"You could, if you'd known her."

"But I'd have to tell them her name, wouldn't I?" She continued to polish the fingernail and avoided his eye. He possessed himself in patience, not knowing where this was leading.

"Yes, you would."

"What if I couldn't do that?"

"I'm afraid you'd have to abandon the idea."

She raised her head at last with a look of fierce determination.

"But I must! I must, or I'll go mad. Think of something. There must be some way around it. If you think of something, perhaps I will too."

He drew a deep breath. "Frau Bender, can't we discuss this another time? It's a very complicated matter. I'll have to see if there's some way out of the problem – and I will, I promise you. But now you must tell me the name of the hospital that treated you. If you don't know the name, tell me what town it was in. Give me some clue – something that will enable me to prove you weren't a drug-addicted whore. You weren't an addict, Herr Grovian has already proved that, and he can't imagine that you ever associated with perverts."

He was hoping that another reference to Grovian would revive her willingness to cooperate, but in vain: she merely stared at him without expression. To hell with Helene and her psychologist's instructions. Being a lawyer, he had different arguments to hand.

"Do you really want to stew in here for the rest of your life, counting to avoid having to think? Wouldn't it be far better to clear your head by thinking things over thoroughly for once? You'll survive a few years in prison – and it won't be more than a few, I promise you. But this place" – he tapped the tabletop – "can drive a person insane. Is that what you want?"

She didn't answer, just looked at him and chewed her lower lip.

"I don't think it is," he said firmly. He had talked himself into form, and his voice carried more and more conviction. "You killed a man, Frau Bender. Only a man, not the Saviour. I don't want to hear you utter that word again. We shall find out why you did it. We shall prove that you had a reason any normal person can understand. And within a few years, Frau Bender, you'll be truly free. Think it over. You're only twenty-four, you can make a fresh —"

Her expression scarcely changed. A trace of bewilderment crossed her face, but that was all. "He knew how old I was," she broke in.

"Aha," he said, not knowing whom she meant and uncertain whether to bring her back to the point. The look on her face betokened concentration.

"How did he know that, when I had no papers on me? Naked by the roadside, he said, badly injured, full of heroin and without any papers. And then he said: 'You aren't even twenty.' Was it guesswork? He couldn't tell from my face, I looked so awful. Check my driving licence – I had to apply for a new one, and I still had some old photos, but the authorities wouldn't accept them. They didn't believe they were of me because I looked so old. He *can't* have known my age."

She fell silent for a few moments, drew a hand across her brow and sighed. "I really don't know his name," she said eventually. "He didn't tell me, and I never even asked him where I was. He didn't tell me that either. I can't remember how I got into the train. A porter told me when to get out. I had a slip of paper with the address on it. I also had money. Someone must have given the cabby the slip of paper and the fare. Grit said I arrived in a taxi."

She sighed again and shrugged apologetically. "If you promise to help me cremate my sister without getting Margret and Achim punished for the death certificate and the dead girl's body, I'll describe the doctor to you. I can't do more. Will you promise me that?"

Brauning did so, and half an hour later he was on the phone to Grovian. "I don't know what to make of it," he said. "She insists there was only a doctor plus a nurse whom she seldom saw. Her room was very small, she says. No window, and just enough room for a bed and a few items of medical equipment. It sounded to me like a box room."

He went on to describe the man. Several seconds' silence followed. "Herr Grovian?" he said, wondering if they'd been cut off.

"Yes, I'm still here. It's just that . . ." Another silence, then: "My God, that's quite impossible. It must be . . . How far is it? Four hundred miles at least. But that's impossible!"

*

She'd been sitting beside him in the car for a good half-hour. Grovian had spent the first few minutes trying to prepare her for the coming confrontation. He'd told her where they were going and why. By arrangement with the district attorney, the examining magistrate, Professor Burthe and Eberhard Brauning, he had rehearsed her at least three times.

It wouldn't have been in the least worthwhile under normal circumstances, but circumstances were anything but normal. Even Professor Burthe was of the opinion – and had convinced the DA and the examining magistrate – that only a crack of the whip could induce her to point a finger and say: "This was the man who treated my head injury."

Being the chief, Grovian needed no whip. She had heard him out in silence. She had even nodded when he asked if she'd understood it all and would do him this favour, considering the time and effort he'd expended on finding the medical man in question.

A consultant neurologist and brain surgeon who headed his own private clinic: Professor Johannes Frankenberg!

He should have withheld the name from her. It wasn't hard to follow her train of thought. If Frankie had been the Saviour, Johannes Frankenberg must logically be God the Father. As such, he must often have stood beside her bed at a stage when she was not yet fully conscious: the Almighty, who had performed a miracle upon her – a miracle in the truest sense – by patching up her shattered skull and transforming it into a serviceable head once more. How often he must have bent over her, shining a little torch on her motionless eyelids and saying: "My son wasn't to blame for this disaster." Perhaps he'd felt it his duty to send her on her way to eternity with that thought in mind. He couldn't have expected her to pull through.

Helene Brauning had pointed out that one could never tell exactly how much a comatose patient takes in.

And Cora Bender had said: "I'll gladly do you a favour, but I don't know if I can. What shall I say to him? My God, don't you understand? He was so kind to me, and I killed his only son. Frankie hadn't done me any harm."

That had been two days ago. Professor Burthe's immediate reaction to his proposal had been less than favourable, and it had taken a long conversation to convince him. Grovian had laid his cards on the table. They didn't amount to much, but Cora Bender had supplied a detailed personal description. Even Professor Burthe had to concede that it couldn't have sprung from her imagination, so he'd permitted Grovian another brief interview with her.

He still remembered vividly how startled she'd been when he came in, how she'd stared at his neck and trembled. She didn't calm down until he'd told her twice why he was there. "I'd like to make a trip with you in the next few days, Frau Bender. Just the two of us. To Frankfurt."

She'd understood two days ago, but when he'd picked her up half an hour before . . . She was staring straight ahead. He tried once more. "Well, Frau Bender, as I already said, you won't have to speak to Herr Frankenberg. Just a quick look at him, then we leave. And then you'll tell me if —"

She reacted at last. "Can't we talk about something else?" she broke in, looking tormented. "I'll do it. I'll look at him when we get there, but we aren't there yet. I don't want to have to think about it till then."

Her speech was slightly slurred. He felt pretty sure they'd given her some kind of medication before they handed her over. He only hoped she wouldn't fall asleep. Talking was a good way of staying awake, but they didn't have to talk about Frankenberg.

"What would you prefer to talk about?"

"I don't know. My head feels like a bucketful of water."

"I know a cure for that."

There was no hurry. They didn't have to be there before one o'clock, which was when Johannes Frankenberg could spare them a few minutes. Grovian had fixed the appointment without mentioning that he wouldn't be alone. A coffee break would do her good.

Soon afterwards he pulled into a service area and sat her down at a window table in the café. She went on pouring sugar into her cup from a dispenser until he gripped her wrist. "You'd better not stir that – it'll be undrinkable. You don't take sugar normally, or am I wrong?"

312

She shook her head and stared out of the window. Her face looked even paler in profile. "I'd like to ask you something."

"Go ahead," he said.

She drew a deep breath and took a sip of coffee. "That girl," she began hesitantly. "You told me that a girl's remains had been found near a military training area. Do you know what happened to them?"

"They were buried, I assume."

"I thought as much. Do you know where?"

"No, but I can find out – if you're interested."

"I am, very. I'd appreciate it if you could find out and tell me."

He merely nodded, speculating on the reasons for her request. The true reason escaped him, however. Although Eberhard Brauning hadn't grasped what death certificate and what strange girl she'd been alluding to, he had naturally kept his promise. Grovian still assumed that Magdalena Rosch had died on 16 August – of cardiac and renal failure.

She picked up her cup again and put it to her lips, but her hand shook so violently, she spilled some coffee on the table. She replaced the cup on its saucer with a clatter. "I can't do this. It can't be right. Work it out for yourself. We didn't drive as far as this. We were in Hamburg, not Frankfurt – I saw the signs on the autobahn. We must turn back. He was such a nice man. Perhaps he really did find me beside the road. I may have walked a long way."

"I don't think you were capable of walking, Frau Bender."

"Oh, you!" She made a dismissive gesture. "Lies are all you ever believe. No one has told you the truth, take it from me." She turned away again and gazed out of the window in silence for several seconds. Still with her head averted, she asked: "What would happen to me if I confessed to a second murder? That would make two. What would I get?"

"For the confession, nothing," he told her. "You'd have to produce another dead body."

She stared into her coffee cup, then raised it to her lips again. Although her hand was still trembling, she managed a sip without spilling any. Having replaced the cup, she said: "You already have one: the girl on Lüneburg Heath."

She gave a fleeting smile. "I killed her. It was me." When he made no comment, she added: "That's a confession. I want you to treat it as such."

He nodded. "Then I'll need more details."

"I know. I lied to you about Magdalena's birthday. I drove back to the Aladdin when she was asleep, but Johnny wasn't there any more, just the girl Tiger had been dancing with. She told me the two of them had gone on somewhere. Johnny had said it wasn't worth waiting for an inhibited prick-teaser. That made me so mad I freaked out, but I remained friendly. I asked her if she'd care to come somewhere else with me. Then I drove her to the heath, where I punched and kicked her to death. I jumped on her chest with both feet and broke her ribs. When she was dead I undressed her so it would look as if some men had done it. I threw her clothes away on the return trip. We'd better go back now, then you can take this all down."

"We aren't going back, Frau Bender," he said firmly. "Your statement can be taken down later. An hour or two won't matter, not after five years."

Her lips twitched as they had on the night he first questioned her, when he still thought she was putting on an act. "But I don't want to go there," she said. "I really can't. He'll ask me why I did it, but my lawyer says I mustn't mention the Saviour. And then he'll say he should have let me die. It would have been better if he had, but he saved my life."

Grovian reached across the table and took her hands. He held them tight – tugged at them until she finally brought herself to look at him. "Listen to me, Frau Bender. Professor Frankenberg saved your life, which was praiseworthy of him. But before he could save it someone must have endangered it, and he didn't want that someone to go to prison. He wouldn't have done such a thing for a stranger. Concentrate on that, just that. Have I made myself clear?" When she nodded he released her hands.

"But I'll have to go to prison for killing that girl?"

"Yes, of course."

"And not just for a year or two?"

"No, it was premeditated murder. That would mean a life sentence."

He paid for the coffee, took her arm and led her back to the car. She seemed to be easier in her mind. While they drove on she told him about her life with Gereon. Three years in a soap bubble. Soap bubbles burst easily. Still, her son was in good hands with his grandparents, she felt sure.

They got there with almost an hour in hand. He pulled up in the car park outside the clinic, a handsome two-storey building in dazzling white stucco. He was hoping for some sign of recognition, but none came. "If it really happened the way she says," the DA had said, "they probably doped her before taking her to the station. But none of this can be proved, unfortunately, even if she recognizes Professor Frankenberg. We would need a confession on his part, and you'd better not count on that."

She sat there for some minutes, shoulders hunched uneasily, peering out of the car window. Then she insisted on his taking down her confession to the girl's wanton murder. Just to be on the safe side, she said. You never could tell. She mightn't feel up to it later on, and she'd sooner get it over.

He humoured her by scribbling a few lines in his notebook and getting her to sign them. She sat back.

"How much time do we have?"

"Almost an hour."

"Could we stretch our legs a little?"

The car park was enclosed by shrubs, the clinic itself by mature trees. "It looks so peaceful," she said.

He opened the passenger door and locked the car behind them, then strolled towards the clinic with her. Frankenberg's private residence, which was situated behind it, was still out of sight, but he knew from his previous visit that it was built in the same style.

Grovian didn't feel like stretching his legs. He shepherded her slowly towards the house, eager to get it over and done with. She was saying something – like a child whistling in the dark, it seemed to him, and he knew so well how she must be feeling: guilty through and through.

His own feelings he strove to ignore. He couldn't help her, nor could Brauning or the district attorney. They might find a thousand plausible reasons for Georg Frankenberg's death, but nothing could unburden her of Magdalena's death. Burthe could try to explain to her that it had been an accident or a mercy killing.

Grovian had grasped that he'd been wrong and fathomed what she'd tried to tell him about the manner of Magdalena's death. He even realized whose skeletal remains had been discovered on the heath in August five years earlier. But jumping on her chest with both feet? What nonsense! She must have exerted a little too much pressure with her hand while masturbating her and hankering for Johnny, that was all.

And her father, who loved her above all else, had kept his mouth shut. Her crazy mother didn't understand, and the neighbour wasn't allowed in the house any more. The body had lain upstairs for a few months until Margret decided to act at last. She'd dumped the remains on the heath and procured the death certificate. It was as simple as that.

The front door of the private residence was approached by three steps. He climbed them ahead of her and rang the bell. Moments later the door opened. A young woman neatly attired in a white coat looked at him enquiringly and cast a dubious glance at his companion.

"May I help you?"

He produced his warrant card. "We've an appointment with Professor Frankenberg at one. I'm afraid we're a little early."

No matter, she said, they could wait in the drawing room. Grovian led the way across the entrance hall. Cora followed, her apprehensive expression and hunched shoulders seeming to suggest that an executioner's block awaited her in the middle of the drawing room. But there was just a sofa and, beside it, an enormous parlour palm whose outspread fronds resembled the spokes of an umbrella. Above the sofa hung an abstract painting in a plain frame. Grovian had been shown into another room on his first visit, so he was seeing it for the first time.

She headed straight for it and came to a halt in front of the sofa. Her face registered a mixture of surprise and bewilderment. She looked down at the floor, then up at the wall beside the sofa.

"It can't be," she said in a low voice. "The stairs have been blocked up." She made a helpless gesture that encompassed the whole room. "They've rebuilt the place." She pointed to the opposite wall. "That's where we were standing, Johnny and me. I was feeling bad because Magdalena . . ." She broke off in mid sentence, shuddering and gagging. Then, haltingly, she went on.

15

I never hated her more than I did at that moment, when she stretched out on the bed. I knew my finger and the candle wouldn't be enough this time. She usually liked to talk and have a cuddle afterwards. If I wanted to make her really tired, I would have to do it with my tongue . . . The very thought of it made me feel sick.

That was when I realized that everything was topsy-turvy. I didn't live for her; she lived my life through me. Father used to call her his little bird, and that's what she was like, a bird pecking the best bits out of my miserable life. All she left me was a sense of disgust.

Maybe it was only the champagne that made my head spin. Maybe it was the thought of Johnny, whom I'd walked out on. I felt I was burning up inside as I kissed and caressed her. Johnny would have been doing that to me, had I stayed with him.

So I proceeded to tell her the truth – all of it. No real boyfriends so far, just a well-meaning wimp. No red-hot sex with randy Casanovas, just a few lukewarm, beer-flavoured kisses. And now this uniquely different boy who had turned my legs to jelly.

She lay still and listened to me. When I started to weep she put her arms round me. I felt her hands on my back. She pulled my T-shirt out of my waistband, slid her hands beneath it and stroked my back. "It's all right," I heard her whisper. "It's all right, sweetheart. I'm sorry. I'm a terrible burden to you, I know, but not for much longer. Not for much longer, sweetheart, I promise you." She slid her hands beneath my arms and cupped them around my breasts. I didn't want her to touch me like that. I wanted to feel Johnny's hands there, yearned for Johnny's whispers, Johnny's kisses, Johnny's body.

I can't recall if I told her that, but I must have done so because she suddenly let go of me and said: "You can have him, sweetheart. Go get him, and I won't ask you afterwards what it was like." She sat up. "Know what we're going to do now? We're going to Johnny."

She always said "we" when she meant me. I couldn't help thinking of the kindly student nurse she'd told me about, and how she'd longed for a cuddle from Mother when things were really grim. And the only person she'd had was me.

I felt sorry for having said such mean things to her. She couldn't help it, but I couldn't help falling in love. I was nineteen! It was normal for a girl of nineteen to fall in love with someone. I couldn't spend the rest of my life inventing imaginary men and showing my sister what it was like to be made love to by them. I wanted to know what it was like *now*, at that very moment.

I wanted to be able to come home afterwards and tell my father: "Now I know what you've been missing all these years. Forgive me, father! Forgive me for all the vile things I've said and thought about you. I think I was simply disgusted with myself. But that's all over now. I'm a woman, a real woman. I've been to bed with a man, and it was wonderful."

All I wanted was to live, to lead an entirely normal life with a man whom I loved and who loved me. With a father who was happy and contented in his old age.

He would never again have to tell stories about Buchholz in order to forget the little children he'd shot in Poland. If he'd been on his own there, he would never have done it, I felt sure. And I wanted him to realize that he was as little to blame for the holes in Magdalena's heart as I was. I wanted him to forget it.

He was only to think of the children I might some day put on his lap, so he could tell them old stories about the railway. I wanted him to be proud of me. I wanted him to stop regarding his children as his punishment – to stop wishing that he'd denied himself for once and bided his time, so Magdalena would never have been born.

She smiled at me. I was a bit woozy from the fizz, from my thoughts and emotions, and I felt so depressed, so wretched inside. "We", she'd said. That meant I was to drive back to the Aladdin and leave her alone with her own wretched thoughts and emotions.

"It wouldn't be right," I said. "Not on your birthday."

"That's just it," she retorted. "That's just why it *would* be right. You must help me to get dressed and . . ."

That was when I grasped what she meant. "You're crazy," I said. She'd scarcely been out of bed all week – she hadn't even come downstairs for meals. Three visits to the bathroom, that's all. I'd given her a bed-bath and held a bowl for her to clean her teeth. She couldn't stand up, even when I helped her. It was impossible.

She didn't see it that way, and she could be very stubborn when she wanted something.

"Don't make a fuss, Cora. If I tell you it'll work, it will. I'm fine, I've been resting all week. I've even put on a bit of weight, hadn't you noticed? Look at my legs. If I'm not careful, I'll get fat. I'm fine, really, I'm not just saying that. I wouldn't suggest it if I knew it was impossible." Her eyes narrowed suspiciously. "Or do you begrudge me an outing? The Aladdin is your personal preserve – you'd sooner I stayed in bed, is that it?"

"No, that's not true."

"But it looks like that. Or are you scared? You've no need to be, I know what I'm capable of." She laughed softly. "There's plenty of time, we've no need to rush. If your Johnny meant what he said, he'll wait – he'll still be there at midnight. Help me get dressed, dab a bit of rouge on my cheeks and paint my nails for me. We can do them last – they can dry on the way there."

"You can't leave the house," I said.

"Of course I can," she insisted. "I'll have to if we go to America; it's the same thing. You'll have to help me downstairs, that's all. In the car I'll be sitting down, and I can easily manage to walk the few yards from the car park. Once we're inside, I'll sit in a corner and watch you dancing with Johnny."

She must have noticed that the idea didn't appeal to me, because she added: "No, I won't watch you. It's your night. I'll sit with his friend. You said he had someone with him. What's he like? The friend, I mean?"

"Not bad," I lied. "An amusing type. He goes by the name of Tiger." I hadn't mentioned that tonight was the first time he'd picked up a girl, and I thought it better not to mention it now.

"Sounds interesting." She grinned. "Does he have stripes and a long tail?"

We both laughed. "No idea," I said. "I've never seen him with his clothes off."

She was still laughing. "Maybe I can take a peek at him if you go off with Johnny." She looked up at me with her head on one side. "It'll be fantastic, you'll see. You'll have a great time, I know."

I still felt reluctant, but what she'd said about America was right. Besides, I thought it might act as a test run.

*

She wanted to wear my dark blue satin blouse and the white skirt with the scalloped hem. The skirt was almost transparent, so her legs showed through the lace. She really had put on weight. Her legs were slender, but not thin any more.

"I'll amuse myself till you get back," she told me while I was helping her to get dressed. "Have a good time, sweetheart. I will too. You've no idea how long I've been wanting to go to the disco. I never thought I'd manage it this year. What a birthday this is!"

She wanted dark red varnish for her nails, so you couldn't see how blue they were. In the car she asked me how much money we really had.

"Only thirty thousand," I said. "Not ninety. I'm sorry."

She shrugged. "Thirty thousand is a tidy sum, though. How did you manage it?"

This time it was my turn to shrug. "I saved it. I always bought the cheapest stuff."

She gave me a funny sidelong glance but said nothing. I was driving slowly and carefully. I was scared of having an accident

321

because of all the champagne I'd drunk, and I was also worried about her. Terribly worried.

"Forget about me," she said. "This isn't the first time I've gone for a drive. Driving to the hospital is more tiring. It's much further too, but I've always survived so far." She was laughing again.

And then, when we got out in the car park, I really did forget my fears. It wasn't as full as usual, but my heart gave a leap when I saw that the silver Golf was still there. Covering the few yards to the entrance was no problem. I put my arm around Magdalena's waist and we took it very slowly. She came to a halt just outside. "Hang on," she said. "Let me savour this for a moment or two."

It was rather breezy, so I couldn't hear how fast she was breathing. "Too much for you?" I asked.

"Is it hell! Let go of me, or they'll think you're carting a tailor's dummy around."

I let go of her but remained poised to catch her if necessary. She took one step and then another, not even holding onto the wall. Then she turned to me and laughed. "You see? I feel absolutely fine."

When I saw the smile on Johnny's face, I felt absolutely fine too. He and Tiger were sitting at a table talking. There was no sign of the unknown girl. Johnny wasn't surprised by my reappearance.

I didn't care for the way he stared at Magdalena and smiled a different smile from the one he'd given me. He obviously fancied her – any man would have. She was a picture, thanks to my handiwork.

She was as aware of this as I was. "Just so there's no misunderstanding," she said, "I've only come to look at a wild animal. I'm told there's a tiger running around loose in here. Mind if I sit down?"

Tiger grinned from ear to ear. He nodded eagerly and made room for her. Magdalena held onto the table with both hands. "I'm rather unsteady on my pins," she said. "I've been lying in bed all day. Not a good idea, bad for the circulation."

She sat down beside Tiger, and I sat down beside Johnny. Having grasped that she was off-limits, he put his arm round my shoulders and gave me a squeeze. "So the lullaby didn't work," he said.

Magdalena heard this. "I'm a bit too old for lullabies," she said with a laugh.

I felt embarrassed – I'd forgotten I'd told him that. Johnny wanted to dance. The DJ was playing an old number by the Beach Boys. He took me in his arms and said: "You don't look alike in the least. Is she really your sister?"

"No," I told him. "My sister's asleep in bed. She really is quite ill. That's Magdalena; I bumped into her in the car park. She suggested pulling your leg a bit."

"I see," was all he said.

I don't know how long we danced. Only a minute or two, it seemed to me, but it must have been half an hour or more. When we returned to the table Magdalena complained that the music was a drag. "Don't they have anything by Queen?"

"Queen be damned!" said Tiger. "Would you like to hear a really good group? Live?"

"Why, got one up your sleeve?"

"In a manner of speaking," said Tiger, "but only a third of it. I play keyboard." He indicated Johnny. "Bass guitar. We left the drummer behind. Frankie didn't feel like making a night of it, he never does. He's scared his parents will turn up unexpectedly."

Almost in the same breath, he said: "Hey, guys, how about giving him a surprise? This place is dullsville. Let's go and make our own party – let's drag Frankie away from his books."

Magdalena leaped at the idea. I didn't want to drive too far after all the champagne I'd drunk, but Johnny said they'd take us and bring us back afterwards.

Magdalena leaned on Tiger on the way out, not that it aroused comment. Being taller than him, she draped one arm around his shoulders – much to his satisfaction – as if she'd known him for years. The two of us got in the back with Johnny and Tiger in front.

I was terribly anxious on Magdalena's account. I felt it was wrong, what we were doing – wrong and far too risky – but it was also exciting because of Johnny. He kept turning around during the drive. He didn't say anything, just gazed at me as if we were alone together in a bedroom or somewhere.

I took no notice of our route, and I can't recall what the house looked like. I only know the two boys got out when the Golf pulled up. Each of them reached into the back and held out his hand. Johnny pulled me straight into his arms. Tiger helped Magdalena out.

He treated her very nicely and considerately. While they were sitting at the table on their own she'd told him she'd been in bed with gastritis. He said she was in safe hands with him. He was studying medicine, he said, and so was Frankie. Frankie was a grade-A student – he'd be bound to become a top consultant some day, like his old man. She told me that before she . . . I think she told me in the car, but I don't remember.

They got to the front door first. I didn't notice whether Tiger had a key or had to ring the bell, but he and Magdalena were inside long before us. I had my eyes shut, and Johnny was propelling me backwards as he kissed me. "Mind the step," he murmured, picking me up. He didn't put me down until we were inside the hallway, that huge white hallway.

He pushed me up against the wall and kissed me some more, and over his shoulder I could see the picture with the stairs beside it. Tiger and Magdalena were already going down. She was managing the stairs by herself, just holding onto the rail with one hand. Damnation, I thought, she'll never make it. I shouldn't have let her go down them on her own. Why doesn't she get him to help her?

I think I know why. She must have seen Frankie as soon as she entered the house. Maybe he'd opened the door to them; and he was several cuts above the pink piglet.

She turned and called: "Coming, you two? You can carry on downstairs. I bet it's cosier down there." I could hear the sound of drums from below. And Johnny said: "She's right, come on."

*

Magdalena was already sitting on the sofa when we entered the cellar, gazing fixedly at the corner where the musical instruments were. Frankie was seated behind the drums, but he was only toying with them. He couldn't take his eyes off Magdalena.

Tiger was standing at the bar, slicing a lemon. "First a slug of hooch," I heard him say. He looked over at Magdalena. "How about you?"

She shook her head. "Just a soft drink, if you have one. No hard stuff, it would only upset my stomach again."

Then they played for us, although more for Magdalena than for me. She was the star. I think they'd all have liked to go to bed with her, but she only had eyes for Frankie. She told me to dance, and I did.

Johnny was smiling at me the whole time. It was very hot down there. Magdalena looked wonderful in that flickering, multicoloured light. The dark blue blouse went well with her fair hair, and her slender legs shimmered beneath the almost transparent lace. Her skin was bluish beneath the make-up, but you couldn't see that. She looked as if she'd just come in out of the sun.

Then Frankie tossed his drumsticks away. He went over to the sofa and sat down beside her. Tiger returned to the bar and knocked back a couple more glasses. Johnny turned on the stereo rig – the tape was also one of theirs – and came over to me. We danced, and although the music was pretty wild, he held me in his arms and gradually undressed me.

I felt his hands on my back and his lips on my neck. Then we were lying on the floor together. It was lovely, but I couldn't enjoy it to the full because I simply couldn't concentrate on him. I kept looking sideways.

Frankie had draped one arm over the back of the sofa – and around Magdalena, or so it seemed. They were talking together, but the music was too loud for me to hear what they were saying. I only saw how they were looking at each other, she at him and he at her. Eventually he kissed her. Well, why not, I thought – it won't hurt her. Besides, he was being very gentle with her, I could see. And then he took off her blouse . . .

He naturally noticed the scars. He ran his finger over them very lightly, very gently, and asked what they were. There was a short

325

break in the music, so I heard every word. I also heard Magdalena's answer.

"My Jacob's Ladder," she said.

For a while I took no more notice of her or of Tiger, who was standing at the bar, presumably snorting his first line of coke. Then he strolled over and stood looking down at us. I didn't like that – I'd sooner have been alone with Johnny, but I didn't dare suggest it. I couldn't leave Magdalena alone with two strange men.

Tiger was holding a small mirror and a drinking straw. Johnny sat up and snorted some of the stuff. Tiger turned to the sofa. "How about you, Frankie?" he called.

Frankie wasn't interested; he was kissing Magdalena.

Then Tiger kneeled down beside me and started stroking my breasts. I thought Johnny would tell him to get lost, but he didn't do a thing. "Stop that," I told him. "Keep your hands to yourself, I don't like it!" – or words to that effect.

Magdalena, who had heard me, called: "Don't be so stuffy, it doesn't mean anything." And, to Tiger: "Give her a shot, it'll relax her. She's a bit inhibited."

He held out the mirror, but I didn't want any of the stuff. "Don't be a spoilsport, sweetie," Magdalena called. "It's a crazy sensation, I've told you a hundred times. Take some. Relax and give yourself a treat."

I wanted nothing to do with what was on that confounded mirror; all I wanted was Johnny. He stuck a finger in my mouth and dipped it in the powder, then rubbed it on me down below.

"Wipe it off!" I pleaded.

"Just what I had in mind," he said and slid down me.

I felt him kissing me there. It was . . . It was heaven.

Magdalena was taking no notice of me. Frankie didn't give her a chance to watch; he had pulled her half onto his lap and was kissing and caressing her. I'll never forget the look on her face. She was very happy, I think.

So was I. Tiger had stopped stroking my breasts. For a while he merely kneeled beside my head and watched. Then he opened his fly, but by that time I didn't care. It didn't disgust me – it wasn't

326

much different from sucking one's thumb. I thought of Mother. What would she have thought if she could see me lying on the floor doing it with two men at once?

It was wrong – all wrong – but it was wonderful. I had fire in my belly, champagne in my head, cocaine in my blood, and Johnny everywhere.

At some stage I looked over at the sofa. I couldn't see much because Tiger's leg was blocking my view. I could only see a broad, bare back. For a moment I didn't grasp its significance: Magdalena was no longer draped across Frankie's lap, she was stretched out beneath him. The blouse and the white skirt were trailing over the edge of the sofa.

It all happened so fast, but I seemed to see it in slow motion. Frankie was making love to her, slowly at first, then more and more fiercely. All at once, he stopped short and straightened up with a jerk, kneeled between her legs and thumped her chest with his fist. "Breathe!" he shouted.

Then he threw himself on top of her, kissed her again, pinching her nostrils, straightened up once more and went on thumping her, this time with both fists at once. "Come on, breathe!" he shouted. "Breathe! Breathe! Breathe!" And he thumped her chest with both fists each time he yelled the word.

Her head was jerking to and fro, her right leg dangling over the edge of the sofa, her left leg resting on the back. Then it too slid off.

There was another short break between two numbers. As he hit her again in that momentary silence I heard a cracking, splintering sound and knew it must be her ribs breaking. But I couldn't go to her – I couldn't do anything but think of the knife on the bar and where I would have to stab him to stop him killing her.

Johnny was now on top of me, pinning me to the floor beneath him, with Tiger holding my head in both hands. I couldn't even scream with his penis in my mouth. The music started again, and Frankie shouted above the din: "Help me! Help me! She's stopped breathing!" There was madness in his eyes.

Johnny had finally grasped that something was wrong. "Are you crazy?" he shouted back. "What are you doing, you idiot?" But he made no move to let me go, just stared in the direction of the sofa.

Frankie didn't reply. Like a man possessed, he went on pounding Magdalena's chest with both fists.

Tiger uttered a sudden yelp. "She bit me, the bitch!" I saw him reach for the ashtray on the table and raise it above his head. The tape was still playing "Tiger's Song". Then everything went dark and silent.

*

She wept quietly to herself on the drive back. Sometimes she shook her head, and the weeping intensified for a moment or two. Grovian left her in peace. Standing in front of that picture, she had spoken like someone in a trance, eyes shut, both hands clenched. She had seemed frozen, he thought involuntarily, and now she was gradually thawing out. He hoped she understood.

All his doubts were dispelled. Magdalena had wanted it that way. She knew she was done for. No possibility of another operation, her heart wouldn't have stood the strain. He wondered what would have happened had Cora refused her request – had she said it was out of the question. "No, we're staying at home!" Magdalena would probably have sought death in her arms – and found it. Cora would still have felt as guilty.

But making that clear to her wasn't his job any more. As for what Johannes Frankenberg had told them, the court would have to decide. "My son wasn't to blame for this . . ."

Innocent he undoubtedly was. Grovian remembered what Grit Adigar had said about Magdalena's beauty and nature's way of compensating for her physical defects. Unfortunately, nature had failed to allow for her willpower, which had lured a man to his doom. Grovian could only see the matter in that light. Had he been able to, he would have given Magdalena a piece of his mind. To him, she was on a par with the irresponsible idiots who choose a stretch of motorway on which to end their lives and those of a few innocent victims.

Georg Frankenberg had been a serious young man who only pursued his hobby at weekends. And because his parents disapproved, he and his two friends devoted themselves to their passion in secret at his grandmother's house in Wedel, a Hamburg suburb.

That house, his mother's parental home, had been empty for months. It was on the market, but no prospective buyer had yet been willing to pay the asking price. Georg often drove there at weekends to check that all was well – or so he said, but his mother had long suspected that he was motivated by something more than filial duty.

There was this friend of his, the tubby little youth from Bonn, Ottmar Denner. Georg had brought him to Frankfurt on two occasions, and Frau Frankenberg hadn't cared for the sly, self-indulgent look in his eye. Then came that Saturday in May . . .

Frau Frankenberg had made several attempts to reach her son at his student digs in Cologne but without success. Shortly after midday she called the house in Wedel, and who should answer the phone but Ottmar Denner!

"Hey, Billy-Goat!" he blurted out. "About time too! I thought you'd sunk without trace again. I've been waiting for you to call for a good hour. Get a move on and pick up a bottle of hooch on the way, Frankie forgot again. We'll get some coke this evening – make a real night of it. Hey, man, cat got your tongue?"

Frau Frankenberg had hung up without a word and insisted on driving to Hamburg right away. "I knew something was wrong," she told her husband, "but this is too much. You're going to give Georg a serious talking-to."

They got there at two in the morning. The front door was open. Georg was sitting on the cellar floor with a naked girl's bloodstained head in his lap, saying over and over again: "She wouldn't breathe, she wouldn't! She suddenly stopped breathing."

Johannes Frankenberg didn't understand what his son meant. Although badly injured and unconscious, the girl with her head on Frankie's lap was definitely alive – just! His wife didn't realize that another girl must have been there until she noticed a second heap of discarded clothes. It wasn't until three days later that Georg revealed that Hans Bueckler and Ottmar Denner had removed her naked body shortly before his parents arrived.

Denner and Bueckler had wanted to take Cora too, but Georg wouldn't let them. "I didn't kill the girl," he kept insisting. "She suddenly stopped breathing."

Heart failure, thought Grovian, or the exertion had proved too much for her aneurysm, and it burst. At all events, it had been a natural death – and possibly, from Magdalena's point of view, a happy one. Frankie had given her what she'd always wanted.

What Cora Bender had described sounded like an attempt to resuscitate her. Grovian was reminded of the young female patient Winfried Meilhofer had mentioned, the one whose ribs Frankie had broken because he couldn't come to terms with her death. Perhaps he had seen her as a second Magdalena. The Saviour, thought Grovian. That's what he had been. He had delivered Magdalena from her sufferings and Cora from her burden of responsibility. But he couldn't rid her of her sense of guilt. On the contrary, his death had rendered her guilty under the law.

She was still weeping. Over an hour went by before she finally turned to him and asked: "How could anyone forget such a thing?"

He shrugged. "Frau Bender, you must speak to Professor Burthe about that. Ask him; I'm sure he'll be able to explain it."

"But I'm asking you. How could I forget such a thing?"

"It happens to a lot of people," he said after a moment or two. "You often encounter it after an accident. All they remember is that they were approaching a road junction. They've no idea what happened after that."

"Approaching a road junction," she murmured. "Or driving home just before eleven at night." She started shaking her head again. She was silent for several minutes. The next time she spoke there was a trace of bitterness in her voice. "Five years!"

She heaved a tremulous sigh. "For five years I believed I'd killed my sister. Everyone thought so. My father, Margret, Grit. No, not Grit. She always said she didn't think me capable of it. But she also said she didn't think I'd taken drugs, when I only had to look at my arms to believe it whether I wanted to or not."

Abruptly, she flung her arm out sideways. It landed on top of the steering wheel.

"Careful, Frau Bender!" he yelled. His palms went moist. The speedometer was reading ninety. The crash barrier loomed on their left, a column of trucks on their right.

She took no notice and left the arm where it was. "Why did he do it?"

He slowed down gradually, unable to decelerate fast without risking a collision with the driver behind. Then he took hold of her arm and replaced it on her lap. "Don't do that again unless you mean to kill us both."

"Why did he do it?" she repeated.

"You must know that."

"No!" she snapped. "I don't know why. He didn't have to make a mess of my arms to put Frankie in the clear. He need only have said I'd walked out in front of his car. I so dearly wished it had been a normal accident. He also said I had vaginal lesions. I can't have had; Johnny didn't rape me. Why did he tell me such a thing? My God, I can still hear him: 'The circumstances and nature of your injuries allow of only one conclusion.' Why did he say that?"

She was absolutely beside herself. He wished she would calm down. He couldn't pull over onto the hard shoulder: there wasn't a gap between the trucks. "You must know why, Frau Bender."

"Yes, I do, but I want to hear if you know too. Go on, tell me. Go on! I've got to hear it once from someone else. It doesn't help if I only think it."

It went against the grain. He had left his emotions behind and was all policeman once more. A satisfied policeman who had done a good job. As such, he didn't want to put any words into her mouth and send her back to Burthe with a ready-made opinion.

But then, despite himself, he said: "He wanted to prevent you from going to the police. He couldn't depend on your amnesia being permanent. If a drug-addicted whore remembered what had happened in the cellar, who would have believed her? After all,

331

nearly six months had elapsed. Only he, his wife and his son knew that you'd been confined to bed in his house all that time. And now, Frau Bender, calm down. Discuss everything with Professor Burthe when we get back. I'll have a word with him too and with the DA and the examining magistrate. I'll tell them all what we learned from Herr Frankenberg."

They'd learned a great deal, starting with the first aid administered in the cellar. Then came an hours-long drive through the night. Frankie had sat in the back with her head pillowed on his lap and his fingertips on her throat, feverishly announcing, every few minutes, that he could still feel her pulse.

Only experts could gauge how great a risk there had been that she wouldn't survive the journey. What would have happened to her if that tiny little flame had gone out?

Perhaps they'd hoped it would. Not Frankie, his parents. Professor Frankenberg could then have saved himself the trouble of breaking his son's arm. Just another dead woman lying beside the road, stripped and unidentifiable like the poor creature on Lüneburg Heath. Whether the latter really was Magdalena, only Ottmar Denner and Hans Bueckler could say – if they could be found.

"I shouldn't have taken her with me," she said, breaking in on his thoughts. "I knew I shouldn't have, I knew it perfectly well. Perhaps I didn't care if she died, I was so obsessed with Johnny. My mother always said the desires of the flesh bring nothing but disaster."

"Your mother is deranged, Frau Bender," he said. "She always was."

"No," she murmured, "not always. Margret told me once . . ." She broke off. "What will happen to Margret?"

She gave him no time to reply. "Look," she said eagerly, "can't we put it this way? I told Johnny my sister was at home in bed and I'd run into this other girl in the car park. We can stick to that story. No one can disprove it."

"Frau Bender, do me a favour and take your aunt's advice to heart. Think of yourself for once. I'm not the only one who heard what you said. Quite apart from that, Professor Frankenberg knows from his son that the girl's name was Magdalena, and you yourself told him you had to get home to your invalid sister."

"Of course, that proves she was at home, and Frankie couldn't have known otherwise. The girl told him her name was Magdalena and she was my sister, but that was just a game – I'd arranged it with the girl in the car park. The doctors at Eppendorf will confirm that it couldn't have been my sister. Magdalena was far too ill to leave the house. That'll work. You only have to want it to."

He shook his head. "It won't work, Frau Bender. You can't keep your aunt out of this."

"But she only did it for my sake – she can't be locked up for that. Promise me you won't arrest Margret!"

He could promise her that with a clear conscience. Margret Rosch didn't come within his sphere of jurisdiction; his north German colleagues would have to deal with the matter. Besides, what could she be charged with? It wasn't a punishable offence to arrange a burial – or rather, a cremation. He remembered now.

Grit Adigar had spoken of it. Everything had been done in the regulation manner. First a cremation, then the scattering of the ashes. A private ceremony. Only Margret had known what was in the urn. Grit Adigar had seen the ashes trickle into the sea.

He wondered whom or what they'd sent to the crematorium and whether, as was customary, someone had taken a last look into the coffin. Then he had a sudden, scalding recollection of what she'd said about Margret's theft. Damnation! It was absurd, but it could hardly be proved at this stage, if no one had noticed five years ago that a body had gone missing somewhere.

He couldn't help smiling. With a little skill and imagination . . . Margret Rosch had plenty of both. She's right, he thought. It not only could work; it was bound to do so, what with Magdalena's medical history, Grit Adigar's testimony, and Hans Bueckler. As for Achim Miek, who had made out the death certificate, he would sooner bite off his tongue than admit that he had stood beside an empty bed and his girlfriend had had to organize a dead body.

She stood at the window, staring out at the bleak day. It had rained that morning, and everything was cold and damp outside. It was February now, and her last day behind bars had come. She knew that, but she couldn't believe it.

"I'll pick you up early in the afternoon, Frau Bender," Eberhard Brauning had told her on his last visit. "I'm afraid I can't give you an exact time."

A few minutes either way didn't matter. She had plenty of time – far too much, in fact. The others had none. The professor had spared her a bare fifteen minutes shortly after lunch. Lunch was mashed potatoes, mushy peas and an emaciated leg of chicken with flabby skin. Afterwards Mario had escorted her to the professor's office. He wanted to explain a few more things and express his good wishes for the future. He had authorized her release, provided she underwent a course of therapy.

She had ceased to be important to anyone including the judiciary. Cora Bender had never been brought to trial. No indictment for murder or even for manslaughter. No life sentence. That might have put things right in some way, but nobody was interested in what she thought.

She had only made it as far as the examining magistrate's office. In view of the psychologist's report, the district attorney had requested that no proceedings be initiated. Cora Bender was "not criminally responsible", he said. A conviction was unlikely in any case.

But they had all been interviewed. Rudolf Grovian, Johannes Frankenberg – even Hans Bueckler, whom the police had run to earth in Kiel. She hadn't set eyes on him, and it was better that way.

Recalling that night in May five years earlier, Hans Bueckler stated under oath that he and Ottmar Denner had left the house in a hurry after discovering that Georg Frankenberg had killed a girl. Who the girl was, he didn't know. All he could remember was that he and Denner had picked up two girls at a disco who claimed to be sisters but weren't. Hans Bueckler didn't know what had happened to the dead body or the other girl. His story could not be disproved.

The psychologist's report dealt at length with the scene in the cellar and in even greater detail with Cora Bender's black soul. Born guilty, she had served nineteen years' imprisonment in a medieval dungeon. But the ultimate criminal was a father. No, not her father – hers didn't come into it. The real culprit was Frankie's father, although the psychologist's report didn't say so. Only her attorney did.

Eberhard Brauning had been magnificent. With his mother's active support, he had composed a speech and delivered it to the examining magistrate as if he were in court. He hadn't been able to keep his promise, however. No limited term of imprisonment. She'd been sent back to the psychiatric ward, there to wait until the professor considered her mature enough to think for herself again.

The time had gone quicker than she'd expected. On the bed behind her reposed the small suitcase Margret had brought to the chief's office an eternity ago, or at least in another life.

She thought of Margret's little apartment. Margret couldn't offer her more than a place on the couch, and the shower room was so small, you grazed your knees on the door when you sat on the toilet. A fresh start in the place where she had once begun to live again. She would leave it in the morning and return there in the evening. It would be almost like going off to work, except that this time she would be attending a day clinic instead of waiting table in the café on Herzogstrasse.

The professor was convinced that she would make it because Margret was her ideal of a woman with revolutionary views. He was also convinced that he had brought her to the point denied her five years earlier. That wasn't altogether correct – the chief had brought her to that point – but she didn't contradict the professor, not wanting to offend him or prompt him to revise his opinion of her progress yet again.

Eberhard Brauning had said: "We're entitled to feel extremely satisfied, Frau Bender."

She wasn't satisfied. She could still see Frankie's face, see the way he'd looked at her and let go of her hand, see him release his wife's hand shortly before, hear him say: "No, Ute, that's enough. Not that, give me a break!" Ute had done nothing to him.

During one of her sessions with Burthe, the professor had said that Frankie had sought his own death. She'd pondered that remark for a long time but had come to no conclusion.

Brauning turned up just before four o'clock. He offered to carry her suitcase, but she declined. She said goodbye to Mario and followed him outside.

"I had another word with your husband yesterday, Frau Bender," he said when she was sitting beside him in the car. "I got nowhere, I'm sorry to say."

She shrugged, staring straight ahead. Gereon had filed a petition for divorce. She hadn't expected anything else, although she'd hoped, in view of the fact that she hadn't really done anything bad until that moment beside the lake . . . "It doesn't matter," she said. "I thought he might have reconsidered it, that's all, but if his mind is made up there's nothing to be done. Perhaps it's better this way. Water under the bridge."

Brauning nodded and concentrated on the traffic. "Must I be there?" she asked. "I'm sure you can settle matters without me. Just say I have to be at this clinic all day long. I'm only allowed out in the evening. Tell Gereon I want the fitted kitchen and my personal belongings. And the right to see our child now and then, not often and not for long. A few hours once a month would do me. While I'm still living at Margret's, Gereon could drop in with him after work. I just want to see if the boy's all right."

She didn't expect a reply, nor did she look to see if Brauning nodded. "How long is this therapy likely to take?" she asked after a brief silence. "A year? Two years?"

"I can't say, Frau Bender. It depends on a number of things. Mainly, of course, on you."

"That's what I thought. Everything depends mainly on me, it always does." She gave a low laugh. "In that case, I'll do my best. I can't stay with Margret forever, and it's not worth looking for a place of my own. I must get home as soon as possible. Any news of my father?"

He didn't know what to say. Rudolf Grovian had undertaken to inform her that her father was dead. "Leave it to me," he'd said. "I'm her scapegoat in any case." He had told her shortly before their visit to Frankfurt, Brauning knew that for a fact.

She stared at the road ahead. "I guessed Gereon wouldn't withdraw his petition. Anyway, it'll be best if I go where I'm needed. I've decided to look after my father – wash him, comb his hair, feed him and do whatever else one has to do for a bedridden old man. I'll also send for my mother. They'll have to let me have her back if I ask, won't they? She isn't dangerous – she wouldn't harm anyone. And then I'll make sure Magdalena gets her cremation. I don't know how I'll manage it, but I will, even if I have to dig her up in the middle of the night. I'll manage it somehow."

She fell silent for a few moments, then started to smile. "Don't worry," she said, glancing at him sideways, "I didn't mean that. The chief said it would be desecration of the dead or something. I've no wish to desecrate or disturb anyone, and I haven't forgotten where my father is. I'll never forget anything again, I'm afraid. It's purely theoretical. I like to imagine myself sitting beside his bed, talking to him. I'd like to have explained everything to him."

She squared her shoulders, and her voice hardened. "Don't forget about the fitted kitchen. I'm going to have it dismantled and carted off to Buchholz right away. And my personal belongings. I don't want any money, I've got enough. I've also got a house and a car. They're old but they're still there, and someone's got to see they don't go to rack and ruin. Can you imagine what the front garden looks like? The front garden and the curtains were Father's pride and joy. It didn't matter to him so much what the house looked like inside, but the curtains had to be spotless. Herr Grovian said everything looked clean and tidy on his last visit, but that's a long time ago."

She sighed. "Have you heard from Herr Grovian?" Brauning shook his head. She gave another shrug. Water under the bridge flowed fast.

But she could never forget it all, not now. Only the ultimate sin of suicide could bring oblivion. She would have to see. If she couldn't bear it any longer . . . A day clinic. And the nights in Margret's apartment. Margret was often on night duty, and she always kept plenty of pills in the little cupboard beside her bed.

D.B.

Elwood Reid

"Raunchy, seamy, cocksure, perversely juicy, so surprising in its vivid convolutions of plot and character that you keep turning back a few pages to see how the author is getting away with it." Jim Harrison, author of *Legends of the Fall*

In 1971 a man calling himself D.B. Cooper hijacked a flight, claimed his ransom without harming a soul and vanished. He parachuted out of the plane over the dense woods of the Pacific Northwest with $200,000 strapped to his body. Elwood Reid uses this true story as a starting point, imagining Cooper as Phil Fitch, a Vietnam vet with a failed marriage who decides the time has come to do something that will save him from a life of punching time cards and wondering what could have been. Fitch ends up in Mexico, where he drifts until a turn of bad luck forces him to return home.

Meanwhile, retired FBI agent Frank Marshall, struggling with his new life of leisure – fishing, drinking too much, tempted to embark on an affair with a female witness – decides to help a young agent determined to solve the case of D.B. Cooper. An odyssey, a manhunt, a gripping and frequently hilarious tale.

PRAISE FOR *D.B.*

"Wild and alive, an epic manhunt and brutal social portrait, *D.B.* is the road trip of your dreams – Hunter Thompson does the driving, but John Steinbeck holds the map." Mark Costello, author of *Big If*

"Masterfully told, *D.B.* ranks among the best and most entertaining books of the year." *Pittsburgh Tribune*

"Elwood Reid ascends to the top of his generation with this novel." Mark Richard, author of *Fishboy*

"Smart and direct prose . . . By shifting the reader's attention from the overtly dramatic to the psychological, Reid has written something much more engaging than the mere suspense novel *D.B.* might have been." *The New York Times Book Review*

£9.99
Crime paperback original
ISBN 1–904738–19–2/978–1904738–19–0
www.bitterlemonpress.com

FEVER

Friedrich Glauser

"With good reason, the German language prize for detective fiction is named after Glauser. . . He has Simenon's ability to turn a stereotype into a person, and the moral complexity to appeal to justice over the head of police procedure."
Times Literary Supplement

When two women are "accidentally" killed by gas leaks, Sergeant Studer investigates the thinly disguised double murder in Bern and Basel. The trail leads to a geologist dead from a tropical fever in a Moroccan Foreign Legion post and a murky oil deal involving rapacious politicians and their henchmen. With the help of a hashish-induced dream and the common sense of his stay-at-home wife, Studer solves the multiple riddles on offer. But assigning guilt remains an elusive affair.

Fever, a European crime classic, was first published in 1936 and is the third in the Sergeant Studer series published by Bitter Lemon Press.

Praise for Glauser's other Sergeant Studer novels

"*Thumbprint* is a fine example of the craft of detective writing in a period which fans will regard as the golden age of crime fiction." *Sunday Telegraph*

"*Thumbprint* is a genuine curiosity that compares to the dank poetry of Simenon and reveals the enormous debt owed by Dürenmatt, Switzerland's most famous crime writer, for whom this should be seen as a template." *Guardian*

"A despairing plot about the reality of madness and life, leavened at regular intervals with strong doses of bittersweet irony. The idiosyncratic investigation of *In Matto's Realm* and its laconic detective have not aged one iota." *Guardian*

"Glauser was among the best European crime writers of the inter-war years. The detail, place and sinister characters are so intelligently sculpted that the sense of foreboding is palpable." *Glasgow Herald*

£9.99/$14.95
Crime paperback original
ISBN 1–904738–14–1/978–1904738–14–5
www.bitterlemonpress.com

FRAMED

Tonino Benacquista

"One of France's leading crime and mystery authors."
Guardian

Antoine's life is good. During the day he hangs pictures for the most fashionable art galleries in Paris. Evenings he dedicates to the silky moves and subtle tactics of billiards, his true passion. But when Antoine is attacked by an art thief in a gallery his world begins to fall apart. His maverick investigation triggers two murders – he finds himself the prime suspect for one of them – as he uncovers a cesspool of art fraud. A game of billiards decides the outcome of this violently funny tale, laced with brilliant riffs about the world of modern art and the parasites that infest it.

In 2004 Bitter Lemon Press introduced Tonino Benacquista to English-speaking readers with the critically acclaimed novel *Holy Smoke*.

PRAISE FOR *FRAMED*

"Screenwriter for the award-winning French crime movie *The Beat That My Heart Skipped*, Tonino Benacquista is also a wonderful observer of everyday life, petty evil and the ordinariness of crime. The pace never falters as personal grief collides with outrageous humour and a biting running commentary on the crooked world of modern art."
Guardian

"Edgy, offbeat black comedy." *The Times*

"Flip and frantic foray into art galleries and billiards halls of modern Paris." *Evening Standard*

"A black comedy that is set in Paris but reflects its author's boisterous Italian sensibility. The manic tale is told by an apprentice picture-hanger who encounters a thief in a fashionable art gallery and becomes so caught up in a case of art fraud that he himself 'touches up' a Kandinsky."
New York Times

£9.99/$14.95
Crime paperback original
ISBN 1–904738–16–8/978–1904738–16–9
www.bitterlemonpress.com

HAVANA BLACK

Leonardo Padura

A MARIO CONDE MYSTERY

"The mission of that enterprising Bitter Lemon Press is to publish English translations of the best foreign crime fiction. The newest addition to its list is the prize-winning Cuban novelist Leonardo Padura" *The Telegraph*

The brutally mutilated body of Miguel Forcade is discovered washed up on a Havana beach. Head smashed in by a baseball bat, genitals cut off with a blunt knife. Forcade was once responsible for confiscating art works from the bourgeoisie fleeing the revolution. Had he really returned from exile just to visit his ailing father?

Lieutenant Mario Conde immerses himself in Cuba's dark history, expropriations of priceless paintings now vanished without trace, corruption and old families who appear to have lost much, but not everything.

Padura evokes the disillusionment of a generation, yet this novel is a eulogy to Cuba, and to the great friendships of those who chose to stay and fight for survival.

PRAISE FOR *HAVANA BLACK*

"A great plot, perfectly executed with huge atmosphere. You can almost smell the cigar smoke, rum and cheap women." *Daily Mirror*

"This is a strong tasting book. A rich feast of wit and feeling." *The Independent*

"Well-plotted second volume of Padura's seething, steamy Havana Quartet. This densely packed mystery should attract readers outside the genre." *Publishers Weekly*

"Lt. Mario Conde, known on the street as 'the Count,' is prone to metaphysical reflection on the history of his melancholy land but the city of Havana keeps bursting through his meditations, looking very much alive." *New York Times*

£9.99/$14.95
Crime paperback original
ISBN 1–904738–15–X/978–1904738–15–2
www.bitterlemonpress.com

THE MANNEQUIN MAN

Luca Di Fulvio

Shortlisted for the European Crime Writing Prize

"Di Fulvio exposes souls with the skills of a surgeon, It's like turning the pages of something forbidden – seduction, elegant and dangerous." *Alan Rickman*

"Know why she's smiling?" he asked, pointing a small torch at the corpse. "Fish hooks. Two fish hooks at the corners of her mouth, a bit of nylon, pull it round the back of the head and tie a knot. Pretty straightforward, right?" Amaldi noticed the metallic glint at the corners of the taut mouth.

Inspector Amaldi has enough problems. A city choked by a pestilent rubbish strike, a beautiful student harassed by a telephone stalker, a colleague dying of cancer and the mysterious disappearance of arson files concerning the city's orphanage. Then the bodies begin to appear.

This novel of violence and decay, with its vividly portrayed characters, takes place over a few oppressive weeks in an unnamed Italian city that strongly evokes Genoa.

The Italian press refers to Di Fulvio as a grittier, Italian Thomas Harris, and *Eyes of Crystal*, the film of the novel, was launched at the 2004 Venice Film Festival.

" A novel that caresses and kisses in order to violate the reader with greater ease." *Rolling Stone*

"A powerful psycho-thriller of spine-shivering intensity . . . written with immense intelligence and passionate menace. Not to be read alone at night." *The Times*

"A wonderful first novel that will seduce the fans of deranged murderers in the style of Hannibal Lecter. And beautifully written to boot." *RTL*

£9.99/$14.95
Crime paperback original
ISBN 1–904738–13–3/978–1904738–13–8
www.bitterlemonpress.com

SOMEONE ELSE

Tonino Benacquista

"A great read from one of France's best crime writers.
A tale peppered with humour, unpredictable twists and a
healthy dose of suspense. It all makes for a cracking read,
with witty insights into the vagaries of human nature."
Guardian

Who hasn't wanted to become "someone else"? The person
you've always wanted to be . . . the person who won't give up
half way to your dreams and desires?

One evening two men who have just met at a Paris tennis
club make a bet: they give each other exactly three years to
radically alter their lives. Thierry, a picture framer with a
steady clientele, has always wanted to be a private investigator. Nicolas is a shy, teetotal executive trying not to fall off
the corporate ladder. But becoming someone else is not
without risk; at the very least, the risk of finding yourself.

"Benacquista writes with humor and verve. This novel is less
a mystery than a deftly constructed diptych of existential
escapism: each story offers a unique map to new possibilities
in the midst of suffocating lives." *Rain Taxi*

"This has been a big hit in France, and it is easy to see why –
Thierry's attempts to slip into a story by Simenon and
Nicolas's explosive encounter with vodka make for
unexpected, cynical comedy." *The Times*

"Exuberantly written, Benacquista's book is another triumph
for the genre-bending approach to crime fiction."
Tangled Web

Winner of the RTL-LIRE Prize.

£9.99/$14.95
Crime paperback original
ISBN 1–904738–12–5/978–1904738–12–1
www.bitterlemonpress.com

A WALK IN THE DARK

Gianrico Carofiglio

"Carofiglio writes crisp, ironical novels that are as much love stories and philosophical treatises as they are legal thrillers."
New Yorker

When Martina accuses her ex-boyfriend – the son of a powerful local judge – of assault and battery, no witnesses can be persuaded to testify on her behalf and one lawyer after another refuses to represent her. Guido Guerrieri knows the case could bring his legal career to a premature and messy end but he cannot resist the appeal of a hopeless cause. Nor deny an attraction to Sister Claudia, the young woman in charge of the shelter where Martina is living, who shares his love of martial arts and his virulent hatred of injustice.

Gianrico Carofiglio is an anti-Mafia prosecutor in southern Italy. *A Walk in the Dark,* his second novel featuring defence counsel Guerrieri, follows on from the success of *Involuntary Witness.*

PRAISE FOR *A WALK IN THE DARK*

"This novel raises the standard for crime fiction. Carofiglio's deft touch has given us a story that is both literary and gritty – and one that speeds along like the best legal thrillers. His insights into human nature – good and bad – are breathtaking." *Jeffery Deaver*

"*A Walk in the Dark,* features an engagingly complex, emotional and moody defence lawyer, Guido Guerrieri, who takes on cases shunned by his colleagues. In passing, Carofiglio provides a fascinating insight into the workings of the Italian criminal justice system." *Observer*

"Part legal thriller, part insight into a man fighting his own demons. Every character in Carofiglio's fiction has a story to tell and they are always worth hearing . . . this powerfully affecting novel benefits from veracity as well as tight writing." *Daily Mail*

£9.99/$14.95
Crime paperback original
ISBN 1–904738–17–6/978–1904738–17–6
www.bitterlemonpress.com